# THY FATHER'S SON

## ALSO BY LEO RUTMAN

Clash of Eagles

Spear of Destiny

Five Good Boys

# THY FATHER'S SON

**LEO RUTMAN**

ST. MARTIN'S PRESS ≈ NEW YORK

www.stmartins.com

Design by Kathryn Parise

LIBRARY OF CONGRESS CATALOGING-IN-PUBLICATION DATA
Rutman, Leo.
    Thy father's son : a novel / Leo Rutman.—1st ed.
        p. cm.
    ISBN 0-312-29061-6
    1. Italian American families—Fiction.    2. Fathers and sons—Fiction.
3. New York (N.Y.)—Fiction.    4. Boxers (Sports)—Fiction.    5. Kidnapping—
Fiction.    6. Mafia—Fiction.    I. Title.

PS3568.U826 T47 2002
813'.54—dc21

                                                                    2002068355

First Edition: September 2002

10  9  8  7  6  5  4  3  2  1

*For Bette*

# Acknowledgments

**WITH THANKS** to Nick Ellison for getting me back in the game.

To Detective (Ret.) Pete Caram for insights into organized crime.

To George Witte for his good eye and deft touch.

And to *The Last Testament of Lucky Luciano* which got me started.

And finally to all my invaluable computer consultants . . . you know who you are. I couldn't have made it without you.

# THY FATHER'S SON

# Prologue

**EVER SINCE** I was a little boy I have always had the feeling of being watched. I can best describe it as eyes searching you out. Seeking to discern what you know and what you will do. It is a look that is commonplace to the world I was raised in and one I came to accept.

Just before my thirteenth birthday, my father, the don, Vince Rossi, told me I was adopted. It came after Richie Tedesco needled me about being circumcised, in the locker room after gym class at Fordham Prep. Vince explained to me that the fact that I was circumcised did not mean I was not a true Catholic. I had been christened in church by Father Francis, with Vince and my mother, Rosalia, watching. And St. Mary's Foundling home accepted only Catholic children for adoption. He did not know why I was circumcised, but there was nothing wrong with it. He said he would have told me I was adopted.

I was shaken but tried hard to conceal it. I had been taught by Vince and his business associates not to show emotion in a tight spot. It was a sign of character. I remember Vince put his arm around me and said he and Rosalia loved me very much. Vince is not a man who uses a word like *love* easily, and I was aware that he was trying to reassure me and also say what he felt at the same time. As I thought about what he had told me, I could see Vince watching me. A strange expression had come to his face. I asked who my real parents were and his Adam's apple seemed to knot up and bulge in his throat. But then he only shook his head. It wasn't known who my parents were. In the days and weeks that followed, it seemed his eyes never left me. I fell asleep seeing those eyes.

I grew up Mafia. It is not an ordinary life. If you look into the eyes of a mafioso you will observe a quality of detachment, a glacial hardness that derives from knowing that everyone can be bent, that all friendship is transitory, that mortality is measured by fragile alliances, and that the only link to survival is having the edge. When you acknowledge the limits of your mortality at an age when you are just beginning, then you get that look in your eyes. All life, and in particular your own, is held cheap.

Once I asked Vince about the risks he took to become a don. I didn't say it, but I was really asking if he had been scared to die. Vince has tight dark eyes, the kind that are described as hooded. Those eyes can become slivers of fury or glint with an insight so shrewd and knowing, it will chill you. I have since come to realize that it was a question he had considered many times. He looked into some private place and then said softly, "I always thought I was going to wind up on a slab someplace." He was quiet for a moment, but I knew he wasn't finished. "It's called seeing to the end, Davey. Seeing to the end of all things."

To see to the end of your days is a prerequisite for any man who wishes to rise to the position of Mafia don. Vince is father to me and Godfather to the Rossi crime family. For many, there is a mystical reverence for the rank they have achieved. Frank Bruno, before he became a don, had earned the title "the Executioner." At a Christmas party, he took me aside and said in heavy, ominous tones, "This thing, our Life, is a calling." For those who realize that they could be dead by nightfall, who accept so readily that they will wind up on a slab someday, such a calling conditions a man to seek the edge. To have the edge, you must be able to judge a man. So you are always looking. Watching. Searching even as you break bread and eat pasta, share anisette and espresso, bring him gifts for his children at Christmas, toast his anniversary, flatter his accomplishments, praise his loyalty. For what you know about his life may save your own. That is what it means to gain the edge and survive the Life. And just as you gauge the dimensions of your enemy, you also take the measure of your friend. For the difference in the Life between one's friend and one's enemy can change with the sunrise.

When I was sixteen, there was a big party for Dino Manfredi, who had just beaten a murder rap. There is no love lost between Dino and Vince, but Dino had been hiding out in Italy for ten years, and if you didn't come to the party, Dino would put you on his list. People were trying to forget how ambitious and violent he was and give him a chance to start again. At one point, Dino got me into a corner and asked me how tough I was. He was testing me, like he tested everybody. Dino always figured that he might come up against you someday and he wanted to know how tough you were. He asked me to punch him in the arm. I declined. Suddenly, he hit me so hard, my arm went numb. It hurt so much, I couldn't talk. Dino, then as now, looked like a rapacious, starved wolf. He pointed a finger at me and said, "Never, never give anyone the first shot at you."

Vince wanted something better for me, like the law. But I knew that sooner or later I would have become Vince's consigliere. Consiglieres spend their lives watching others and being watched. Always plotting to remove or replace someone. I didn't want that for myself. There were other possibilities, but they didn't suit me. The trouble was that I had been raised around men who regarded violence as a viable solution to a problem. Men who lived each day with the threat of the hit always there. I didn't crave danger, but neither did I shun it. During my second year of college, I decided on a profession that also had the elements of chance and danger in it. I needed help to get started. I needed the kind of touch that Tommy Costanza could give it.

Tommy Costanza fixes everything and everybody in New York for the Five Families. Judges, cops, politicians, Tommy owns them. He's the don with class. Tommy took a liking and an interest in me as I grew up. Vince is my father, but Tommy and my brother, Johnny Baca, dubbed by the mob "Johnny Silk," have been my role models. Tommy is known as the "Gray Eminence," the Pope of the underworld. Johnny is his cardinal-in-waiting. One sets policy, the other carries it out. Nobody who listens to them ever got hurt.

I spent a lot of time as a boy dropping in on both of them. Johnny lives in a beautiful penthouse apartment facing Central Park West. On Sunday afternoons, he and I would go over to Tommy's place on Sutton Place South and Tommy would tell us about the twenties, when he made his first million. Tommy came from nothing, from dirt-poor peasants; by 1930, he was the consigliere for the mob. He would sit in his favorite chair on the terrace of his apartment facing the East River and tell us how he bought everybody for the Syndicate. At one time, Tommy had the governor, the mayor, the police commissioner, and Tammany Hall on the pad. When Tommy moved up to become a don, he recommended Johnny for his job. Tommy has manicured fingers and wears the best pigskin leather gloves, but his hands needed a lot of washing. He knows everybody now; he dines out every night in the best restaurants. Johnny once told me that Tommy hasn't eaten at home in forty years. One evening, a reporter found him alone at dinner and asked about the terrible things he did on the way up. Tommy should have laughed it off, but instead he just got quiet and said, "You do a lot of things once."

Tommy not only takes care of his own family; he takes care of the mob. Dino Manfredi came back to New York in 1949, and everybody figured there would be a war. When Dino went away, he was the don, but in his absence, the Mafia Council put Tommy in his place. Ten years is a long time to be away and then come back and think you can take over the family again. Tommy sat down with Dino and convinced him to let things stay the same, in exchange for an equal share in the family business and a piece of the casino deals Johnny was setting up in Cuba for the Syndicate. The Council was so grateful, they let Dino run his own drug pipeline and looked the other way. That's how it stayed until 1956, when Dino got ten years on drug-dealing charges. It was a frame. Set up by Tommy on behalf of the Syndicate, which feared Dino's ambition.

I knew if I got into the rackets, I would have to do things that I would regret later on. Violence comes easy in the Life. It was from Johnny and Tommy that I learned to distrust it. Vince uses violence; Johnny accepts it but thinks it stupid; Tommy despises it. Even though Vince would never admit it, danger thrills him—Johnny and Tommy are like clones. They see things without passion. And yet Tommy, who lives for the sure thing, loves to bet on an honest fight. Vince and Tommy shaped me. I discovered the traits of both of them in myself. Danger makes my blood run; taking a chance gives me a high. Put them together and you have what I turned out to be: a prizefighter.

When I went to Tommy and said that I wanted to fight, he didn't say anything for a few moments. He was figuring the angles. I had my angles covered before I went in. I knew the only thing that would get Tommy interested was a fighter who was good enough to win the championship without any tank jobs. That was the only kind of fighter he would put time and money into. So the first thing he wanted to know was if I expected him to "fix it." If I did, then he would get me a manager, but he wouldn't have any part of it. You might think that a gangster would want the fix to be in, but Tommy didn't look upon boxing as his business. He viewed it as a great sport and he had tremendous admiration for men who performed like champions. To be a champion was to have heart in what Tommy called "the most brutal business in the world." "It's tougher than my racket anytime," he always said to me. So I knew when I went to him that I had to make Tommy use the word *fix* and turn him down. To figure that, I needed the edge, and that came from knowing Tommy all my life and knowing what he would respond to. By seeing to the end of all things.

I remember Tommy saying, "This ain't college; you'll be fighting hungry spics and niggers. The Latinos are dynamite. They're hungry for the money and the title and the fame. Are you hungry?" "I'm starved," I said. Tommy looked into my eyes, and I guess he liked what he saw, because his eyes twinkled. "I'll make some calls," he said.

When I told Vince about what I wanted to do, he didn't say anything or show any emotion. I knew he didn't like boxing. For a man who had used the gun, that might seem strange, but I understood. Violence was a thing to be used if you had to, not something to be displayed. He went to the liquor cabinet and poured two glasses of red wine. Then he turned to me and said, "I am surprised, though I should have expected this. You are more civilized than your father. More clever at the games that are played. They will let you hurt someone and pay you for this senseless violence. They will take your picture and celebrate you. They will ask for your autograph. Women will also celebrate you. 'Bravo, il bruto.' " He raised his glass and we both drank. "Only be good at this thing you do, or you will suffer, and I will not allow that." I saw the pain in his eyes then and realized his disappointment. He had hoped my calling would be something more noble. I was struck by the irony of it that night as I tossed in my bed. Tommy, the man who played all the angles and never carried a gun, embraced my choice. Vince, who lived all his life amid vendetta and murder, called it "senseless violence." Vince made only one condition: Johnny would be my manager. He always believed you should have family with you when you went to war. Vince gave me two years to make good. We shook hands and finished the wine to seal our bargain.

By the time I became a fighter, I had developed an instinctive affinity for survival. By the time I fought for the title, I had cultivated it into an art form. I would leave my dressing room surrounded by my entourage. In front of me would be my trainer, Sy Morris, and my cut man, the old black welterweight Joe Dunn. Once we reached the arena, there was the crowd, which got bigger and bigger as I fought my way up to the rank of contender. When I got down to ringside, there were the reporters, studying me through pools of smoke, and there down in front, at ringside, the men I had known all my life. The dons who ran the Five Families. Joe Dante, the "Papa" of Staten Island and the Brooklyn waterfront; Frank Bruno, "the Executioner," carefully gauging me; Dino Manfredi, looking like a starved wolf ready to devour me; Carlo Scola, with his wizened face and the child's staring eyes which missed nothing. And alongside them, a flurry of mob guys, big, fat, bald, in dark suits, diamond ring fingers pointing me out to a blonde glittering with ice around her neck. The thug wondering how I would perform that night and his lady thinking the same thing about a different venue. Then I would search for Vince and see him standing there, eyes full of warmth and affection for his son, as well as distaste for this bloody spectacle. Next to him, a cigarette lazily ladled in his mouth, all snappy in a black suit, shoes shined to a high gloss, carrying his Camel topper, the little man, Tommy Costanza.

It was from Tommy that I got my ring face and game plan. Look alert, keep coming, and never appear discouraged or down. Never let the other guy see what you're feeling. Even after I won, I would keep my feelings in check. Tommy would give me a quick salute and raise his eyebrows a little. I would nod back. He taught me that if you didn't celebrate too much when you beat the other guy, it showed respect. "Never rub defeat in anyone's face," he told me. "We all go down. If you have respect, some guy who knocked you down will help you up."

I was brought along at just the right pace. I didn't have to worry about fighting for peanuts or about taking a fight too quick for the first big purse somebody dangled in front of me. And I got all the close decisions. I didn't fight in the Garden until I had twenty-two bouts under my belt. My opponent was Tony Romero, who had held the lightweight championship of the world for over three years before losing it. When I got the match, Tommy had me come over to his apartment. It was an autumn day. Tommy pointed in the direction of Queens, just across the East River, to make his point about the world. "It's close enough to grab, Davey, and after you beat Tony tonight, a lot of people will offer it to you. Don't be in a hurry. And don't be conned. Tony was a great fighter, but he's not the champ no more. He's just a stepping-stone." Tommy scrubbed out his cigarette and his voice dropped. "Don't carry him; if you can finish him, do it."

I didn't screw up. In the third round, I hit Tony with a combination left hook and right cross and he went down. I knew I had him. I also knew that he was nowhere near the fighter he'd once been; that was his sorrow. When the bell rang for the fourth round, Tony came right off his stool, but I could see he was wobbly. Instead of boxing him, I moved in fast and put him down with a right. He fell backward on his haunches and sat looking at me, a stunned expression on his face. He got to one knee and then stayed there, listening to the referee's count. I could see Dino Manfredi right below him at ringside. His mouth was slightly parted and there was a beatific smile on his face. I saw Tony was out on his feet. But the referee wasn't going to stop it while he was still standing. Tony had earned the respect of being counted out. I ended the fight with a quick combination that left Tony on his back, staring sightlessly at the big overhead lights of Madison Square Garden.

There was a party for me after the fight at Umberto's Clam House in Little Italy. All the mob guys were there, and their eyes were suffused with a kindred spiritual glow. I had done the job on a fighter they all admired. A perfectly executed hit. A naked display of fury. The best and worst of these men got to the top because that fury resided in them. But their passion was reserved for violent deeds executed in private. Mine had become a kind of exalted exercise, made more authentic by the fact of its public display. It gave me a legitimacy that could not be questioned. Christened with the name and identity of fighter.

Frank Bruno stared at me with those brooding brown eyes all evening, as if unable to comprehend that the thin boy he had seen at Christmas gatherings had grown into this apostle of violence. At the end of the evening, he took me aside and said, "Davey, you have a gift and you used it. You had him and you killed him. Farlo fuori." He embraced me as if we were a breed apart from the others at the party. As if only he and I knew what "Farlo fuori" truly meant. Vince came over and hugged me. In his eyes was some indefinable expression that merged love and pride with disbelief. A recognition that this boy he had raised and loved possessed qualities of unknown strength that made him both a son and a stranger. There was a layer of emotion in his eyes that suggested his encounter with an experience both mysterious and profound. As if there resided within him a dark creature that had possessed him. Vince turned to me and for a moment seemed as though he would show me the nature of this creature and tell me its name. Then I recalled the expression he'd had on his face the day he told me I was adopted.

At just this moment, Johnny approached us. Johnny is a handsome man. His hair is streaked with white, even though he is still in his forties. When he smiles, women find him irresistible. My brother was elegant as always in a gray suit over a light-colored shirt and paisley tie. His blue eyes were ablaze with light as he hugged both Vince and me. I could see him whispering softly in Sicilian to Vince, who nodded and smiled. Father and brother sharing a moment of pride and joy. And yet something more was occurring. In embracing Vince, Johnny seemed to impose himself on the creature birthing within Vince.

I noticed Johnny's hand squeezing Vince's arm. As if by the strength of his embrace he could still the creature within Vince and prevent him from telling me what it was. Whatever passed between them caused Vince great pain, for his face went white. Then abruptly, Vince broke Johnny's hold and excused himself, his face sheathed in a mask of sweat. I watched Vince get himself a drink. Johnny squeezed the biceps of my left arm and said, "You were an artist tonight, a prince deposing a king. You'll be greater than Tony ever was. You will bring great honor to the family and to Vince. I guarantee your future, Davey."

I knew Johnny meant what he said. But I was angry and hurt for Vince. I looked at him, and I don't know where the words came from, because I had no sense of them forming. I held up my fists and said, "These guarantee my future. Not you." We stood together, eyes locked, and finally he nodded. "The boy has become a man." In that moment, I knew he had confirmed a long-held perception that I was unlike Vince. Johnny could not outsmart or outthink me. He could not treat me as a clever pug who was so intoxicated with his rise up the ladder that he would look the other way and not involve himself in a family cruelty. Johnny nodded as if to affirm silently what he had seen within me. "Remember, Davey," he whispered, "no matter what honors you achieve, how much money and fame, remember who the father is. Loyalty is always to the family." There was an ironic glint in his eyes to counter the mystic tone of his words. What was he saying? Was he pointing the finger at himself for pricking Vince, or pointing that finger at me in anticipation of my insurrection against Vince? What did he know that I didn't? I only knew that there was some secret between him and Vince. One that I was excluded from.

Nineteen fifty-six became my year. My twenty-seventh fight, against Lulu Perez, was for the lightweight championship. I celebrated the signing of the bout with Tommy and Johnny at Toots Shors. We ate manicotti and antipasto and toasted with good dago red. Johnny gripped my left hand, my Michelangelo, and straightened it into a jab. "Use it all night, Davey, and remember that Lulu knows all the tricks. He likes to slow down and make you think you got him, and then he flurries. He steals a lot of rounds that way. People think they can knock him out, but no one ever has. He likes the title and he's going to make you bleed to take it away from him."

Johnny was right. We both bled a lot. I came out fast and took the early rounds. In the middle rounds, Lulu made me miss with some beautiful head feinting and found my face more often than he should have with his left jab. In the eighth round, I came on again as Lulu started to fade, and Sy Morris warned me during the rest period. "He's tired; he'll try to steal the next couple of rounds. Stay on top of him and don't let up. Watch for the flurry and flurry back." So we traded flurries for four rounds, which Lester Bromberg described in the *World Telegram* as the best display of left jabs he'd ever seen. By the thirteenth round, Lulu was out of gas and holding on. When it was over and my hand had been held up and I'd been proclaimed the new lightweight champion of the world, Lulu hugged me while whispering into my ear, "You're a great fighter, Davey, great . . . great." Then Johnny was there massaging my neck, telling me I was going to be champion for a long time. Sy was dancing around the ring, his eyes aglow, while Joe Dunn kept saying, "How you feel, champ?" Vince had never come to my dressing room—he didn't want the don to overshadow his son—but this time he was there. We hugged and Vince kissed me. He kept whispering in my ear, "Champion, champion." Then he and Johnny turned to each other and I pleaded silently for an embrace. They shook hands. Whatever it was was still there. They could not bury it.

Johnny threw a big bash for me that night at Mangicore's on the East Side. As Walter Winchell wrote in his column the next day, it was "Mob à la mode." Everybody turned out. Friends, enemies, dons, consiglieres, and even the ancient wise man, Don Carlo Scola, who sits at the head of the table at the nationwide Mafia Commission meetings. They come from Detroit, Los Angeles, and Miami to seek his wisdom. He has stopped and started bloody wars. Of all the dons, he is the most respected and serves as senior statesman. If Tommy Costanza is the Eminence, then Carlo Scola is the power behind the throne of Rome. He is a small man with white hair neatly parted and very big eyes. As a boy, I called him "Uncle Carlo." Of all the mob people I grew up with, he always seemed to be searching for something inside me. In those large childlike eyes were a detachment and a shrewdness I found frightening. As I started over to his table, Tommy caught my arm and whispered to me. "When he finishes talking with you, he'll expect you to kiss the ring. If you do, he'll always think of you as a soldato." A *soldato* is a soldier, a man of limited intelligence with unwavering loyalty to his don. Tommy said, "I make it two to one; you'll kiss the ring."

I made my decision as I was led over to him. Scola was flanked by two fierce-looking men with Doberman faces and prominent bulges in their coats. Scola gestured for me to sit down. His small wrinkled left hand was on the table and showed a big ring with a diamond inside it. I had been raised knowing the power of Carlo Scola. As a young boy, I was brought before him at a party as he threw the bocci ball with friends. I remember he said to Vince, "*Bene*, Vince, he is a beautiful boy. Be proud." He turned to me then with those saucer eyes and gave me a piercing stare. It was like nothing I had ever experienced before. as though he knew something about me that I didn't know myself. Then he held out his right hand and I dutifully kissed it, as my brother Johnny had instructed me to do. Carlo Scola smiled and patted my head. When I asked Vince about it, he didn't say anything, but there was a look on his face, as if he'd swallowed something distasteful. As a boy, it seemed to me that Vince deferred to him. Vince never knuckled to anyone, but it always felt like Uncle Carlo had some kind of hold on Vince.

Scola began talking about the fight. I don't remember what he said so much as the way he said it, like his vocal chords had been pickled in brine. There was a searing noise every time he spoke. It was a congratulatory speech, in which he praised me and my dedication. I just listened. I wasn't supposed to say anything. Carlo Scola was holding audience. I knew Tommy was watching me just as closely as he had watched me during the fight. Scola finished, looked across the room, and waited. I could see his hand extended on the table and the glittering ring before me. Kiss the ring; kiss the ring. For some reason, I turned, and there was Vince, who had just come in. He was dressed in a blue suit with a white shirt open at the neck. Vince has the eyes of an assassin. He is still lean, but his hair has gone gray. His once-dark pencil-thin mustache is fuller and grayer. It makes him look more human. Often, those assassin's eyes are filled with some private pain. But just then he saw me, and his expression was one of fierce pride. That gave me courage. Scola turned to me, the full weight of those saucer eyes upon me. I saw his hand again and the lights flashing on the diamond inside the ring. He waited a beat, and when he saw I wasn't going to lower my head and kiss the ring, a startling change appeared in those eyes. They went from regarding me with a mild beneficence to registering surprise and then flashed scorn. In that moment, I realized the reason. In my place, Carlo Scola would have not made himself known as a man who had contempt for the gesture of bowing his head. He marked me as a headstrong young man. He made that clear when I rose and offered to shake his hand and saw it slide away under the table. He turned from me as others came to pay him tribute.

When I rejoined Tommy, he pressed a sheath of bills into my pocket. I attempted to return the bills, but he pushed them back toward me. "I always pay up, kid. And you won that bet on moxie." I looked back and saw Johnny greet Scola. Then suddenly, he dipped his head and put his lips on the cold ring. Moments later, he turned and stared at me. Now Johnny was definitely not a *soldato*, but he was sending me a message. It was his way of telling me what I had done was not smart. I got very cold and looked over at Vince. He had been watching the scene, a grim smile painted on his lips. He focused intently on Johnny and Scola, as if he saw much more than what was actually there. Vince seldom gave himself away, but this time I could see an expression of hurt. It reminded me that there was something bad between Johnny and Vince. Something I was not a part of.

Later that evening, I slipped out to the garden in the back of restaurant and stood watching the water cascading down upon a cluster of black rocks. Somebody coughed and I whirled around. It was Dino Manfredi. He had on a gleaming gray silk suit and a blue shirt. His tie had been unknotted and flowed loosely down the shirt. I noticed the trail of leaping white fish on the tie. He pulled the cigarette from his mouth and pinched the end of it between stubby talonlike fingers. "Remember once," he began, "when you were a kid and I offered to trade shot for shot with you?" I told him I remembered. "I didn't think you had a taste for fighting. Turned out I was wrong. You remind me a little of Benny Leonard. He was a Jewish kid. Fought in the twenties. Great fighter. There are no more Hebe fighters around anymore. Used to be a lot of Hebe gangsters in them days. Very tough guys. They thought no one could take them. There was one named

Nails Gordon. What a mob he had. Somebody had to put the hit on them." He stopped and eyed me. Why was he telling me about a Jewish gangster? "Ask Vince about Nails Gordon," Dino urged. "He got rubbed out. Vince remembers. It was a big story. Made all the front pages. Vince knew Nails Gordon. Ask him." Dino had a funny look on his face. He was needling me, but I didn't know about what. His eyes were mocking me. What was I missing? He pointed at the stars. "Enjoy tonight, kid, because the best part is over. It's the hunt for the crown that is the best. When you get there and become king of the hill, everybody is looking to knock you off. And in your game, there is always somebody better. Somebody will catch up to you. That's what's better about my game. The hit is final. No rematches." He flipped the cigarette into the fountain. "He's out there now, the guy with your name on his gloves. So sock it away, because he's coming for you." Dino stood there smiling, as if in the playful white foam in front of us, he could read my destiny. But he couldn't read his own. The next day, he was nailed on the narcotics rap Tommy and Vince set up, and he got ten years in the slammer.

I held the title for five and a half years and defended it nine times. I beat them all. I fought with courage, with heart, with smarts and the best left jab in the game. The mob loved me and bet their money on me. If you fought me for the title, I got 70 percent. I bought into a steak house on the East Side. Johnny suggested I think about getting out after a couple more fights. I told him I'd sleep on it. But the nap took place in my car on the Palisades Parkway and I woke up wrapped around a pole. I broke a lot of ribs, ripped up my shoulder and knee, and cracked some teeth. And I did something to my back. It was almost a year before I agreed to a title fight with a tough kid from Harlem, Sandy Simpson, who was moving up from the featherweight division. People had been touting Sandy for years. He was big and rangy with a punch. We had fought in the Golden Gloves when we were young and I'd put him in my pocket. Johnny didn't want me to make the match, but I told him and Sy that I had too many moves for Sandy, and besides, I was getting sixty very large for the fight. It was held in Madison Square Garden on a warm Friday night in May. A night full of excitement in New York because President Kennedy had come to speak at the United Nations.

I made a mistake with Sandy Simpson, a mistake Tommy had warned me about a long time ago. Never take anyone lightly. Simpson hit me with punches that I felt all the way down my aching spine. He knocked me down once in the third and twice in the fourth round. Sy wanted to stop it, but I wouldn't let him. It was my title to lose in the ring. In the world I was raised in, you win or you get carried out. There was no question of not going on. In the eighth round, my left shoulder came out of its socket. I couldn't punch with any zip, and Sandy Simpson busted me up. By the eleventh round, I couldn't use the left anymore, and Simpson put me down again. Between rounds, Teddy Gaines, the referee, came over. "How's it going, Davey?" Sy touched my shoulder and I almost jumped off the stool. "It's dislocated," Sy screamed. Teddy leaned over me. "I gotta stop it, Davey. I got to."

The papers the next day showed me slumped in my corner, a towel over my face. I was beat up bad. Simpson had put me down five times and made me quit in my corner. The mob was in shock. Around street corners and poolrooms, in sharp cars, in cushy restaurants and hot nightspots, the word was the same: "The nigger busted up Davey. He made him quit."

I had dinner with Johnny a few nights later, and he put it to me the way he always did. Looking ahead. Cutting to the conclusion. "You gotta quit, Davey. You're still a good fighter, but Simpson is a great one. Walk away now. You've got enough money. Don't do a script with a predictable ending. Walk away with class."

The words hurt worse than Simpson's punches. "I can beat him," I flared. "The accident hurt me."

Johnny was quiet and he looked deep into his scotch glass. "You're twenty-nine. In this racket, that's ancient. Simpson's twenty-six. That's his three punches to your two. That's the left hook he'll catch you with after he muscles you into the ropes. You can't beat youth."

I went to bed and kept hearing Johnny's words, and the eloquent logic of Dino Manfredi that night I won the championship. "He's out there now, the guy with your name on his gloves. So sock it away, because he's coming for you. He's coming for you."

# 1

**AUTUMN IS** my favorite time of the year. It holds the promise of things to come. The days are warm and the nights cool. But there's also something sad about autumn. You can see the summer slipping away, a seemingly endless string of days now gone. Stolen away by an unseen hand. Like a life: one day you wake up and you're old.

But there is something else in the air in the autumn of 1962. If you were raised in the world I come from, you could smell it. It hangs there sharp and pungent, like a rancid piece of meat crawling with maggots. The smell of fear permeated the mob. After six years, Dino Manfredi had been released from federal prison in Atlanta on August 28. The witness who had sent him away on a drug rap had recanted his testimony. When Dino got caught, it was very convenient for a lot of people. Convenience in the underworld is a euphemism for set-up. Vince told me about it one night over dinner. A neat, tight frame, which featured the canarylike voice of a street fly and drug pusher named Gaspare Manzo, who swore that he was part of a drug deal and witnessed Dino buying a lot of little bags of heroin. It got Dino ten years, until Gaspare Manzo suddenly recanted his testimony before a federal appeals judge. Somebody had taken an ax to that tight little frame. Gaspare had been paid a lot of money to take a perjury rap. The edge is a funny bird. It doesn't play favorites. Now Dino was free and everybody waited for his next move.

I've been training in Pompton Lakes for the Kid Bassett fight. Today Johnny drove up from the city to see me work out. We are just
sitting down for lunch on a small patio outside my cottage when the
telephone rings. One of my sparring partners answers. It's for Johnny.
He goes inside and doesn't come out for some minutes. When he
returns, the smile is gone from his face and his eyes are somber and
heavy. It's a warm October day, but suddenly there is a chill in the
air. He indicates with a gesture of his head. Let's walk. We go some
distance in silence. Johnny doesn't speak until we reach a group of
trees. I can see the sun jumping in sparkling lines off the blue lake as
he speaks. "That was Vince. Tommy got hit this morning. In a barber
chair." It's like taking a bullet. Sunspots leap in front of my eyes and
the lake seems to freeze. I picture Tommy lying on the floor of a
barbershop amid shards of glass from the mirror, which only a few
moments earlier had encompassed his reflection. He is a small, compact
man, who parts his hair down the middle, and has a prominent nose
and small, alert blue eyes. He always dresses for the occasion, and I'm
sure he was neatly and expensively dressed this day. He favors gray
or blue striped suits and his shoes are always shined till they glisten.
I knew I was thinking in the present because I was in shock. How
could this happen? Tommy is a fixture. He's the Eminence. He never
carries a gun. "Dino," I finally said.

Johnny's forehead is bathed in sweat. A tight little smile creeps
across his face. With Johnny, that's always a cover for the emotion
underneath. Guys like Tommy and Johnny never show their feelings.
For them, logic and smarts must come first. That's why the mob relies
on them. They never hustle themselves into a decision based on emotion. Johnny took out a cigarette. "With Dino, it's never just business;
there's always a little personal signature. Dino never forgets anything.
Tommy's been going to that barbershop for forty years. Back in the
thirties, he ran numbers out of there. It's a little place on the Lower
East Side. The same guy owns it. Augie Donadio. Nice man. Plays
opera music and talks all day. Every Wednesday, Tommy would have
a cut and shave there. He loved to sit in the chair, drink espresso, and
gossip. He told me once that he knew he had it made when he could
afford hot towels every day. That's how they got him. Sitting under
some hot towels. They pumped twelve slugs into him."

Johnny stops talking. We both know what happened. Dino Manfredi knew about the barbershop and waited for the time when he
could use the information. That's what Johnny meant when he said,
"Dino never forgets anything." What will Vince do? Tommy was his
closest friend. If he goes after Dino, there will be a war. A big one. I
remember the day Dino was sent away to Atlanta and Vince poured
himself a big glass of wine. "Salud," he said, and smiled. "There was
going to be a lot of killing, and I am too old for that kind of business.
But Tommy fixed it. He is my patron saint now. Salud, Tommy."

We walk along the edge of the lake, watching it glint back fiercely
at us, past the hut that housed the ring I sparred in. I know what
Johnny is thinking. The alliance that has kept the Five Families out
of drug trafficking has been shattered. Tommy, Vince, and Frank
Bruno always voted together when the Five Families met at the Mafia
Council. They held the balance of power. Now that balance was blown
away. Dino would take over Tommy's family. Nobody was going to
oppose the man who had just knocked off Tommy Costanza.

"What will Dino tell the Council?"

Johnny kicks at the ground. "He'll say he didn't have to ask for a
table on killing Tommy because Tommy was the one got him sent
away to Atlanta. Then he'll bring up the drug thing again. He's been
working on getting the Five Families into the narcotics business since
1949. Narcotics was the next gold mine, he kept saying. A million
times bigger than Prohibition. He got Joe Dante hooked on the drug
operation. That will carry a lot of weight with the Council now.
There's just Vince and Frank Bruno against it, and without Tommy,
I don't know if Frank will hold out. Frank is a greedy bastard. Dino
will offer Frank a chance to come in on the drug deals and Frank will
jump at it. And then Dino will have all the dons up to their elbows
in heroin except Vince. He'll stick out like a sore thumb."

"What about you?" I ask. "You're Tommy's consigliere. What will
he do about you?"

Johnny doesn't answer right away. "Dino and I will have a talk."

"A talk."

Johnny smiles. His Hollywood number. "Sure. We'll talk. Johnny
Silk is good for business."

Johnny grinds out his cigarette. "Dino would never have done this without getting Scola's okay."

"When will the funeral be?"

Johnny pulls another cigarette from his expensive silver case. He smokes Salems. "I'll let you know."

"What will Vince do?"

Johnny eyes me. "I don't know. We'll have to talk about it."

"Since when do you and Vince talk?"

Johnny picks up a large pebble and throws it into the water. It churns up some spray and disappears. "This is business, so we'll talk."

"Is this just about drugs?"

Johnny lights a new Salem with a very expensive lighter, the line of fire jumping in the wind. "It's about Dino anointing himself capo di tutti capi. Boss of all bosses. That's always been the thing that mean little son of a bitch wanted."

I have been around the edges of this stuff all my life, but now it has struck home. This is the way the big boys play. And it is rough. I recall that night when Dino told me, "Never, never give anyone the first shot at you." Dino Manfredi had made his move. A move that Tommy, wherever he is now, understands very well.

Johnny suddenly looks wan and tired. I want to find some words that will make it better, but can't. This is too real.

His shrewd blue eyes follow the flight of a bird. "C'mon kid. Let's get back. We both have work to do."

He doesn't say anything more. We walk in silence around the fringes of the lake, which looks so peaceful and inviting. I realize what a blow this is going to be for Vince. Six years ago, when Dino got sent up, Vince was fifty-seven. It is late in the day for war and mattresses.

We finish our walk. Johnny doesn't bring up Dino or the hit again. We talk about the odds for the Bassett fight and the date for the return bout with Sandy Simpson. You would never guess that this was a consigliere faced with a terrible adversary who has just killed off his don. But at least Johnny is still young and vital. Vince is sixty-three. To be a gangster, facing a war when the vitality of youth can no longer sustain you is a terrible prospect.

We stop in front of the gym and I look at Johnny. "You going to watch me spar?"

He lights yet another cigarette and now impatiently puts it out. "I gotta get back. I'll try to drive up on Friday." He smiles. "My money is on you, kid. You look in the pink. Just don't take Bassett lightly. He's got a punch like a horse and he butts. I'll see you, Davey."

I watch Johnny walk away. He has a graceful gait and a knack for landing on his feet, but the bounce isn't there in his step.

As I circle around the sparring partners trying to impersonate Kid Bassett, all I can see is Tommy lying dead on the floor of the barbershop, the towels covering his face soaked in blood. The tabloids will carry that image tomorrow. With Dino loose, Tommy should have known better than to go in a public place exposed and unprotected. But he must have felt he was beyond retribution. That's what gave Dino the edge. Tommy thought he was an immortal, when all he really was was old.

I try to concentrate on the sparring, but I am more worried about Vince than Kid Bassett. Bassett is a club fighter with a brawling style. At long range, I will pick him to pieces with my left jab. The Kid likes to get you in the corner and pound away at your body. So Sy Morris has hired fighters who fight that way. I go six rounds with Ab Riley, Harry Black, and Casey Mendez. I slip their clinches and their right-hand leads, hook them with my left, and stay off the ropes. Sy keeps yelling, "Bassett will kill you if you stay still. Skip . . . skip . . . trip the light fantastic." Then it's over and Sy drapes my robe over my shoulder and wraps a towel over my neck as he whispers, "Stick and move and Bassett will never see you. Be gorgeous. Not a scratch."

I duck under the ropes, and there are fans waiting for me. I sign the autographs. They are mostly older people. Fight fans, retirees, old boxers. A guy is holding a folded piece of paper in front of me and I open it and get ready to sign it when I notice the writing. It's a note. "If you want to know about your real father, then you'll meet me. I'll be in touch. It's worth a lot."

I look up in time to see a slope-shouldered man hurrying down the aisle toward the exit.

After dinner, which I don't finish, I walk down to the lake and sit down on a log. The sun has already set and dark shadows are covering the water. The knot in my throat seems to have permanently settled there. I keep seeing the note. "If you want to know about your real father . . ." Vince is my father, not some ghost who gave me up twenty-nine years ago. I tried calling Vince before dinner, but he wasn't reachable. He would be sitting in a restaurant or a car somewhere, trying to figure the next move. Maybe a meeting with Johnny this evening and more Sicilian strategy. And inside that scarred and aching heart would be the hurt that came from their having fallen out. Vince brought Johnny up just like he did me. He rescued both of us. Now Tommy is dead. I should be there for Vince. Look at Davey smart, getting all emotional. That note really got under your skin. Some guy is just trying to touch you up. Forget him. Tear up the note. This is no good. You have a fight in ten days. Fighting is your business. Vince understands that. He doesn't expect you to be there. He knows you're thinking about him. Finish your business, he would say, and then we'll talk. I pick up a pebble and throw it into the water. Damn that note. It's like having a knife stuck in me. Your real father. It is something I have known was coming since I was thirteen and Vince told me I was adopted. I throw more stones into the lake, stirring the waters like the note had stirred something inside me. It has been a day of bad omens. Tommy is dead and then the note. Night has fallen and I am alone in the dark. I can't see anything.

Footsteps behind me. I jump up. There are four men. Stocky, with mashed, battered faces. My fists close and I prepare to defend myself, until I recognize the scarred face of "Dago" Pete Canzone, Vince's capo. Standing behind him are Mario Brugatti, Tiny "the Wop" Luca and Joe Rico. I have known these men since I was a little boy. They are Vince's *sgarrista*, all made men. They surround me and there are gentle bear hugs, muffled, throaty exclamations, rough but affectionate words of greeting. They have watched me grow up. They are simple men who are loyal to Vince. They have seen a great deal of history, survived other wars, but they are like their don, older now. Worry lines deepen their faces and they squint at the night with angry expectation. The unthinkable had occurred. Tommy Costanza has been hit. The Eminence has been violently deposed. They are facing a war against a violent, ruthless opponent. War is not good for business. It interrupts the flow of their lives. It stops the loan-sharking and the payoffs, the extortion and the collections. It stops the late-hour dinners of soup, antipasto, and calamari, the easy comraderie over drinks late at night.

It disrupts order, makes them travel in packs, haunts their dreams, and makes sleep impossible. No, war is not good for business or for living to a ripe old age. Dago Pete takes my arm and guides me toward my training camp. At the same time, he whispers in my ear, "Beat the shit out of this spic Bassett."

I see the Cadillac. Suddenly, Vince is there beside me. A creature of the night who has materialized out of nowhere. Wearing a coat and hat over his suit. Still hard and coiled, though his hair is streaked with white, as is his mustache. If I had to use a word to describe him even at the age of sixty-three, I would choose *dangerous*. Or perhaps that is the memory of my youth. Rosalia died twelve years ago, and part of Vince died with her. He often looks peaked and resigned to what the future holds. Once he seemed like an avenger to me. Dago Pete moves away as we embrace and Vince kisses my cheek. I feel his mustache scrape my face. It is an old and familiar sensation. He steps back and looks at me. "You look fit and ready for this brute you fight. Are you ready?"

I raise my left hand, my Michelangelo, and show it to him. "I'm ready."

Vince nods. "Come. We will walk."

We make our way around the edge of the lake with an entourage of husky soldiers behind us.

"The funeral for Tommy is Thursday. I want you to stay here."

I turn to protest, but the pressure from his hand on my shoulder is a silent message for me to wait. "This is a dangerous time and many different signals are being sent. Your presence at the funeral would be a show of respect for Tommy. I do not wish to take that away from you, but I must. You are not involved in this."

I stop and face him. "Others who are not involved will attend."

Vince has my arm again. "You are my son, and anyone close to me is involved. This game has many players. Attention will be focused on you. Perhaps someone will have an idea. All my options must remain open."

"Someone may approach me anyway."

Vince nods. "But you will not suggest it to them."

We walk in silence. A breeze coming off the lake blows the scent of water at us. "I want to pay my respects to Tommy; you know that."

Vince's arms goes around me. "I know what I ask you is not easy, but it must be. Tommy would understand. Today was just the first dealing of the cards. Tomorrow another hand will be played, and then another." He stops, his eyes fixed on an intricate and invisible journey. Staring into a maze of myriad possibilities in a dark tunnel of treachery. His ability to evade and anticipate each one will determine his survival.

I shake my head. "I can't understand how it could happen. Tommy could always see around a corner."

"It was carefully worked out. Dino planned his great revenge all the time he was in prison. But he waited until he was out to act. Like a crab stuck in the sand, waiting for the water to come. Then when the tide is full, he strikes."

I look at Vince, full of concern for him. "You can't stop the drugs. They all want it."

Vince looks back at me, his dark eyes like twin stilettos. "I know that. Old Scola has been whetting his beak for some time."

"So let it go, Vince. Let them sell their drugs. Turn your back."

Vince is silent, but I know he will answer me. We turn and walk toward the hut where the ring is housed. "It is about drugs, but it is also about me and him. He will not rest until he finishes me."

"Why?"

"Because Dino still thinks of me as I was before. He has been afraid of me ever since that day."

"What day?"

"The day I put hands upon him. It was 1926 or '27. We were making a run of scotch to New Jersey. I brought in some people to protect our trucks—we called it riding shotgun. They were Jews. Dino made a protest. I remember he said, 'You're loading us up with Hebes.' I was furious. . . . I could have killed him. It was a great insult you see. We were all the same. We were none of us dagos better than the Jews or the Irish. Only a fool would think differently. But this was worse, for the leader of the Jews was my friend. Dino insulted him with those words and he insulted me. We were in a warehouse and I pushed Dino back against the wall. In those days, I was never without a knife. It was a habit from my youth in Palermo. I put the blade to Dino's throat and I said, 'And what are you but a dirty dago? Is your blood richer than his. Let us see.' Then I gave the knife a little turn, and Dino thought I would open him up right there. He went white. I almost cut his heart out once, and that will always be between us."

We get to the gym and I open the door and the smell of old sweat and liniment comes to me. "What about Johnny? He's right in the eye of the storm."

Vince steps inside the gym where I train. He looks into the enveloping darkness at the ring bathed in moonlight. Does he see something his terrible adversary does not? Something that will give him the edge? Vince has been here before. The question is, does he see as good as he once did?

Vince's hands now rest on the apron of the ring and he looks up at the ropes. He takes out a cigar, bites off the end, and lights it. I can see its red ember as he continues to contemplate the darkness. A stranger would think Vince is ignoring me, but I know better.

"The day I found Johnny, he was sitting in a coal bin. It was in the basement of a house we were going to make into a still. He was up to his eyes in coal. I remember his face was all black and his eyes were fierce like those of a panther. I took him home so he would have a meal and a bath before I gave him to the nuns. Rosalia said, "Let him stay the night; he is exhausted." The next day, I made inquiries and learned his mother had died of the typhus and his father had deserted them many years before. Each day, I was ready to give him to the nuns, but Rosalia would say wait. I let it go on too long because we had lost a child and I knew she had an ache inside her. A week became two weeks and then a month and then two."

Vince releases a long puff of smoke above our heads. "He followed me everywhere I went. I cuffed him around a little, but always he was there. I got used to him. One day, I looked back and he wasn't there. I felt abandoned. Then he came out from a tobacco store with a cigar in his mouth and a bandit's smile. I knew I couldn't let him go to the nuns. Right from the beginning, he wanted to be in the business with me. He was very smart and he learned fast. It was not possible to keep Johnny away from the Life."

"What happened with you and Johnny?"

Vince blows another smoke ring and watches it evaporate into the air. "Life happened, Davey. Johnny grew up and made a decision. He didn't consult me. He just made it."

"Isn't it his life?"

"No, Davey, it wasn't just his life."

Thrashing blindly, instinctively, I lash out. "You can't forgive him, can you?"

"I could forgive him if I could understand. I am not God."

No, you are perhaps even greater. You are the don.

Vince waves his hands at some smoke in the air. "But in this thing with Dino, Johnny and I are together. Dino knows he will have to deal with both of us."

The subject of their falling-out is closed. Both of them will observe *omertà* as to what separates them.

Vince climbs up on to the apron of the ring and ducks under the ropes. He turns and looks down at me. "Tell me what it feels like up here? When the bell rings and the other brute comes to you, does your blood run and your heart pound with fear and excitement? Do you throb with the desire to kill and then go cold and know this is a business and you must trap him?"

"All those things."

Vince dances to the center of the ring in a pantomime of me. "How do I seem?"

"You're wide open."

"I did not want you to become a fighter because I didn't want you to be like me. But we are the same. Men who have violence in us and have used it to make our way. I love you, Davey. From the first when we brought you home from the foundling home, I loved you."

He comes to the ropes, climbs through and down. He holds me tight and I feel the emotion in my chest. Feel our hearts beating against each other. He is right: I *am* like him. Inside me, there is a creature whose blood runs hot when he stalks his prey. The ring is my habitat. In the end, we are neither of us tame men.

But as we press against each other, our hearts beating in time, the note comes back to me: "If you want to know about your real father." Suddenly, I am cold and I withdraw from our embrace. Vince drops his hands awkwardly. He thinks I am embarrassed by this display of feeling. We are men who have loved each other as we have kept our distance. It is our way. But now the note is there and something has changed for me.

Vince has walked back toward the ring and stands there admiring it. He is perfectly still as he stares at it. He is like a painter admiring an invisible canvas on which a panoply of characters and events are depicted. I know he is moving those characters back and forth in a sequence of logic and illogic known only to him. Filtered through a labyrinth of events and motives that go back forty years, through history he has experienced with men like Dino Manfredi, Joe Dante, and Carlo Scola. Tommy is on that canvas. In the mist of the Sicilian night, the dead have their hold on the living, their tortured souls crying out for revenge.

We are back outside. A soft mist has formed, obscuring the moon. We approach the car and the four brutes who will shadow Vince in the days to come. He turns back to me. "Do you remember that Thanksgiving day when you had the thin Irish boy from your class for dinner? And Johnny brought a girl. I thought your friend would never stop eating all the turkey and stuffing and sweet potatoes. He didn't know we were only beginning. You remember what Rosalia said then?"

"I remember. She said, 'Now dinner is served,' and she brought out the antipasto . . . and then the soup."

"And then the meatballs. He got sick. Do you remember? He bolted for the bathroom, and when he came back, there was steaming lasagna waiting for him. He was green in the face. How she could cook, your mother. That was a good time, wasn't it, Davey? We were all together then."

He looks at me and I search for the words. "Yes, it was."

For a second, there is a flicker of movement from his hand, as if he wants to touch me, but the impulse is stilled and the past is swallowed by the mist. Then he is gone into the car as all the gunsels pile in. The car pulls away and Vince is again one with the night.

# 2

WE BREAK CAMP and come back to the city. Johnny never showed for my last few sparring sessions. I spoke to Vince on the phone once. I could hear the tightness in his voice. "I know you will fight bravely," he said before hanging up. And you, Vince, how will you fight? Who will stand by you?

Back in New York, I run through Fort Tryon Park at dawn, a couple of sparring partners just behind me. I like the quiet to think and plan my fight, but I keep seeing the note. Keep rereading it. "If you want to know about your real father . . . It's worth a lot." It tumbles through my head.

I stand under a shower that is no longer hot, trying to snap out of it. There's always someone trying to put the touch on you when you make it in the fight game. I've made big bucks and I'm a target. This guy can point to anybody and say, That's him . . . that's your father. But I have been raised too smart to fall for this kind of theatrical game. And this guy knows it. He has to be right on the money.

There's a haze to the sky and night falls as I leave the gym. A kid slides over, looking for an autograph. He hands me an envelope. I know it's from my pen pal. I give the kid a buck and duck into a Nedick's stand. I take a deep breath and tear it open.

"If you're interested in hearing about your father, come to 113 West Eighty-seventh Street tomorrow night at ten o'clock. Ring apartment

4A. And bring five grand in hundred-dollar bills. No bargaining. What I have to sell is hotter than fresh bagels. It could burn your fingertips. Your dago friends will find it saucy. Come alone."

The letter, like the last one, is printed on lined paper. The kind you buy in the five-and-ten. My information peddler isn't exactly flush. It reads like a cheap attempt to hold me up. But in my bones, I can feel he's the real thing.

For dinner, Becky, Sy's wife, has made pot roast swimming in gravy, with fresh rye and pumpernickel bread to mop it up with. There are thick potatoes and lots of vegetables. Dessert is ice cream, stewed fruit, and tea. Usually, it's a nice, quiet time filled with conversation, jokes, and old stories Sy likes to tell. He's a man of fifty-five, who grew up in the gyms of the Lower East Side. He has a round cherub's face and his eyes are forever young. He loves fighters and fight stories. He's a middle-aged kid who has never outgrown his love of the fight game. But tonight, the stories are flat because a part of his audience is surly. I haven't eaten as much as usual, and Becky notices it. She is about to say something, but Sy shakes his head. I send them off to the movies, saying I need a nap. I turn out the light and lie on the living room couch.

In the darkness, I smell the remnants of our pot-roast dinner. I try to think about Kid Bassett and plan my fight, but nothing comes. I'm a six-to-one favorite. Bassett is the fifth-rated contender, but I'm the former champion, the wizard of legs, with the jab of Michelangelo. To beat me, Bassett has to wear me down. He needs a standing target, and I never stop moving. He's a tune-up for the Simpson rematch, nothing more. It's not that I'm cocky, just confident. The Kid has a good right hand, but you can see it coming. His left hook is awkward and he seldom uses it. He's a one-armed fighter, and as long as I circle to my left . . . But then thoughts of the fight leave me. Tomorrow night, I have a date with my past—with my real father's identity.

I sleep poorly. In the morning, I get the money on the way down to the gym and have Sy hold it for me. I know he's wondering what's going on with his boy. The fight business has never been a sure thing. I shadowbox and skip rope my way through the day but remember none of it.

We are home by late afternoon and I try to nap before dinner. I finally doze off and wake up to the aroma of lamb chops cooking. It's my favorite. Sy and I sit down and start eating. Becky, still holding the potatoes and vegetables, doesn't set them down.

Sy looks at her. "What's the matter? It's a mitzvah, this meat."

Becky is a small woman with curly gray hair. She has lots of wrinkles in her face, and just now they're all showing. She shrugs. "I don't know. Suddenly, they announce the president is going on television tonight. Nine o'clock. I don't like it."

Sy waves his hand in dismissal. "Big deal. He wants to jack up his ratings. What could happen? C'mon, tsatskeh, I got a hungry fighter here. We got a fight Friday night. Feed him."

Reluctantly, Becky joins us. We get through what should be a jovial dinner in poor shape. Becky keeps looking at the clock. At 8:30, she has the tube on. When I return to the living room at nine o'clock, they're both sitting on the couch, wearing glasses. Sy looks at me funny.

"Let me have the gelt."

His face drops and his mouth opens. Jesus, he thinks I'm giving someone money to bet on the fight.

I ride through his protest. He looks into my eyes and clams up.

"Where you going?"

"Downtown."

I can see Sy struggling, like a mother with a child going to the dance alone.

"Don't use the subway; take a cab. Jesus, Davey."

I laugh. "Who's going to roll the ex–lightweight champion of the world?"

"Tell that to Bummy Davis."

Bummy Davis was a left hooker from Brownsville who got killed in a restaurant stickup. President Kennedy comes on the tube as I get my coat. I stop in the bathroom for a water deposit, and when I come out, Becky is holding her cheeks, saying over and over, "Vai iz mir, oi vai." Sy takes her hand.

The president looks grim. He announces the Russians have missiles in Cuba. Ninety miles from the American coast. Becky looks worse than the president. Sy doesn't look so good, either. I leave without saying good night. I hear Becky saying, "Vaiz mir, we're at war with the Russians."

I think of the possibility of missiles hitting New York City as I step outside and decide I'm better off underground in the subway. It has become a very interesting week. I am fighting in the Garden on Friday night, if there is a Friday night. In the meantime, I'm carrying five thousand large to give to a man who said he has information about my real father.

# 3

**I GET OFF THE TRAIN** at Broadway and Eighty-sixth and walk in the direction of Central Park West. Broadway seems light on traffic and devoid of people. The pungent aroma of fresh bread baking makes me hungry. I'm all keyed up. There's something in the air on this October night. It's intoxicating, all-suffusing, exciting, and dangerous. I feel my nerves grip me in that way that comes to you as you wait for the bell for the first round. So taut and tight, you can hardly breathe, and for a moment you think you're going to fall down. Then the bell sounds and it goes away. I pick up my pace.

At Amsterdam Avenue, I head north to Eighty-seventh Street and turn right, heading toward a row of brownstone houses. I slow my pace as I reach a brownstone that shows the numerals 125. One thirteen would be just a few houses away. I cross the street so I can get a better look at 113. It's my Sicilian heritage. I grew up with the belief that nothing is as it seems. I'm not ready to walk in there cold. Not yet.

I slip down the steps of a short enclosure used to stack garbage cans. From this vantage point, I can check out the fourth floor of the building. There are no lights on. The tight feeling is back. I feel the roll of money in my pocket. For someone raised by a don, I'm not acting very smart. Maybe this is all a mistake.

I take a deep breath and walk to the building, and seconds later I am inside the vestibule. Number 4A has no name on it. I check the impulse to ring the buzzer and try turning the doorknob. It goes all the way around to the right, and then I am inside, underneath a small overhead light in the foyer, which reveals a worn brown rug and faded, yellowing wallpaper. There is a musty smell, as if the building hasn't been aired out in decades. As I climb the stairs, I listen to my footsteps and feel the residual pounding of my heart.

I am facing an apartment with a large but crooked *A* affixed to it. The door is ajar. A record is on. A woman's voice. The note repeats itself. The record is stuck. I stand there listening to the same one note, smelling the old house I am in. The odor seems to permeate my brain and sets off a warning chord. As I approach the door, I feel the tightness return. I take a deep breath and push it open.

The room, lighted by a dim table lamp, is a combination living room and kitchen. The smell of recently fried meat lingers in the air. Two stacks of newspapers are piled in the corner. There is an armchair next to the newspaper stacks. An old green-and-gold-print rug seems embedded in the floor. Plaid drapes hang listlessly from above the two windows facing the street. They are drawn. The music is coming from the bedroom. I walk slowly toward it, wanting to speak but instinctively knowing I shouldn't. I can see the small light in the bedroom. I hesitate and then go inside. There is a tumble of sheets on an unmade bed, a sheaf of newspaper clips strewn on the floor next to a cigar box, and then I see the body—lying faceup underneath a table that holds an old television set and the record player.

The hit. The word I have been taught to respect for its terrible finality. The solution to all disputes. The resolution that makes a beggar into a king and a king into a legend. And what manner of beggar or king lies on the floor beneath me? Wearing a checked suit, which he must have gotten from a department store rack, over a brown tie and white shirt. The collar of the shirt is turned up and dirty. He has an unshaven, pouchy face and his hair is a thinning mixture of brown and white. The eyes are open. Eyes that have seen all manner of things, including the face of his killer. He is up there in years—sixty-five or more. He has taken a couple of slugs behind the ear. On the floor at his feet is one of those heaters you plug in. A dull, inadequate light touches its bent strands. I fight the impulse to run. I lean over him and touch his neck. Not stone-cold. The hit was recent. What did this washed-up has-been with the lifeless eyes have to sell me that was worth five thousand dollars?

Though I have heard countless stories of the hit, I have never witnessed one, never seen a victim of one. But the stories have served me well, for I don't feel fear, though I am repulsed. Yet it is hard to breathe, and the stuck record fills the tiny room. I walk over and lift the needle; the record slows down. I look at the label. Dolly Irving. *Torch Time*. Next to it lies an album. The picture on the cover is of a beautiful flapper, hair glistening, wearing an evening gown. Some indefinable emotion is registered on her face. Something hungry, love-haunted. Looking out after the lover who got away. I look again at the corpse, take a deep breath, and, raising him slightly, feel for a wallet. It is in his back pocket. The wallet is a cheap brown and wrinkled thing. There are cards, a pawn ticket. Nothing identifies him until I come to a Social Security card in the name of Harold Green. It is not a name that jogs anything for me. The wallet has no money. He was either cleaned out or he was broke. Taking another breath, I fish into his pockets.

He was heavily into the ponies. There are track tickets and slips of paper with horses' names on them. Fix It . . . Shy Guy in the fifth . . . in a scribbled circle are the words *win, place*, and *show* and an arrow leading to the name Heart Felt. Another slip of paper is filled with numbers. They add up to $5,100. So the magic number was five thousand. That's why I was here.

One of the newspaper clippings on the floor catches my eye. It is faded and yellow. The headline reads: MOTHER OF SLAIN GANGSTER PLEADS FOR BROTHER'S LIFE. It is a copy of the *Daily Mirror*, dated Saturday, June 17, 1933. The article is by Herb Lawrence. As I unfold it, a small end breaks off.

*They are sitting in the kitchen and a copy of the* Daily Mirror *is lying on the floor next to them. There's a picture of Benny Wagman all stitched up from machine-gun bullets. Ruth Wagman, Benny's mother, is a small, pinched woman with wispy gray-brown hair. Her birdlike brown eyes keep flittering from Nails Gordon to the copy of the* Daily Mirror *lying on the floor. She has on a long black dress and slippers. They are seated across a table covered with a faded red-and-white tablecloth. The kitchen is a little bandbox with peeling, cracked walls, but I don't see a speck of dirt on the floors. The icebox rests against the wall. Just beneath it is a case of seltzer water. Next to the icebox is the sink. Its faucet has a perpetual drip. An exclamation point to everything this grieving mother is saying.*

"This I always waited for, Max. This I knew was coming."

*Max "Nails" Gordon has bushy eyebrows, which just now are furrowed up, thick black hair, and mesmerizing dark eyes. He is wearing an expensive pinstriped blue suit, white shirt, and pale blue tie. His hand flickers. He drums his fingers on the old cloth that covers the table separating them.*

"Al," *Ruth Wagman says.* "You are going to save Al?"

*Nails Gordon tries to reassure her.* "Nothing will happen to Al."

*She looks plaintively at him.* "Benny was the baby, but he had always a terrible temper. I couldn't keep him from the street. That's where he ended up."

*There is a painful silence, broken only by the drip of the faucet.*

*She sips tea from a cup.* "Where is Al? His brother is dead and he's not here."

*Nails Gordon's fingers resume their nervous run on the table.* "Al will come."

"Benny is buried tomorrow."

"I'm trying to arrange—soon he'll come."

*She shook her head.* "On Shabbas they killed him. In front of my house." *Ruth Wagman is pulling at his arm.* "I want Al. Tell them to spare my Al. Send him back to me."

"Soon he'll come," *Nails reassures her.*

*The tea in her cup must be cold and bitter by now, but she takes a long swallow.* "The boys wanted me to move, but this is where I raised them. Morris and me. But we couldn't keep them from the street."

*Nails Gordon knows all about the street. There has been bad blood between the Gordon mob and the Mazzoti gang for years. Climaxed by the killing of Larky Mauro and Joey "the Plumber" Doto in front of the Hot Spot on West Fourth Street in the early hours of the morning of February 18. Mauro was the cousin of Ace Mazzoti, leader of the Mazzoti outfit. Now the war has claimed Benny Wagman, and his brother, Al, is in hiding. Sources along Broadway say the Mazzoti gang is highly placed in the emerging underworld combination that has come out of Prohibition. The Gordon mob has lost its crack killer, Benny Wagman. Benny Wagman was one of the New York Police Department's chief suspects in the murder of Legs Diamond, but Benny came up with an alibi the men in blue couldn't crack. The same Broadway sources say the Gordon gang doesn't have the fire power to match up with the Mazzoti mob and the hired guns of the combination.*

*Nails Gordon leans over and says something I cannot catch. I move closer and hear these words. "I'm working on something. We're gonna talk. Something will be worked out."*

*Does that mean a truce is in the works? Is Nails Gordon offering concessions to Ace Mazzoti and the combination?*

*Ruth Wagman points to the back bedroom. "That's where Benny slept."*

*Nails Gordon is whispering to her now. She listens carefully and nods her head. He takes her hand now and pats it. Ruth Wagman seems to recede into her dress of mourning. She looks very frail. One of Nails Gordon's "boys" comes into the room. His name is Bo Sussman. He indicates with a nod of his head that he wants to speak to his boss. Bo is a big, tough-looking man with immense shoulders. There is a conspicuous bulge under his jacket. Nails Gordon whispers some final words and goes out, leaving Ruth Wagman alone. She stares toward the back of the apartment. Toward the bedroom where her boys Al and Benny grew up. She is hardly aware of my presence. She wonders if Al Wagman will come tomorrow or if he will ever come.*

An old killing out of another time. A mother mourning for her son asks pardon for the other. And Nails Gordon, leader of the gang that Benny Wagman served, tries to console her with promises he cannot keep. There is no forgiveness in the "Life." There will be no pardon for Ruth Wagman's son. Nails Gordon knows that. Why has he exposed himself to a reporter? Is he sending a message by going public? Is that it? Why is his name familiar to me? Is this what was being sold to me?

I pick up the next clipping. It is dated Sunday, June 18, 1933. Again the *Daily Mirror* under the byline of Herb Lawrence. GANG WAR ERUPTS. MOBSTER GUNNED DOWN ON BROADWAY.

*The gang war that has been simmering between the Gordon mob and the Mazzoti gang erupted yesterday when Nick Rossi, the younger brother of gangland chieftain Vince Rossi, was gunned down outside the Broadway Cafeteria at five o'clock in the afternoon. Rossi, who had been eating inside the cafeteria located at Eighteenth Street and Broadway, had just emerged when a gunman in a green DeSoto sedan parked outside opened fire with a machine gun. Several witnesses who saw the daring broad-daylight murder told police that the killer called Rossi by name before opening fire. Cries of "Nick, Nick" were heard by witnesses. Rossi, who was dressed in a blue suit, tie, and shirt looked up and started toward the car. He was met by a deadly volley of bullets, which killed him instantly.*

I sink to my knees like a fighter who has just been dropped by a left hook. I have seen pictures of Uncle Nick, and the story was that he died from pneumonia. Vince never wanted to talk about it, and I let it go at that. I remember now the look in Rosalia's eyes when Nick's name came up. Some indefinable, trembling emotion, which I interpreted as grief. It wasn't grief; it was guilt over the lie that was being told me. I go back to the column and fight blurry vision.

*Detectives working on the case believe that the murder of Nick Rossi was an act of retaliation by the Gordon mob for the killing of Benny Wagman by hired killers from the Mazzoti gang. Ace Mazzoti is a cousin of Vince Rossi, who controls the action for the Syndicate in the Bronx. A detective questioned by this reporter said that the killing means "All-out war. The killing of Nick Rossi will bring Vince Rossi and his guns in on this. It was the worst thing Nails Gordon could ever have thought up."*

The name comes back at me again. Nails Gordon. Where have I heard the name? This is what the corpse wanted to talk to me about— that much I realize. What was the connection? A twenty-nine-year-old murder. Harold Green was a mob guy. Somehow he was involved in this. My eyes fall to another clipping lying at my feet.

MOB MASSACRE

NAILS GORDON AND 3 OTHERS KILLED

IN EAST SIDE HOTEL

*The simmering gangland war that has pitted the Jewish East Side mob of Nails Gordon against the Ace Mazzoti gang exploded into four violent murders early this morning. Four men carrying pistols broke into rooms on the seventh floor of the Rodman Arms Hotel on East 28th Street and opened fire. Killed in the fusillade of bullets were legendary East Side mobster Nails Gordon and three members of his gang. Morris "Bo" Sussman, Abner "Abba Dabba" Bernstein, and Al Wagman. Al Wagman is the brother of Benny Wagman, who was cut down in his car on Friday night. It was the murder of Benny Wagman that started the bloody war that has claimed the lives of six on this bloody weekend. Also wounded in the attack was Sam "Red" Miller. Miller was in serious condition at Madison Square Hospital.*

*The brutal massacre began at 4:20 A.M., when six gangsters apparently acting on a tip entered rooms 728, 729, 730, and 736 and began blasting away. Gunshots and terrible screams erupted on the seventh floor. Witnesses reported to the police that the victims died horrible deaths. None of the men was dressed, and several were lying in bed when their killers broke in and opened fire. Police reports indicate that more than forty bullets were fired during the ambush. Nails Gordon was apparently lying in bed in his shorts and undershirt, smoking a cigarette, when the door burst open. He took six bullets in his head, chest, and abdomen. Sharing another room were Bo Sussman, Red Miller, and Al Wagman. Round after round of bullets tore into Sussman and Wagman and they died instantly. Somehow Miller, while wounded in the arms and legs, managed to get off several shots from his pistol, and police believe he may have wounded one of the killers. While Miller lay seemingly dead, the killers broke into room 730 and began firing. Killed while lying on his bed and shooting at the deadly crew of murderers was Abba Dabba Bernstein. His companion in the room, Joe Axler, who had been awakened by the gunfire, was able to crawl under his bed and escaped injury. As the victims' screams tore through the night, awakening hotel guests, the gunmen pounded down the back stairs, where they sped away in cars parked outside the hotel for a quick getaway.*

*Arriving at the hotel owned by Broadway bootlegger Waxy Green, the police found the four dead bodies, and had Miller transported to Madison Square Hospital, where he underwent surgery. Joe Axler was taken downtown for questioning, where he is being held as a material witness. Chief of detectives Joe Hurley said, "This is a very professional job. The killers must have been tipped off. Nails Gordon was a smart, tough guy who's been around. For somebody to catch him and five of his boys asleep in bed this way means they were ratted on."*

*Police are speculating that Gordon and his men were holed up in the Rodman Arms while rumors spread that the Syndicate was trying to strike a deal with them. There are reports that several guests at the hotel noted six "showgirls" coming in just after midnight. The girls, who were described as young and attractive, were seen getting off on the seventh floor. It is believed that they had been brought in by the Gordon mob for some late-hour socializing. Several of them were seen getting into taxi's at 3:30 in the morning, about an hour before the killers appeared. The police believe that one of these girls may have tipped off the men who killed Nails Gordon.*

*Contacted at his Manhattan apartment, Waxy Green, king of the beer barons in New York, said he had been trying to arrange a truce within the mob. Green said, "I have known Nails Gordon since he was a little kid and I knew he was in bad trouble. I told him to lie low at the hotel till something could be worked out. But I guess somebody found out where he was. The Gordon mob was a bunch of tough kids who grew up on the East Side together. They made a lot of noise, got into the rackets, and made plenty of money in Prohibition. I knew them all. They were tough kids who got a little wild. They made a lot of enemies, and this time I think some of them got together and wiped them out."*

There are pictures of the four dead gangsters. The other three look like fireplugs, but Nails Gordon is a man with dark good looks and arresting eyes. Eyes haunted by the life he has led. I stare down at the corpse. Harold Green, his Social Security card says, but his obituary will read "Waxy Green, king of the beer barons during Prohibition."

He had taken a long fall. A small-time crumb reduced to peddling information. But what did this crumb know? What does this sheath of clippings that fell out of a cigar box mean? Is this what he was going to tell me? It's linked to Vince. His brother was murdered by the Gordon mob. Did Vince have anything to do with the wipeout in the Rodman Arms Hotel? Why is Uncle Nick's murder a family secret?

I look down at the floor. There's a slew of clippings, which I pick up and stuff in the old cigar box, Waxy Green's Exhibit A. The final days of Nails Gordon. Nails Gordon, the legendary East Side mobster. Now I remember where I heard his name—that night in Mangicore's, after I won the lightweight championship. It was Dino Manfredi who mentioned him. He was talking about the Gordon mob. "Ask Vince about Nails Gordon. He got rubbed out. It was a big story. Made all the front pages. Ask him."

What does Vince know? What does it have to do with me, with my real father? I didn't ask the right questions when I was thirteen. Because I didn't want to know. But now the past has reached out for me. Nineteen thirty-three. The year I was born. The year Vince's brother Nick was killed. I stand up and I am very dizzy. The airless room is getting to me. Get out of here.

Some impulse brings me back inside the room. I go to the record player and lift the record from it. I check the label. It belongs in the album with the picture of the beautiful Dolly Irving on it. *Torch Time*. The first song on it is "The Man I Love."

# 4

THE WALK I HAVE TAKEN so many times begins as always in my dressing room, robe tied around me, a towel wrapped around my neck. Sy is in front of me, next to him, carrying a bucket, is Joe Dunn. It is a short walk down a darkened runway and then a blast of warm air as I come into the Garden. The smoke hits my eyes and the crowd ahead comes to its feet as it becomes aware of my presence. It is a ritual long observed. With the towel covering my head and neck, surrounded by my entourage, it is as if I am a holy man being escorted to investiture. The crowd is applauding, remembering those nights when I have been an artist and also that night last May when I offered them the ultimate gift, the spectacle of the artist fallen, the champion dethroned. Now they want to see if there is anything left beyond the heart of a champion. It is a cruel business not only for the physical punishment you absorb but for the manner in which you are discarded by the crowd. If Kid Bassett hammers me tonight, I will be consigned to the junk heap by the crowd and by the reporters. Dismissed as "Poor Davey, he's shot." But for the moment, I am Davey Rossi on the comeback trail. The great little Italian boxer, slippery, artful, smooth, possessed of a dazzling left jab. Poker-faced, a pro, a former champion. But beneath the mask, I am unsteady. There is a dead man whose murder made all the newspapers in town. A dead man who claimed to have known about my real father. Why has Vince kept the real story about my uncle Nick's death from me? Why the lies? What doesn't he want me to know? As I stare down at the canvas, I see the dead face and eyes of Waxy Green. And a stuck record plays the same one-note lament of love by Dolly Irving.

As I shuffle in my corner, I can see my backers at ringside. Mob guys with their dolls. Lumpen faces with cutout sockets for eyes that have lost their capacity for expression, as if they had been permanently anesthetized. In their midst is Joe Dante, don of all Brooklyn, dressed in a tightly fitted black suit and a maroon striped tie, his eyes tiny slits. Then I catch sight of Frank Bruno in a brown suit, those somber killer's eyes surveying me, wondering if the skinny kid has anything left. A few seats away, dressed in a dark suit, is Johnny, and next to him sits the dark lady of my dreams. Regal as a princess in a black two-piece suit with high collar, her hair worn up. I stare at her. She has a face I have been searching for all my life. Her lips are soft and voluptuous, her nose a perfect line, the eyelashes long and dark over eyes that never leave me. They are eyes pierced by intelligence. Watching my every move. I turn away, looking for Vince, knowing he will not be there. He has never liked to see me take punishment. And now he is at war and will not be seen in a public place. I am grateful he is not here. Johnny has moved down to ringside and is conferring with Sy.

I look across the ring at the face of José "Kid" Bassett, his eyes intently searching me out. He is wondering how much the fight with Sandy Simpson took out of me. They are big dumb eyes, like those of a grazing cow. His face is without expression. He has large, flaring nostrils and thick oval lips. The black hair is greased back, tight to his scalp. He gives me the evil eye now, meant to intimidate me. It is a game we boxers play. I pay no attention.

Referee Herb Gretz beckons us to the center of the ring to give us our instructions. It is like listening to a worn record of the catechism being recited. Phrases heard endless times: "Keep your punches up. No hitting below the belt, no rabbit punches. When I say break, break. Good luck. Come out fighting at the bell." Bassett's eyes stay on me. He is game and determined. If he beats me, he could get a shot at Simpson. We'll see how much those eyes like a good jab that will be in his face all night. Back in my corner, Sy pulls the robe off me and

Joe puts the mouthpiece in. "Box him," Sy tells me. "Move, stick and move. Make his tongue hang out. He's muscle-bound. Every punch he telegraphs." I nod and skip in my corner. The bell rings. I make the sign of the cross, a silent appeal to the Virgin Mary for her protection. I take a quick look at the girl. God, she is beautiful, and she keeps watching me.

I am slow getting out of my corner as Bassett comes rushing across the ring at me. He leads with a long, wild right, as if he would end the fight right there. The crowd surges, and in its collective voice is hope for the underdog. I slip under the punch, tie him up, and slide away. We are in the center of the ring, at long range. I circle left, going counterclockwise, giving him no target for that explosive right hand. It is like a hundred training sessions and dozens of fights. He gets impatient and lunges. I spear him with the left, and the crowd acknowledges my punch. I move in and out, bobbing my head, feinting left and right. Bassett thinks he sees an opening and fires the right. I step back and let it graze me. I could have evaded it completely but I am teasing Bassett. I want him to take a chance. And he does. He comes wading in and I pepper him with a left-right-left combination. The crowd roars. His face is red and a trickle of blood descends from his nose. I keep circling and stick him three more times with my left. The crowd picks up the noise level. This is the Davey Rossi they know. A deft, skillful boxer with million-dollar legs and the jab of a Michelangelo.

Bassett tries to cut down the size of the ring so he can catch me in a corner. "Move . . . move," I hear Sy yell. I spin away, but Bassett is there lunging again, and I tie him up. He pounds my arms in the clinch. He is very strong. The idea is to make my arms heavy so that later in the fight, my hands will come down and leave him an opening for the right. Gretz breaks us and I move to the center of the ring. Pop, pop, pop, I drill a tattoo on Bassett's face. Sharp punches. Not knockout ones, just stinging blows that will wear on him. But he is like a bull and keeps coming. I drill him four times with left jabs and then cross with a right. It is a strong punch, landing on the bridge of his nose. It slows Bassett. He is down in a low crouch, head bobbing. He shifts his weight and throws the right; I duck under it as the bell sounds.

Joe washes me down and Sy is a relentless machine-gun splatter of words. "You let him get you in the corner and almost got tagged with the right. Don't play with his right just to sucker him. If he tags you with it, it's nighty-night. Stay away, Davey. Move and jab; get him tired. There's a long way to go." I rinse out and Joe puts the mouth-piece back. I see Bassett standing in his corner and I come off my stool. The bell.

Bip, bip, bip. I paint the left all over his face. I move, stop, feint, and drill him, moving left all the time, away from Bassett. The crowd makes a lot of noise when he throws the flailing rights, but fight people will tell you that it is all for the unwashed. Bassett is being undressed in public. A wild, brawling fighter who is out of his league. As the round ends, I stick him with a series of six straight lefts and he takes them all, standing there in a frozen cameo of frustration.

Back on my stool Sy croons in my ear. "Beautiful. Keep sticking and the bull will bleed." All the while he is talking, I keep peeking at Johnny and the beauty. She sees me looking. She seems very serious. Very beautiful.

In the third round, the bull keeps bleeding as I plant the left in his face and frustrate his charges. But Bassett is game. He keeps com-ing, his swarthy body glistening under the hot lights, his black hair oily from sweat and water. In the last minute of the round, Bassett gets me in a corner and pounds at my body. Big heavy blows to my kidneys and ribs. They hurt. They are clubbing heavy punches. I tie up his hands until Herb Gretz breaks us. We are at close range near the ropes and Bassett thinks he sees a chance. He comes barreling in the right, cocked, and I beat him to the punch with a stinging left hook. The crowd roars. Still at close range, I rake his face with the left. Jab, jab, jab, and then I hook with the right. The dumb cow eyes show pain. I skip away to the center of the ring, where I am waiting for him with a series of scorching jabs to end the round.

There is a Yiddish word *kvelen.* It means "to glow with pride and joy." As I stand up waiting for the bell for the fourth round, Sy whis-pers, "You're beautiful, boychik. I'm kveling. Use the hook. Get the bull crazy. And stay off the ropes."

There is a moment in a fight when you achieve a rhythm. That is, you don't have to think about what comes next, you just do it. It's as if an actor could throw down his script in rehearsal and the words would come to him anyway. That's how it is for me in the fourth round. I know just what to do and just how Bassett will respond. I always have the answer for his moves, while creating my own. When he gets near, there are a series of combinations, starting with jabs, ending with hooks. Enraged, he puts his head down, trying to get in. I waltz away, flutter like a butterfly at long range, and then start again. I am way ahead on points.

Near the end of the round, I put another cute move on Bassett. I let him pin me near the ropes so he will get bold. He throws a very wild right and his follow-through sends him sailing into the ropes. The crowd raises its voice at the action, cheering as the artist makes the puncher play the buffoon. I stop to admire my artistry, instead of skipping away. Bassett hits the ropes, but rather then hang there, he bounces off and whirls in the same motion. The big bull head thuds squarely into my forehead and eye. It is the worst butt I have ever taken. The impact detonates a bomb in my brain and blood spurts from above my eye. I can't think or move. My knees go soft; my hands fall to my side. Bassett, momentarily stunned, straightens himself and sees me standing there, no longer skipping, darting or able to punch. He hits me with a clubbing right on the side of the head. My legs give way and I sink down to meet the floor.

I hear the amazed cry of exultation from the crowd, like you hear the sound of a massive ocean wave before you see it. The chopping force of the punch has numbed me. I lie inert on the canvas, groping to focus on the misty image of someone standing over me. I can't hear the count. I can't move to get up. Then I see the referee's hand coming down and hear the tail end of a word and then another. Five. Instinctively, I get to one knee. Six. I shake my head to clear it. Seven. I can hear him clearly now. I let him count to eight, and at nine, I get up. Herb Gretz wipes my gloves. The Garden is pandemonium. Somebody is yelling for me to hold on. The blood gushes down over and into my right eye. I can't see at all out of it. I use the left eye to focus and then I see Bassett cross the ring in three steps, positioning himself to throw a right. He flings himself at me and I go under the punch and half-tackle him. We are all caught up in each other, knotted together and stumbling about the ring when the bell sounds. The raucous voice of the crowd blows the roof off the Garden as I wobble to my corner.

My corner is a frantic commotion of noise and motion. Joe gives me a long whiff of smelling salts to clear my head. He swabs my face and sutures the cut while Sy barks strategy at me. First a jab at my arrogance. "You got cute and you got caught. Now he smells blood. Box him, use the bicycle, and stay off the fucking ropes. Box him, Davey. Stick and run." He looks into my eyes and I nod. Joe has cleaned the cut and used all his skill to close it. He smears it with salve to give it some protection. Sy looks at the cut, then at Joe.

"It's nasty," Joe says solemnly.

Sy is like a worried mother. "He'll try to use his head again. Watch out for the butt." The bell rings and I come off my stool, hearing Sy's instructions. "Box him. Stay away."

My head is clear, but I am still shaky. My legs are like jelly. That's what a paralyzing punch does to the nervous system, to your brain, to your sense of order. Another strong punch and the system will self-destruct. Bassett has been given a huge chance. He doesn't even have to knock me out. Just open the cut over my eye again. It is bad; it will gush blood. The referee will stop the fight.

Run, jab, run, jab. Bassett pursues me relentlessly. The crowd cheers Bassett and boos me. Let them boo. The points are mine. He keeps boring in. His leaden eyes are filled with excitement. He knows he can finish me, get a shot at the title. But he is too excited, too anxious. He uncorks wild rights and throws himself headlong after me. I rap him with the left, spin away. He pursues. An enraged bull chasing a bee that repeatedly stings him. The bell.

In my corner, Joe swabs my face and covers the eye with more salve while Sy chatters like a magpie. "Good. Now listen, he's very anxious. Run for a while, then fight him in flurries. A couple of combinations, then you get on the bicycle. You have to get control of the fight again. Wear him out." I can see Bassett's corner frantically imploring him to finish me. His manager, Doc Kramer, is whispering something in his ear. Bassett nods. The bell.

The restless voice of the crowd is there urging Bassett to attack. It seems like a replay of the last round. Bassett throws a furious right, but when you are fighting a one-armed opponent, he is incredibly easy to anticipate. We move to long range. Suddenly, he is there to confront me. I dip, bob my head as I see him set himself for the right, but he throws a short left hook. It is completely unexpected. He doesn't have a left. Not until this minute. It lands heavy and leaden on the side of my head. It is a punch of tremendous force and has caught me flush. My knees buckle, the crowd roars its acclamation, and Bassett, stepping in, follows this punch with a vicious right uppercut that explodes on my jaw.

I am gratefully at rest on the canvas. I pick up the count at three. The crowd is a cacophony of voices imploring Bassett to finish it, me to get up. I wait on one knee till the count of nine. Herb Gretz checks me carefully and then, seeing I am all right, says, "Fight." Bassett closes on me. I need to run, but my reflexes are not there. Bassett bulls me into the ropes, frantically throwing punches. The crowd screams in affirmation of his fury. But the punches are not landing. I take them on my elbows, on my gloves; I make him miss and we clinch. As Gretz separates us, Bassett lowers his head and brings it up. The butt savages my right eye, opening it anew, and the gush of blood blinds me. The pain is excruciating. Bassett is afire. He batters me relentlessly with punches from close in and I sink to the canvas. This time, I am not coming back from anywhere. This time, it is easier. I take the nine count and assure Herb Gretz I am okay. It is not my assurance he is interested in, but my eye. My face is a crimson mask. I push him away and beckon to Bassett to come on. The crowd loves it.

I hear Sy yelling, "Thirty seconds, thirty seconds." I backpedal, but there is no spring to my legs. Somewhere in the crush of sound, I pick up the ringside broadcaster doing the fight. "Rossi is badly hurt. Here comes the Kid." I plant my legs and meet his head-on charge. Blood streaming down my face, I throw a flurry of punches. I am fighting for my life, and from somewhere comes the adrenaline that keeps my blood pumping and the punches coming as the bell rings and the crowd erupts in tribute, a beastlike voice eternally grateful at having its appetite for violence fed.

Joe is trying to work miracles on my eye as Sy hits me with smelling salts twice. Sy is raving. "The lousy bastard, Kramer. He told Bassett to use his head that way. He's got a left, Davey. They suckered us."

I nod. Now I know what Doc Kramer was whispering in Bassett's ear. Telling him to use the butt and then the left—the punch they had worked on for months in training camp but told him to save.

Sy looks at me. There is no quit in those eyes. "You have to run and then flurry. Bring him in, beat him with combinations, and get out of there."

Herb Gretz is there looking at my eye. "One more time, Davey, and I'll have to stop it. It's deep."

Sy is in his face. "Sure it is. The son of a bitch uses his head like a razor."

"I've warned him."

"Thanks a lot. That really helps."

The bell rings and the crowd roars its approval. We circle each other. Bassett is in a low crouch, looking to get in. I spin away, trying to bounce on my toes, reaching for leg strength that isn't there. Without those legs, I can't set the pace. Stepping in, I nail Bassett with a left hook and right cross. The right is from short range and perfectly timed. He is surprised; his legs bend and he goes down on his right knee. The crowd screams in ecstasy. Herb Gretz waves me off and starts to count. Bassett is up at the count of one. He is not badly hurt. He comes at me. I step to my left and catch him with a sharp left lead. He counters, but I slip the punch and nail him with a right-left combination. The crowd roars from its belly. Bassett's nostrils flare in fury and he clubs me with a straight right. I take it on the head and fire back with another quick combination. They are good, hard punches. They hurt and make Bassett realize I am not a stretcher case. But he is not to be discouraged.

I let him chase me for twenty seconds and then meet him again with another flurry of punches. A succession of lefts, a sneak right, and then a bolo right uppercut. I am playing to the screaming gallery, to the referee and judges. Outmaneuvering and outpunching Bassett. But the stamina and legs to get away aren't there. Bassett rolls his shoulder for the right and bangs me with the left again, catching me flush on the temple. My legs buckle and I try to hold on, but he is there with two incredibly quick and numbing right hands. I feel the ropes at my back and try to duck, but the right lead is there, delivered with tremendous follow-through. A punch with which he propels himself off his legs. It impacts on my jaw with crushing force.

The noise in my ear abruptly fades and I fall forward on my face. I hear dissonant noises and Herb Gretz is there counting over me. Somehow I'm on my feet. "I'm okay," I tell him as he wipes off my gloves. I lurch forward before he can do anything. Champions get the respect of being knocked out.

Bassett is in front of me. I reach for him and grab his hands. He yanks them away and I wrap my arms around him. Gretz breaks us. Bassett rakes my body and ribs with thudding blows. My hands come down and Bassett catches me with a short chopping left, followed by a right thrown in a swift, powerful arc.

I crumble and fall. I lie there hugging the canvas, a man in love with his pillow. It would be wonderful to sleep. But I have to get out of bed and do something. I push myself up and go to answer the door. Somebody is knocking. Three, four, five, six, seven, eight, nine. I desperately throw it open and see his face. What is he saying? It is Gretz; he is trying to throw up his hands and say it's over, but I won't let him. I grab his hands as the bell rings and then lurch on drunken legs toward my corner.

There is a terrible odor, a popping noise in my head, and the smell of ammonia in my nostrils. But it works. My head clears and I can see Sy in front of me. I can hear him. "I'm going to stop it, Davey."

"No."

"Five times you been down."

"No."

"You're meshuga. Fix his eye, Joe. His eye."

I grab Sy's arm. "You don't stop it. No towel. You hear? You got that, Joe. No towel."

Joe Dunn leans in. "Let me see the eye."

Once again, he sutures it. It hurts, but not so much anymore. Sy holds my neck. "You're behind. We got the first three rounds, but he's got everything else since."

"What's the round?"

Sy shakes his head. "It's the eighth round. You need to take the last three rounds. You need to make him look bad. If you can't do that, don't go out there. It's a freak . . . that lousy butt."

Herb Gretz is there. "Davey . . ."

"It's the eighth round and I'm fighting Kid Bassett in Madison Square Garden. I'm behind on points, but I'm going to win. And the Russians have missiles in Cuba. Good enough?"

"One more round like the last one, Davey . . ."

"Go away."

I turn to Joe. "Give me the mouthpiece."

Sy is saying something. The bell sounds for the eighth round. "Box him."

"You box him."

Look into a fighter's eyes and you can tell how the fight is going. The Kid's eyes are brimming with confidence. And he is hungry. He has a better fighter rocky and bleeding. He knows I don't have the legs left to run for three rounds. He is confident he will catch me. It is seeing to the end of all things.

Look into my eyes and you will see a hurt fighter. A fighter who has taken a pounding, a fighter who has lost his legs. Not a confident fighter. "Davey is game," they are saying in the press box, "but he's beaten. He can run, but he can't win." They are right. I can't win by trying to run. I can win only by knocking you out, Kid. That is also seeing to the end of all things.

The crowd is strangely quiet. Bassett is stalking me so he can throw combinations from short range. I stop and fire a weak left jab. The snap isn't there. The Kid grunts and smiles. He has taken the decoy. He bulls me toward the ropes. This is where it is supposed to happen. I fake the left and he gets ready to shoot the right. I step in with a right and dig it into his belly. This time, it is not a grunt of dismissal. I rip him with two short lefts to the head, go back to the belly with a right, and then shoot the right hand to his head. The crowd's roar is sweet music. His back is to the ropes now as I bang him with a combination of punches while making him miss. He comes brawling back at me, but I evade the rush and move to the center of the ring.

The Kid bores in after me. How much hand speed do I have left? How many punches can I put together? Pop the left in his face. Another time. The right. I am hitting Bassett with two and three shot flurries. The crowd is going mad. I bang him five times with a series of punches and the blood flows from his mouth. He flurries back and we are inches apart, trading punches. The Garden is bedlam. I see the right coming over my left and it lands flush. The reaction is almost a delayed one. I am still coming forward and then my legs buckle and I fall to my knees, gripping Bassett's legs, holding him in the corner.

Flashbulbs are popping, capturing the knockdown that will be featured in the sports pages in a sequence of three blown-up pictures. The caption under the photo will read "Davey Rossi on his knees, down for the sixth time, holding desperately to Kid Bassett's legs." The next photo will feature the Kid standing over me, bringing a brutal right across the top of my head. In the last one, I fall over on my back. Gretz is waving Bassett to a neutral corner and now, picking up the count from the timekeeper, he tolls the numbers over me. Four, five, six. I get up. I should have waited, but I am no longer thinking. It is all instinct. Get up and fight. Survive or die.

The Kid is incensed. He comes at me, a swollen lion's head with engorged eyes, mad to kill. I meet him in the center of the ring. His head is huge—a two-headed beast. There is nothing to do but hit the both of them. I throw the left and connect. Another time and another time. He is so easy to hit. But so am I. We stand there trading now. Nobody is backing off. This is about killing and about will. The crowd is up on its feet, chanting a tribute of noise to the spectacle it is witnessing.

He hits me hard and a fog descends. I can't see him, but I can smell him. This is not how I was trained to fight. Without caution, without regard for survival. Punching at some dim figure in front of me. Taking his best shots and giving mine. There is a furious rush of adrenaline. My chest is bursting. From somewhere, I hear, or think I hear, Frank Bruno's voice. "Farlo fuori." I keep throwing more punches. The Kid is going backward, and a crazy rush of emotion grips me. My hands are pistons. My heart is going to fly out of me. Farlo fuori. He is getting weaker. Fight. Fight or die. The surging rush of blood clogs my throat, spilling out in a wild cry of exultation as I land a right. The pure impact of the punch causes the most wonderful tingle to travel up my arm. I look for the Kid, but he isn't there. My feet get tangled up with him. He is lying on the floor and Herb Gretz is pushing me to a neutral corner. The Kid is lying on his side. He moves finally and gets up on his knees. Gretz wipes his gloves off. The Kid lurches toward me his eyes no longer filled with confidence. Squinting out of my good eye, I grope my way toward him. He bangs me with a right and I want to lie down. Never. I bang back and then his back is against the ropes and I begin throwing punches again. Hands never stopping, heart thumping. I will die throwing punches . . . I will die . . . I will die . . . He is there in front of me, eyes glassy and unseeing. Hands down. Kill him. The left hook I hit him with is a killer's punch, learned from hundreds of drill hours in the gym. The best punch I have ever thrown. Six inches of pure muscular coordination and viciousness landing exactly at the point of his jaw. Through the mist, I can see the impact of the blow twist Bassett's neck halfway around; he crumples slowly, body sagging, and lands on his face. He lies there, unable to move, gloves extended in some kind of homage to the savagery we have just committed upon each other. In front of all these witnesses who have joined in one glorious voice to acclaim me.

Then somehow I am in a neutral corner and Gretz is waving his hands over the Kid to indicate it is ended. Sy and Joe are embracing me and Joe is whispering, "Sweet thing" in my ear. I think Sy is crying, or maybe that is me. The robe goes around me; Joe is bathing my face with a bloody towel, saying words I cannot understand. The crowd is up on its feet now as ring announcer Johnny Addie recites the words, always the words. The litany of the ring. "The winner by a knockout at two thirty-eight of the eighth round." The crowd noise swallows my name. But I can read it on their lips. "Davey . . . Davey . . . Davey." I look for brother Johnny at ringside. It takes a moment, because I have only one eye to use. He is whispering something to the beauty as I lean against the ropes, using them for support. I look at the girl and she stares back. A vision of beauty all in black. There is real emotion in her eyes. Is it for me? Did I move you? Did you see what I did? Do you see how much courage I have? Did you see what I did to the Kid? Johnny climbs up into the ring. He knows what I did. Tommy would have known also. He would have loved it. You know how much it took, don't you, Tommy? Just then, Sy whispers, "Mazel tov" in my ear. Johnny throws his arms around me and kisses me. I can't hear all his words. Just something about "great." I look for Vince, knowing he won't be there, and see Frank Bruno. He brings his right hand up in a salute and mouths the words, "Farlo fuori."

# 5

My FACE IS A SWOLLEN, lumpy, sewn-up mask. It took twenty-nine stitches to close the gash opened by the Kid's head. The eye is closed. Both my cheekbones seem as if they will explode out of my face and my lips are puffy and discolored. All the ice packs did little for me. I lie on the table giving a few minutes to Pat Gavin of the *Daily Mirror*. That's the only reporter Sy would let in. Pat says that I looked worse than the Kid, and he is nothing to write home about, either. Sy says it was the third-best fight he's ever seen. Pat, a little guy with million-year-old eyes, gives Sy a look. "C'mon, Sy, cut it out. It was the second-best." Pat and Sy both laugh; I do my best to smile. Then Pat asks me, "You still want to fight Simpson?" I make a little joke, pretending not to know who Simpson is. But we all know better. Davey Rossi can still fight, but he isn't the same anymore. The Davey Rossi of a few years ago wouldn't have been hit by Kid Bassett. I'm twenty-nine and I've lost a half step, a split second off my reflexes. I'm still the darling of the fight crowd, the man of the hour, but I'm not the same as I was. And that's what it will take to beat Sandy Simpson.

"I'll be there," I tell Pat.

Pat goes over and says a few words to Joe Dunn. Johnny comes over. I am on my back, my face covered in ice.

He speaks softly. "I brought Nandy with me. He'll give you a shot."

Felix "Nandy" Pecora is the New York State Athletic Commission's doctor, as high-priced as he is good. He has been around the fight game for a long time. Nandy looks at my face and shakes his head. "I told the Kid to box you, but he wouldn't listen."

"You know me, Nandy. I'll take three punches to give one."

Johnny smiles. "After Nandy looks you over, how about some dinner at Gaston's?"

Gaston's is the best French restaurant in New York.

"I don't know if I can open my mouth."

Johnny leans over and whispers. "There's somebody wants to meet you. I asked her to have dinner with us."

My heart is fluttering crazily, but it is a happy feeling. I see her face now and the eyes, the wonderful eyes.

Joe Dunn brings me some bouillon in a paper cup. I try to sip the hot broth, but my torn lips scream in protest and the cup splatters all over the floor.

Nandy, dandy as always in a blue-striped suit and white shirt with blue tie, sets his bag down on the table. "How are you, David? I've never seen you look worse. But the fight was a great spectacle." Nandy has owl eyes and his thinning white hair is parted down the middle like an old-time barber. This wise old owl has seen all the great fighters of the last twenty-five years. He opens his black bag, takes out the syringe, then neatly picks out some bottles. It is a vitamin B-12 shot, along with some other stuff that will give me a jolt.

I feel myself slipping away and close my eyes. Nandy has my arm and whispers, "Easy." The needle goes in soft and graceful. Nandy is an artist. "Thanks," I say.

He packs up his bag. "Give me a call in the morning, let me know how you feel." Nandy closes up his bag, leans over and whispers again, "No more of these kind of nights, David. Go out a winner. Simpson would have finished you in the fifth round."

I nod. I am the toast of New York and Nandy is telling me to quit. But Nandy was also Tommy's doctor. He knows how to look down the road to the end of the line. And he is right. If I fight Sandy Simpson this way, it will be a short fight. Sentiment is for show business, not for the people I know.

I step into the shower and let the hot water run down on me. A jumble of thoughts pursues me; images of the fight come hauntingly alive. Nandy's words ring in my ear, Pat Gavin asking me if I want to fight Simpson. The girl. Who is she? What was she doing with Johnny? Where is Vince?

"Jesus, you look horrible."

I look up, and Johnny is there. He throws me a towel and I turn off the faucets. I rub myself dry, ignoring Johnny's eyes appraising me. I slip on the robe and walk gingerly toward my clothes, which are hanging from a large hook protruding from the wall. As I slip into my shorts, I stumble and Johnny catches me.

"You need some food."

He hands me my shirt. We eye each other warily. I got tagged good tonight. I won ugly, as the saying goes, and Johnny Silk knows better than anyone how much I've slipped.

"The spic was tough."

I shrug, then pull on my trousers and reach for my shirt. Johnny uses an expensive silver lighter to torch his cigarette. "I never saw you take those kind of punches."

"I'm training my face for the Simpson fight." I try to smile, but it hurts too much.

"You really want the Simpson fight?"

I button up the shirt and Johnny hands me my tie. "It was a great fight for the sports pages, but you got tagged. Bassett is like ham and eggs."

"I won, didn't I? Just get me the Simpson fight."

Johnny stares at me. Emotion has brought color to his face. "I'll call Matty Clark tomorrow. He never saw you punch before; now he's got something to think about." But the facade is paper-thin. Johnny doesn't think I have it anymore. It's the second fight in a row where I've taken a pounding. I am like a thousand other pugs before me. Davey Smart doesn't know it's over.

I knot the tie. "Who's the girl?"

A fleeting smile crosses Johnny's mouth. "She was working for Tommy on his taxes. When they nailed him on the tax rap, Tommy wanted to make sure it never happened again."

"She's an accountant?"

"Julie is a tax lawyer with very good contacts in Washington. Tommy met her in Sag Harbor and hired her."

"Tommy always had an eye for the ladies. Anything going on with them?"

Johnny doesn't say anything.

"What's her last name?"

"Alpert."

"She's Jewish?"

"She's a classy lady. As far as her and Tommy, I never got that message. They went to dinner, but everybody goes to dinner with—" He catches himself. "Hey, there's social and there's social. I recommended Julie. I met her down in Miami. She's good."

The "good" digs at me. Johnny has bedded them all down. He's Johnny Silk. Get away from this.

Johnny claps me on the shoulder. "C'mon, Davey, we'll eat some French food and you'll find out for yourself if she's too young, or maybe too old."

But neither of us makes a move to leave. I haven't seen Johnny since the day at Pompton Lakes when we got the news about Tommy's hit. And saying his name as we talked of the girl has brought us into the present. The Mafia is at war, and Johnny is a prime player.

"Where's Vince?" I ask.

"I don't know, Davey. I don't know what page he's on."

I am knotting my shoe laces and look up. "What does that mean?"

"You talk to him. Maybe he'll listen to you."

"I'm not a player in this. Suddenly, you want me to be a coach."

Johnny yanks the cigarette from his mouth. "You're his son. You can talk to him."

"So are you."

We are in each other's faces and breathing hard. The pressure is taking its toll. Johnny holds up his hand. "I already talked to Vince and nothing was accomplished. But you're right—it's not for you to get into this. It's just that you're close to him and I'm not. He'll hear you in a way he won't hear me."

Johnny has left himself open and I throw the left hook. "What happened between the two of you? He found you in the streets, raised you. He still loves you, Johnny."

Johnny shakes his head. "It's just something that happened. We came down on opposite sides of something. You know how stubborn Vince is . . . he doesn't forgive."

Yeah, I do know. And that is all Johnny is going to tell me. We stand in the suddenly eerie quiet of my dressing room, the stone floor wet, the drip of the shower punctuating the silence and the smell of blood, sweat, and liniment pungent in the air.

"You have to stand with him, Johnny, no matter what."

"Listen to me, Davey. I was a kid when they purged the mustache Petes, but I remember what it was like. Bam-bam and a lot of old bastards fell down dead. It was the young guys taking over. Vince was one of them. They didn't have time to sit around talking about the old times. They were the future. Well, drugs are the future now. Either you become part of it or you're the past."

Everything Johnny says makes sense and yet I find myself angry. Tommy is less than two weeks dead and Johnny is talking accommodation. It is not a word in Vince's vocabulary.

Johnny throws away his cigarette and snatches another one. "Davey, Vince talks to you. Since Rosalia died, you're the one he confides in. Tell him there's too much money in this for any one man to stop it. It's good business. Vince may not like it, but he has to be smart. Like you're smart, Davey. I never said this to you, but I always thought if you got into the business, you'd give us all lessons."

"I'm happy where I am." I am angry at Johnny because I feel like he is ready to jump ship. At the same time, I understand that at this point in time he is a lot more pragmatic than Vince. I put on my jacket. "I'll do what I can. Let's get something to eat."

Johnny watches me closing up the brown canvas athletic bag I will leave for Joe Dunn. "Davey, there was a hit this week on Waxy Green. Ever hear of him?"

My heart does a little dance across my chest. "Should I have?"

"He got it in his apartment over on the West Side. Waxy was just scuffling along, trying to make it. Living on the balls of his ass. But during Prohibition, he must have been worth five million bucks. They got him on a tax rap. Twenty-five years and he served every one of them. The word is out that he was peddling some information. Maybe a little blackmail. Somebody didn't like it and whacked him. Waxy had a list of people he was trying to squeeze or peddle information to. A lot of names. We have our sources downtown in the precincts." Johnny carefully lights his cigarette. "It's like this, Davey. Your name was on a piece of paper in Green's apartment. Papa Joe asked me to talk to you about it."

I bend down and fumble with the bag. This is business. Mob business. The mob hears about everything, and Johnny is a fixer as well as my brother.

"Davey, did Green try to reach you?"

Johnny either knows the answer and wants to see how I'll play it or he doesn't know and he's fishing. But if I lie to Johnny and Joe Dante catches him on it, then we'd both be in trouble. Yet dangerous as a lie may be, I am not prepared to talk about what I have learned. "I don't know who this guy is. After I left Pompton Lakes, I stayed with Sy. He keeps me shut up like a monk fasting for Lent."

There is an expression of relief in Johnny's eyes. His brother is clean. He doesn't know about my going to Waxy Green's apartment.

"What's going on, Johnny? What is this about Waxy Green?"

Johnny acts as if the matter is closed. "He was just a fish peddler trying to get by. Could be he sent you a letter or something. When you get home, check the mail."

I close my eyes. It's been a long night. Everything aches. It will be worse in the morning. I put my hand on Johnny's arm. "Stick by Vince. The heart attacks have taken a lot out of him. He's not the man he was, but he is still the don. Still father to us both."

Johnny nods and we move toward the door. It is time for us to leave the dressing room for dinner at Gaston's.

We walk out into the October night and the girl is there, dressed in a white raincoat, her hair long now. It's for me. We both know it. I walk toward her. She extends her hand. "I'm Julie." Her voice is husky and up close her eyes are kind.

"I know. Johnny's told me about you." Her mouth is even more inviting at this distance. "I made sure to ask."

She smiles.

"Is this your first fight?"

"It was so awful. I don't know how you did it."

I try to smile. "I was dumb. But don't say it was your last fight."

It is like neither of us can move. We stand there in the soft October night and I hope Johnny has disappeared.

Her hand touches my face. Just the barest touch. Her fingertips are soft and I tingle inside. "Will you be able to eat?"

"I can always eat."

It is just at that moment that the fleeting image crosses my field of vision. I sense trouble. Like an unexpected punch. I turn and see somebody big and brutish. He has engaged Johnny in a conversation. The proprietary hand is on Johnny's arm. The gesture is not lost on me. It means he has been sent for Johnny. The hulk is Nuñez Otonio, Joe Dante's premier muscle man. His bulky shoulders distort the shape and contour of his suit. He has bulging cheekbones and sunken eyes. Behind him are several muscle heads, and there is a car. Escorts for the ride that is to follow.

I touch Julie's hand briefly. "Excuse me." I walk toward them and Nuñez sizes me up. "Joe is waiting for Johnny in the car. You, too, Davey. Let's go."

He steps backward so we can cross in front of him. This is not an invitation to be declined. Johnny gives it a try anyway. "Davey's kind of beat-up. He's taking the lady to dinner. I'll talk to Joe."

Nuñez has been around. "I think you both better get in the car. I'll cover you with the lady."

He has my arm and I spin free of him. "I'll take care of it."

The look we exchange is not a pleasant one. Mine says, don't handle me like you own me. I'm not meat from your slaughterhouse. Julie steps between us.

"Everything all right?"

I shake my head. "Something's come up."

She looks at me, then over at Johnny, who has joined us. "There's a surprise party for Davey. An old friend. I'd invite you, but it's family."

Julie stares at both of us and then at Nuñez. "Can I do anything?" She's not afraid.

"I could get the lady a cab," Nuñez rumbles.

"It's okay." I take her arm. "It's real family. Know what I mean?"

Julie's hand is in mine. "I'll give you a rain check." I can feel the slip of paper in my hand and my heart starts up again. "A rain check is a promise."

My hand closes around the paper. "I won't lose it."

Nuñez intercedes. "C'mon, Davey."

Nobody is going to dispute him any further. Awaiting us is Joe Dante's big black sedan. The cadre of hoods flanking it moves to meet us. It is a perfect match. An entourage of grotesques escorting me, the prince of gargoyles, to Joe Dante's for a late-night ride. I will be congratulated, but we are not driving to Brooklyn to talk about the fight. I check Johnny. Nothing registers on his face. I look back at Julie. She has been watching the entire procession and she knows this is not a trip I want to take. The black Cadillac opens and I catch a glimpse of my face in the glass. It is bloated and distorted. I have taken a lot of punches this night. And it is still not over. I slide in next to Joe Dante.

He smiles broadly, but only with his face, not his eyes. "Davey, you did the spic good. You made the families proud. Bravo." He enfolds me in his arms and kisses me on both cheeks. His lips are cold, like death in the night.

# 6

WE SLIDE INTO the back of the limousine, each with our own thoughts. Johnny has been here before. He is eighteen years older than I am. As I grew up, he had already taken his position at Vince's side. He has learned well, for now he smiles as he greets Joe Dante. The mob's consigliere greeting one of his clients. The car glides away and I focus on Joe Dante dressed in a light topcoat and hat. My eyes have adjusted to the dark and I can see his cunning mouth and piercing eyes. He is a true son of Sicily.

The ride is made to seem like a casual one in celebration of my victory. A ride offered by my father's longtime friend and fellow don Joe Dante. Papa Joe has embraced me and saluted my accomplishment in the ring this night. I left the spic for dead.

We are heading across town and Joe leans over and pats my cheek. I can smell his expensive cologne. "You are a good boy, Davey. Like a second son to me. But I worry about you. You took a lot of punches tonight. Simpson is a much better fighter than the spic."

Johnny intercedes on my behalf. "The Kid was tougher than we thought he would be."

Joe produces a cigar, bites off the end, and, rolling down the window, spits it out. "You should take some time off. Someplace in the sun. Think about what you want to do after you retire." I am wedged in next to Joe and he taps my leg. "Davey, the legs don't last forever.

You are approaching thirty. Time to use your head for something besides taking punches. Talk to Vince. Tell him what is in your heart. He'll do the right thing for you. After all, he is your father. You have made him proud, as you have made us all proud. You have brought glory to us. We are grateful." There is a brief pause as he rolls the cigar in his mouth to taste it. "You know I have invested in Las Vegas. There are people who owe me. Let Vince just say the word and I will speak to them on your behalf. You are a smart boy, Davey. There are people in Vegas who would pay for that. Pay well. If you want, I will put out some feelers."

He primes the cigar and waits for Johnny to light it. Joe Dante is playing the role of the benevolent don. See, I celebrate your victory. Trust me, for I am your father's friend. It is a carefully planned preamble.

He must be answered in kind. I let my head sag wearily, the picture of the exhausted, compliant warrior. One who could never be viewed as an adversary when we get to the real matter at hand. "I know you have always looked out for me, Joe. There are not too many fights left, and then I will talk to Vince and you. I know you will both look out for my best interests."

It is the right answer, the appropriate one. Joe is watching me intently. Johnny crosses his legs. Just a little impatient flourish. Now begins the second act. We are on the FDR Drive, heading toward the Brooklyn Bridge, the East River a glacial palace of light. Joe puffs on his cigar and gives Johnny a sign. Johnny leans forward and closes the partition so Nuñez and the musclehead at the wheel can't hear us.

He rests a hand on my shoulder and begins. "We must dispose of this business with Waxy Green. He was a peddler. Men like that sleep with the fishes. I know Johnny has spoken with you about this, but it disturbs me that he wished to contact you. Tell me, Davey. Why do you think your name was written on a piece of paper?"

When you are dealing with a Sicilian, you must do two things. The second and most important thing is to anticipate his agenda. That takes time. The more immediate goal is to answer his question so he will not see you trying to anticipate him. I must do it well. Joe Dante is no fool.

"He had something to sell."

Joe's eyes gleam shrewdly. "What could that be?"

"Only the fishes know that."

"Sometimes," he replies, "the fishes can tell us things. They can speak to the dead, Davey. This Waxy was a Jew." He says *Jew* with distaste. "You are an Italian. Why did he come to you?"

There is a trap in the question. His words imply a meeting. A meeting I must disavow. That is how Sicilians work. He will keep implying I am guilty, and I must protest my innocence at every turn.

"You mean why would a Jewish gangster want to approach me? We will never know."

"How many Jews do you know, Davey?"

"My trainer is a Jew."

Johnny carefully injects himself into our discussion. "Did Sy ever mention this Green to you?"

It is a question meant to make me look good. It supplies a possible connection and enables me to disassociate myself from it.

"Never."

Johnny Silk works diligently on spreading the false trail. "Green had connections to the Jewish bookies. Maybe they wanted to see if Davey was interested in doing some business on the Bassett fight. Could be Sy came up short, needed some quick money, and spoke to Green."

Doing business means getting me to ease off. I could lead Joe Dante further along Johnny's false trail, but I don't want anyone leaning on Sy. "Sy is clean. He never borrowed a quarter from anyone. He doesn't owe anybody. He lives very simply up in Washington Heights. People like Green would be chased from my camp."

Joe nods and continues the game. "Do you know many Jews, Davey?"

"Barney Grosset. Nobody else."

We all know who Barney Grosset is. King of the bookies in New York. Everybody in the mob lays bets through one of his gambling parlors.

Joe reaches over and runs his fingers deftly across my bad eye. "The spic left his mark, didn't he?" He uses the moment to stare into my good eye. To read me. He wants to know if I would lie to him. If Joe determines I have lied to Johnny and gotten away with it, Johnny will be given poor marks for letting sentiment get in the way of business. My lie will engulf us both.

The don puts his hand on my arm. There is just enough pressure to make me aware of exactly whom I am dealing with. He has lived as a mafiosi since his earliest days in Palermo. He has learned his craft, just as I have trained for the ring. But for him, it is a lifetime's work in a profession in which to get old, you must be cunning and devious. Joe Dante is fond of saying he comes from an honorable tradition. In truth, he was nothing more than a pistola when he came here. He has known me all my life, but I don't doubt for a moment that if he ever saw me as a threat, he would strike at me. With his hand still on my arm, he speaks softly. "The police will visit you, Davey. They will ask about Green."

"I don't know anything."

"They may let something slip. Let them talk. You listen; then you ask a question."

"I understand."

Joe draws on his cigar and exhales smoke. "You know, Davey, perhaps Las Vegas is not the right situation for you. You have wisdom beyond your years. It is not something that can be taught, only refined. Maybe in this delicate time, you can sit beside Vince. Tell him what you think."

It is a rebuke meant for Johnny, who has not been able to make Vince see that drugs are the wave of the future. The whole performance of Joe Dante angers me. He has stepped over the line with his condescending arrogance. Vince would never sit still for it. But I am Tommy's pupil. Anger is a luxury. A wise man doesn't show his true feelings.

"I don't really have any thoughts about this delicate time, Joe. I'm not in the Life. I leave talking to my father up to Johnny."

Joe knows how to observe the ritual also. "You are a good son, Davey. You do Vince great honor. Enough of business for this night. We will let Waxy Green sleep. This was a man who should have paid for his treachery a long time ago. Isn't that true, Johnny?"

Joe has turned to my brother, expecting an answer. Again, Johnny crosses his legs. "He did twenty-five big ones. Took him right out of the Life. He paid pretty good."

We cross over the Brooklyn Bridge and start winding down the ramp toward the empty streets of Brooklyn. Joe Dante has provided me with an opening and I grasp it. "What did he do?"

Joe looks over at the mob's consigliere. "Tell him, Johnny."

Johnny looks out the window and tries to be offhand. "There was a hit that went down a long time ago. The Gordon mob. They were caught in the Rodman Arms Hotel and wiped out. The Wax Man fingered them for the hit."

Joe has a mocking smile of contempt on his face. "This was a Jew who sold other Jews."

Nothing registers on my face, but inside me there is lots of turbulence. Waxy Green was selling information about a man he had fingered for a rubout.

"Nails Gordon?"

I catch Johnny's hard stare. He is wondering how do I know and what do I know. The same thing Joe Dante is wondering about. I move to cover my tracks.

"Remember the party Tommy threw for me after I won the championship?"

Johnny nods. "At Mangicore's."

"Dino told me about him. He said it was a big story. Did you know Nails Gordon?"

"I knew him." Johnny turns away and looks out at the street. He doesn't want me to see his face.

"We all knew Nails," Joe Dante cuts in. "But Vince knew him best of all. Didn't he, Johnny?"

Johnny pointedly ignores Joe's remark.

"So what happened?" I ask.

Johnny still doesn't want to look at me. "He got hit."

"Why?"

Joe is right there with the answer. "He had a mob full of kill-crazy Jews. The Syndicate cracked down."

I should let it go for later, but I can't. "What made it such a big story?"

Johnny tosses his butt out the window. "Everything was a big story then. Al Capone had been sent away and the papers needed to jack up circulation. You had guys like Dutch Schultz and Mad Dog Coll shooting at each other in broad daylight. People were scared. Then Nails gets hit and the papers played it up."

There's something about the way Johnny says "Nails." Like he has said it many times. You knew him a lot better than you're letting on, didn't you, Johnny?

Joe puts his arm around my right shoulder and it throbs violently. "How come, Davey, you're so interested in an old war story? Didn't Vince ever tell you about Nails Gordon?"

I look at Joe Dante and then I see it. The whole charade about Waxy Green was so that we could get into the Nails Gordon hit. Nails Gordon, whose mob hit Uncle Nick. This is all aimed at Vince. Joe set me up for it and I played the chump. Davey Smart and Johnny Silk, and Joe Dante has driven a wedge between us. He made the assumption that I spoke to Waxy Green. Then he led me to the bait and I took it in my mouth.

I stare out at downtown Brooklyn. "Where are we going, Joe?"

"Didn't I tell you? We're going to break some bread at my place. Anna has cooked a wonderful meal for you. You know how much she cares for you. For an Italian woman, food is love. The steak will melt in your mouth. We're just going to make one little stop to pick up somebody."

We go some way in silence, passing deserted streets and empty warehouses. As we peel into a right turn, Joe squeezes my throbbing shoulder again. "Tell me, Davey. Do you think much about Tommy? I know how close you were with him."

"I think of him."

"We all do. He set the table for us. But we have to go on. Isn't that so, Johnny?"

Johnny gives me a probing stare. "Tommy lived each day to its peak, but he'd be the first to tell you that in this racket, yesterday doesn't mean much."

The car slows, there is a squealing of the brakes, and then we pull into an old deserted parking lot. Another car is waiting for us. "Wait here," Joe Dante tells us, and gets out.

We watch him walk over to another Cadillac, a replica of the one we are in. Johnny and I exchange glances. We both know whatever

Joe Dante's agenda is, it's not over. Waxy Green was just the beginning.

Johnny shakes his head. "You got suckered, kid. Don't wash dirty underwear in public. You should have waited. What do you know?"

"Not enough. What happened?"

"Life happened. Our Life. Nails and Vince were a great team."

"Couldn't Vince square it?"

Johnny shakes his head and says very softly, "When your time comes, nobody can square it."

We lock eyes, and then abruptly the door swings open and a short man with unruly white hair is looking at us. I haven't seen him in six years, but he still looks like a hungry wolf. The way he did when I first met him as a boy. Dino Manfredi beckons with his hand. "C'mon, Davey, I'll give you a lift."

I step out of the car and he sizes me up. "Remember what I told you that night when you were a kid. Never give anyone the first shot at you. Okay, I'm giving you first crack. Go ahead. Do it. Go ahead."

It's been a long night. I look at the grinning wolf's face. Dino is always testing. Something snaps in me and my fist is cocked and ready to go. I hear a voice and turn. "Don't do it, Davey." I see Buster Minetta, Dino's triggerman. "Keep your cool, Davey."

Dino surveys me and steps up close. "You're getting better, but you still ain't Vince. When you raise your hand, Davey, use it. In an alley, you would have been dead."

# 7

**WE EAT STEAK** by candlelight. Cooked to perfection in a rich pizzaiola sauce in the big old kitchen of the Dante house. Illuminated just above the sink is a statuette of the dying figure of Christ. Head tilted to one side, mouth open, hands pinioned and rent by nails. It has been made to seem like a casual celebration of my victory. Hosted by Joe Dante. No one will seem to be leaning on anyone else. No disrespect intended to Don Vince Rossi or his sons. In front of all assembled, Joe Dante and Dino Manfredi have toasted my prowess. Benedictions have been said on my behalf. The supplicants have paid their worshipful homage to Prince David for vanquishing the reincarnation of the Spanish Inquisition. Dago lineage has been proven better in the ultimate arena of public brutality before the eyes of the mob and the Mob. The dons and their capos, dressed in rich suits and custom-made shirts, could rejoice and hold their heads high. They could walk away from the fight, having watched the spic twitching numbly on the canvas while I, the proclaimed winner, shed noble dago blood on their behalf. They are grateful to me far beyond their limited ability to express it, for as much as I have graced them with victory, I have confirmed their heritage. Proclaimed and anointed them as *men* while saving them from *disgrazia*—the disgrace of defeat.

Over steak, two separate pastas, and heaping salad bowls, the coarse macho jokes fill the air. For the moment, there is no distinction according to rank. Johnny sits next to Nuñez Otonio and Buster Minetta. Joe Dante rubs elbows with his driver, Cancelero Ruggerio. All except Dino, who sits at the head of the table in isolated splendor. Judas at the Last Supper. The hot food keeps coming, all under the watchful eye of Anna Dante, who in middle age is still a striking woman. She has classic features, a perfect nose, a provocative mouth, and dark, haunting eyes. Her hair is as black as a storm-tossed night, marred by a few patches of white. She first caught me staring at her when I was a little boy, at a gathering hosted by Joe. She has always returned that gaze with a warmth I've never believed I deserve. There have been thoughtful presents on my birthday and at Christmas, always accompanied by a card. I have come to realize that Anna has a warm and protective feeling for me. Once at a party held somewhere on the Long Island estate of "Tough Tony" Esposito, I ran into a couple of the older children and a game of football got rough. I had inadvertently flattened Tony's nephew, Caesar. Caesar and Tony's son Dominick advanced on me. Suddenly, Anna was there, angrily defending me. The conviction she brought to a children's dispute startled me and frightened my attackers. It was made clear not only that they were bullies, whom she would report to Tough Tony, but if there were any attempts at retaliation, she would take care of it personally. Since then, I have always regarded Anna as a patron saint, a woman who holds a special place in her heart for me. Tonight when I entered Joe Dante's house with my stitched and battered face, she showed her revulsion and a deep compassion, which manifested itself in tears.

I eat the steak slowly, its protein juices reviving me. Anna stands over me, watching each mouthful I ingest with great pleasure. Silently imploring me to eat. *Mangia, mangia.* She has even cut the pieces for me. I eat the pasta and sip from a glass of wine. The steak replenishes me and my blood runs warm and happy in my body. I remember this table from when I was a boy and Vince would sometimes bring me here when he had business with Joe. I would play outside with Joe junior. In the winter, we would go downstairs into the finished basement and shoot pool or throw darts. Anna would bring us cookies she had baked herself. They were happy times. It was not always that way. Mafia children grow up lonely. There are compensations for your unique status. You learn that there will always be special dispensations and favors. Rules can be bent. There will always be a career for you. But as I matured, I sensed, as Joe junior must have, that we would never be welcomed by others who also grew up advantaged. We had gained entrance because our fathers were adept with a gun. It became my secret conviction that the rich kids at the private academies we attended thought of us as freaks. I never for a moment believed we would be accepted into the club the ruling class presides over. The sons of mafiosi have become generals, lawyers, doctors. But the society of respectability our fathers craved for us could never be ours. Because whatever we achieved rang false. Who in society could or would refuse us? So when my time came to pick a profession, I also chose a racket: boxing. Inside a twenty-foot ring, I was on my own. No fixed fights. But I am still one of the freaks who lives in a world that society abhors. We are tolerated, patronized, feared, but never accepted. I am a prodigal son, but I know the rules. I will always be the mob's Davey. And so the world will view me.

The war stories are over. Dino stands up first and the others wait. Clearly, protocol has been established. He walks from the room and Joe follows. Now Johnny leaves, and finally the loyal soldiers are free to stand up and stretch. This is the prelude to pastries and steaming espresso, anisette and cigars. Anna clears the table. She is wearing a long green dress that accentuates her dark beauty. If she led me to a bed now, I would happily collapse. She brings me the espresso in a demitasse with green flowers. A piece of lemon rests in the saucer. I spoon a little sugar into it and drop in the lemon. The espresso is hot and bitter. But the sugar fights back. I taste it on the tip of my tongue. I am content.

Anna lays her hand on my arm. "Handsome boy, what have they done to you?"

Her eyes are filled with compassion and something indefinable. She has been married to a mafioso for thirty-eight years. The evil devised by her husband must leave its mark. One cannot live with a mafioso without absorbing some essence of malefaction. Now she whispers, "It is a monstrous life."

Is it my own or hers that she speaks of? I saw what it did to my mother. The Life spares no one.

"It was a wonderful meal, Anna."

She gives me a sparkling smile. "Come more often and I will make you ten pounds heavier."

I smile back. "Then I will have to retire. How is Joe junior?"

Her smile fades and her eyes are marred by pain. "He is away on business for his father. You should call him, Davey. He misses you. You played so well together when you were boys."

"I will try." Joe junior always had a quick smile and a quicker temper. He has broad shoulders and curly hair and looks like an All-American football player. He has never been able to get out from under his father's shadow. He never should have been drawn into the Life. He lacks Joe's cruelty and gifts of survival and cunning. His attempts to compensate led him to become a bully. Once as kids, we fought on a snowy day. I was much too fast for him. I left him bloody and tearful, trying to explain it to his father. Joe Dante took in the scene, and after whispering in his son's ear words that hurt worse than any blows I had delivered, he walked over to me. I remember he lifted me up by my shoulders and said, "Joe is bigger than you and still you are the better fighter. Vince will never have to fight your battles. Come. I have a gift for you." We went inside, where Joe gave me some rare gold coins from his collection. Vince told me later they were worth hundreds of dollars. But what I will never forget is holding those coins in my hand and looking out the window at Joe junior sitting in the snow, his head in his hands. And then Anna was there, kneeling beside her sobbing son, enfolding him in her arms. Joe Dante looked out at the scene and never blinked. All the while, he kept his arm around me and extolled my courage.

I look up at Anna. Joe junior married a beautiful girl, and now they are separated. Their wedding was a lavish affair, which cost Joe Dante more than fifteen thousand dollars. His first two grandchildren were girls. There is no grandson, and Joe junior works for his father, seeking redemption for falling short of the standard set by the man who is more don than father.

"Please tell Joe to call me when he returns. Tell him I miss him."

Anna gives me a radiant smile and then an impulsive kiss. Her delicate fragrance sweeps over me. "You are a good boy, Davey. Always you have been good. Vince is a fortunate man."

She turns abruptly and goes out. Her husband and his guests will be expecting their espresso. I fight the urge to sleep, but the hour is late and I feel myself drifting. Somehow, I am back in the ring and Christ on the cross has become Kid Bassett. He comes forward and taunts me. Fight, fight. He removes his boxing gloves. I can see the tape on his hands. They are black and grimy, flecked with touches of blood. I am trying to explain that the fight is over, but the Kid keeps beckoning me to continue. In his eyes is the poverty of defeat. It is like a portrait of hunger. A terrible gnawing emotion transforms those eyes into beady little dots of fury. He stalks me. I cannot bring myself to hit him again. He swings and I see the nails in his hand. Driven through them. Bright silver nails . . . nails . . . nails. A raspy but commanding voice demands my attention.

"Davey, Davey." A hand is on my shoulder. I open my eyes and see the flickering candles and the crucified Messiah. Joe Dante is looking at me. The candles flare up, framing the diamondlike glint in those tight eyes. Nothing in Kid Bassett's eyes tonight could be a match for what resides in those of Joe Dante. He has seen all manner of treachery. He has seen himself on a slab. He is beyond death.

I look for Dino and Johnny, but they are nowhere in sight. That means they are locked in a room upstairs. Private negotiations are taking place. From the moment we arrived, Johnny retreated, becoming a second to the illustrious prizefighter. Where I filled myself with steak and pasta, he ate sparingly, as if to keep himself lean and ready for what is ensuing now. The drivers and muscle men have evaporated. They are on standby while the deft maneuvers continue. And where in the midst of the endless positioning by deadly men is Vince? He is not the man he was once, but his instinct for survival remains his strong suit. It has been bred into him by generations who came before him in Sicily. All this is about him—that, I know. The feast of our patron saint of victory is over.

Joe pours anisette for us and offers me a fat Havana, which I decline. He carefully lights his cigar and leans back. He implies in his physical gesture a tableau of intimate confidentiality. "Davey, we are in a delicate time. The Five Families must draw together. The death of Tommy Costanza makes everything very fragile. We must restore order. I have explained that to Johnny."

He stops and watches for a response from me. I offer him my best poker face. Tommy would be proud.

"This is not like the old days. The business has gotten very big. One man's recklessness can bring us all down. Don't you agree?"

"Reckless men are not wise men."

Joe nods and picks up his glass. He stares into it the way a seer might, looking for elusive portents of the future. "Reckless men have a way of leaving much destruction. In difficult times, it is better to accommodate."

Joe Dante, like Vince, still has a touch of Sicily in his inflection. The stress is on the last four letters of the word. It makes *accommodate* sound sinister.

Joe is looking at me, waiting for some kind of response. I decide to give him one with a little barbed edge to it.

"Accommodate a reckless man and he may devour you."

There is a glint in Joe's eye. A hint of anger resides there. I have turned it around and pointed to Dino.

Joe puts his hand on my arm. The candles flicker brilliantly, illuminating our little theatrical. I sit facing the don across a table.

"Davey," he begins, "this is a country with a great appetite. We have all made a life for ourselves because we feed this appetite. When I came here as young man from Palermo with your father, it was the booze. I never understood how the Congress could be so stupid as to make a law against the booze. It was a great thing for us. By the time they changed the law, we were all rich men. And what did we do? Nothing more than feed the people what they wanted. We were suppliers. Oh, there was killing, but it was between us. We hurt no one else. In time, the people got their legal booze. Then they wanted something else they could do that was illegal and risky. So we gave them the gambling, and finally came Las Vegas. Now they have the whiskey and the gambling and they want something else. They want to stick this shit into their arms and get high. They want to sniff it. I am like Vince: I don't like it. It is a primitive habit. But if we do not give it to them, then somebody else will."

I am tired of Joe Dante and his little history lesson. "But you have already given it to them, Joe. So you are different from Vince."

"I am a businessman, Davey. I know what I do is good for all of us. But Vince doesn't want to do what's good for us. Why is that?"

The hour is late. His performance grates on me. "Maybe because with the powder, it's not like the booze. The booze gave people a hangover, but the powder makes them sick."

Morality is not a message a don will respond favorably to. It is like baiting a bull.

"We didn't hook these people. They want it. The niggers and the spics want it. We can't stop that. Tell Vince. It's everywhere. Kansas City, St. Louis, Detroit. The nigger and the chink gangs are organizing. If we let them take over the drugs, they'll come after us next. The drugs will feed us for thirty years."

Behind Joe Dante, the dying Messiah holds out his right arm, the vein bulging. Waiting for his fix.

Joe speaks softly to me. The caress is still with the velvet glove. "Davey, in Vince's family, there are those who sell drugs. The future is here. The future is drugs."

I'm trying to follow the line of all this. I'm dizzy, and I crave sleep. I drain my anisette and turn to the don. "With all due respect, Joe, I think Vince has considered this, but I will tell him what you have said. I know Johnny will also."

Once again, we are at an impasse. There is just a hint of impatience in his expression. His gaze goes to the large clock above the sink. It is just past 2:00 A.M. Joe Dante is waiting for something or someone. "I have known you for so long. As I have known Vince. What has been done is to end the bloodshed quickly so we can resume our lives."

Joe takes a careful puff of his cigar. "Remember it isn't personal. We all go back together. Tommy was godfather to my son, Joe."

The air is suffocating and I have had enough of the pious sanctity of Saint Joseph.

"Well, Tommy's dead, and I think Vince is still lighting candles for him. Maybe I am, too."

A grainy voice comes to me. Vocal chords scraped by sandpaper. Dino stands silhouetted under the crucified Christ. He pours himself some anisette and hoists his glass in the air. "Here's to Tommy. I make it two to one he's already got the ice concession down in hell."

Joe Dante stands up and backs off. He clearly has deferred to Dino as our script unfolds. Johnny steps back into the room. I try to read his eyes, but there is no emotion there. Dino has made him an offer.

That's the main course. My conversation with Joe Dante was strictly an appetizer.

Dino's eyes glitter like ice picks. This is the man who would be king, and he fears Vince. Joe Dante has positioned himself so he is just to the rear of Dino. In the back of the kitchen, the flickering candles briefly illuminate the hulking figure of Buster Minetta.

Dino sets his glass down. "It's like this. In the end, we're all in business, and war ain't good for it. That's what I been talking to Johnny about." His eyes never leave me.

Johnny is watching Dino intently. It is a time for both of us to listen.

Dino's eyes rotate toward us. "You get it over with and we all make money. When we wiped out the Mustache Petes, it was necessary so we could form the Syndicate. It's the same way with Tommy. He was in the way of progress. Besides, Tommy set me up and he had it coming. All those years when I was in Atlanta doing time, I thought about how to get even. If I hadn't gone away, Tommy would have been dead six years ago, but no sense in putting the knock on him and not be around to take over. No, that was all in place. It was the rest of it."

Johnny is biting his lip. The don has admitted his murderous deed. He is very sure of himself in front of Vince Rossi's sons.

Dino stares at me. "It was Vince I thought about. Vince has muscle around him all the time. Vince is tough and smart. You don't catch him alone in no barbershop."

Dino is just in front of me, a malefic smile painted across his face. "Your old man is smart as they come. He thought up the best rubout that ever happened. The hit on Boss Joe Lucchio. What a genius idea. Joe was paranoid about every dago in New York trying to knock him off. He had a bulletproof car and ten guys around him all the time. Nobody knew how to get to him. But Vince came up with perfection. Lucchio was cheating on his taxes, and the T-men used to check his books every few months. So Vince brought in four Jews to act like T-men. Joe Lucchio hated Jews. He figured none of them was equal to a Sicilian. And only a Sicilian would have the balls to kill him. When the hit team got there, dressed just right, Joe gives them a big smile, takes them into his office, and they iced him right there. Guess where Vince got those Jews from?"

My blood is pounding, as if the bell has just sounded. "Nails Gordon."

"That's right."

It is like Kid Bassett has me pinned on the ropes again. But this time, I have to think, not react. Dino and Joe are a team. Working in tandem. One softens you up; the other pistol-whips you. The car ride out here was the prelude to this. Play it like Tommy would have. Don't get suckered.

Dino is right in front of me. I am a couple of inches taller, but he is heavier. In a fight, I can take him. That's what he's thinking. He looks over at Johnny. He is working us both over. "You knew Nails pretty good, too, didn't you, Johnny?"

Johnny keeps a lid on, refusing to be baited. "Sure, I knew him, but Vince knew him better."

Dino shakes his head. "Yeah, he did. It was too bad about Nails. He took the rap for those cowboys of his. If you see Vince again, you should ask him about Nails, Davey."

Dino's words hang in the air. I move forward and Dino points a finger at me. "Listen up, because Dino is talking. Now, it's no secret I don't get along with Vince, but business is business. He should leave off the drugs and look the other way, but not your old man. That son of a bitch has been making inquiries about me. I got reports. That means he's getting ready to put the knock on me, and that ain't going to happen. Now, I'm for business first, and I made your brother Johnny an offer tonight. He takes over for Vince. Vince is stepping down. What do you think of that?"

I speak in a voice I can barely recognize. "That's not going to happen, Dino."

Dino grins at me. "Yeah, that's what Johnny said. Well, we'll see. Anybody can be taken, even Vince." Dino lights a Camel, using a book of matches. He has thick, stubby, nail-bitten fingers. "Like I said, your old man can see around a corner. But I had six years to look around the corner. Everybody has his soft spot. With Vince, it's family. You know what I mean?"

My heart is racing.

"Vince goes to the Bronx on Friday nights to meet your uncle Mike for dinner. Ain't that right, Davey?"

Dino bares his teeth. "Tonight's Friday, ain't it? That's maybe why he couldn't come to the fight. He went up to the Bronx to eat, and I been waiting six years for that. That's what gives me the edge."

I keep thinking Dino's bluffing. Vince wouldn't go up there alone. Not now. Tommy got careless, but not Vince.

Buster Minetta has come up behind his don. Dino has turned his attention to Johnny. "You understand, Johnny. It's got to be so that the war will be over and we can all make money. And Vince had it coming, just like Tommy did. They put the frame in and sent me up. Six years' worth. Tonight, I took Vince."

I fly forward, the roar in my mouth. But Buster bars my way. His piece is aimed directly at me. Buster is a tall, swarthy man with a pockmarked face and a penchant for flashy suits and shirts. He is very sure of himself as he speaks. "Easy, Davey. You were a winner tonight. Nothing you do is going to change anything. Sit down. I said sit down."

I step back and look over at Johnny. He is very cool, very composed. Like he is waiting for a stock market quote.

"This official or unofficial?"

Dino wipes his mouth with the back of his hand and pulls out a cigarette. "Johnny Silk. I like that name. You're not going to give me trouble after this, are you, Johnny? You and Vince haven't seen things the same for a long time. You got nothing against drugs, do you? You get to run the family in Vince's place. That'll show there's no hard feelings."

I lose my cool and the words fly out. "Fuck you, Dino."

Dino's malevolent eyes dance by candlelight. "Shut up and hold your water. You don't see your brother losing his cool. I got a proposition for you, Johnny. You're a deal maker. I think this is a good one for all of us."

For some reason, I turn to Joe Dante. His eyes are hard diamonds. There is no room for sentiment here. One day, it will be his turn.

Dino approaches Johnny. "We grabbed Vince. He's okay. He's safe. Here's the deal. He steps down and I make you the head of the family. That's it. You take over and Vince lives."

It is faster than any fight I have ever been in. In the underworld, to "take" someone means to hit him. But Dino has abducted Vince. Why not finish him? Think fast, Johnny.

Johnny registers no emotion. "What if Vince won't step down?"

Dino's hand cuts through the air like scythe. "He's got no choice. I'll give you twenty-four hours. Don't think too long. Albert Molina wants the job. I know where I stand with him. Just remember this. Whatever happens, Vince is through. And if you don't make the deal, he's dead."

The pressure is on Johnny to cut the deal now. Declare himself for Dino. Bind the blood wounds with a deal.

I turn toward Dino, Joe, and Buster Minetta. I look at their faces. It is like they have assumed one face, the mask of evil, malignant betrayal.

Cool Johnny lights a cigarette. "I'll think about it. How do I know you have Vince?"

Dino turns to Buster. "Tell him."

"We got him on Arthur Avenue just after he left Arturo's."

It sounds like the real thing. That's where Vince likes to go with my uncle Mike. But why the snatch and not the hit?

Dino exchanges a glance with Joe Dante. "Call your uncle Mike, only don't think about it too long, consigliere. I have to know who my friends are—real soon."

The air is very close as we all eye each other. This is what the Life is about. About heart-stopping waits, about your insides rotted and quivering from fear. From never knowing when you're next. From living fast days and endless nights. Waiting. Waiting.

Everything is throbbing inside me. Something is off. Why was I brought here? I know a lot of things only those in the know are privileged to hear. I could finger Dino for Tommy's murder.

Dino pours himself another anisette and throws it down. "Hey, Johnny, haven't you guys ever told Davey yet?"

A surge of breathlessness overtakes me and my knees go soft.

Johnny's eyes never flicker. "What's that?"

Dino is again right in front of me. "They been holding out on you, Davey. Vince is your old man, but he ain't your father."

Swallowing is hard. "I know that."

"Yeah, well before you bleed for Vince, you should know who your father really was. You ain't no dago; you're a Jew. Your old man, your real old man, was Nails Gordon, and Vince put the hit on him." The left-right combination sends me reeling. Dino's malefic smile is back.

"On account of Nails's mob hitting Vince's brother. So Vince squared the deal. Ain't that right, Johnny?"

Johnny is biting his lip again and a trickle of blood appears. "Davey. It just came down that way. Nails wasn't supposed to be there."

Dino is right there to finish me. "Sure he was. Everybody was there for that hit. Me and Joe and Vince. Taught those Hebes something. So don't bleed too much for Vince, Davey. He put the knock on your father. It's a tough racket. When someone goes down, you go on. And something else: What was said here ends here. Johnny will teach you that. As far as the world is concerned, this is a gathering to celebrate Davey's fight. And then we heard the terrible news about Vince. We're all covered." Dino turns back to Johnny. "You got twenty-four hours."

Dino strides from the room while Buster's gun stays trained on me.

Joe Dante approaches Johnny, never for a moment looking at me. "Take the deal, Johnny. You'll be saving Vince's life. Whatever happens, Vince's time is finished. This is not the moment to be reckless. You have a great opportunity. Remember: Twenty-four hours, and then Dino will go to Albert Molina."

Joe Dante slips from the room as an assassin vanishes, hugging the night with furtive elegance. The two of us are alone. The sons of Vince Rossi. Davey Smart and Johnny Silk.

The adrenaline is pumping furiously through me. All these years, and everybody knew about Nails but me. I turn to Johnny. "How could you let them set me up that way?"

Johnny's face shows the sweat he has somehow suppressed till now. "We're going to walk out of here in a minute. Don't do anything stupid. Don't swing on anybody, and keep your mouth shut. I have to find out what went down. You gotta be tough, kid. Tougher than you've ever been. Tough as Vince has always been. I'll explain it to you when we get back."

My fists unclench and I stand there, trying to comprehend it all. This is a swift tide, a surging ride around the Sicilian bends, and I am in over my head. "Talk to me, Johnny."

Johnny comes toward me. "I'll tell you all of it, but not here. Whatever they said, Vince is your father. He's the one who raised you, Davey."

His voice cracks with emotion and his eyes silently plead. I try to take it all in. I know what he is saying is right. Johnny extends his arms, but I cannot embrace him. He covers by throwing down a drink. "I'll get us a car." Then he is gone from the room.

Dizzy and swaying, I hold the table for support. Suddenly, there is the scent of perfume and Anna is there. Her eyes are moist. Her hand starts out to me, then halts. This is not the first time she has eavesdropped on the muted words of treachery and murder.

"Leave this place, Davey. Go back to Vince."

"They've taken him."

Her eyes are lacerated by an emotion that she is only too familiar with. "Leave them all. Save yourself. Don't let them do to you what they did to young Joe. Don't let them. . . ." She puts her hands to her mouth as if her words were an admission of original sin. "Sleep, you need sleep."

Someone calls to me. "Davey." I turn and see Johnny. "Let's go."

I am all in. I start to sag, but Johnny has my arm. He leads me outside. My head is pounding. The night has turned cool and dank. I miss a step, and Johnny grabs my arm again. When we reach the car, our eyes meet in acknowledgment of this thing that he has twenty-four hours to decide about. I look back at the house of Joe Dante. Our candlelight drama is over, but in the study, the lights burn brightly. There will be no sleeping this night for Dino Manfredi and Joe Dante. They will sit up for hours, trying to anticipate our next move. What will Johnny Silk do? What if Vince agrees to step down and then crosses them? Uneasy lies the head of the usurper. And somewhere else in this house, in a darkened bedroom, is a Mafia wife whose heart is cleaved by pain, saying novenas for a life she never had.

We are inside the car and I smell new, soft leather. Johnny leans over and slams the door shut. His face is impenetrable, devoid of feeling or expression. Our driver is Cancelero Ruggerio. He has a face like Quasimodo's. "Did ya hear, Davey? Kennedy made the fucking Russians back down. That dirty fucking Khrushchev is getting out of Cuba." He cackles furiously. "I knew he was a punk."

# 8

THE CAR TURNS onto Spring Street and slows down. It is almost three o'clock, and an eerie quiet permeates the night. A time for stealth, plotting, abduction, and murder. Someplace out there in the fumes and night vapors is Vince, waiting. As Dino and Joe Dante are waiting. Waiting for Johnny to give them the word that will spell the end of Vince's reign as head of the Rossi crime family. And yet, like others before him, Vince is fodder for the morning newspapers. To be featured in a gruesome photo, showing him fished from the bottom of a lake or lying trundled up in a ditch with multiple gunshot wounds. A topic for breakfast conversation, to be discarded as abruptly as the newspaper will be thrown into a trash can. The don has been abducted, and Johnny Silk has been designated pretender to the throne. The stakes are high for them both. The cost of ransoming the don is his abdication and disgrace. The price of Johnny's refusal is Vince's life. Albert Molina, a pig-faced hood with a snout of a nose, would plunge the Rossi family into the cesspool of drugs—something Vince would consider an infamy. There is no way Johnny can win in this situation. Dino is holding the best hand. But if Vince is released, he will not consider himself bound by any deal Johnny makes with Dino. That is the wild card. A wild card that carries with it the terrible burden of the family split asunder. Vince will forgive no deal Johnny makes with Dino. Not even the one that saves his life.

We have done no talking, Johnny and I, on the ride home. The moment and its possibilities are too real. The past and its finality too stark. We reach Prince Street and the car slows to a halt. Just in front of us is the house I grew up in. It has two levels, and every spring, Vince has a fresh coat of white paint added on. It was Rosalia's favorite color. There are several cars in front of the house and I can see a light on the ground floor. We leave the car and walk toward the waiting group of men assembled in front of the house.

Pete Canzone is there, Mario Brugatti, "Wop" Luca, and "Harp" Fonza. I look for Joe Rico. He is Vince's driver. He had to be a witness to the abduction. Pete Canzone is saying something to Johnny and ignoring me. That's how the chain of command works. Johnny is in the business. I am a celebrity pug. The don has been kidnapped and Johnny Silk will run the family.

I go inside and there is the smell of flowers. Rosalia always kept fresh bouquets of flowers in the kitchen and the living room. The housekeeper, Mrs. Lamberti, has preserved that tradition faithfully. I enter the living room, noting Vince's favorite chair, the rocker, which rests directly opposite the fish tank. There is a red light above the tank, and I can see the diving red fish and their striped black counterparts leaping above and below one another.

I walk toward the tank, half-expecting to see Vince sitting in the chair, watching the fish in endless fascination, his angular face framed by the light, his eyes fathomless sockets of darkness. Sitting in his shirtsleeves, holding a drink, a decanter of whiskey resting on the coffee table. The lights from the tank giving the whiskey a fiery color. Vince has taken to whiskey since Rosalia died. He dislikes its bitter taste, but it soothes the pain in his aching heart. I sink down on the long couch and blend into the room's darkness, watching the fish, hearing the soft hum of the tank's heater.

Johnny has gone upstairs with Pete and Wop Luca. They will report all the news and then the mental machinations will begin. Put yourself in the shoes of your adversary. The endless tracing and retracing of the night's events. Johnny will be in touch with Uncle Mike. More intrigue. Steps and countersteps. Plots and counterplots. After hearing the consensus, Johnny will make his decision in the dawn or at noontime tomorrow or perhaps at the last minute, just before Dino's deadline. But in the end, it will come down to nerve or the lack of it. Sometime in between the plotting and the counterplotting, we will have our talk.

Harp Fonza comes over and hands me a stiff whiskey. He is a brute of a man, with a pockmarked face and curly hair. The name Harp comes from his facial resemblance to Harpo Marx. Like Harpo, he has laughing eyes, as if he knows some kind of mad secret. Whiskey is not a drink I favor. Harp pats me on the shoulder. "Drink it down, Davey. It will make you feel better. I think Johnny might need you later. Sweet fight, Davey. Sweet fight."

His voice is so gentle and full of concern, he could be saying, Sweet night, sleep tight.

I gesture toward the whiskey, indicating he should help himself, but Harp gives me a short negative shake of his head. It is Vince's whiskey. There is an exact protocol in Harp's world: A soldier does not drink his don's whiskey. I raise my glass and say, "Salud." The whiskey goes down smoothly and the fire inside me ignites immediately. Vince keeps good stuff in his house. I let my head loll back on the couch, the soft velvet caressing my neck. I close my eyes briefly, fighting the desire to sleep. When I open them, Vince is there, staring at the darting fish.

*Many times, he says, when I cannot sleep, I come here and watch the fish. Somehow, it gives me great peace. Or perhaps it is just age. Once in Central Park, I saw an old man with shaking hands staring at a pigeon. He had the palsy. Yet his eyes never left the bird. He could not stop his hands from quivering even when he pressed them together. But the pigeon gave him great satisfaction.*

*Did you see the fight? I ask him.*

*I saw it on the television.*

*What did you think?*

*I think Bassett is a terrible brute. He is like a crab in a shell. Even when you hit him, you are being punished. I kept wondering why you would want to take such punishment.*

*It is a question he has always asked me with his eyes, but he has never spoken the words.*

*That's what fighting is about, I explain to the ghost. Sooner or later, it catches up to you.*

*He pours more whiskey for himself. The Life also catches up to you,* *he says.*

The clock above the fireplace softly chimes and the apparition disappears. So many times we have sat down here in the late hours and talked. It is only in this moment that I fully comprehend how much I miss him, how much I love him. I admired Tommy and was seduced by Johnny. But it is my father I want now. The father who killed my father. The acid-dipped pain is back. I'm a Jew, a Jew.

I slosh down some more whiskey to ease the hurt. I need Vince. There have been many nights together in this room since Rosalia died. Paradoxically, now that I no longer live at home, we have grown closer. Our late-evening talks have become special. Sometimes, we've even achieved intimacy. I would listen to the deep voice and take comfort in his knowledge of the violent world I am facing now. If he were here, we would talk of what has happened and Vince would explain his kidnapping to me.

I remember sitting here with him after Rosalia died. I was seventeen then. Vince poured us some wine. He drank it slowly, choosing his words carefully. "They will be watching you at the wake for a sign whether you cry as a woman does. If you do, they will take it as a sign you are weak. They will come here afterward and drink wine, taste the food, and always they will be watching us. Am I getting soft? Are you strong? They will kiss your cheek and mine, say good night, but they will mark us. You must not let them see anything. So always they will think the Rossi family is still to be feared."

The quiet darkness silently mocks me. I call out to him. "We're not finished yet. Come back. What are they doing to you, Vince?"

Then I see him again outlined by the tank's red light. Staring at the night. *I suffer or I am dead. Perhaps we should ask the fishes,* he says, turning toward the tank and the red light that outlines their darting, bright bodies.

I cannot respond to his terrifying logic. For the first time in my life, I see Vince's private vision. The dark waters rushing at him. The terrible tides and undertows that form the Sicilian bends. And the slab that carries his body. I try to hold on to him for just a few seconds more, but I have taken too many punches. I find myself falling away and a great pillow rushes to soothe me.

I hear the humming noise of the fish tank's heater, see the red bulb above it, and I blink my eyes. The smell of a cigar comes to me. I hear the clock chiming and I stir. My kidneys and shoulders throb violently. My face feels like a bloated pomegranate. I shake my head to refocus, and I recognize Johnny.

The clock chimes, but I am still disoriented. "What time is it?"

Johnny puffs on the cigar and I see the red ember flare up. "Quarter of five. How do you feel, kid?"

"Like I ran into a wall. What's the news?"

Johnny takes a thoughtful drag on the cigar. "No news."

In the Mafia, no news is not good news. The question is whether it's bad news.

"The police are holding Joe Rico for questioning. He managed to call in and told Pete two men with guns grabbed Vince as they came out on the street. It was late and there weren't a lot of people out. He said one of them looked like a Jew. Mike was inside the restaurant when it happened, paying the check."

I try to make sense of it as Johnny continues. "Dino uses a Jewish hit man named Ed Levy."

"Why would Dino kidnap Vince?"

Johnny picks up a coffee cup and drinks from it. "Hitting Tommy didn't go over big with a lot of the guys in the outfit. Tommy was a deal guy, a moneymaker. Hitting Vince on top of it would make Dino look very reckless. That has a way of boomeranging on you."

The role of devil's advocate falls to me. "The way for Dino to make a big point to the Five Families is to take out Tommy and Vince. That's a language they all understand."

Johnny turns to me. "That's the way Vince would figure it. You sound just like him."

Johnny leans back and puffs on the cigar. Large smoke rings flit over his head like ominous clouds.

"What are you going to do?"

Johnny doesn't answer. Instead, he gets up. "You want some coffee?"

"Just ice water." I watch Johnny walk toward the kitchen. He's Johnny Silk, but he's never been in the catbird seat during a war. He's going hand-to-hand against Dino Manfredi, and now there's no Tommy or Vince to back him.

Johnny comes back holding a tray with a pitcher of ice water and a tall glass. I take the first cool sip and realize how thirsty I am. I drain the glass and reach for more.

"Here," he says. He holds out a couple of pills. "Aspirin."

Once again, smooth Johnny has anticipated the moment. Everything aches. I crave sleep. I down the tablets and look up at Johnny. "We have to talk."

Johnny sips his coffee before answering. "I knew someday it would come down to this. I told Vince that a long time ago, but he wanted it kept secret from you."

"How could it be a secret when everybody knew? Everybody but me."

"Vince made a mistake. If he had known it would come down to your being in a room and getting the word from Dino like that..."

"It was always headed in that direction, Johnny. It was there to be used."

The anger is clearly visible in Johnny's face, no longer layered over by the slick facade. "Dino's really asking for it this time."

"Skip the dancing and the moralizing, Johnny. Just tell me how it happened."

Johnny looks over me. He has discarded his jacket and his shirtsleeves are rolled up. He sets his coffee down. The clock chimes five o'clock and we stare at each other. It's twilight time. The light is somewhere between full night and morning. We don't know if Vince is dead or alive and we have to talk about that which he never wanted discussed.

"Nails wasn't supposed to be there," he says in a resigned voice. "Vince sent me over to the Waldorf, where he lived, but he wasn't there. I left word for Nails to wait for me, not to go out, but he never got the message. I went down to the East Side, where his mob hung out, but nobody would talk. I mean, here is a dago in the Jewish ghetto asking about a Jewish hero who's in trouble. They all loved Nails. Nobody would tell me spit. I tried to reach Vince, but he had left already."

"Left?"

Johnny bites his lip. "You have to understand what was happening then. The Gordon mob had been living on the edge for a long time. Hitting Nick to even up the Benny Wagman hit went beyond our rules. It meant Nails had lost control of them. Nick was a civilian. The Council met and said wipe out the Gordon mob. Vince was crazy with grief. He adored Nick. Nick was just a kid. He was studying pharmacy at Fordham. Vince was going to buy him a drugstore when he graduated. Nick was going to marry a beautiful girl from Naples, Elizabeth Gatti. When Nick got killed, she became a nun. Vince knew the hit on Nick couldn't have been ordered by Nails, but every dago in New York was looking for him and the rest of his gang. There was no question they were going to be wiped out."

"And then Vince got the tip from Waxy Green."

Johnny nods his head. "They were at the Rodman Arms and a bunch of Polly Adler's girls had been over to entertain them. Everybody on Broadway knew Nails. The girls would have recognized him. Before the hit team broke in, the girls were questioned. They swore Nails wasn't there."

"So they went in, and Vince was right up front, wasn't he?"

Johnny looks away. "The room was dark. No way Vince could know Nails was there."

There is a long silence before Johnny continues. "What probably happened is that between the time the girls left and the hit went down, Nails slipped in. Vince and I went over it a thousand times. Why did he go there? Why?"

Johnny reaches for Vince's whiskey decanter and laces his coffee. "That's the way it happened. Nobody was thinking too good, Davey."

"It was a real slaughter, wasn't it?"

Johnny drains his bitter cup. "It shouldn't have been."

"Tell me about Waxy Green. Why would a Jew sell out another Jew?"

Johnny shakes his head. "He and Nails had been in a lot of deals together, but Waxy was in trouble. Prohibition was going out and the feds were after him. The Gordon mob was finished no matter what happened. Waxy must have figured the Syndicate would owe him when his tax case came up. He figured wrong."

Johnny fills his cup again, and this time it's all booze. It goes down fast but not easy.

Look at me, Johnny, I think. Vince would.

"No one knew about you when Nails died. Maybe a month later, we found out. There was a girl in show business. She left town. Nails had a lot of women. We couldn't find her."

It is like being stunned with a sucker punch. One I should have seen coming when I was thirteen and Richie Tedesco wanted to know why I was circumcised. I remember he said only the kikes were circumcised. I can still hear Richie's taunting words. "Goddamn Jew boys are Christ killers."

Johnny sees where I am and tries to neutralize the feelings with talk. "When Vince learned about you, he sat up all night drinking. I found him in the Broadway Hotel, in a room on the fourth floor. He must have consumed four bottles of scotch. I put him to bed and waited. In the morning, he came downstairs to the hotel restaurant and ordered steak and eggs, finished a pot of coffee, and told me he was going to arrange things. He worked it through St. Mary's, and a few weeks later he and Rosalia brought you home. He said to us that night that you were never to know. Nobody was to ever discuss what happened to Uncle Nick. He died of pneumonia; that was the story. I remember you started to cry and Rosalia jumped up and ran to your crib. Vince said to me that you would be very good for her. She needed a baby to take care of and love. Vince was right. You made her very happy. She was crazy about you from the beginning." Johnny pours more whiskey and downs it. "And that's how it happened."

Once upon a time, there was a little Jewish baby whose father was killed by his friend, a tall, dark mafioso. Filled with pity and remorse, the mafioso took in the baby. The room is spinning.

"Who named me?"

Johnny takes a deep breath. "Vince did. For David. King of the Jews. He said Nails's son should be named after a great warrior."

The breath is gone from me. As if Kid Bassett had hit me with a body shot. And King David though I may be, I respond like the dago son of a mafioso. "Dino, how did he know? And Joe Dante?"

Johnny shakes his head. "I always thought it was just me, Vince, and Rosalia. I told Vince it wasn't a secret he could keep. Somehow,

Dino found out and he held on to it all these years. Till the time was right to use it."

I struggle to gain control of myself. "Who told Vince that Nails had a son?"

Johnny takes a deep breath. "I never found out."

I'd seen the moonfaced corpse that was Waxy Green. He knew. How? The man who betrayed Nails Gordon was ready to sell his son the information about his father. Who else did he approach? Why was he killed? What other secrets was Waxy ready to peddle?

Johnny is watching me closely. "What is it, Davey?"

I shake my head. "Nothing. I could use some of that coffee."

Johnny heads for the kitchen and I have my respite. He hasn't told me all there is to be told and this isn't the time to press him. There are answers that only Vince can give me. There is more to the death of Nails Gordon than anybody is letting on. Who else knows? Who else will reach out to me? I hurt all over from the blows of this evening. Kid Bassett's punches I can handle, but I gave Dino the first shot and he finished me off. I am a Jew in the house of the Mafia.

# 9

I AM RUNNING through a long, dark cavern, fleeing from the men pursuing me. Breathless, I come out on the tracks. I hear their voices behind me as they draw closer. I am in a tunnel within a tunnel and there are no lights. I pick up the pace and hear my strangled, desperate breaths. My chest throbs. The tunnel narrows; the track beneath me has fused into one single hot rail that singes my feet. The ceiling is touching my neck; the walls close around me. Boxed in, all boxed in. I lunge forward into someone's embrace. Rough, hairy arms embrace me. I smell his sweat—pungent, sour-smelling. I stare up into the face of Kid Bassett. The Kid nods to me, smiling, and leads me down the track. We are inside another tunnel, walking toward a man illuminated under a single light. His face is hidden by shadows. His hand is extended and I see the gleaming gold crucifix. A shaft of light crosses his face. It is Joe Dante, a knowing, conspiratorial smile on his face. He thrusts the crucifix at me.

Someone is shaking my shoulder. I cry out and come up swinging. A hand grabs my fist. The blurred image before me shapes and reshapes itself and then I see Johnny. He pats me on the shoulder and releases my fist. "Easy, kid, the fight's over." He drops a pile of newspapers on the bed. "The papers say you won." The top one is the *Journal-American*, open to the sports pages. There is a huge photo of me on my knees, clinging to the legs of Kid Bassett as his right hand descends toward my head. How did I ever survive that punch? How did I win the fight?

I sift through the others, all with similar photos and captions. The headline over a series of photos in the *Daily News* reads BLOODBATH IN THE GARDEN. My eyes go to the story as Mrs. Lamberti pokes her wrinkled face through the door. "Would you like your breakfast now?" She has kept house for Vince for a long time now and knows about the Life, but the sight of my face makes her wince.

Johnny nods to her. "Better have it, Davey."

I start reading Bill Devlin's account of the fight in the *News*.

*In a furious waterfront brawl that featured nine knockdowns, the once-great boxing master, Davey Rossi, came off the canvas to knock out slugger Kid Bassett and position himself for a return match with Sandy Simpson, who lifted his crown six months ago. What was expected to be a walkover for the former champion became a wild slugfest after a series of butts by Bassett left Rossi dazed and wide open for a mugging by the Kid. Knocked down by the Kid five times between the fourth and seventh rounds, Rossi came out for the eighth round knowing it was do or die. Meeting the Kid in the center of the ring, Rossi became a punching machine. In a furious display of nonstop punching, fighting for his ring life, Rossi weathered a knockdown and left the Kid for dead at 2:38 of the eighth round. It was 10:57 P.M. when referee Herb Gertz held up Rossi's hand, signifying his victory only minutes after his father, underworld boss Vince Rossi, was kidnapped outside of a Bronx restaurant where he had just eaten dinner.*

I groan and look up at Johnny. He is dapper as always in a gray suit with a blue shirt and a blue-and-black-striped tie. "They're all that way," he says.

I turn to the front page of the *News* and the headline screams at me BOSS TAKEN FOR A RIDE AS SON WINS BRAWL AT GARDEN. The inside pages feature pictures of Vince and me. There are prominent biographies of us both. It is a relationship that the press has always known about but never focused on, primarily because they knew it would not make the don happy. And Tommy and Johnny were always there to spread a little grease around so that the great engine that fuels the media would grind out only boxing stories. But Tommy is dead, Vince abducted, and all bets are off.

"The *Daily Mirror* is even better," Johnny says. "That's got pictures of all of us." Under a banner headline are photos of Vince, Johnny, and me. The bold black type reads DON ABDUCTED WHILE CHAMP SLUGS IT OUT. Johnny shrugs, "That's the least of our worries right now. When you fight Simpson, it'll be the hottest ticket in town."

I toss the paper aside. "The Simpson fight won't be for a while."

"It'll be a lot sooner than you think, if you want a shot at him."

I give Johnny a hard look as Mrs. Lamberti enters with my breakfast tray. The smell of crisp bacon permeates the room. She sets the tray and the stand down on my bed. "What does that mean, Johnny?"

He waits until Mrs. Lamberti goes out before answering. "Matty Clark called me this morning. The fight's in ten weeks."

"I won't be ready."

"That's the deal if you want the title shot. Simpson's going to fight for the welterweight title this spring."

This is not the way it's done. You get three months to heal up and then you start training. That's standard. Nobody dictates those kinds of terms to the Rossi family. "What's going on, Johnny?"

He takes big breath. "We're being squeezed. Tommy's dead and Vince is out of circulation. We lost a couple of big hitters."

"Who's doing the squeezing?"

"Dino, through Carlo Scola. Scola owns Sandy Simpson."

"I never knew that."

"It's like everything else Scola does. He keeps a low profile, but he pulls the strings." He reaches over and touches my face. "I know, your cuts need four weeks to heal. They know it, too."

"And if I wait?"

"They'll stall it around eighteen months, maybe longer."

"I'll be a million years old by then."

"You're in a tough business, Davey."

The smell of the bacon suddenly makes me nauseous. I push the tray away. "I can't eat this."

"You better eat it; last night was just the beginning." Johnny stands up and reaches for the coffeepot. There is an ironic smile painted on his mouth. "Wake up and smell the coffee."

There are scrambled eggs to go with the bacon, lots of toast with marmalade, orange juice, and milk. Johnny watches me eat. He is right. Last night was just the beginning, and we haven't spoken about Vince yet.

I eat mechanically because the good appetite isn't there. For the first time in my life, the pressure is on the Rossi family, and I am a part of it. The part of the Life that has never touched mine had suddenly intruded upon my sheltered existence, squeezing like a hand upon my throat. Vince has always lived with the picture of himself lying on a slab. Now that picture is there for me. I can see him lying on a table, eyes open but sightless. I drink the hot black coffee to wash away the grim photo I have conjured up, taste the eggs flavored with cheese that Mrs. Lamberti has made, smother the toast with gobs of dripping marmalade. And it is all good. Life goes on, every single waking moment of it. I am eating this food with Johnny at my side, while somewhere Vince is lying tied up, eating doughy submarine sandwiches served by his captors, if he is able to eat at all.

I push the tray aside while Johnny pours coffee for us. "Tell me about Vince."

"No news. I sent a message that we wanted some sign that Vince was still alive."

"And?"

"No word yet."

I drink more coffee to steady myself. "If I were Dino, I wouldn't give us that courtesy."

Johnny nods. "You're learning fast. No, I wouldn't either. I'd just let you sweat. Dangle in the wind and sweat."

"And if you don't hear from Dino?"

Johnny drains his coffee and looks down at the floor. "If I don't hear, then I'll have to call him back and tell him something."

We both stare at each other and then at the clock on the table next to my bed. It's just after two o'clock. Ten hours to save Vince's life or give it up and go to war with Dino Manfredi. It is Johnny's choice.

I look over at Johnny. "What about Frank Bruno?"

"What about him?"

"He stood with Vince and Tommy. If he's on our side now, Dino and Joe will have second thoughts about a war."

Johnny stands up and lights a cigarette. "I'm meeting with him this afternoon."

Johnny bites his lip. There is no need of words. Frank Bruno is the ball game. If he sides with the Rossi family, then the numbers even out. If he doesn't . . .

Johnny tosses a note on the bed. "Letter from a fan."

It's a message taken by Mrs. Lamberti: "Call Julie." I note the number, trying to subdue my racing pulse. I look up at Johnny.

He nods his head toward the slip of paper. "Better lay low, kid."

I fold the note up. "Am I a civilian or not?"

"Once you were, Davey, but no more. Dino used you to get at the family last night. You may not be a player yet, but you're not a spectator."

"They wouldn't touch me. They do that and it's open season on their kids. The whole system is built on one foundation. Family gets safe passage."

"Rules are made to be broken, Davey. That's how people get to the top. Anywhere you go, take Harp and one of the other boys. And I mean anywhere, even if you wind up in the sack."

"I don't share well."

He cuffs me in the head with a pillow. "You do now."

For a moment, it is like it used to be, full of quips and affection, and then last night comes back to me and I feel an ache. The knot is in my throat. Johnny reads it and his arm rests on my shoulder. "C'mon, Davey, that's the way the hand was dealt, but you're one of us. You're a Rossi."

I swallow hard. "I'm a Jew."

"You're still a Rossi."

It all lies there and neither of us can say anything. "We have to save Vince," Johnny says softly.

I don't say anything for a long beat. "I know." I wave the note in the air. "I want to see her, Johnny."

Johnny starts to say something and then decides not to. He is trying to smile, and so am I, but it is not right. Last night is still there. Nails Gordon is still there. I get out of bed and reach for the robe in the closet. "I want to know about Nails, Johnny. I want to know it all."

It is there now, right in front of us as the phone rings. Someone downstairs picks it up on the third ring. Never look too anxious.

Johnny and I stand there eyeing each other, waiting. A voice calls from downstairs and Johnny picks up. "Hello." His eyes glitter with a dark anger as he says, "Yeah, I understand." He hangs up and looks over at me. "We have eight hours. The deadline is ten o'clock tonight."

I look at Johnny and try to read him. Johnny Silk, deal maker extraordinaire, has eight hours to decide on whether to go to war. And the price is Vince's head.

"What are you going to do?"

Johnny rubs his chin. "I'll decide that tonight. I have a few things working." He checks his watch. "You better get moving. I want you back here by six o'clock."

We stare at each other and then I nod. I am still a Rossi. I reach for the phone.

The hot shower reminds me of what a good job the Kid did on me. My shoulders are stiff and sore; my rib cage is a massive ache. It will be a week before the effects of the clubbing blows leave me. The Kid will have his own set of body-deep bruises. We have both left our signature on the other. But the hurt inside him runs deeper this morning. That's what the knockout means. The water cascades down on me, balm for my aches and pains. A continual spray of tingling moments. Like Vince must be feeling right now. The luck of the draw. I'm here, safe and clean, while he ... cut it out, I tell myself. No pity. Vince wouldn't want that or want me thinking that way. He's lived the life, knowing this was always coming. He's lived a long time and it's not over yet. It's a long time between now and ten o'clock tonight.

I put it into another compartment and think about Julie's voice on the phone, cool and yet husky with a tremor of emotion. "I'm glad you got back from your ride."

"Me, too."

"Are you okay?"

"I'm fine."

"I'm sorry about your father."

"Thanks."

"Is this a bad time?"

"No, I'm glad you called. I was going to call you."

There is a moment of silence before I can speak again. "I was hoping       "

"What?"

"Could you come out . . . meet me?"

"When?"

"I don't have much time."

"Where, Davey?"

"Do you know Harcourts on East Fifty-sixth, off Madison?"

"Yes. That was Tommy's favorite spot, wasn't it?"

The mention of Tommy makes something inside me turn over. "Wait, let's go to Bonsignore's. It's just a couple of blocks over, on Third Avenue. In about an hour. Is that okay?"

"I'll see you then, Davey."

There's something about the way she says my name. Like she knows me, like it means something to her. What am I doing going over to meet a girl now? Downstairs, the capos are gathered around Johnny. Outside, there are more groups of soldiers. The family is at war. Vince's life is at stake and you're going out to meet a girl. It can wait. She'll be there. But somehow I need to escape the family under siege, the war mentality, the dumb, brute men drinking espresso, pacing, waiting, in their eyes the expression of forlorn hope, desperately wishing their don to survive and things to go back to the way they were. Like Vince, they've all been around a long time. Maybe too long.

It is gray and overcast as I leave the house. Johnny is whispering something to Harp. Harp sees me and his body language changes immediately. He straightens up, approaches me, and obediently hovers at my side. Just behind him is "Fat Louie" Toldano. He will be my driver. Johnny takes me aside. "Don't get sidetracked. It all changes hour by hour."

"I'll be at Bonsignore's and then right back here."

Johnny claps me on the back. "Want to carry a piece?" He is smiling.

"What for?"

He laughs. "I hear she's a tough broad."

He leads me over to the car and I can see the crew watching me. Dago Pete, Mario Brugatti, Wop Luca, Joe Rico, who was with Vince when they snatched him. Joe looks down at the ground. He seems a little ashamed. The don was taken right out from under him. That

makes him less in the eyes of the others. Even though I am not important to the matters at hand, Harp and Fat Louie regard me the
way a farmer going to market watches over his prize pig. I slide into
the back of the dark Buick and Fat Louie pulls away. As we leave, I
can see all of them watching us. There are looks of apprehension. Only
Johnny seems pensive. He waves with his right hand.

We roll slowly out of Prince Street and into the network of little
blocks that will lead us uptown. The raincoat I grabbed as I left the
house is folded over my legs.

Harp looks back at me. "Jesus, look at the fog, Davey." There is a
worried expression on his face.

I choose not to answer. Something is nagging at me. Why when
Julie mentioned Tommy's name did I change restaurants? Harcourts
is a classy place with excellent food. It is because Tommy always did
business there and the association is too painful? Or is it because I am
still unsure of Julie's relationship to him? Why am I rushing to meet
this girl? Just to block out the atmosphere at the house? No, that's not
it. It's to escape the strangers in it. Vince and Johnny and the history
of a father I never met.

Fat Louie guides the car up Third Avenue. He sneaks a quick glance
at me. "Best fight I ever saw, Davey."

"Thanks."

Fat Louie is infinitely patient with the traffic, cruising behind cabs,
slowing for pedestrians. Up the block, I see Bonsignore's. Unlike Harcourts, nobody does business here. It's not a mob social club like the
Gold Band over on Fifty-second Street. It caters to tourists and New
Yorkers who like big Italian meals while being serenaded by a strolling
band. It's on the chichi side, but it won't be crowded at this time of
day. The fast singles will gather around the bar at five, but I'll be
checking out then. As we pull in, I see Julie. She is wearing a navy
blue suit with a crisp white collar showing. In daylight, her hair is
brown, not black, and she is wearing it down. I am suddenly aware
that my mouth is open and there is not a thought in my head.

Harp's hand on my arm brings me back. "We'll be right out in
front. Louie in the car and me on the door. If there's anything not
kosher, I'll give you the high sign."

I nod and clap Harp on the shoulder. "Thanks, guys. I really appreciate this."

Harp gives me a resigned, weary smile. "Don't worry, Davey, we'll get Vince back."

As I walk toward Julie, Harp is right there behind me.

She turns and, seeing me, flashes a vivid smile. It seems to run all through me. I fight the impulse to touch her and there is an unsteady moment that she diffuses by taking my hand.

She notices Harp and I take her arm. "Let's go inside."

As you step inside Bonsignore's, there is a hatcheck, but no one minding the store. Muted lighting greets us and the air is suffused with the smell of lunch. At night, the lights built into the wall gleam brightly. To our left is the bar, occupied by a lone drinker. Harp walks over and cases him. Satisfied, he comes back and walks through the dining room, passing Alfredo, the maître d', without even pausing. Alfredo starts to call after him, but the instinct that serves him so well in his profession sounds a warning and Harp is allowed his walk through the dining room uninterrupted.

Alfredo spots me and comes over. He is a small, pointy man with a receding hairline. Sweat glistens on his forehead. He gives me his professional smile. "Mr. Rossi, so glad to see you."

Clearly, he is uncomfortable with my arrival. Alfredo has read the papers; he knows what's going on. The meaning of Harp's stroll through the dining room is suddenly very clear.

"Could we have something in the alcove?"

"Of course."

Bonsignore's is a wide oval-shaped room with corner nooks that allow you to see the rest of room without being seen yourself. Large chandeliers encompass the room and a red rug, brilliant with medieval scenes, covers the floor. It is all overdone, but the tourists flock here.

Alfredo leads to us to the alcove, where a round table is surrounded by a leather-upholstered bench seat. I am careful to take the side that faces the bar. Harp gives me a signal that he has covered the room and then walks toward the entrance. Alfredo watches him leave and licks his lips nervously.

"Alfredo, we'd like a bottle of wine. Something chilled."

"A Chardonnay perhaps?"

"You pick it."

He gives me a nervous smile. "Anything to eat?"

I look at Julie and she shakes her head. "Nothing right now. Maybe some espresso later."

"Of course."

He walks abruptly away as we both watch him. "He wouldn't last long in a poker game, would he?"

Julie shifts her bag on the table. "What do you mean?"

"Well, generally he calls me Davey, but today it's Mr. Rossi. He's read the papers, and then Harp makes his promenade through the restaurant." I shrug. "It's a nervous time."

We both acknowledge that silently and Julie lights a cigarette. It is that awkward moment when you are with someone you want to be with and don't want to stare. But there is nothing else to do. She's so beautiful, and swallowing is difficult.

A small smile forms around the corners of her mouth. "That ride you went on last night . . . I knew it wasn't a celebration."

"Well, I came back and I'm here. With you."

"I know."

Alfredo returns with the wine and we lapse into silence. There is the perfunctory show of the label, my approval, and then he busies himself with opening it. He works hard, but his nerves give him away. I try not to stare at the sweaty, flushed face. Finally, the cork comes out and he pours some in my glass. "It's fine, Alfredo."

"Anything else?"

"Nothing."

"I'll bring the espresso."

"In awhile."

"Of course."

We watch him back off. I try to ease the moment between us. "Like I said, it's a nervous time."

"Do you want to talk about it?"

I pour the wine for us. "I don't know. Right now, it's about waiting."

Julie holds the glass in her hand. She has long, graceful hands, the nails painted a deep red. There is something about them that rivets me. Something about the glow of her skin and the green eyes. The fingers on the idle hand drum on the table. She is all charged underneath.

"Have you had any word about your father?"

"He's okay, I guess."

The flashing green eyes leap out at me. "What does that mean?"

Her directness has caught me off guard, but I like it. She is not going to accept evasion. I look into the cold glass of Chardonnay and then back at Julie. "It means there's a time factor."

"Are you negotiating?"

She is quick and it's too close to home. "I really can't say anything more. Let's drink to something."

"You make that toast, Davey."

Hearing her say my name sends the river running again. I hold up my glass. "To here and now. To what is and what could be."

A soft smile creases her lips and she extends her glass to mine. I'll bet she smiles that way when she wakes up in the morning and some-one's made her happy.

Alfredo has picked a good Chardonnay. It goes down dry and easy.

"Johnny told me you did work for Tommy."

Julie doesn't say anything and I wonder why I have gone directly to this. But I can't let it go. "Who introduced you to Tommy?"

She inhales a lungful of smoke. "Tommy introduced himself. It was at a party in Sag Harbor. He had a place out there and he liked to socialize. We met at the bar and he asked me what I did. When I told him, he said, 'What's a looker like you doing in a courtroom?' Then I told him I did tax law, and he said, 'Maybe we should talk, because I pay a lot of money to accountants and all I got was eighteen months in the slammer to show for it.'"

I find myself grinning. "That sounds like Tommy."

"We went to lunch a few times and just talked. We became friends. He was a very interesting man."

"Just talked" reverberates in my head. "Just talked," "an interesting man," "became friends." None of Tommy's ladies were friends.

"One day, he asked me if I wanted to work for him."

I sip some wine to steady myself. "Aren't taxes boring?"

"I don't do that part of it. When people like Tommy come to us, they're in trouble. He had already done eighteen months, and the government was trying to deport him."

"Deport Tommy?"

"The case was all ready. Tommy lied about being a bootlegger when he was naturalized. It was one mistake he couldn't fix with a bribe."

"How were you doing?"

"Pretty good. We were in the process of showing Immigration that we had grounds to take it all the way to the Supreme Court. We would have challenged the legality of the deportation order. Immigration was doing a little dance around us. It would have been very interesting."

"Who is 'we'?"

"Alpert and Bates. My father is Alpert. Ben Alpert. He's been down in Washington for twenty-five years. Came to work for Roosevelt and met Sandy Bates. Sandy does the legal work; Dad has all the contacts."

"And he passed them on to you?"

Julie smiles. "Something like that. More vino. I could make a habit of this."

I pour and look into her eyes. "Me, too."

Julie runs her finger around the glass. "You know, I got to be very fond of Tommy. He had done a lot, seen a lot, and he was sorry."

"Sorry about the way he lived."

Julie gives me a sharp look. "Yes, and for what he had missed. 'The normal things,' he called them. When he was young, he beat men for money. He said that always stayed with him. He was being treated by a psychiatrist for depression."

The Life always leaves its mark. Vince had a bad ulcer.

"Is your father that way?"

It is a long beat before I answer. "Yeah, there's a lot to be sorry for."

"You look so sad when you say that. As if you're sorry."

"Maybe I am."

Julie reaches across the table and runs her hand across my face. "Don't be sorry, Davey. We just met. Your face. Your poor face."

"Imagine what Kid Bassett feels like today."

"But he's so ugly, it doesn't matter."

"So you like my face better."

The warm hand traces a line from my cheek down to my lips. "Oh, much better."

The hand lingers there, soft, inviting, and then is gone.

"Would you like that espresso?"

"Yes, and I hope it's raining out, so I can't get a cab to my office and work on a Saturday. Excuse me."

I watch Julie walk across the room. Watch the trim body and the firm, leggy walk. Watch and wonder. And want.

A waiter comes by and I order espresso. I gaze around the room. The lone drinker has left the bar. Diners having a late lunch occupy a few of the tables in the room. Twenty of four. There is that late-afternoon lull that descends on a restaurant in the time between lunch and dinner. Harp comes padding across the room, signaling with his hand that everything is okay.

"Listen, Davey, how long you think you will be?"

"Awhile. Any problem?"

"Just that Louie has gotten rousted a few times in the car. The law won't let him sit there. I'll have him put it in a garage. No sweat, Davey. Enjoy." Then a small smile. "She's a beautiful girl, Davey."

Harp leaves and a waiter passes by him, bearing a large pot of espresso. He sets it down and places cups, saucers, and lemons for the espresso on the table.

"Where's Alfredo?"

The waiter, who is tall and balding, purses his lips. He speaks with a thick accent. "He has some business. Anything else I can get you?"

"It's fine."

I watch him walk away. The wine has made me lazy and tired. I feel like making love. I am all tight inside. Julie walks briskly across the room and sits down, rewarding me with a warm smile.

"Espresso in the afternoon. How sinful. I'm never going back to work."

"I used to have a teacher in college who said days like this are meant for creative leisure."

"How did he define that?"

"Lying in bed with a bottle of wine, some espresso, and ..."

"And?"

"And thou."

Our eyes meet and there is no need for words.

The espresso is piping hot and strong. I keep devouring Julie with my eyes, and she has a wonderful way of knowing it and not being bothered.

We make small but pleasurable talk. The minutes pass by and neither of us pays any notice. Everything we say seems terribly important. Just as everything we don't say but feel is wonderful in the same way. I almost reach for her hand, but I can't do it. Not yet. Instead, I talk some more. "Tell me about your father and Washington."

"It's an ongoing story. My parents were divorced when I was very young. I grew up with my mother."

"Where?"

"Long Island. The Five Towns. My parents split up when I was five. I didn't see my father very much after that. He set up a practice in Washington and lived for his career. When I got older, I would visit him on the holidays. I really didn't spend much time with him till I went to law school and clerked in Washington. It was only then that I realized how much I had missed. This was my father, and I had spent a lifetime without him. I'm still getting to know him."

The newspaper photo of Nails Gordon the day after he was killed leaps before me like a close-up in a movie.

Julie sees my distress and honors it with silence, for which I am grateful. I need to regroup. I finish my drink and stand up. "I think I've had a lot of wine."

I start to walk away, and Julie calls to me. "Davey." It is like hearing music. I turn. "Come back."

Her look stays with me as I make my way to the men's room. The wine and coffee make for an endless stream. My kidneys complain about working on this day, after Kid Bassett massaged them. Then I am at the sink, staring at my face in the bathroom mirror. I look grotesque: eyes stitched and lumpy, cheekbones swollen and distorted, a monumental discolored bruise above the left cheek. Everything is lopsided and out of proportion. My eyes are tiny slits. What can she see in me?

I wash my hands and dab water gently on my face, take a deep breath, and head back toward Julie. There is a man just outside the door. He is large, somehow familiar.

"Davey, how are you?"

I smell the hair tonic he uses and the cologne. Joe Dante Jr. always splashed himself with the stuff when we went to high school at LaSalle Academy.

"Hey, Joe." I stand back, warily watching him. "What are you doing here?"

"I just came in for a drink."

We played together as kids, attended high school together, and then went our separate ways. He into the Life and me to the ring. Now our fathers separate us. I recall last night. Anna said he was away.

"You with somebody?"

"Yeah. A lady. Over there." I point to Julie.

Joe turns, then whistles softly. "*Madone*. That's okay, Davey. Listen, great fight. Great fight."

"Thanks."

We stand there surveying each other. Joe junior is tall, maybe six feet two, and goes over two hundred pounds. He has a thick mop of glossy hair and a nice face, which he has stuffed with too much manicotti and alcohol. He is wearing a sharp blue suit over a white shirt and red tie. The yesterdays seem like minutes ago. But it is still a bad moment for us.

"Listen, Davey, it's an accident. Here." A big smile. "Frisk me. Go ahead."

I go through the motions and he forces my hands over his body. "You see. No hard feelings. You're not carrying, are you, Davey?" He gives me the once-over, but it is expert. Too good to be casual. "Okay, we're both clean. Now can I go to the louie? Look at your hand, Davey." He points to my clenched fist.

"Sorry."

"That's okay, Davey." He glances back at Julie. "She's a real dish."

"Join us for a drink."

Joe measures me. "It's okay?"

"Just a short one."

"It's on me, Davey."

Joe Dante Jr. pushes his way into the men's room and I walk toward Julie. It could be a coincidence, but it isn't. Joe junior didn't just show up. Someone sent him. In the Life, there is no such thing as coincidence.

# 10

**A THOUSAND RACING THOUGHTS.** Joe junior here. Yeah, Bonsignore's is a hangout, but this is war. Vince has been taken. Nobody just hangs out. Except you, because you're getting hooked on a looker. That's what Tommy called her. Tommy, who knew all the angles, and got whacked in a barbershop. Vince, who went out for dinner and got picked up off the street. And Davey, who slipped out for an afternoon cocktail and suddenly runs into Joe Dante Jr. for a fast frisk. Joe's got backup. You're not a civilian; you're Vince Rossi's son, and they're going to snatch you.

I walk across the ornate rug, and its exotic patterns jump out in front of me. Abruptly, I catch sight of Alfredo, and rather than look at me, his eyes divert and then, catching himself, he nods. You son of a bitch, you fingered me. You sent one of your waiters to serve me espresso and you slipped away and called Joe Dante. Joe Dante put the word out: If Davey shows up anywhere, I want to know about it. He was figuring my next move because this is a time of war. And like Vince, I was smug. In the history of the mob, there have been a thousand hits and snatches, and every one of them at a bar, or a restaurant, or a hangout the victim liked to frequent. And yet nobody learns.

Julie looks at me expectantly as I sit down, lean over, and whisper,

"Take a cigarette out and wait for me to light it for you. Do what I say."

Her eyes get big with surprise, but she is a quick study. I pick up the matches on the table and then we close together in an intimate tableau. Just a couple getting chummy and the man is putting the move on. Dumb Davey. Punchy Davey.

"They're going to grab me." Her eyes go wide. "It won't be long now. When we finish talking, I want you to go to the powder room. Count to thirty, slip out, and call my brother, Johnny. Use the same number you called this morning. Tell whoever answers that it's very important, that they're snatching Davey. They must get here fast. No stops, no traffic lights. Can you remember that?"

Her hands go around my neck and stroke it. There is a big smile on her face. Julie is a terrific actress.

"I have a gun in my purse. Would that help?"

I smile back. Big smile. "Joe junior just put the frisk on me, but they'll do it again."

"Is that the man I saw you with?"

"Yes. He's the son of one of my father's enemies."

"Why are they doing this?"

"I'm not sure. They're squeezing Johnny."

"Why are you so sure they're going to snatch you?"

"Because there's no way that Harp would have let Joe junior in here without letting me know about it. That means they took care of him and Fat Louie."

Julie leans closer. "I'm going to kiss you. Don't look surprised. I've wanted to do it all afternoon. Don't you want to kiss me?"

"All my life."

"Good. Then while I kiss you, I'm going to slip you the gun."

"Do it this way. Take my raincoat with you to the powder room. Put the gun in the pocket. When you come back, drop the coat next to me."

"You're smart, Davey. Come here."

Her lips are moist and infinitely soft, tasting of wine and something fruity. I could live in them.

We break it and I light her cigarette. "Stand up. Hold on to my hand for a beat and then get out of here. Take the coat."

I watch Julie walk to the ladies' room. They don't want her; they only want you. Chances are, they'll detain her by the powder room till the grab is completed.

I look up and Joe junior is walking toward me. Two hoods in trench coats and hats are in the room, about ten yards behind him. Play dumb. Maybe that will help you catch a break later.

"Hey, Davey, where's your lady?"

"Powdering her nose."

"That's a shame. I would really like to have met her."

"Stick around."

"I can't. Neither can you. Let's go, Davey."

"Where?"

"You know."

"For a ride?"

"To the country. Get some fresh air."

"What's this for, Joe?"

"For nothing really, Davey. For being Vince's son."

"What happened to Harp and Fat Louie?"

"They were detained."

"Are they okay?"

"Sure."

"Stand up, Davey. I got to pat you down again."

"You know I don't carry."

"I know, but it's part of the job. My old man places great stock in that stuff."

He pats me down efficiently, thoroughly.

"Now you see the two hitters behind me, Davey?"

"I see them."

"Good. Walk toward them. They'll take your arm. Don't do anything stupid. There's three of us and one of you, and they don't know you since we were kids. They only know about taking orders from my father. *Capisce?*"

"I know you'll speak highly of me, Joe."

"Let's go, Davey."

The proprietary hand is on my arm. The gesture used by the mob to say, I own you. He guides me toward the two sluggers. One of them is Nunez Otonio, looming massive in front of me. The first team is definitely here. I try to pick up a sign of Julie, but she is nowhere in sight.

I am guided toward the exit, flanked by the three-man escort. No one is in a hurry. No one is going to interrupt us. As we pass the hatcheck, Nuñez whispers to Joe.

Joe turns to me. "You must have come on too strong. Your lady cut out on you. I don't know where she went, but she did us a favor."

We are through the door and out into the street. It is still light out. They won't turn the clocks back till tonight. But it is gray and misty. A black Chrysler sits at the curb, a driver at the wheel. Joe reaches for the door, I hear Julie.

She has interposed herself between us, pressing her body against mine. "Davey, where are you going? You said you would wait."

Joe moves quickly to deflect her. "Something important came up. Tell her, Davey."

"It's important, Julie."

"He'll call you, Julie."

She looks at Joe and then at the open door. Her face set, the words fly out. "I'm going with you." She throws herself into the car.

Her bold maneuver stuns them. Julie has taken possession of the backseat car. Nuñez comes to life. "I'll get her." He starts around the car but stops short as Julie calls out.

"C'mon, Davey. Davey!"

Her cries have caught the attention of several people across the street. Heads turn. Joe junior grabs my arm. "Get in." He pushes me in and calls out to Nuñez. "Never mind, let's go. C'mon."

Joe jumps in back and barks instructions to the remaining hood. "Vito, call the house. Tell them we're on our way."

Nuñez thrusts himself in front as Joe turns to Julie. "You just made a big mistake, lady."

My feisty girl doesn't back off. "Maybe you did. You just can't go around picking up people all the time." She edges forward, her voice shrill, and the raincoat falls over my lap.

Nuñez intercedes. "You want I should deposit her?"

Joe junior has a moment of indecision while looking across the street at the gathering crowd.

Julie cries out again. "Who do you think you are?"

"Get out of here," Joe yells at his driver. "C'mon, Tulio, move it."

The Chrysler, which has been idling, starts up and we head east. Turning back, I can see several people watching us. Witnesses. Not clean, not neat, Joe. Papa Joe will not be happy. Witnesses can identify people. Joe junior reads my thought and sneers. "Don't worry your head about it, Davey. Maybe somebody recognized you, but when they read about what happened, all those people will be D and D."

Julie pipes in. "What's that?"

Seeing she has his attention, she pushes the raincoat farther over and touches my hand.

"Deaf and dumb, lady."

I touch the pocket of the coat and feel the gun—a small revolver. It will be easier to get out of the coat if I can create a diversion at the right time.

We turn up First Avenue and slide into the uptown traffic. It is Saturday afternoon and midtown lacks the bustle of a weekday. In a few moments, we blend into the uptown traffic.

"Take it to Ninety-sixth Street and then through the park." Joe tells his driver.

I look at Julie and for the first time see the fear in her eyes. What she did was brave and impulsive, but it was not seeing to the end of things. If I come back from this ride, I will not speak of it. But Julie is not one of us, and Joe junior knows that. I reach over and take her hand. It is no longer warm as it was when we were having drinks. I can feel the sweat.

The Chrysler speeds up First Avenue and makes a left at Ninety-sixth Street. I see Joe regarding Julie with heavy eyes. He turns and looks at me. "I hear you're a Hebe, Davey." Joe junior has a malevolent smile on his lips. "All those years, and I couldn't figure out why your meat was sliced in front." Joe's words have lanced me in the right place. All the pain and anger from last night leap and bubble inside me.

Joe turns back to Julie, the broad who has humiliated him. "Can you imagine, all these years, Davey Rossi, son of the don, was a Yid hiding out with dagos. What's the matter, Julie, can't you talk? You wanted to come along for a ride, now you're on one."

We are through Central Park and steaming toward Columbus Avenue. Moments later, we cross Broadway and the driver slows for the light on West End Avenue.

"Don't stop," Joe yells.

The driver calls out, "There's a light."

"Run it."

"Hey, Joe," Nuñez calls out. "Cops park around here. We don't need to be stopped."

"Old lady Nuñez. Run it."

The car darts through the red light and then we sweep under the crosswalk and onto the West Side Highway, the gray mist over the Hudson makes the river look magical as we speed alongside it. I remember as a kid how reckless Joe junior became when he was angry. Sometimes we would fight, and the anger always led him into a mistake. A mistake I learned to wait for. The thought comforts me as we dance up the highway in the powerful Chrysler, while the tall old tenements of upper Manhattan look down silently upon us.

# 11

**WE SETTLE IN** for the ride and the talking stops. I need the space to think about my next move. I have a gun they don't know about, but there are three of them. And this is not a rubout; it's a snatch. Maybe Dino is just covering his bet. If he has both Vince and me, then how can Johnny hold out? But Julie coming along for the ride changes the strategy. She is an innocent spectator and Papa Joe cannot hold her a long time without a large search developing. Vince once told me, "As long as it's us dagos cutting each other up, no one cares. But if we touch an innocent, then the roof comes down. So the rule is, when we have a war, it stays in-house. The one who brings down the outside world on us is our enemy." I look over at Joe. He knows the rules. He knows what he has done. He has put his father on the spot. Once again, he has failed a mission his father would have handled easily as a young man. And it is this knowledge of what Joe is feeling now that gives me the edge, not the gun in my raincoat.

I watch him out of the corner of my eye. What is he feeling, thinking? There was always an unhappiness to Joe when I used to visit his house. He was too heavy as a kid, one more way that he failed a father he desperately wanted to emulate. I always thought he was closer in character to Anna, who is a soft person. The knowledge that his son was more like his mother must have rubbed the don the wrong way. Joe junior knew that in the way only a son could. I remember

Anna's ravaged face last night. I recall her words: "It is a monstrous life." Anna has always been kind to me, made me feel wanted, even special. But she has never been able to remake the world that holds Joe junior and me as hostages.

The signs marking the upper and lower ramps of the George Washington Bridge loom before us. Joe junior leans forward. "The lower one, Tulio."

I can see the driver's face in the rearview mirror. It is swarthy and pitted, marks from a losing bout with the pox in childhood. There is a look in his eye, an expression of his contempt for Joe junior. Tulio is a professional wheelman. He doesn't need Joe to tell him what ramp to take.

We wind up and around and then we are on the lower roadway of the GW Bridge. Down below us is the Hudson, serene in the mist. Julie and I exchange glances. She doesn't expect me to outgun three sluggers. It wasn't smart to come along. It was emotion. Smart would have been to stay behind and make that call.

When we come off the bridge, we are in New Jersey. There are the signs for the Palisades Parkway and Fort Lee, the town that we have to ride through to reach it. I see a string of garden apartments and then hear Tulio's voice. "I think we got someone on our tail."

Joe's head swivels. His dark brown eyes open wide. I see a blue Chevrolet behind us. Still watching the car, Joe bites off each word. "When did you see him?"

"On the West Side Highway. He's tailing us; I can smell him."

"Let's find out. Hit the gas when we get on to the Palisades."

Tulio guides the car into the right lane and follows the signs onto the parkway. "Go," Joe yells.

The big Chrysler has lots of power and it jumps out as Tulio floors the pedal. We charge into the left lane. Traffic is light and there is lots of room for maneuvering. The Chevy pulls out after us.

"I told you," Tulio trumpets from the front.

"Son of a bitch," Joe snarls. "All right, lose him."

Again, I look at Julie. Maybe she made the call after all. But if it were Johnny, there would be backup, and the Chevy is not a new car. All Vince's cars are new and up-to-the-minute.

"Let's see what you got," Tulio calls out as he challenges our pursuer.

He shifts into the right lane and then back into the left, spinning deftly around two cars. My hand tightens on the revolver resting in my raincoat. The Chevy stays on our tail.

"Lose him, lose him," Joe is yelling.

Another burst of speed as Tulio lets the car all out and we blaze a path in the passing lane. In front of us is a station wagon. Tulio wheels around him and then cuts in front of the wagon. But the Chevy is still there, passing the station wagon and gaining on us.

"Jesus, can't you lose him?" Joe cries out.

Nuñez Otonio has turned to look back and is staring directly at me. There is an impassive expression in the small eyes. If there is a confrontation, he's the one I will have to take out.

"I can't lose him; he's all souped up," Tulio yells back.

"C'mon."

"I got it to the floor."

We burst pass the Rockefeller Lookout, where a group of five people are peering through telescopes back at the mists of Manhattan. Heads turn to watch us. I reach for Julie's hand. Tulio weaves in and around two cars and for the moment the Chevy is blocked. But then he is there again, gaining, gaining. Nuñez has raised himself up.

"Let him get closer," he rumbles.

Joe gives him a startled look.

"Do like I say, Tulio."

There is something about Nuñez's manner that is very commanding. There is an imperceptible slowing down of our car. Nuñez is carrying out orders from his don. When the real heat is on, you take over.

But Joe junior is feeling the heat, too. "What the hell are you doing?"

The Chevy is still behind us. "It's just one guy," Nuñez announces. "I could take him."

Joe does a double take and checks our pursuer. Looking back, I can see the lone driver. It doesn't seem like there is anybody else in the car.

Joe flashes his teeth as he makes the decision. "All right, let's take him." He pulls a gun from his inside coat pocket.

Nuñez has his piece out. "Tulio, get into the right lane. There's another spot coming in maybe a mile. Pull in there and make a sharp U. I want to be waiting to meet this guy when he pulls in."

We speed along in the right lane while the Chevy races along even with us in the left. Joe nudges me with the gun. "Don't get any ideas, Davey, or you, either, lady. When we stop, just get down low. I'll be right here with you."

Julie's hand releases mine and I slide it into the pocket of the raincoat. My fingers tighten around the trigger of the small gun.

"Ease off, Tulio," Nuñez commands. "It's just up ahead."

Tulio abruptly eases off on the pedal and we are gliding now. Up ahead, maybe forty yards, is the Alpine Lookout. I palm the gun now, all the while staring at the clock in the car, which reads 5:57.

There is a clanging thump and Tulio yells out in surprise. The Chevy is ramming us, its looming fins making it look like an angry shark. A terrific whack sends us sprawling over the divider and onto the grass.

Julie screams and falls toward me as we bounce along, Tulio trying to gentle the brakes. Joe is yelling something unintelligible while Nuñez orders Tulio, "Bring it around, bring it around."

But Tulio still doesn't have command of the car, and the Chevy is leaning on us. Another knock sends us off the grass and into the parking area of the lookout. Somehow, the Chevy has disengaged and is up ahead of us, pulling to a stop. We spin; there is the screeching sound of our brakes, tires screaming, as Tulio manages to swerve and stop the car. We are on a diagonal, facing the Chevy, and I can see the driver getting out. He is not a young man and has a thinning fringe of reddish hair.

Nuñez is bellowing at Tulio, "Get out, get out. Take him from both sides."

Joe slams the gun into my chest. "Get out."

Julie is frozen. I reach over and thrust open the door. We stumble out. Joe orders us, "Get down, get down." I slip the gun into my jacket pocket as we drop to our knees.

The lookout is empty. The deadly stalk begins. They have come on both sides of our mysterious rescuer, who waits implacably for them. He is wearing a suit, his shirt open at the neck, and holds the gun directly out in front of him. He doesn't look dangerous, but at the same time he seems poised. His stillness conveys both confidence and courage. This is a cool professional.

Nuñez is yelling something to Tulio and now they converge from opposite directions. The idea is to get close and pin our pursuer in a cross fire. But this is not a hit aimed at a helpless victim. This is walking straight toward a gun aimed by another professional. For a moment, the three men are like figures in a Dodge City mural. The menacing Nuñez and the short, swarthy Tulio closing on the lone gunman. Abruptly, he turns and walks toward Tulio, who freezes and then, giving way to his nerves, fires two shots. This forces Nuñez to open up from long range. The man fires back at Nuñez and then runs directly at Tulio, as if Tulio had been spotlighted and immobilized. Tulio shoots wildly. In an awful instant, his attacker is just steps away from him and fires point-blank. Tulio takes two bullets in the chest and falls over, screaming in protest over his death.

Instead of turning to face Nuñez, the gunman sprints to the Chrysler and jumps in. Moments later, the car roars to life. It is a brilliantly planned improvisation—knowing he would isolate one man, kill him, and that the keys would be left in the ignition of the car he forced off the road. He heads the car straight at Nuñez, who lacks not courage but imagination. Nuñez in the middle of the lookout, fires directly at the car bearing down at him. There is the sound of splintering glass as Nuñez's bullet pierces the windshield and then the car plows right into him. For a moment, it is as if two immovable objects had hit each other, then Nuñez flies backward and the car rolls to a stop. Nuñez is on the ground, moving but badly hurt. The stranger advances toward him, holding the gun, and puts two bullets into Nuñez's head. I feel the jab of Joe's gun in my back. "Move. Both of you." He prods Julie with the gun and we run along the edge of the lookout.

We are approaching a green fence. Through the trees, I can see the Hudson River and the lights of the city. I try to look back, but Joe pushes me with his gun. I can't make out if the gunman has given chase.

The fence runs along the edge of a thicket dense with trees and underbrush that slopes down to the river. The trail we are on runs parallel with it. From the corner of my eye, I see the darting figure of the stranger. He is running at an angle on a grassy incline just above us. Joe sees him also and gets off two rounds, which makes the mystery man duck for cover. For a moment, Joe debates checking the damage, but now there is a cry from the man. "Let them go."

Joe's eyes dart wildly back and forth. He puts the gun to my neck and pulls me to him.

"Let her loose, Joe. I'll go with you. You can't escape with us both. There's no percentage."

Joe considers it and nods. "Okay, get over the fence and then lie on the ground. If you try to escape, I'll clip her. Go ahead, Davey."

Julie reaches out her hand. "Don't, Davey."

"It's the only way, Julie."

It is an iron-barred fence and there is wire looped in between the bars, which enables me to get a hold with my hands and hoist myself over. "Get on the ground, Davey," Joe commands. I sink down, feeling the cool, moist earth.

Joe calls out to his pursuer. "All right, I'm letting the girl go. If you open up, I'll kill Davey. We got a deal?"

There is a long silence, and it almost seems as if I can see Joe shiver. Lying there in the darkness, the smell of the ground pungent in my nostrils, I remember a long-ago winter night, playing in the snow with Joe. The Irish kids came then and surrounded us. That was the first time I saw Joe junior shiver.

"Do we have a deal?"

Again the silence and then a shout from the ground above us. "No deals. Just let them go."

Joe has made his decision. "Start walking, Julie baby. Right toward the big hero. Go ahead."

I call to Julie. "Do what he says. It's okay."

She looks toward where I am lying and then turns and begins walking. Joe calls out, "All right, I'm giving you the broad first. Then we'll talk about Davey. I want a deal. I get my car so I can split and you get Davey."

Julie is walking toward the grassy incline that leads up into some trees, where the gunman is hiding. "This way," he calls to her. In that instant, Joe opens fire and Julie screams. She runs desperately for the trees while Joe turns and scales the fence, jumping and landing beside me.

"All right, Davey, that was just a little diversion. Move."

I raise up and feel the gun pressed into my back. We are walking downhill through trees and thicket. The ground is covered by a heavy coating of leaves. It is slow going because the drop-off is steep and the footing treacherous.

"Where we going, Joe?"

"I'll tell you when."

I grab a tree to brace myself as the thicket intensifies around us. Joe stops behind me. "Hold it."

He is casting around for something. The breathing spell allows me to figure the next move. Down below is the river. The only reason to go down there is to set yourself up to wait for your enemy. Joe has to be thinking about where to position himself. He knows the mystery guest will be coming down after him. Joe could have negotiated an exchange. Our freedom and he walks. But that would mean returning to his father in disgrace. He has made his choice. I feel the press of his gun in the small of my back.

"All right, Davey, move."

I go forward, fighting the urge to pull the gun from my pocket. What would you do with it? You've never used one. But Joe has. Somewhere along the way, he made the choice to go into the Life, and his father had him blooded. Joe was sent somewhere like Kansas City or Miami, where the Outfit is well set up, so he could make his bones. Sure he's scared now, but there's something different in his eyes—something I should have recognized before. I have been viewing him through the prism of childhood. He is more dangerous than I have given him credit for.

"That way, Davey, to your left."

We veer on a long diagonal down a steep patch of ground, the tree branches scraping my face. The smell of the water is like an exotic aphrodisiac, conjuring up memories of other times. Hidden, artful stories that my mind has retained without my permission. Roasting mickies with a gang of kids to end a winter afternoon of adventure. Piercing the baking potatoes with a long stick and watching them turn black. Our faces chafed from the cold, framed in the orange hues of the leaping fire, nothing ever tasting as good as those potatoes.

We reach the water's edge and Joe shoves me into a V-shaped shelter formed by a network of trees. He flattens himself against the tree, listening for the sound of pursuit. The light is disappearing quickly. It is after six, and the sky is already shrouded by the oncoming night.

Joe has the advantage here. Anyone coming after us will announce his presence.

"Get down, Davey."

I drop to one knee and feel the gun barrel in the back of my head.

"This is how it feels just before you get it, Davey. When the trigger gets pulled, the bullet takes the top of your head off."

Breathing becomes very difficult. I am acutely aware of the darkness and the sound of the Hudson River lapping at our feet.

The pressure of the gun on my head suddenly evaporates. I hear the pistol shot and my heart leaps and congeals in the same instant. Joe has fired the shot into the air. A single shot meant to sound like an execution. Meant to draw my rescuer down here.

Joe speaks in a very soft voice. "Don't say a word, Davey. If I get out of here, so do you."

And if you don't, Joe, what happens to me? Will you plug me? How did it come down to this? Those days at the beach, the touch-football games, Anna bringing us hot cocoa while Vince and Joe talked in the house. I can reach out and touch those times. Remember the night the Irish kids caught us alone and they formed a vigilante posse and rushed us? You took a hard snowball right in the eye and went down crying. You thought they would let you go, but they wouldn't. I had to fight for our honor. Remember how Joe and Vince came, and when they heard the terms, they agreed, and I fought the Irish kid, Grogan, and beat him?

As if we are somehow linked by this umbilical cord of memory, we stare at each other. There is a crackling sound, like someone stepping on a twig, and Joe whirls. It is from the right, above us. The gunman is coming from the other side. I peer into the darkness. For a moment, I see him and then he takes cover.

Joe dips down and scoops something up. His arm extends in the darkness and an object flies from it. The rock hits the ground and the figure in the darkness reappears. Joe junior has made the right call. The figure of poise and assurance up above becomes just an old man stumbling in the darkness.

Joe whispers in my ear. "Lay down flat, Davey, and not a peep."

The gun in my head drives my face into the earth. Joe junior has become an experienced practitioner of fear. I hug the wet ground as Joe moves away. I raise myself up and catch sight of him down at the water's edge. The gun is in his right hand, while in his left are several large rocks. He loops around to his right and, positioning himself, throws one, then launches another. They hit like precision bombs. They are meant to cause confusion, disarray, and give Joe cover. He disappears into the thicket. I am on my knees, staring into the wooded landscape. There is the fleeting image of a man moving. Then a startled cry as he trips and tumbles through the brush, landing just a few yards from me. He lies there dazed, this deadly killer, better at the hit than at hide-and-seek.

Joe is right there above him. "Don't fucking move." I hear the quiver in his voice. He is close to going off. As he points the gun, my hand moves to the revolver in my pocket. Then it is in my hand, pointed at Joe. I hear my voice, but I don't recognize it. "I have a gun, Joe. Don't make me use it."

For a second, he doesn't move, and then he looks in my direction. "Where the fuck did you get that?" He is trying to figure the angle. The gun is a fact of life. The question is whether I will use it.

"The broad gave it to you, didn't she? That's the only way it could have happened."

"Just get out of here, Joe."

"C'mon, Davey, you're not going to use it."

I don't want to. Talk, you could always distract Joe that way. I call to the man on the ground. "Who sent you?"

He has a stoic face and a bald spot. He blinks up at me. "Your father sent me."

Joe's voice is harsh with disbelief. "Vince sent an old piece of shit like you?"

The old guy massages his leg and then looks directly at Joe. "Tell the don that Nails Gordon sent me."

Joe's face creases into a harsh look of contempt. "I don't believe it. Some old Hebe just popped Nuñez."

There is no fear in the old shooter. "That's the way we did it in Prohibition when we rode shotgun. Lots of them tried to hijack us. You walk toward the shooter, sonny, and he shits his pants. Like you're doing now."

Joe is stunned.

This ghost from my past looks up at me. "Take him, Davey."

He's talking so he can divert Joe and go for his gun. But Joe isn't buying. He kicks the piece away and aims the gun. "Who's got the shits now?"

"Fuck you, sonny boy. Kill him, Davey."

His words lie there in the stillness around us. He is reminding me of what I have to do if Joe decides he can't go home to his father empty-handed and tell him that two of his best men were clipped by an old Jewish mobster from the Nails Gordon gang.

Joe is weighing what I will do. "You ever seen a hit, Davey? Could you pop a guy under a hot towel with a gun in your hand?"

My hand closes around the gun. "You killed Tommy."

Joe smiles. "I did it the old Sicilian way, right to his face. Twelve slugs. One of them tore his eye out. Guns are for keeps, Davey. It's not the fights on Friday night."

The hot feeling is there in my throat and my voice is tight with rage. "Get the fuck out of here, Joe. Now."

We stand there, trying to read each other. Did I see him quiver, or am I remembering that time in the snow?

Uncannily, Joe speaks the words. "Remember the time when those micks trapped us? Jesus, you fought like a bastard, Davey."

He looks at me and I know why he won't try it head-on. He still thinks of me as a hot blood, like I was on that snowy day. Joe gives me a little wave with his free hand. He turns, takes a step, then pivots and comes back. The fury within me breaks free into a savage cry and my finger is squeezing nonstop on the trigger. The gun jolts in my hand and Joe takes the three rounds in his chest. He crumples over on his back, and all I can think is how slow he's always been. You have no reflexes, Joe. You're not a big-time hit man; you're a loser.

He lies there, trying to figure it out, eyes blinking, mouth trying to form words. Instead, they become a cough, and then he is reaching for my hand. For a second, I try to pull away. His lips tremble and I feel the pressure of his dying hand. "I could never beat you, Davey . . . just this once . . . this once."

My fury has flown away now, replaced by a great emptiness and sorrow. Nothing I have ever known has felt like this. Knocking out the Kid was a reflex, a headline and a memory. This is forever.

Joe junior struggles to comprehend the meaning of his life and the imminence of death. "Davey," he says, and then, as it is for all of us, the distance between life and death merges and he closes his eyes to rest.

I am left holding his hand, eyes blinking back moisture. From behind me comes the voice of the old Jewish gunman. "I wasn't sure you could do it till you told him to get the fuck out of here. You sounded like Nails. That's when I knew you would kill him. When he got into your gut. That's what Nails was like. When you reached into his insides, where he lived, there was no fear of anything happening to him. 'Someday it'll get me killed.' That's what he always used to tell me."

# 12

**THE OLD HIT MAN** picks up his gun and I feel his hand on my shoulder. "We got to go. The cops will be here very soon."

I look into his lined face. The eyes are alert and ageless. They have seen more than I can imagine.

"Where's Julie?"

"Waiting for us with the car at the next lookout. I said I'd bring you back soon. C'mon, let's get up on the trail. We can talk as we go."

The journey up the incline is slow, and after a few slips, he hooks his hand through my belt. "It's my knees, Davey. They're shot."

"Who are you?"

It is a long beat before he replies. "Sam Miller. When I had a little more on top, it was Red Miller."

The name is like a chime sounding. Two men survived the massacre in the Rodman Arms Hotel. One of them was this man. Samuel "Red" Miller.

It is slow going, but we finally reach the fence. I go over first, then help Red over. He lands heavily and falls to his knees. "Jesus, I'm an old cocker."

"You didn't look so old a little while ago."

"That's something you never forget."

We move to our right along a trail that runs parallel with the parkway, although soon we are under the safety of tall trees. We walk side by side, while to our left the cars streaming along the parkway make abrupt whizzing sounds. The beams from their lights appear and disappear at regular intervals.

Red whistles softly. "The cars they got now. What we could have done back in the old days. We used to outrun the law with souped-up engines, but we were always having trouble with each other. Once we took a convoy of booze from Joe Kennedy. It was a special favor to Nig Rosen."

I recall the chase and Red's souped-up Chevy driving the Chrysler off the road. "Who sent you, Red?"

"You know it's Shabbas, don't you? You know what that is? It's the Sabbath. It starts at sundown on Friday and goes till sundown on Saturday. We light candles and read from the Torah. I'm not supposed to touch money. I broke the Sabbath for a dago." He laughs softly. "That's not to say I haven't broken it before. This is not a business where you can afford to be off on Friday and Saturday nights. Max tried to respect the Sabbath. I always called your father Max. If you knew him good, that's what you called him. When we spoke of him to others in our profession, then it was Nails. Sometimes he would call me and say, 'Red, I got you a special dispensation.' That meant it was a hit. I hated like hell to kill a guy on a Friday night. Saturday night wasn't bad, because Shabbas was over, but Fridays was tough."

It hits me now. I killed Joe junior. Anna won't know how it happened, but Joe Dante will want to know. If he finds out, he'll come after me. There's no squaring it with Joe, but Anna—I owe her something. How do I tell her?

Red stops me. He knows what I'm feeling. "He didn't give you any choice. He could have walked. Yeah, you knew him from way back, but he went after you." We trudge in silence, the beams from the car lights reflecting in our eyes. "That's the terrible thing about this business. When you have to do someone you've known a long time."

"What were you doing here tonight, Red? Who sent you?"

Red prods me with his rough, grainy voice. "Why would they want you when they have Vince?"

"Vince sent you to keep an eye out for me. That's it, isn't it? Vince faked his abduction. Before Dino could move, Vince made his own."

A car speeds by and the light thrown off by it frames his eyes.

There is the glint of approval there. I am Nails Gordon's son and I have Red's loyalty.

We resume our walk and Red picks up the pace. "I been on the run for a long time, Davey. After they wiped us out, you'd think they'd a been satisfied. We weren't a threat no more. Joe Axler and me were the only ones to escape. But the word went out to get us. The Syndicate sent hit men to find us. They trapped Joe in a gin mill in Minnesota four years later. The fuckin' dagos would never let it rest. I moved from city to city. I was in Toledo, Akron, Cleveland, Miami for a while, Tucson. I got rid of a few guys they sent after me, and then it got easier. A new generation came in, and it wasn't such a cushy job to go after Red Miller. I'm not that old, Davey. I'm fifty-eight, and nothing shakes. It was just tough making a living for a long while, but then one day I got a message to go to the dog track in Miami, and Vince was there. Now, going wasn't easy after that night in the Rodman Arms, but I took the chance because I didn't know how much longer I could hold out. We came to an agreement and Vince said he would square it for me, and he did. He also told me that one day he would need me. When that time came, he would send for me."

Johnny told me that one of the men who kidnapped Vince looked like a Jew. So all these years, Red Miller was Vince's wild card.

"Where is Vince?"

"Nearby, but he's not ready to talk yet. He said he would send for you very soon."

"What about Johnny?"

Red has stopped to light a cigar. He is very calm and methodical about it. We are here on this soft October night while behind us are three dead men. Two killed by him and the other by me. Red blows out the light. "You can tell Johnny about me but not about Vince."

From behind us comes the wailing sound of the police siren. Red claps me on the shoulder. "C'mon, let's move."

We walk briskly, the red ember of his cigar serving as our guiding light.

"It won't take Johnny long to figure out Vince is alive."

"Sure he'll figure it, just don't you suggest it. That's what Vince wants."

What game is Vince playing and why is he playing it alone? And what does it have to do with this refugee from the Nails Gordon mob? Johnny gave me a quick walk through the past the other night, but there's a lot more to it than I know. Red was a survivor of the massacre in the Rodman Arms. Why would he and Vince make a pact?

More sirens behind us. I look back and Red chuckles. "They'll never dream we're this close. They'll stand over the bodies and the lab boys will come down and there'll be lots of flashing lights and they'll rope off the Alpine Lookout point."

And down below is the body of a kid I grew up with who never should have been in the rackets. I'm the one who killed him, and it hurts, it really hurts. I never met Nails Gordon. He's just a name to me. I may be his son, but Vince Rossi raised me and I'm a lot more dago than I am Jew. I turn to Red. "Did you know about me?"

Red stares impassively into the night. "I didn't know about you until Vince told me. Max never said anything."

"Who was my . . . who was she?"

Red puffs away a cloud of smoke. "There were a lot of girls around him, but that was a long time ago."

"Ever hear of Dolly Irving?"

That stops him.

"Sure I heard of her. She was a big star on Broadway. As big as any of them. Once you saw her, you never forgot her."

"Did she know Nails?"

He reflects on it. Long enough to make me realize he is not going to tell me the truth. "If you were from the ghetto, you knew everybody else. She grew up on Hester Street. Most of the guys knew her."

"Did you?"

"I didn't grow up in New York, but I met her a few times."

"And Nails?"

"He knew everybody."

"Were they . . ."

"That was a long time ago. I can't say."

You're lying, Red.

"What about Waxy Green? Did you know him?"

"Sure I knew the Wax Man." Red bites down on his cigar. "That was all a long time ago, Davey, and I've been away. Sometime we'll talk about it."

The emotion dissolves and I am alone with the mystery of the past and the bitter knowledge that I killed Joe junior. We walk on in silence until the path flares out and we reach the parking area of yet another lookout. There are several cars pulled in next to a small inn advertising beer. I see someone moving toward us. Julie. She runs toward me but stops short of embracing me. I see the expression in her eyes and the hurt inside me dissolves. I am alive with the night, intoxicated by the mist and the magic of possibility.

# 13

**RED DRIFTS OVER** to the car so we can be alone. I reach over and take her hand. "You're cold."

"Not anymore. When I was driving away, I heard a shot from down where you were. . . ."

"That was Joe trying to be cute."

"Is he . . ."

I nod my head.

"What happened?"

"I'll tell you later. That was a gutsy thing you did."

"I didn't think; I just reacted. Both times I've been with you, someone has taken you off for a ride. I couldn't let it happen again."

Red moves in and interrupts us. "We could all use some black coffee, and then we get out of here." He hands Julie a bill. "It would be better if you bought it. The cops will wind up here, asking about anybody who might have pulled in. Nobody will be looking for a girl. I take sugar in mine. Davey?"

"Fine."

He watches Julie walk off. "Lots of class. Nice suit. How did she slip you the gun?"

"In my raincoat."

"Let me see the piece."

I hand it to him. Red hefts the gun and then checks it over. He slips the magazine out and looks at it, then jams it back in. "Thirty-two, semiautomatic. Easy to handle. What's she do?"

"She's a lawyer."

An awry grin shows on Red's face. "I guess the law can be dangerous. It's a lucky thing for you she was carrying. Tell her I did the hit."

"Why?"

"Because it's neat and she doesn't need to know any more than she does. If the girl shows up as a witness, the trail will lead back to you. I know she saved you, but they'll do ballistics tests and they'll know two different guns were used. As long as no one talks, it'll stay a mystery." Red shoves a piece of paper in my hand. "That's the number of a place you can leave a message for me if something comes up. Just say Nails recommended you. They'll reach me."

Julie is back. Red turns to her. "I was just saying to Davey that you did a brave thing, slipping him the gun."

"Who are you?"

Red takes a container of coffee. "Just an old friend who was keeping an eye on Davey. What's your name?"

"Julie Alpert."

"I thought you might be from the tribe. I'm Red. I was just saying to Davey that this should all be left a mystery. Can we arrange that?"

Julie hands me my coffee. "I don't know. Sweeping everything under the rug will encourage these people to try again."

The smoke pours from Red's coffee container and drifts over his head. "If they find me, who's going to keep an eye on Davey?" Their eyes meet and stay glued there until Red breaks it. "I come from the Lower East Side. Down there, we all protect each other. A Jew is responsible for a Jew. Think it over. Let's get out of here."

The coffee is hot and strong and the sugar gives me a lift. Red tools the Chevy to the next exit and brings us back on the Palisades. As we drive south, he points to the flashing lights on the other side of the parkway. "That's the scene of the crime."

The Alpine Lookout is full of squad cars and milling police. It has been cordoned off and red lights placed in the right lane, next to it. A policeman directs the traffic, which is backed up into the left lane. I take peek at Julie. She is mulling over Red's words: "A Jew is responsible for a Jew." Minutes later, we are back on the George Washington Bridge. The rest of the ride is made in silence.

# 14

JULIE'S BUILDING is a redbrick postwar structure on East Seventy-eighth Street, between Second and Third avenues. The lobby is marble, gold, and chrome. A doorman is posted under the new green awning. As we exit the car, there is an uncertain moment on the curb. All we have gone through has changed the feeling we shared at Bonsignore's.

"You never reached Johnny, did you?"

Julie shakes her head. "I couldn't. There was a goon by the telephone, so I went out in the street and waited till they brought you out."

"Once I call him, he'll want me back at the house."

"Do you have to call him?"

"I should."

"Right away? You look like you could use a drink."

It is all hanging there. Everything that happened before . . . Nails . . . Vince . . . Joe junior.

"I need to talk."

She looks at me with those piercing eyes. "Yes, Davey, we should talk."

I walk over to Red, who is seated at the wheel of his car. "I'll take over from here."

The stub of the cigar is in his mouth. "I'll be watching you. That's what Vince wanted me to do, and it paid off. As long as Vince is underground, they'll be interested in you. Don't travel alone, and tell your brother to get some new talent. Those old dagos he sent with you are rotting away in some morgue. Tell him to borrow some fresh Jewish talent from Abe Mortkoff over in Williamsburg. Don't look so surprised; we were always saving the dagos from each other. The difference between a Hebe and a dago is that they kill each other and we kill *for* each other." He turns the car on. "Remember, I killed the dago down by the river." Now he smiles. "Spill your milk, not your guts." He gives me a wave and then the Chevy speeds up to the corner and hooks a right downtown on Second Avenue.

We ride up the elevator in silence. I keep staring at her hair, at the delicate hands holding the keys. I watch those hands as she inserts the key into the lock and turns it. A perfect fit. The door opens and we go inside. The apartment is cool and dark. We are in the foyer. Somehow, I don't want to go any farther. I want to stay in the still darkness. The nakedness of my desire is unnerving. Julie reaches for the light and I say, "Don't."

She switches on the closet light and hangs up my coat. She has removed the gun from it. The gun I used on Joe junior. I grip those charged fingers and coil them around the gun. Julie pushes me into her and we meld into a long kiss. My hands are all over her. She is saying something I can't understand as my hand rides up her skirt. Then somehow she is leading me through the apartment, her hand wrapped around my hand, which still holds the gun. We are in her bedroom and everything is a dizzying blur as clothes fly from us and I approach her, still holding the gun. She takes my hand and presses it to her lips. Her breasts are rich and full, her body incredibly lush. She pulls the gun from me and lies back on the bed. I am above her, my hands running in concentric patterns around her body till I find the moist crevice. I hear a gasp that becomes my name and I follow the path I have traced into Julie. She raises her legs and I surge inside her. Everything is all silky and wet. Each successive thrust evokes tingling music. That is for last night, for Kid Bassett, for me all cut and bleeding, for Joe Dante and his assassin's eyes, for Dino and his malevolent tongue, for Vince, for Nails, for Joe junior. From Davey to Julie. For me to you. And as all manner of words and expression leap from my feverish brain and fevered lips, Julie locks me in, calms me, and we move in a languid rhythm, bits and pieces flying out of me. Sweaty and possessed, I lunge into that lush valley again, hearing her say my name as I keep spilling into her, feeling the end of pain and hurt. Hearing Julie's throbbing cry as she finishes, I lie across her chest, sweet and spent. An exhausted pilgrim who has come to rest in paradise.

I fall gratefully asleep, floating on something velvety and soft. The sensation of being in a strange place where I have known intimacy brings me awake, and then seeing Julie, her eyes closed, reassures me and I give myself back to sleep. But this time, the place I have come to is ugly and dark and I am thrust into a pit where they want me to fight. A hideous old hag throws coins at me and then wraps herself around me, seeking to kiss me. She is a parody of lascivious desire, her teeth nothing but black stumps. This laughing old strumpet tears off her veil and becomes Dino pointing to Anna Dante, her face an anguished mask as she bends over Joe junior. He pushes me toward her, laughing. I lurch forward, landing on dead Joe, and cry out. I come awake, my hand resting on something cold and hard. The gun I killed Joe with.

I look at Julie. "I have to go."

"Not yet," she says. She lies against my chest, stroking the back of my hair. "Why did he call you a Jew?"

There is no escape for me. "I was adopted. My real father was a Jewish mobster named Nails Gordon."

"Is that why Red was there?"

"Something like that."

"Have you always known that?"

I search for the right words. "I knew I was adopted, but I didn't know about Nails Gordon until last night."

"Those men told you. That's it, isn't it?"

I lie back, remembering Red telling me not to spill my guts. But I need to spill. I don't want to be alone with a past I don't know enough about.

Julie reaches for something in a little chest on the night stand. Abruptly, a cigarette lighter flares up and I see her full breasts as she sits up. The smell of the fire eating away at the tobacco blends with the scent of her perfume and the pungent aroma of our lovemaking.

My hand moves across the bed and comes to rest on the gun. We both are riveted by it.

"What are you going to do, Julie?"

"Do?"

"You witnessed a big-time hit. If you go to the police, they'll want to question me also."

"You didn't do anything."

"Why do you carry a gun, Julie?"

"For protection. Something happened once."

I coil my hand around the gun. I feel its power; my hand is on the trigger and then I am shaking."

"Davey, what is it?"

"Take it out of my hand."

She reaches for it and I feel her soft hand. "What happened, Davey?"

"You can't go to the police, Julie; then they'll all know."

Her hand covers mine. "Tell me what happened."

I don't know where to begin, but then I see the river and Joe and the words come tumbling out. I can't help it, Red. It feels good to spill to Julie.

She squeezes my hand. "Oh Davey."

"I've known him since we were little kids. It's funny, but I was always quicker than Joe. I could always beat him. I think that's why he tried it. Just once he wanted to feel like he'd won."

"How terrible . . ." She sees my stricken face and her expression changes. "I mean for you, Davey. How terrible that it should end this way."

"Yeah, Ma, but you should see the other guy. You have something to drink?"

"Wine, or something harder?"

"I don't care."

She glides into her closet and comes out in a robe. Moments later, there is soft music and a tray with wine. It goes down easy and Julie refills my glass. She is watching me closely.

"What are you thinking?"

"What they're doing to you is so awful. You're just a pawn they're using in this game of power they're playing. And where is your father? Why would they want to kidnap you also ... unless ..." Julie looks at me. "Was he kidnapped?"

I take refuge in the role of the bewildered pug. This is not something I want to spill about. "That was the message we got."

Julie guides her hand across my neck. "How does a Jew wind up as Davey Rossi?"

"Vince adopted me, but he never told me the rest of it." I look up at her. "He was one of them ... who killed my father."

Julie's hand goes to her mouth to cover the surprised exclamation, as if she might catch the words with her hand. She sets the drink down and her arms go around me. We lie that way in the dark, huddled next to each other.

"You have to keep tonight in a box, Julie, until I can figure it all out. If the police get me for doing Joe, then Vince will have more problems."

"What about you? Why do you have to pay the price for all of them?"

"I need time. If I get hauled in by the police, they'll box me in. They'll use me, too."

We fall away from each other, separated by what each of us is bound by. Julie pours more wine. "I want to call my father and discuss it."

"You can't. It either belongs between us or it belongs to everybody." I hold up the gun. "This is evidence. If you can't sit on it, don't call your father; call the police. It's the same thing." I get up.

"What are you doing?"

"I have to call Johnny. He'll be worried. What time is it?"

She turns toward the clock radio. "Ten-fifteen."

"I need to do this in private."

"In the living room, on the table next to the couch."

I fumble my way in the dark till I find it. There is a small desk light and I flick it on. I listen to the dial tone, knowing this is not a call I want to make. Dago Pete comes on, his voice a little breathless.

"It's Davey. Let me speak to Johnny."

I picture Johnny as I tell him briefly what happened. In shirtsleeves, silk tie knotted smoothly against his collar, smoking a cigarette. "I'll tell you the rest when I see you. Yeah, she saw it all. She'll play. I'm at her apartment."

Julie's voice comes to me. "Two twelve East Seventy-eighth Street."

"Two twelve East Seventy-eighth, between Second and Third." I click off.

Julie glides toward me. "When will they be here?"

"Soon. I have to get dressed."

Her finger traces a line down my body. "I like it the way you are. Right down there."

"There's no time."

Her hand is still resting there. "How do you know that I'll play?"

I look up at Julie. "I don't. It was just easier to say it. Will you?"

Her hand tightens around me. "I'll sleep on it."

"They'll be here soon."

"There's time. There's always time for this."

"Here?"

"It's a soft rug." She lets the robe fall away from her and she is all there for me. My hand moves up her leg until I find just the right spot. She sinks down on the rug and pulls me down with her. Her arms go around me. "Will I play? Will I?"

I come to life and then leap forward inside her. She arches her back and I am where I want to be. She's right. There's always time for this.

We finish together and I cry out, then fall back, sweaty, gasping. I lie there wet and warm, Julie's arms around me, drifting to sleep on gentle, lapping waves. Something brings me back and I identify the third ring as the intercom. It is like the ten-second warning before the next round, and for a moment the roar of the crowd is in my ears. Julie slips on her robe and answers it. She calls to me. "They're here."

"Tell them I'll be right down."

I throw water on my face and dress quickly. I come out of the bathroom and Julie is holding the gun. "I'll get rid of it."

"Okay. I'll call you in the morning. Where will you be?"

"In my office."

The buzzer rings again. This time, it's the door. "I have to go."

There should be some better way to say good-bye, but it is the mob

out in the hall. Its hand reaching out to grab me by the throat and
cut off words of intimacy. Julie hands me the raincoat and I toss it
over my shoulder as I open the door. Framed in the light are two
hulking men I have never seen before. Johnny has reached out for
new talent. Once I saw a picture of Primo Carnera in his boxing prime.
A primordial creature. These are his lineal descendants. I step outside.
The elevator is waiting. We ride down in silence. I realize now that
it was always coming to this. The Life is a bitch whore of a lascivious
old woman with rotted teeth who let me go on all these years thinking
I was a visitor. The door opens and we step into the lobby, where
Dago Pete and another hood I don't recognize await us. Out in front
are several cars, with still more men standing next to them. I step into
the street and walk toward the car. The men form a circle around me;
then the line magically breaks and Johnny is there.

"You okay?"

"I'm hungry."

He lights a cigarette. "I could use something, too. We'll get a bite
and talk." We slide into a blue sedan. "Al, you know Manuchi's?"

"Sure."

He turns on the motor as Johnny slides the window down and calls
to Dago Pete. "Manuchi's. One car in front and one car in back. *Capisce?*"

Dago Pete nods and calls out to the others. Everybody jumps into
cars and we pull out. Johnny is watching me closely. A little bit of a
smile is there. "Son of a bitch, you're here. You made it, Davey." He
slaps me on the shoulder. "Was she good?" I don't answer, and the
smile is a big one now. "I know you. She must be good." He waits
and then sinks the hook. "The question is, Were you good enough?
Good enough to keep her quiet?"

"She'll play, Johnny. That answer your question?"

He grins. "Yeah. That means we got the edge."

# 15

I REMEMBER ANOTHER TIME eating veal shanks with Johnny at Man-uchi's. I had just turned twenty and I was fighting Sandy Simpson in the semifinals of the Golden Gloves at the Garden. There had been a weigh-in for the fighters at the New York Athletic Commission and Simpson played cock of the walk. Everybody was touting him, even though he was only seventeen. He was tall and slender and he hit very hard. But he was more of a boxer then. He had that way of smiling like he knew he had you. Part of it was for show, but there was an arrogance in the smile you couldn't ignore. I remember Johnny waving the veal shank, saying, "Did you see that boogie! He's all whipped cream, isn't he? But he's good . . . damned good."

I smiled but said nothing. I was going to surprise my brother and give him a big victory. I remember how close I felt to Johnny then. I remember catching the veal shank Johnny was waving and saying, "Cream melts when you turn on the heat, Johnny." He broke into a big smile and tossed a wad of money on the table. "This goes on your back."

I beat Simpson two nights later. I took the fight to him and that confused him. Afterward, Johnny hugged me and slipped a roll of money into my pocket. He chuckled and said, "For Christmas."

God, I wish I could have that time back. All those days when we ate in Manuchi's and the future belonged to me. I knew everything I did then was right. But now I have a secret to keep from Johnny.

"They knew you were there and they had plenty of time to figure out their next move. They trailed Fats back to the garage and slipped a shiv inside him, left him slumped over the wheel. Then they came back and got Harp. Chances are, they just pulled up in a car and surrounded him. They did him in the car and then waited while some-one drove Fats's car out into the street. They loaded Harp in there and left them to be found. It was a message."

Ray, the owner, comes over. He is a short, fat man with thinning jet black hair and mustache. He has changed little over the years. He wears the same clothes—dark pants and a white shirt buttoned to the top. "Johnny, I keep the place open just for you. Stay as long as you wish. The food is good?"

Ray is plainly nervous; his tongue keeps flickering in and out of his mouth. In this time of the hit, he doesn't need the "boys" around.

"It's terrific, Ray. In fact, bring me another bowl of stracciatella. Best I ever tasted."

"Right away, Johnny. I do it myself. You like, huh?"

As he starts to move, Johnny puts some money in his hand. "That's for you, Ray, and for the staff."

Ray bows obsequiously as he backs off. Johnny nods and waves him away. "Jesus, I hate this," he says. "Fuckin' war. It's just bad for business. Scares the shit out of good people." Johnny looks over at the goon squad sitting a few tables away. There are more hoods outside. Manuchi's is an old place on the Lower East Side. There is nothing fancy about it. The walls are a varnished old yellow and the wooden tables are scarred and chipped. It is not a fancy trattoria, but the food is sensational. The veal shank and the linguine smothered in putta-nesca sauce are wonderful. Johnny lets me eat without pressing me for details. Now as a second bowl of steaming stracciatella arrives, he lights a cigarette and dumps some cheese on it. Johnny has eaten sparingly, skipping the pasta and nibbling on some salad, leaving the veal shank half-finished. But Johnny has always loved soup.

"I think it was Alfredo who called it in."

Johnny pushes the bowl away. "Could be. They spread the word that if you came in alone, they wanted to know about it." Johnny takes the palm of his hand and slaps it into his forehead. "And I let you go."

"Julie saved me. She pushed her way in the car and slipped a piece into my raincoat. Joe lost his cool. He was afraid of a scene and witnesses. For Joe, it was always about not screwing up in front of papa."

Johnny nods. "What did Joe say?"

"He called me a Jew after I needled him."

"Go ahead."

"A blue Chevy came up behind us and we tried to outrun him on the Palisades. The plan was to spin inside one of the lookouts, wait, and nail the driver, but he rammed us, took out Tulio. Then he jumped in our car and ran over Nuñez. Joe got me over the fence and we were in the woods."

"What about Julie?"

"He let her go. It was me Papa Joe wanted."

"Lucky you had the piece."

"The guy came down after us. Joe got the drop on him. I showed the piece and told Joe to get out. He turned like he was going to take off, but then he came around firing. I nailed him with three shots."

Johnny brings the bowl back and spoons out some more soup. "Who was the shooter?"

"Red Miller."

That jolts him. "From the Gordon mob? Christ, I didn't know he was still alive."

Johnny's blue eyes are now shrewd and tight. "Vince sent him. That's the only way it adds up." He watches me closely. "What did he say?"

"Just that he'd be around."

"You didn't ask him?"

"I was shook up, Johnny, and he wasn't telling me anything. We had to get the hell out of there."

"He didn't say anything more?"

"Yeah, he did. He said you should get some Jewish talent from Abe Mortkoff over in Williamsburg."

Johnny's eyes flare. "I don't need an old shooter from a hundred years ago to tell me who to get to ..." He waves the rest off with his hand. "You got Joe with her gun. Let me have it."

I shrug. "Julie's got it."

"Davey, your brain must be mush from that fight."

"Don't worry, Johnny, it's on ice."

"Davey, it's got to be lost. Your prints are all over it. Tomorrow, it gets taken care of." He is quiet now as he mulls it over. "Vince is out there, playing his cards very close. Dino tried to pick you up because he didn't have Vince."

"Dino looks kind of dumb now."

"Not so dumb. Bluffing was the smart play. If we fell for it, he splits the family."

Johnny lights another butt off the old one. I know what he is thinking: I'm holding out on him. Maybe Vince and I have something going and Johnny is on the outs. I have to get him away from this. Give him something so he thinks I am safe.

"Johnny, there is something I haven't told you. I should have, but I didn't feel right."

Johnny waits. He learned that from Tommy. Look interested but never commit yourself.

"I got a note in training camp from somebody who watched me spar. It said he knew who my real father was and it was worth money. We set up a meet when I got back to the city. I went to the guy's house, only he had been hit. It was Waxy Green."

Johnny's eyes have become very hard.

"When you brought it up in the dressing room after the fight, I wasn't ready to talk about it. I'm sorry, I should have trusted you, but I was off. I guess I had a feeling everyone was holding out on me ... and I was right."

The smoke from Johnny's cigarette swirls around us. He has his poker face on now. "What else, Davey?"

"There was some old newspaper clips about the Gordon mob being rubbed out. That's what he was going to sell me before someone put the knock on him. What do you hear about that, Johnny?"

But he is not about to let me off the hook so fast. "What else did you find?"

"There was a record playing from an album by Dolly Irving. Who's that?"

"Anything else?"

"That's it. Who is she?"

"A long time ago, she lit up Broadway."

"Was she with Nails?"

"She had a big torch for him."

There is something behind the facade, some essence of feeling he is trying to keep in place.

"What happened?"

"That was a bright time, you know. There were a lot of torches."

"What happened to her?"

"She's around."

"Around?"

"If people aren't dead, they're around."

"Could you find her for me?"

"Listen, Davey, we got enough to handle right now."

"And I have my own record to set straight. Did you forget that, Johnny?"

"You held out on me, Davey. Are you forgetting that?"

The tension between us is thicker than the smoke circling above us.

"That's pretty good, Johnny. You and Vince held out on me all my life. But what the hell, so I'm a Jew instead of a dago. I don't mind so much. One ghetto or another, it's all the same. But you let me play the chump for Joe Dante and Dino."

He holds up his hand. "Okay, you got a right to be sore. I told Vince a couple of times that he couldn't sit on it forever. But I can't have you trying to square up the past while we're in a war. We have to be on the same track. Deal?"

I take a deep breath. "Okay. What happens now?"

Johnny scrubs out the cigarette. "We lie low and wait."

"Wait?"

"Wait for Vince . . . wait for some word. My guess is that Vince will try to work something with the Council."

"But why is he out there alone?"

Johnny pours more wine for us and pushes my glass toward me.

"Vince has got some ace up his sleeve. One of us will hear from him, Davey."

Johnny is letting me know that he will be watching me.

"Johnny, I want the fight with Simpson."

"He'll cut you up and they'll stop it."

"That's my risk."

"Sleep on it, and then if you still want it, we'll take it. In the morning, I'm sending one of the boys over to pick up the gun from Julie."

"I'll get it."

"Davey . . ."

"I'm not going alone. Send an army with me."

"All right, but it gets done. You have to keep your eye on the ball. Julie's a hot number, but you're a player now. We got suckered once."

"I'll be careful."

"You don't go anywhere without clearing it so we can case it."

"Anywhere?"

"Anywhere. You shack up, the boys are outside."

I don't respond.

"You hear me, Davey?"

"I hear you. I want to know where the funeral will be for Joe."

"What are you going to do, send flowers?"

"Maybe. Can we skip the espresso? I'm tired."

Johnny purses his lips. "I drank enough of Pete's espresso to float a battleship." He takes out the roll and leaves some bills on the table. As we stand up, Johnny claps me on the shoulder. "Not too many guys come back from a ride, you know that, don't you? That's how Lucky Luciano got his name."

He's trying to lighten up, but it's uneasy between us. He's wondering if I have a secret agenda with Vince.

Flanked on both sides by muscle and artillery, we come out onto the street. It has turned cool and there are some raindrops. Was it just a few hours ago that guns blazed and I killed Joe junior? I feel the food in my belly, the first trickling drops of rain, smell the cool night air while somewhere in the city Joe junior lies sightless on a slab.

Prince Street is deserted as we turn onto it. The lights in the houses have been turned off as if in tribute to the ongoing hostilities. Vendetta and murder are things of the darkness. When it is over, the lights will go on again and the people will come out to the street and their allegiance will be to the new feudal lord, whoever he may be.

We pull up in front of the house and Dago Pete gets out first. He is a stocky man with sharp eyes. He looks like a predatory bird. He would lay down his life for Vince, and I find it odd that Vince didn't take Pete with him that night when he staged his kidnapping. And then it comes to me. Vince took Joe Rico, whom he knew would be easily overpowered. No one expected a lot from Joe. Pete wasn't there because he was in on it.

Pete leads the way inside and I follow Johnny into the living room. He fixes himself a drink and gestures to me. I shake my head. Johnny tops the scotch off with water and stands holding it in his hand. The light from the fish tank frames his face. He is a handsome man, my brother. A man of late-night dinners and drinks. A man of the smooth deal, the fix, the seduction. This thing of the mattresses is not for him. Is that why Vince is playing his cards so close to the vest?

"I'm going up, Johnny. I'm really tired."

He watches me. He is thinking about Joe junior. He knows it's on my mind. "Davey, it shouldn't have come down to what it did, but you had no choice. You never tried to set Joe up. You understand what I'm telling you?"

Somehow, I don't. I just want to turn it all off. "Johnny, what did Waxy Green have to do with Dolly Irving?"

"The Wax Man put a lot of ghelt into the shows. I know he backed a couple of musicals she was in."

"Did you know her?"

"Dolly? Sure. I used to see her around with Nails."

"What happened to her?"

"She faded after he died. She was a torch singer. Times change."

"What was Nails like?"

"He had more guts than anyone I ever saw." I sense he wants to say more. Like I want to ask more. He gazes out into the night. I walk to the window and look down the block at the trees. The leaves are falling from them, the wind blowing the frail little things into the night. We go through life forgetting who we were.

I hear the phone ring and someone picks up. Dago Pete looks in. "Phone call, Johnny."

He walks from the room. Rain begins to fall. I can see Dago Pete's reflection in the windowpane.

"You okay, Davey?"

"Yeah? You like the rain, Pete?"

"Sometimes it's a good sign. Cleans the streets, you know?"

I watch the rain streak the windows. In the soft tattoo it beats on the windows is the code I must find. "Sometimes, Pete, you can look at things and not see them. Know what I mean?"

I watch his reflection, note his impassive face. "I believe Vince will be back, but till then, someone has to look out for things. And you being someone Vince trusts, you could do that. Vince would want you to keep your eyes open. I think he had someone in mind, don't you?"

"Could be."

"I would like you to watch Johnny."

There is a brief silence and then Pete speaks. "Vince said you would figure it out."

"I want to know where Johnny goes. I want to know about everyone he sees."

"I could do that, Davey."

"And if I need to reach out to Vince?"

"He'll be in touch."

The rain is falling harder now, much harder, making it difficult to see. That's what Vince wanted to do, to see clearly. By disappearing, he's letting everyone else take the spotlight. He can see them and they must wait for him to appear.

Johnny is back. "Something's come up. I have to go out. I'll see you in the morning, kid. Remember what I told you about the fight."

"I'll remember."

"Let's go, Pete."

I continue looking out at the night. Johnny is whispering something to Dago Pete as they go out. Outside, the lights of a car flash on. Escorted by three men, Johnny stands on the curb, talking to one of them. The man nods and inclines his head. The trappings of power.

How does it feel, Johnny, to be number one while the search for Vince continues? The search that has made me a killer. Johnny slips into the backseat of the Cadillac. Another car angles in front of his. Both cars pull away. Remember, Johnny. Uneasy lies the head of the pretender.

# 16

**JULIE'S VOICE** comes to me just seconds after I pick up the phone. "Hi. Are you all right?"

"I'm okay. How about you?"

"I didn't sleep that well."

"I guess you shouldn't sleep alone."

My words hang there for the moment and images of last night return. Julie moving beneath me, the two of us consumed by fire. "Can I see you tonight?"

"I'll make us dinner."

"If you don't mind my friends outside your door."

"As long as they're outside."

"Why don't I come by and pick up that package."

"I'll be at my office. I have to go in and catch up on some work. Three forty-eight Park Avenue." There's something in her voice. Something not right.

"Davey?"

"Yeah."

"Nothing . . . I'll see you later."

In the shower, I plan the day. I was just falling off to sleep when I heard the cars pull in. Whatever Johnny's business was, it kept him late. Several minutes later, something was slipped under my door. I felt around on the floor till my fingers touched the small piece of paper. An address was scrawled on it: 424 East Sixty-seventh Street. Dago Pete is right on the job. That's not far from my apartment on the East Side—brownstone country. Johnny wasn't meeting anyone from the fraternity of blood brothers when he went there. Johnny, like Vince, has a private agenda.

I call down for Mrs. Lamberti to bring me breakfast in my room. Downstairs is like a fortress; scowling men with bulging guns, pots and pots of red and white sauces cooking for the hungry troops.

Dago Pete enters, carrying my breakfast of hot rolls, juice, and espresso. He inclines his head toward downstairs. "Mrs. Lamberti said she'd be back when Vince comes back. So I'm doing the cooking this morning."

He sets the tray down on the bed and pours coffee for me. I bend over and help myself to a breakfast roll, which I cover with marmalade. We are just inches apart and I whisper, "Thanks, Pete."

Johnny enters the room, looking as if he had gone to bed at eight o'clock instead of four in the morning. "How's Dago's espresso?"

"It would grow hair on Mussolini's head."

Dago grunts and Johnny gives him a clap on the shoulder. "Just what I need."

Johnny pours a cup for himself and Pete leaves the room. "Sleep okay?"

"I miss my bed."

Johnny smiles. "Sleepovers are tough."

"I'm going back home tonight. You can put some guys on my building."

"It's a lot easier if you're here."

"I just had a tough two days, Johnny. The fight and the other stuff took a lot out of me."

"Now I need a favor from you."

I cover another roll with marmalade and bite into it.

"I want you to run up to St. Cecilia's Convent in Bronxville and see Sister Mary Elizabeth. She called this morning and she's worried about Vince. She's got some lucky crucifix or something. Says it's been blessed. She was Uncle Nick's inamorata. He got killed just a month before they were going to get married. She asked for you. Says she's never met you and it's time she did. She prays for you before every fight." Johnny drains his espresso. "Are we on?"

"We're on."

"I'll have Tiny and Vito drive you up. This is one ride you can relax and enjoy."

The ride I came back from brings back the face of Joe junior.

"When's the funeral?"

Johnny stops smiling. "Tomorrow. Don't get any crazy ideas. Joe and Dino will be there. You won't. We're sending a big wreath. You turn up and Joe Dante will take it very personal. After we make the peace, then you take his hand."

"Do I tell him then that I whacked his son?"

"You tell him nothing and let it lie."

"He's going to want to know, Johnny. How did his son wind up down by the river while his goons got it in the lookout?"

"He's never going to know about the gun you were carrying. Speaking of the gun . . ."

"I'm picking it up this afternoon."

"No slipups. It's got to disappear. Finish up your breakfast. Tiny and Vito are waiting for you in the car."

As he heads out of the room, I call to him. "I want the fight, Johnny."

He is halfway out of the room and stops. "I know you do. I'll talk to Scola."


The car rolls up a driveway that intersects the green carpet that is the lawn of St. Cecilia's. I get out of the car and look over at the slate gray–bricked church with stained-glass windows. In front of me is the gate, which fronts the convent, a large white-and-green shuttered building. As I walk toward the gate and the guard, I can see Tiny and Vito watching me. They both have the drooping faces of mastiffs. Their eyes lack the quality of possibility. They see only what is there. I reach the gate and tell the guard I am here to see Sister Mary Elizabeth. He calls, and moments later I am walking toward the large building.

She is waiting for me in one of the reception areas. It is a high-ceilinged room ringed with pictures of martyrs and eminences. The floor is bare, but there are several expensive armchairs and a long burgundy couch on which to recline. In the corner of the room is a desk and chair, undoubtedly for those who wish to transcribe their meditations. There is one large window, which is closed. As I enter, she stands up and walks to meet me. I have seen pictures of her and my uncle Nick, but those are from over a quarter of a century ago. In those pictures, Elizabeth was a strikingly pretty woman with thick brown hair. Now the habit covers that hair and her face has lost its resilience and beauty. The skin seems devoid of tonality. There has been a great deal of meditation on a life lost. Elizabeth has become Sister Mary. Resignation and acceptance have replaced the sparkle of youth in the blue-gray eyes that jumped vivaciously from the photographs. But they are not weak eyes. Rather, they are the eyes of someone who has gained strength through denial. She has purged the juices of her youth and learned to live through intellect and abnegation.

We shake hands and Sister Mary looks at me. What does she think of my battered face?

"You are not the conventional portrait of a gladiator."

"What do you mean?"

"You seem more intelligent."

"I wasn't so smart the other night."

"Perhaps, but still you attained your goal. Come sit down."

She leads me over to the chairs. As she talks to me, her hand wanders to the large crucifix that rests just below her neck.

"Vincent has spoken of you many times. He takes great pride in you."

"I know he must have a special feeling for you."

She nods her head as a small smile touches her lips. "Do you think he's all right?"

"Yes, I do."

I wonder how she's existed all these years with the knowledge of who Vince is and what he does. That certainly must add time to her devotions.

She is studying me carefully. What does she think? Do I remind her of what might have been had she married? Does she see the child she might have had?

"I am sorry that we have never met."

I shift my weight in the chair. "I think Vince always had a difficult time over what happened with my uncle Nick. Somehow, bringing us together would have opened it up in a way he would have been uncomfortable with."

"Perhaps that is so, but I also played my part in it. I am glad we have come to meet at last."

An awkward silence falls over us, and yet she is not uncomfortable with silence. She has learned to live with it.

"Johnny told me you had something for me."

"It's something for Vince. It's over in the rectory. We'll get it in a few minutes."

"What is it?"

"A Saint Christopher's medal that's been blessed. It possesses the miracle of survival."

The silence descends again and I wonder how far I can go with her. There are so many pieces in the puzzle, and she is not fragile china.

"Tell me about Uncle Nick."

Her eyes flicker with surprise but not hurt. "He was gentle; that's what I remember best about him. He had a remarkable smile and a great capacity for laughter."

"Vince loved him a lot. . . . He still does."

"Vince punishes himself a great deal for what he thinks he brought upon Nick."

She is much more solid than I have been led to believe.

"Vince thinks it was because of who he was that Nick was killed. Vince's cross is his guilt."

"He couldn't help what happened."

She watches me, eyes searching me out. We have come to one of those rare moments. People who have a history and yet are strangers.

"Nick died . . ." she begins and then pauses, holding her secret close to her. But she sees the hunger in my eyes and finds it irresistible. "Nick died for what he did as much as for what he did not do."

I do battle with her cryptic words. Nick died because he was Vince's brother and there was a war going on. "I don't understand."

"You will have to ask Vince that."

"Vince won't talk about that time."

"He'll tell you."

"I'm not so sure."

"You must be patient. It took me a long time to understand. In the beginning, there is only anguish and tears. Then there is rage and resignation. And then finally you are ready for the last stage, the most important one."

"What's that?"

"Wisdom."

She's saying I'm not ready. "Sometimes we don't have choices. . . . It's forced upon us. Sometimes answers must be learned in other ways than by questions."

She stands up. "Come with me."

"Where are we going?"

"To get what you came for."

She leads me out of the room to some stairs that go down a back entrance. We reach a door that leads outside. She pushes it open. It is gray and overcast; the grass is wet. I watch the long hem of her black skirt catch and hold the water. We walk to the church, and at the door, she stops and lets me open it. The room is small and dark, with a small light as its front. I see a row of candles burning and a long burgundy curtain. The Messiah hangs down from a cross mounted on a black stone slab. The candles jump as the cool air fans them. I see a hooded priest standing next to the candles.

"Go to him," she whispers. "He has the medal, the blessed medal."

The whole scene seems surreal. I look at her and then back at the priest. There is something about his stance.

Her hand softly presses my side and I go forward on shaky legs toward the candles and the hooded man. He is dangling something from his hand. The hood falls away and I see Vince.

# 17

**As I REACH VINCE,** he embraces me. The gesture, so atypical, seems to mirror his position. The don has his back to the wall; his friends are few. Yet I cannot reciprocate. He must be aware of it, though his face betrays no expression.

"The fight has left its mark."

Which fight is he referring to?

He guides me over to the pews. I look back for Sister Mary, but she is gone. We sit facing each other. I note the tension on his face. It is one thing to be hunted and on the run when you are twenty. But Vince is sixty-three now and the dark, implacable eyes move up and down in quick, darting flurries. There is a throbbing movement around his throat. The flesh around his Adam's apple seems to yield to some nervous impulse, recoil, and then snap back. And there is something I have never seen in those dark eyes: uncertainty.

His hand rests on my shoulder. "I could not tell you what was going to happen. It had to seem absolutely real. But I made a miscalculation. I didn't think they would respond so quickly. I knew they would try to strike at me right away, but I forgot about you."

"That's why you didn't want me to go to the funeral."

"I didn't want to give them any ideas about you. But they are a deadly force. They moved against me through you."

"Rod told you all of it."

"He told me."

"Then you did anticipate them."

"I didn't anticipate well enough. I didn't want you to become a pistola."

"Maybe there never was a choice."

The thought sits there for a moment and then we both move away from it. Vince looks about the small church as if expecting an intruder to burst from behind the curtains. He turns back to me. "I wanted to tell you, Davey. All these years, I wanted to, but the words stuck inside me. Rosalia begged me. And I would say, 'What can I tell him? That his father was murdered by me and that I took him in because of my remorse?' "

"Is that why you did it? Remorse? Why didn't you let a Jewish family raise me? I didn't need to be brought up by a father who had killed my real father. I didn't need to be raised in a world of dagos who kept my secret in a little box they could use when they were ready to carve me up."

Anger is running through me. I stand up as Vince answers. "I did it because Nails asked me to."

I whirl toward him. "Asked you—how could he?"

"He left a note behind. He knew it had all caught up to him. I don't know how he knew his number was up. He was afraid if you were raised as a Jew, you would become a target. You would always be the warrior son of Nails Gordon and they would fear you, retaliate against you. You would have no chance."

"So I was brought up as a dago by the dago who killed him."

Vince comes off the bench. "I didn't know how it would all come out. He wanted you to be safe."

"Dago-safe. If you can't fight them, join them. But you didn't have to do it, Vince. Not after you had killed Nails. You could have given me to someone else. I could have been raised by some wop baker or a . . ."

"Or what? It was 1933 when Nails died. The heart of the depression. Jew or dago, who needed another mouth to feed?"

"There's more to it, isn't there, Vince? It took more than a note from Nails."

Vince looks at me with those hard dark eyes. He is struggling with the same emotion I remember from that night at Umberto's Clam House. Stillborn words searching for expression.

Then I am graced with knowledge. "You didn't take good-enough care of Nick and I became his replacement. I was another chance for you."

He speaks slowly now, each word etched by his inner pain. "Nick was an innocent and I stopped watching out for him. We were making money, a lot of it, and I gave him some. He began to hang around the shows, to see a woman. He was a good-looking boy, and he was engaged, but he was not prepared. Everything was fast on Broadway. I knew nothing about it. Finally, Johnny told me. I was furious. How could he disgrace us and Elizabeth this way? 'Give her up,' I told this consumed boy. My threats only drove him further away." His voice falters. "It was his woman—don't you understand? Nails's woman."

We stand there, eyes locked, and one of the veils from the past falls. "Dolly Irving," I say.

His eyes register shock. "Johnny told you."

"Not Johnny. Go ahead, Vince."

"When my cousin Ace Mazzoti called to tell me he was at war with Nails Gordon, I said I would not be part of it. I told Nails whatever happened, I would not be involved in a war against him. And then it all happened so fast. Ace hit Benny Wagman and Nick was killed by the Gordon mob. I cannot tell you what losing Nick meant, and I could not forgive. Even if they were just some of his crazy cowboys, Nails should have controlled them. Nick was not part of the Life. So we went out like vigilantes, and when the call came that they were at the hotel, I went with a gun in my hand. Nails was not supposed to be there. When it was finished, there came the letter from Nails. He told me where to find you . . . and asked me to take you in. Then it came to me there was nothing else to do. Nothing would bring back Nick. Or Nails. I had lost them both. So I would sit in your room at night, thinking about what happened, rocking your cradle, a drink in my other hand, playing and replaying it like some film you cannot escape from."

Vince sits back down, his eyes riveted on the floor. His hands nervously flick through his hair. He looks up at me with haunted eyes. "Don't you see? It was a magic show."

"What was?"

"All of it. Benny Wagman was the first trick. He was the best shooter Nails had. That began the war. Then Nick was killed to bring me in. That was the second trick."

"Why do you call it a trick?"

"A trick is a thing a magician does for an audience. The audience for this show was all of us. The tricks worked because they were logical. So when Nick went down, all the dumb dagos in town lined up with shotguns in their hands. And I was first in line. The magician had done his tricks well. Only one man wasn't fooled."

"Tommy."

"Tommy made inquiries and he undid the trick. The magician was Scola. He set it up so that Nails and I would be turned against each other. He ordered the hit on Benny Wagman and then he sealed it with a kiss by having Nick shot down in the street."

"Why?"

"When we purged the old greaseballs and put together the Syndicate in 1931, rules were made about hitting those who stepped out of line. There would be a hearing, then a vote, and then the hit. The Jews wanted Nails to be the enforcer. The dagos got scared of that, so they put me and Frank Bruno in charge. But Tommy told me that Scola feared I would join with Nails and form an alliance to control everything. He was afraid we would take over the Syndicate and do away with him. So he gave us some hocus pocus. Now you see Nails, now you don't. And so I lost a brother and my best friend."

The air is suddenly very close. This is confession that eviscerates the soul.

"Why didn't you go after him?"

"When I found out about Scola, you were a little boy. Rosalia, Johnny, and I, we all loved you. I met Tommy for coffee and he laid it out. I remember he said to me, 'You can't do nothing now, Vince. The cards are all stacked against you. The Council would never back you, even if you could prove it. Nails Gordon was a troublesome Jew and a lot of people were scared to death of him. Scola has a thousand chits that are owed to him. If you go out on your own and start something, no one will back you. There's no percentage. You have to lay low and wait for Scola to make a mistake. Everybody's making a shitful of money and no one wants to go back and worry about who killed Nails Gordon.' "

Vince balls and unballs his fist. "Right after that I got an invitation to go to Scola's house. It was a family party. He patted your head and told me what a good boy I had. That was code. He was pointing to where the bullet would go. You became his hostage. If I moved on him, you would be the first to get it. And then he got his hooks into Johnny."

"Did you tell Johnny what you learned from Tommy?"

"Sure I told him. He was my son. I told him right away. And he says that there's nothing you can do. He didn't say there's nothing *we* can do till Davey grows up, he just says there's nothing you can do. Then a few weeks later, I found out that he was going with Dolly Irving. And I started to remember that night when Nails got killed and Johnny said he went looking for him. Why couldn't he find him, Davey? Johnny knew everywhere to look for Nails. But his story was always that he couldn't find Nails. Johnny was twenty then. A big boy. Plenty big enough to be hot for this ... this Broadway Dolly."

It is all happening so fast. So much to assimilate. "Is that what you fought about that night?"

Vince takes a deep breath. "I wanted him to give her up, but he wouldn't. I told him that she was bad for Nick, that she's the kiss of death. He says you don't tell me what to do. I ask him about that night—why he couldn't find Nails—and he wouldn't talk about it. I already told you, he says. And then I ask about him and Scola."

Still agitated, Vince begins pacing.

"Johnny and Scola?"

"I told Johnny, 'You kiss the ring, you are Scola's man. You are with him or with me.' He don't say anything so I told him to go and the next day I call Tommy and tell him to take Johnny in. But I warned him maybe Johnny is a spy."

Vince pulls out a cigar and holds it, but his trembling fingers give him away.

# 18

So WHAT HAPPENS NOW, VINCE?"

His eyes are filled with an ominous anger. "It is time to settle my account with Carlo Scola."

"You have to deal with Dino and Joe Dante first."

"I will deal with them all. But it is always about Scola. Dino planned everything with him. But they didn't figure I'd disappear. Now they don't sleep so good."

"What about Johnny?"

"Say nothing to Johnny. When I finish Scola, then we will see about Johnny."

"But you put him in such an unfair position. You wanted to see what he would do. That's it, isn't it?"

Vince lights the cigar now and blows out a ring of smoke. "If I had really been kidnapped, there was only one choice. He should have told Dino, no deal. No matter what you do to Vince, no deal. But he didn't do that. He stayed in the middle to hedge his bet. I don't know what happened to Johnny. When he was a boy, he was crazy with courage. But now he is Scola's man."

"You have proof?"

Vince taps his chest. "I feel it in my heart. That is my proof."

Vince paces now, smoking the cigar and musing on what must be done.

"You have a plan, don't you?"

"Perhaps."

What can Vince have arranged? He is alone; he doesn't trust Johnny. All he has are Dago Pete and Red Miller, a relic of the Gordon mob.

Vince reads my thoughts. "You think I hold few cards."

"Something like that."

"Perhaps you are right, but they have a fatal weakness—their arrogance. They think they cannot lose and so they are over confident. They don't believe I would attack them, and that is how I will get them. And you will help me when the time is right."

"When will that be?"

"Soon. I don't like to involve you. This thing with you and Joe junior gives me great pain. I saw you both grow up. I never wanted any part of the Life for you. It seems I cannot spare those around me. That is the way of things. But now we must be finished with it, both of us."

"I want to know the rest of it, Vince. How did Dino know about me and Nails?"

"Dino was Scola's shooter in those days. He killed Nick. And Joe Dante was part of it also. He turned up the night we were ready to raid the Rodman Arms. He was crazy for blood. You would have thought he had something very personal to settle. At some point after you were born, Scola told them about our secret."

"It's all come around, hasn't it?"

We are all of us joined by that bloody night back in 1933 when Nails Gordon and his mob were rubbed out by a dago hit squad. Fathers and sons. Joe junior and me.

"We must finish it once and for all. Are you in?"

I remember Friday night and Dino's mocking words. "Everybody was there for that hit. Me and Joe and Vince. Taught those Hebes something."

"I'm in," I hear myself say.

Vince's expression doesn't change, but his body language does. He flexes his arm and points the cigar at me as if it were a weapon. "Sister Mary will contact you and tell you to arrange a meeting. Here is a number for you to call. Memorize it and get rid of it. Tell the person who answers that you wish to speak with the abbot. When the abbot comes on, tell him the priest is finished with his devotions. He seeks an audience with a higher authority. Repeat what I have told you."

"I ask for the abbot and tell him the priest is finished with his devotions. He seeks an audience with a higher authority."

"The message from Sister Mary must be in person. If it is a phone call, then it is a trap. Only if you see Sister Mary do you call the abbot."

"What about Dago or Red?"

"Sister Mary is the only one who comes from me."

He has placed both hands on my shoulder. "When you speak to the abbot, he will give you a time and place to meet him. You will go there with Red. No one else."

"And then?"

"And then your part is finished."

"You're not going to tell me the plan?"

"That would put you in greater danger."

"Nothing could put me in greater danger than I already am."

"Trust me. It is better that you do not know."

"Why did you bring Red back?"

Vince flicks an ash on the floor and then scatters it with his foot. "Perhaps because I want someone who was close to Nails at my side. Red had to run for many years. Scola made sure the Syndicate sent its best killers after him. After Red killed two hitters in Miami Beach and one in Tucson, no one wanted the job. He is like me, Davey. Still dangerous."

"I'm going back to my apartment tonight."

Vince reaches for the priest's robe and slips it over his head. "I have waited a long time for this. Scola is a snake who corrupts. This time, I will cut off his head." He slips the cigar back in his mouth. "Stay five minutes after I leave." He walks toward the curtain, stops, and looks back at me. "Be careful and wait for Sister Mary."

"If I need to reach you?"

He shakes his head. "For this to work, we cannot meet again until it is over. If there is an emergency, give Red a message. You understand why it must be this way. Here, give this to Johnny. Tell him it will bring us all good luck." He presses something into my hand and disappears behind the curtains. In my hand is the medal. It is all gold and has the image of Saint Christopher engraved on it. We are going to need more than luck.

# 19

I CLUTCH THE MEDAL in my hand during the ride back to the city. What does Vince have in mind? Who is the abbot? Johnny is Scola's man, Vince says. Yet his final words are to tell Johnny the medal "will bring us all good luck." Vince is like the man who proclaims he has a faithless woman and yet cannot stop loving her. Has Johnny gone all bad? When the news came about Tommy, it hit us both hard. Johnny wasn't acting. If Johnny is in with Scola, then he would have been tipped. Tommy took all the rough edges off and made him into Johnny the gent. How many times have I sat together with the two of them? Johnny had real affection for Tommy. But in this business, affection is like sentiment; expendable.

I signal one of the muscles in front to get off the West Side Highway at Seventy-ninth Street. Minutes later, we come around the wide circle that leads us toward Riverside Drive. I tap the shoulder of the driver and tell him to pull up next to a phone booth. The first call is to the house. The voice on the other end is one of the new boys Johnny has imported. Johnny is at some meetings, I am informed. I leave word that I'm back in the city and will see Johnny after I pick up some merchandise. Then I call Julie's office. It is only seconds before she picks up, her voice warm and welcoming. How soon will I be there? She wants to know. "In about fifteen minutes," I respond. "Make sure the merchandise is in a bag." "It's all waiting for you," she says. Suddenly, I am uneasy. I am not sure why. "Do you have the address? Three forty-eight Park Avenue. Hurry." I hang up and slip back into the car. My body is alive. There is tonight. Soon. Soon.

We cross the park at Seventy-ninth Street and I give the driver the address on Sixty-seventh Street. The block is a row of brownstones and town houses. Number 424 is a slate-colored town house with ivy growing around the front door and winding around the windows. It is almost as if the ivy had been cultivated to keep the curious eye from seeing in. This is where Johnny went last night. Who did he come to see? Was it business or personal? Moments later we are cruising down Park Avenue.

Because it is Sunday, there is a guard posted in the lobby. He directs me to the elevator. Julie's office is located on the thirtieth floor. It is a big wide room that is truncated by her desk. A leather couch rests in the corner of the room, facing the windows. There is a large bookcase filled with law volumes. Several chrome chairs with leather backing are placed around the room. A thick black rug covers the floor. My eyes peruse the room and then come to rest on Julie. She is wearing a black suit with a soft pink blouse underneath. Long pearl earrings dangle down almost to her neck. My hand involuntarily goes to the gold medal in my pocket. She looks very beautiful and a tingling sensation spreads from my groin and travels up.

She opens the desk, takes out a gray shoe box, and walks toward me. "I think this is what you want."

I open it and look at the .32 semiautomatic I killed Joe junior with. I start to say something to Julie, but the words don't come. Her hand touches mine and she traces a line to my wrist. I feel my pulse jump, and I fight the urge to reach for her.

"What are you going to do with it?"

I close the box. "Lose it. This isn't easy for you."

"No, it's not. It's breaking the law. Its covering up a . . . a killing." She was going to say *murder*. "This is all wrong. You don't have anything to hide, Davey. It was self-defense."

"Julie, I was raised one way, with one cardinal rule. You don't go to the police. You buy them, but you don't go to them."

"You weren't doing anything, Davey, and they took you for a ride. Now you've accepted their primitive ethic. When you cover up what happened, you make yourself part of it. Just because you throw the gun away doesn't mean it's over."

"There's no other way."

She drops my hand and walks toward the window. "You know, Davey, it makes me an accessory. That was my gun."

"I won't tell if you won't. Look, you worked for Tommy. You knew what kind of world he came from. This is the kind of thing that happen."

She dips her head. "I know." She walks to the desk and takes out a cigarette. "Davey, I did some research this morning. I went to the stacks in the library and looked up Nails Gordon. There's a lot to read."

A big ball clots my throat.

She waves a stack of clippings at me. "He was a hero in the ghetto. There was a big parade to honor him after he died. He organized the ghetto against attacks when he was a young man. He was a defender of the faith. They didn't see him as a gangster; they thought of him as a kind of Robin Hood."

"I didn't know anything about him until——"

"Until when?"

The corpse of Waxy Green appears before me. Should I tell her? For a moment, I almost blurt it out, but then some cautionary instinct checks my words. "Someone sent me some clippings. I don't know who."

"You don't owe any of them anything. I know Vince raised you, but——"

"But what?"

"He should have protected you better against this. What a terrible way to find out about who your father really was." Her face softens. "It's not too late, Davey. Go to the police and tell them what happened. There would be a lot of questions and they'd go over and over it for a day, but then it would all be over."

"I can't."

"Why?"

"It would put me on the line for Joe junior."

"But it was self-defense."

"Tell that to Joe Dante. He'll hit me. In my world, anybody can get it."

"It's not your world."

"Yes it is. Dago or Jew, that's where I come from and those are the rules."

"Then you'll always live under a death sentence unless—"

"Unless?"

"Unless Joe Dante is put away."

"Julie, suppose he's put away. What difference does that make?"

Her eyes recoil as if from a punch.

"It has to stay an anonymous death. That's my only chance. If the truth comes out, he'll come after me. I killed his son and it will never be over."

"It could come out anyway."

Julie looks at the gray shoe box. "I'll have to report it as missing. I'll wait awhile and then say I lost it on a trip."

"Why do you carry a gun?"

The intelligent brown eyes flicker for a moment. "I'll tell you that tonight. Kiss me, Davey."

For a moment, we are strangers separated by the terrible void of reality and then we reach across the void to each other. Like a slow descent from a high place and then a wonderful free fall. Her lips taste like crushed flowers. It is a dizzying moment, one from which we both reluctantly part. Swaying, this close to each other, we hang on to the thrill. Then Julie hands me the box. "Do you like pasta?"

"Only if it's kosher."

She goes to her desk and brings back a pad. "Write your address."

I scribble it down and pick up the box. "There'll be a reception squad outside of my building."

"As long as they don't come up." Despite the banter, she seems upset. I'm still vibrating.

"Eight o'clock."

"I have a lot of paperwork. Make it nine."

I open the box and slip the gun into my pocket. I am at the door as she waves good-bye.

I can feel the gun nestled there as I ride down on the elevator. Snug in my pocket. The elevator opens and I head across the lobby toward the glass doors and the car waiting outside for me.

Two men closing on me from either side. "Keep walking, Rossi."

Clean-cut men, tall, closely shaven, neat blue suits with blue-and-red-striped ties. Not from the mob. No one from the mob would call me anything but Davey.

One of them flashes a brilliant gold badge. "Justice Department. Let's have a little talk. There's a car outside."

They take my arm and lead me toward the revolving exit doors. And me carrying.

# 20

**THE BACK EXIT** brings us out on Lexington Avenue. Just around the corner are my two goons, oblivious to what is happening. So much for dago protection. They have me by the arm, guiding me toward a gray Cadillac. Blue suit number one presses me against the car while blue suit number two steps in front of us. A redheaded mick sticks his head out the window and shows me his badge. "Brendan Foley, Department of Justice. We'd like to talk to you about your father. Pat him down boys."

I am the village idiot carrying the chocolate bar he has just stolen from the candy store. How could I get caught with a gun this way?

Number two's hands go down my body and stop as he feels the bulge in my coat pocket. He is also a mick, but without the red hair. He has a pug nose and squinty blue eyes. "We got something here." Foley gives him a nod and Blue Eyes checks around to see if anybody is looking. I am being rousted on Lexington Avenue in broad daylight and nobody gives a damn.

Blue Eyes palms the piece to Foley, who flips open the door. "Let's go for a ride, Rossi."

Blue Eyes pushes me inside and slides in next to me while the other suit hops in the front. The car heads east until we reach First Avenue and then peels a left going uptown.

Foley has been checking the weapon; now he looks up at me. "You got a permit for this?"

"I don't think so."

"Then I guess it's finders keepers."

"What's the matter—you don't have enough guns?"

Foley exhibits a little smile. "You'll acquire another one. I'm not interested in getting you on a gun rap."

He slips the piece into his brown trench coat.

"How did you find me?"

Foley has slipped on a dark fedora that was resting on his lap. He looks like a G-man.

"We've been tailing you all day. That was a nice ride you took to the country."

We swing around toward Second Avenue and pull up in front of a large new apartment house with a driveway that allows you to park in front of the lobby. Blue Eyes jumps out of the car and heads off the doorman while Foley loops his arm through mine. "We go in nice and easy. These are successful people who live here, and we wouldn't want to disturb them."

Flanked by the suits, we walk through the ornate lobby, which has large mirrors on both sides. I catch a fleeting glimpse of myself and my Justice Department partners. They walk briskly, these boys in blue. Not like the soldiers from the mob, who once they have your arm are secure that you belong to them.

The apartment they take me to has a spacious living room that is sparsely furnished with a long couch and a few chairs. The windows face a side street. A rug has been hastily laid down on the floor. The ends are crooked, suggesting this apartment has only recently been rented. Foley tosses his coat and hat onto a chair. Blue Eyes collects it and disappears into the bedroom with the other suit. Foley gestures for me to sit down on the couch while he turns a chair around and sits down, his chin resting on the top of it. He is a born interrogator.

He has sharp features, beginning with a knife of a mouth, which leads up to a thin, angular nose and blue eyes that glint with ambition and courage. This is a man who is not afraid to put his ass on the line, or yours, either. Yours first.

I put the ball into play. Make him answer. "Why the tail on me?"

"Why not? Someone took your father. You could be in danger. Do you have any idea where your father is?"

He's working as a priest at a convent up in Westchester, but I'm not telling you that. "I don't know anything. Why don't you talk to my brother? He's in charge of family matters."

"I thought talking to you would be more interesting. We could help you."

"How?"

"If your father isn't dead, then he needs friends. We could offer him protection."

"You want me to tell him that?"

We watch each other warily. I'm wondering what the sparring is about. Foley is wearing a blue suit over a white shirt with a pinstriped blue tie. These guys must bleed blue.

"What do you want, Foley?"

"I'm giving you a chance."

"A chance?"

"Listen, your father is outnumbered. If he's not lying at the bottom of some swamp and they let him go, he has no friends. We could work a deal."

"What kind of deal?"

"We'll take care of things if he points the way."

"When I see him, I'll tell him."

We lock into hard, unyielding stares. Foley's got the gun, but he doesn't realize he has the edge ... yet. There's always the chance of tracing it back to Joe junior. Think. How are you going to get it back?

"Could I have some water?"

"Sure."

He walks toward the little alcove that forms the kitchenette. I hear the water running. How do I do it? Be casual. Don't make a big thing of it. Do me a favor and I'll speak well of you to Vince. Foley is back, holding the glass of water. I take it and drink some.

He watches me and rubs his chin. Here comes the pitch. "All right, Rossi, listen. You're a civilian, as far as we know. You've had a terrific career, you're clean, and you've been a good citizen. You have to realize that maybe your father isn't coming back. You could help us then or you could help us now. It doesn't sound like there's much of a difference."

"What do you want me to do?"

"Keep your eyes open, listen. You'll hear things."

"That's pretty ballsy, Foley. You give me a glass of water and I'm supposed to be so grateful I'm going to rat these guys out."

Foley's face gets red. "Skip the Cagney dialogue."

"What is all this crap about being a good citizen? You're asking me to inform on my brother."

"I'm asking you to consider helping us get the mob."

"The mob? I've known them all since I was a kid."

"They've grabbed your father, Rossi. Bosses don't come back from rides."

So that's it. The Justice Department is putting in their pitch for a little revenge. But they don't know Vince is alive, and I do. Maybe here is how I get the gun back. He expected me to be angry. Let's shift gears and see what happens.

I drink some more water, as if I'm covering. Foley watches me and waits.

"We don't have any leads on my father. Do you?"

His eyes gleam. "We're watching a lot of people . . . all with connections back to Dino Manfredi. Something might break."

I set the glass down on the floor. "If you could let me know, I'd appreciate it."

"I could do that."

String him along. That's the only chance to get the gun back.

"Listen, Foley, this is a tough time. If Vince is alive, then that's one thing, but if he's not, that's something else."

"Here's my card, Rossi."

I throw up my hands as if singed by fire. "No cards. I'm going back to my apartment. If you hear anything, contact me there."

Foley takes the card back. "I'll be in touch."

I give him a hard stare. "We haven't agreed on anything. Got it?"

But Foley's eyes give him away. He thinks he has the hook into me.

"Can we drop you?"

"No, my escort will be getting antsy. Just let me walk out of here alone."

Foley nods. "Whatever you want."

"And don't get caught tailing me, or everybody will be watching me."

Foley doesn't respond. I get up and head for the door. Now do it. "Oh yeah, could I have my gun?"

It is just right, neither too casual nor too pointed. A guy who's on the edge of things asking for his piece back.

Foley waits a beat and then says, "I can't do that, Rossi. It's unregistered. That's against the law. You know what I mean?"

I read the frozen eyes and the message there. We don't have a deal yet. No deal, no gun. Foley is not going to play the patsy for my little act. You don't get any favors till you put out.

I drift downtown on Second Avenue, trying to figure my next move. The odds on Foley running a check on the gun are long. He is not suddenly going to look for a link between the gun and the bullets that I fired into Joe junior. The gun is going to go into a drawer, along with a file that he is building on Davey Rossi. Johnny will scream that he was right about the gun. It should have been ditched last night. I played footsie with Julie's conscience. Chump. The gun that will link you to Joe junior is with the Justice Department. If they ever put it together . . . I stop for a traffic light and realize I am hungry. I haven't touched anything since breakfast. I reach into my pocket and feel the medal. Where's the luck it's supposed to carry?

Over a hamburger in a Greek coffee shop, I play the next move over in my head. I keep stumbling. People pick me and take me for rides. My protection falls apart. Everybody knows who I am and where I am. Everything I learned growing up around the life hasn't helped. And Vince has trusted me with a message. Trusted me with his ace card. I can't even dump a murder weapon, so how can I carry a message?

I slug down a second coffee, get some change, and call the house. Dago Pete answers. "Dago, it's me. Listen, I got rousted by some Justice Department agents. They picked me up in a building on Park Avenue. I'm okay, but you better send somebody up there to tell Vito and Tiny to cool out. They're probably chewing the fixtures by now. I'm going home. Tell Johnny I got the medal."

"That's good to hear, Davey. He's uptown talking about the Simpson fight."

"I'll be home, Dago. I'll call you when I get there."

I click off and drop another dime. Someone with a deep-seated growl for a voice answers. "This is Davey, Red's friend. The one who chews on nails."

"What's the message?"

"I need some of Abe Mortkoff's boys. And tell Red I'll meet him tomorrow at three o'clock at the boathouse in Central Park."

I hang up and go outside. The lights are on and I check my watch. Daylight saving time has ended. A soft rain has started to fall. I wend my way downtown. So much has happened since Friday night when I fought Kid Bassett. Just forty-eight hours ago. Everybody is in motion and I am in the middle of it. I need to know something that the others don't. I need the edge. I pick up the pace. I know where I'm going.

Somehow, the realization that I'm trying to effect something gives me a lift. Being picked up by strangers is like being caught with a punch while you stand flat-footed. I need to be in motion. I cover the blocks quickly until I reach Sixty-seventh Street. I slow down, wondering what I'm going to do next. The ivy-covered brownstone looms ahead of me. I cross the street, looking for a place to take refuge. A telephone truck is parked there and the entrance to a brownstone is open. I duck inside and watch 424. There is a light on the second floor.

Five minutes go by and then five more. Nothing is going to happen. I close my coat. I'll give it two more minutes. Hell, it's raining harder. I check my watch, but it's too dark to read the numerals. I look up and see the car that has pulled up in front of 424. A gray Caddy. A man gets out; he's wearing a trench coat. A charge runs through me as I recognize Brendan Foley. Foley goes up the steps. He rings the bell and waits. The car drives up the street. Someone has buzzed Foley in. Moments later, his figure is silhouetted against the window on the second floor. He is facing another man, who moves to the window and draws the blinds.

# 21

THE BLINDS HAVE BEEN DRAWN for almost half an hour while I try to piece it all together. Johnny's secret agenda involves Brendan Foley, who tried to squeeze me. That's the only way to read this scenario. The brownstone with its walls of ivy to keep out prying eyes is a safe house. I remember Vince explaining it to me when I was a kid. "It's a place you go to, Davey, where you can hide and meet your friends. A place where you'll be safe." Not safe enough, slick Johnny. Maybe it was you who put the federal boys on me. That story about following me to the country doesn't ring true. Vito or Tiny would have spotted Foley's car. But you knew where I was going. First to the convent and then to Julie's office. What's the game, Johnny, and how do I play it?

No, there's no percentage in confrontation. The question is, Why are you snuggling up with the Justice Department? Why are you letting them roust your brother? What's the slickest deal you've ever made?

The Caddy cruises back down the block and pulls up in front of the house. Ten minutes later, Foley emerges from the brownstone and walks to the car. He leans in and says something. A few moments of conversation, then he gets into the back of the car and it pulls away. I am left hiding in the shadows of the building I have taken refuge in. The lights have gone out on the second floor. I leave my building and come up behind the telephone repair truck. I want a good look at whoever comes out. Five minutes later, a man emerges. Tall and whipcord-thin, he's wearing a dark raincoat and no hat. He walks a few feet and then stops to open an umbrella. He will be an easy tail.

I stay about thirty yards behind him on the other side of the street. He stops once to light a cigarette and I drop in back of a car. A few seconds later, we continue our stroll. At Fifth Avenue, he swings left and heads downtown. The rain has tapered off. Traffic is thin. The lights of Fifth Avenue beckon to me. Ever since my excursions uptown as a kid, it has always seemed to me a block of majesty. Park Avenue is tradition, Madison Avenue class, but Fifth Avenue is the crème de la crème. Well-dressed couples are heading for dinner; the lights of the cabbies flicker in competition with each other like fireflies gone mad.

He closes his umbrella now, this tall, mysterious figure who knows my brother, and continues his walk. I am directly behind him on the same side of the street. Between us is an elegant couple in formal clothes, her arm looped in his. They serve as perfect cover. We cross Sixty-sixth Street as the light changes. At Sixty-first Street, I can see a milling crowd and some long black limousines. They are in front of the Pierre Hotel. That's official stuff. Men in black raincoats linger in front of the building. The tall man stops, flips the cigarette away, and walks inside. Journey's end. Where do I go from here?

I cross the street to where a handsome cab is waiting. The horse is eating from a bucket, chewing methodically. An old blanket is draped over his back. I incline my head in the direction of the hotel. "What's the excitement?"

The driver is a short, stocky young man. He's wearing a jacket patched into a red-and-black quilt design. "Kennedy is there. The attorney general. I guess there won't be a war with the Russians if he's up here in New York."

I turn my head to look at the elegant building. I run the connection through my mind. Attorney general . . . Justice Department.

I look at the gleaming lights of the Pierre. A safe house on Sixty-seventh Street. Robert Kennedy is in New York, a few blocks away. Foley picks me up. What're the odds it's a coincidence?

The driver is looking at me oddly. "Wait a minute. Are you Davey Rossi? With those bruises, who else would you be?"

My silence becomes ready confirmation. "Jesus, this is my night for celebrities."

He has a rich brogue and a ready smile.

"What's your name?"

"Tom Cassidy. I was in the Garden on Friday. Jesus, you took a few. But Bassett's got his lumps to take care of. I won fifty bucks on you, and it's going right on your back for the Simpson fight." His face is all flushed and excited. "When will that be?"

"Soon."

Cassidy is scrambling about under the seat of the cab, looking for something. He comes out with a brown paper bag and a pencil. "Would you sign something for me?"

I take the bag and pencil. "Let's see what I can do."

"Christ, what a fight. When he got you with the butt, I thought you was gone. And that second one, I almost climbed over the back of the ringside swells to get into the ring. Bassett's dirty, dirty as they come."

I hand the bag back to him. "I hope that does it, Tom."

He silently reads what I have written and then a second time aloud. His face beams with delight. " 'To Irish Tom, my second in the ring.' "

"Irish Tom. Jesus, what a night. I get to see the attorney general, the future lightweight champion of the world, and the mob. All in one night."

"What do you mean, the mob?"

Cassidy backs off apologetically. "I didn't mean you. I read about your dad, but I didn't mean that . . . sorry."

"It's okay. Who did you see?"

"Over at St. Patrick's . . . she's praying."

"Who is?"

"You know . . . the mother of the guy who got killed. You know his father is a big chief when he can keep St. Pat's open this late."

"Joe Dante."

"That's him."

"Are you sure it was him?"

"Isn't his picture all over the *Daily News* today? And his son."

It is all racing through my head about St. Patrick's. Something jogged loose from a long time ago. A show at Radio City Music Hall that Anna took us to. Joe junior and me. And we had to wait inside the great church while she prayed. As she does now for the soul of her son.

"And I'll tell you something else. When this boyo . . . this chief got there, I seen His Eminence greet him. Cardinal Spellman himself."

Cassidy is shaking his head in wonder. You shouldn't be shaking your head, Tom boy. When the don and the cardinal talk about breaking bread together, they're talking denominations with serial numbers. For them, the Last Supper is a prix fixe meal.

"When was this?"

"Maybe ten minutes ago. She's there right now I tell ya."

"Thanks, Tom." I slip him a twenty.

He looks at it with astonishment. "Jesus. God bless," he is yelling as I race down Fifth Avenue.

# 22

St. Patrick's stands silhouetted by the lights of Fifth Avenue as I leave the cab. As a kid, I always felt that it was part of a magnificent presentation that showcased the heart of the city. St. Patrick's, Rockefeller Center, and Radio City Music Hall. A little bit of religion, show business, and American enterprise all rolled up into one. The spires of the great church tower over Fifth Avenue. I walk toward it. Why am I doing this? It isn't smart, isn't the percentage play. If she's still here, there will be an escort. They don't want to see me, for I am a reminder of what should have happened and what actually did. They don't know that I killed Joe. I was supposed to be his victim. Somehow, I survived and it is disrespectful in their eyes for me to be here. But I owe Anna something.

As I climb the stone steps, I see a line of trigger boys standing by their cars which are parked on Fiftieth Street. They are smoking and pacing. So much of their time is spent waiting. I am standing in front of the bronze doors, with the Jesus and the twelve disciples depicted on one, and the other featuring the bronzed figures of such notable saints and martyrs as Saint Joseph, Saint Patrick, and Saint Isaac Jogues, martyr and first priest in New York. I go inside. The great cathedral with its soaring nave and marble stanchions is hushed and still. I stand beneath the balcony, looked down upon by the statues of Saint Peter and Saint Paul as well as angels, Popes, and wise men adorning the stained-glass windows. As a kid, when I first saw those windows that rise to every level of the church, I thought heaven must be just beyond them. At the center of the cathedral, hanging opposite each other are the American flag and the yellow, white flag of the Vatican. I stand at the foot of the nave, looking directly at the sanctuary. In its center is the cross mounted on a table of green velvet, with bouquets of white flowers all around it. Tall candles burn on both sides of the pulpit. Up and down the far aisles are altars and to my left are the shrines illuminated by candlelight that are used as confessionals. The last mass of the day was much earlier but a number of people remain in the pews. The lonely, the haunted, the guilty and terrified keep vigil here. These are prayers of duty and obligation. Prayers laced with memory and remembrance. Prayers of repentance and of mourning that will never end.

I stop at the shrine of Saint Stanislaus Kostka. Flickering candles in glass holders become burning symbols of confession. Bless me, father, for I have sinned. I have killed a boy I knew since childhood. He drew first, but I was faster. I couldn't help it—he was taking me for a ride. Rides are sometimes one-way trips, know what I mean? Suddenly, an arm on mine. I look up, and there is Cancelero Ruggerio. His voice comes to me like a rusty buzz saw.

"Davey, you gotta go."

He is a little embarrassed and nervous. He is on the spot in a place where he is not comfortable. Looming behind him is another beast I recognize: Carmine Sincola. Relics of my youth. Faithful beasts of burden. I shake loose from Cancelero and Carmine approaches. He doesn't have enough sense to be awed by St. Patrick's. He is never out of place. He has lost his good friend Nuñez Otonio and I am a part of that. He stands in my way as I start forward. I cock my right, fake with the left, and as he covers, I flip his tie in his face. Then all of us are walking toward the Fifty-first Street exit and the marble tablets that depict the Stations of the Cross. Jesus falls on the way to Cavalry the second time. Veronica presents the linen cloth to Jesus. Jesus assisted by the Cyrenian. Jesus meets his afflicted mother. . . . I spot Anna sitting in the second row of pews. She is alone, dressed in black; a shawl covers her hair. I watch her for a moment, wondering what I am going to say. I didn't mean to do it. Joe made the bad percentage play. It was me or him, Anna. Then I can no longer think, only obey this dumb impulse that brought me to her.

I slide in beside her and lower my head. She is holding a crucifix and I can see her face is heavily rouged. Her dark hair is pulled back. She has on a black dress and a white pearl necklace. This is all a terrible mistake. I have intruded on her grief. I have nothing to say, only a need to be here with her. And I am not sure why. She has been kind to me, but that is not it. Maybe it has something to do with the other night when her husband brought me home and I saw the prison she lives in. When she said, "It is a monstrous life."

She looks up now at me and she doesn't seem surprised. Was she expecting me? I search desperately for something to say. She takes my hand and lowers her head. She wants me to pray with her, and all I can think is that I killed her son. I didn't mean to. I had no choice.

The pervasive silence inside the cathedral fills me up. Once my mother brought me here and the cardinal conducted Mass surrounded by twelve priests, the tableau becoming a re-creation of the Last Supper. Once, there was a Messiah and twelve others. Among them, one who would betray him. I remember after the Mass, the cardinal, dressed in his red robe, sat in the archbishop's throne. It is a great high seat, symbol of his power and authority. Is that power greater than that of the don? Joe Dante brings his Anna here and is received by His Eminence. And what was the subject of the sermon of the Mass held earlier? The promise of youth blighted? Or maybe never trust a Jew. After all, didn't Jewish holy men sell their prince to a dago consulate from Rome? I look toward Anna again. I want to say something that will comfort her, but I am trapped by what I have done. I want to confess and be comforted. When I was a kid, I would sometimes note Anna watching me with a warm look in her eye. I couldn't imagine being worth the attention of this lovely woman. For a time, I thought it was because I was nice-looking. I finally came to realize it was the kindness within her. The kindness and compassion she showed me the other night, when Joe and Dino shredded me, using the past as their weapon. Someone taps my arm. I turn, and there are four of them. Even in this great cathedral, the wafer of the Eucharist is dispensed by Joe Dante.

They lead me away, these four mastiffs, out of the great stained-glass cathedral and onto the stone steps, where their master is waiting. He is wearing an expensive white topper and a soft gray hat. He is pale. His eyes look wounded. You took a shot to the chops, didn't you, Joe?

Joe Dante surveys me for a moment. "You got balls coming here, Davey, for—"

"For a Jew?"

He doesn't respond to that. "What are you doing here?"

"Paying my respects . . . to Anna and to Joe."

"Vince didn't teach you good. We let family bury their dead."

"I was there, Joe, but I shouldn't have been. Joe shouldn't have been either, but you sent him. You figured I'd go quietly with an old friend."

"Who killed my Joe?"

"You did. He was never for the Life, and he paid for it."

A thin smile is painted on his lips. "Sarai lo prossimo."

But his threat fills me with contempt. I came here as much to confront him as I did to see Anna. "Maybe now you know how it feels, Joe. You were there when my father got it, and I was there when your Joe got clipped. It's business—isn't that what you always say? Some people give the business and some people get it."

For a second, I think those eyes will break from fury, and then he laughs it off. "You took too many punches."

"I took your best shot."

"Did you?"

In the coldness of his words and demeanor, there is something that stops me. I have had my moment of bravado. Johnny would call it stupidity.

We stand there, eyes locked. If he knew I pulled the trigger on Joe junior, he would have me hit somewhere in public to emphasize his power and his contempt for me.

Anna has come out, and she stares at us. Something in her expression changes, as if she knows what this exchange is about.

Joe turns from her and spits the words at me. "I will not spare you a second time."

He breaks away and walks toward Anna, followed by his entourage. He takes Anna's arm and they walk slowly toward the car. Carmine

Sincola turns and stares. His finger comes up and he points it at me. I cock my fist and hold it up for him to see. Finally, someone calls Carmine and he disappears down the steps. Moments later, the cars pull away and I am left standing alone under a half-moon on the steps of St. Patrick's Cathedral.

# 23

I HAVE NEVER BEEN able to rid myself of a certain guilt when I make love to a woman—a feeling that I am taking something. It comes at the point of most intense pleasure. It seems in those moments that I am a furtive stranger who has touched upon some deeply concealed nerve that releases passion, a passion that I am manipulating and yet somehow apart from. The cries of ecstasy fall upon me like blows I take during a fight. I am a benumbed creature seeking release. When I was a kid, the end of my climax filled me with fear. How to be alone with a stranger? As I grew older, I handled it, but I never lost that fear. This time, it is different. I am not manipulating her; I am not ashamed of the feeling, hers or mine. So her cries and our words caress me. The fear is gone. And as I am born, the furtive stranger in me dies.

The rich aroma of Julie's cigarette fills my bedroom. Our clothes are strewn about the floor like tattered fragments of a book hastily ripped from its binding. It's as if from the moment we came through the door, each article of clothing was an impediment to touching each other.

Julie turns to me. "Tell me what Johnny said."

"He said we were both fuckups. That I've been walking around on my heels like some kind of punchy pug. And that he was crazy not to have gotten rid of the gun last night. I told him this afternoon that it wouldn't have happened if he'd had better people watching me."

Her hair is long, her lips moist, and for a moment the thoughts and words are not there. "Go on, Davey."

"So then we sparred around for a few minutes. Then he told me I fight Sandy Simpson in late December."

Her fingers run over one of my cuts. "That's only two months away."

"Either I take the shot then or they'll put me in the deep freeze for a year or two. I'm twenty-nine. In this business, that's ancient."

"What about your cuts?"

"They'll heal." They'll also open up and bleed the first good pop I get. But I leave that alone.

"It's all about what's happening to your father, isn't it?"

"Yeah. It's about tightening the screws. They get at Vince through me."

"Who's doing it?"

"Carlo Scola."

"What does he want?"

I roll back over, look at the ceiling. "They want Vince to step down."

"Will he?"

I feel her eyes searching me out. "No."

"Have you heard from him?"

The furtive stranger returns. My chest fills with the lie. "No."

"What's going to happen?"

I flip back over on my side so I can see Julie. "There'll be an accommodation or there'll be more bodies."

"What does Johnny say?"

"He says Vince is holding a bad hand."

"Why?"

"Because he's outnumbered. When Tommy died, the whole thing changed. Tommy was the key. He was the mob's moneyman, the deal guy. Tommy was against drugs on principle. It didn't stop the others from wetting their beaks."

"What does that mean?"

"You know . . . like a bird dips into the water and drinks."

I look at her and she reads my eyes. "Finish it, Davey."

"Tommy and Vince were holding the line against a big investment in drugs by the Five Families. Now Tommy is dead and Vince is an outlaw."

"So why don't they just go into drugs and leave Vince alone?"

"It doesn't work that way."

Julie looks for an ashtray and I scoop one up from the night table. I watch the energy in those hands as she puts the cigarette out. "Fix me a drink."

I walk to the closet to reach for a robe and Julie's voice comes to me. "Make it a scotch over ice. And don't put anything on. I like to watch you."

I grab a Coke from the kitchen and mix the scotch in the living room. I flick the small light on over the bar and there is an autographed picture of Tommy. Who's the abbot, Tommy?

I pad back into the bedroom and hand Julie her drink. "There you go, scotch rocks nude."

She smiles. "I'll drink to that."

The Coke is good. I am very thirsty. Julie watches me as she lights another cigarette. "What does Johnny say?"

"That Vince needs a wild card."

"Does he have one?"

"I don't know."

"Why would he just disappear and not contact you or Johnny?"

"Vince has always been like that."

"Like what?"

"He plays a lone hand."

She puts down the scotch and takes my hand. "You know, I read those clips and I thought of what you must be going through. All these years, and then you find out about Nails Gordon. What's going through you, Davey?"

I shrug. "A lot, but I can't say yet. I just don't know." I dig my fingernails into my hand to stop myself from saying more. I feel like spilling my guts. I'm spilling all over the place. That's why I went to St. Pat's. I wanted to spill to Anna. I remember something Johnny told me once after the hit was put on Augie Lozano, who ran the bookie joints for Frank Bruno's family. "Augie couldn't walk past a confession box booth without spilling his guts. He was going to church twice a day. Some people got suspicious. So one day, Frank put a guy in a priest's outfit inside the box and they found out Augie was meeting a cop every week. He spilled over in confession so he wouldn't feel bad about it." Johnny waved a cigarette and turned those ice blue eyes on me. "If you ever get that way, take a razor and cut your throat." Then Julie's hand is in mine and the words spill out.

"If they trace your gun back to Joe junior, they'll come after me. What do I do, counselor, and why do you carry a gun?"

"Which question should I answer first?"

"The second one."

She takes a long drag of the cigarette, then sets it down. "When I was fifteen, I came home from school one day and there was a man there with my mother. He had come to pick her up. He had on a flashy suit and he had little marble eyes. He was unlike any man I had ever seen my mother with. There had been lots of them. Mother was a sexy dish. She liked sexy men. This one scared me. Right from the beginning. His name was Frankie Tenuto. He was a gangster."

Something tumbles inside me. Some little click of remembrance.

"He was involved with gambling and loan-sharking in Nassau County. Mother had met him at some kind of charity party. She was just at that point where she was getting very vulnerable about her age and how she looked. She would spend hours each day making up. She was ripe for someone like Tenuto. Absolutely ripe. He was the type of violent animal who made her feel young. Everything about each other turned them on. They fought and they screwed, screwed and fought. It was all part of this game they played. That's when I began to visit my father again. I hated Tenuto and I hated what my mother was doing. We lived in Lawrence. Lawrence is a very wealthy Jewish enclave. It didn't take long for word to get around, and I felt like I was a social outcast. I used my trips to Washington to be with my father as my way of escape."

She picks up the cigarette and downs some scotch. "My father said it would end when he got tired of her. It took awhile, but finally Tenuto started to play around. It didn't take mother too long to figure it out. Maybe she was expecting it. She was home more often, and there would be these screaming fights on the phone. Then they'd make up and it would be good for a few days, until he made another excuse and Mother would start screaming at him on the phone. Then she'd go off to the bedroom with a bottle of bourbon. I remember I would lie in bed at night and wonder what it was about him. He was small and oily-looking. He had very powerful shoulders and black hair that was all slick. And his fingers were thick and ugly, like pig's feet. He was so repulsive. What could have made her want him so much?"

I put my hand out to Julie. "I'm still thirsty. You want me to freshen yours?"

"Please."

I am back with Julie, lying across the bed, facing her. I feel the desire building in me. Julie shakes her head. "Why did she want him so much?"

"Because that's the way it is. You see somebody and you want them."

She takes a long hit of scotch. "Once, I went into the bedroom after he had left, and it still reeked of them. It smelled of lust and semen and death. It was overpowering. My mother was in the tub, soaking in a bubble bath. She had a compress over her face. I wasn't sure she knew I was there, and then she said, 'You'll understand someday when you meet a man you'll degrade yourself for. You know what degradation is, Julie? It's wanting a man so much, you'll do it anyplace, anywhere, even though you know he has others. He'll have you tonight and someone else in the morning. And you still have to have him. Someday you'll understand.' You know I tried to understand, but how could I? The only thing I knew was that she couldn't give him up. It got worse that summer, and I gave up trying to save her. I just counted the days till I would go away to college." She shakes her head. "But I didn't escape in time. It was Labor Day weekend and I had been away visiting friends. I came in at ten o'clock and heard their voices. Then my mother screamed. He was hurting her. She was terrified. I ran up the stairs and mother was lying at his feet, all bloody, her fingers scratching at his shoelaces. He was kicking her. I ran and threw myself at him. He hit me with his fist as if I were a man. Then he opened his hand and slapped me over and over. He called me a Jew bitch. I couldn't breathe; there was blood on my face. His eyes were all swollen and black. He's going to kill me, I thought. He had gone completely off. I could see the scratch marks on his face. He raised his leg to kick me and then the shots came. Four, then two more. I remember his little eyes widened and seemed to roll up into his head. . . ."

I hold Julie close and can feel the beat of her heart. "But that was your mother, not you."

"I didn't sleep for a long time after that. I would wake up and reach for something to protect me. About six months later, I got my father to get me a gun permit. I used to tell myself I was afraid they would send someone after me. I guess I got used to it. I've tried being without one, but after a few weeks I start waking up in the middle of the night." She looks up at me, a tear creasing her cheek.

"What happened to your mother?"

"She got probation on a manslaughter charge. My father handled it. She sold the house and moved to Southampton."

Julie's hand moves down my body. "Do you still want me?"

I roll over on top of her. Poised above her come the words of simple admission. "Anytime . . . anyplace."

# 24

**WE CLING TO EACH OTHER,** floating in that void in which you are half-asleep and half-awake. Arms and legs entangled as if we are extensions of each other. I feel the soft pressure of Julie's breasts and I want to spill my guts. Fight it, fight it, the voice in me clamors. Why should I? If I can't trust this, what can I trust?

"Something happened after the Justice Department roust."

Her hand strokes the back of my neck.

"I had this address. It's a town house on East Sixty-seventh Street. I went over to check it out and a car drove up. Foley got out of it."

Her hand stops moving. "The one who grilled you?"

"It's a safe house. He was there to meet someone. It went on for about half an hour and then Foley left. I followed this tall, kind of aristocratic guy who came out to the Pierre. He went inside. Bobby Kennedy is staying there. That's some coincidence, isn't it?"

Julie rolls away, takes a cigarette, and lights it. "It's no coincidence. How did you find the safe house?"

"I had Johnny followed."

I see the surprise register on her face. "Johnny?"

"He was there the night before. Whatever is going on, Johnny is locked into it."

Julie props up some pillows and leans back against them. "Davey, you know there's a lot of intermingling of these worlds."

"Worlds?"

"Gangsters and agents. Deals are cut."

I look at her. "Deals?"

Julie touches my face. "Davey, when I took Tommy's case, he told me to do anything that would save him from being deported. The last word I had from the INS was that they would drop the case if Tommy became an informer."

My stomach coils into a tight fist. "Tommy would never have bought that."

"I don't know. He was killed before I could talk to him. But I don't rule out Tommy making a deal if it would have saved him."

"You think Johnny is tied into something Tommy started?"

"I don't know, Davey. It doesn't mean he's an informer. Johnny has got lots of lines out."

"Lines?" I flip back in time to my dressing room after the fight. What was it Johnny said? "I recommended Julie. I met her down in Miami. She's good." I remember the uneasy feeling and how I shoved it aside.

She sees me studying her. "What is it, Davey?"

"Johnny said he met you in Miami. Was that tied in with Tommy?"

She plays with it and then nods her head. "Tommy ran all the gambling for the Syndicate. When we were preparing his case, he flew to Florida to check on some of the casinos there. He invited us down."

" 'Us'?"

"My father and me. Johnny was there with Tommy. We had dinner one night . . . the four of us. At the San Souci."

I had a fight in Miami a few years ago and Johnny booked me into the San Souci. He said, "It's one of our places, Davey. The house will tab everything."

The image of Julie and Johnny stays with me. He's bedded every woman he's ever been with. That's how he looks at women. How many times he has said to me, "Women are ports of call. A guy would be crazy to anchor in one place." Johnny doesn't have business relationships with women.

Julie's hand finds mine. That is how she reassures me. It's not something we have to talk about. But something is working on me. It's my upbringing—the cynical side of growing up with men who fix everything and believe in nothing. It's Johnny saying to me as he taught me the ways of the world, "There are all kinds of hustles, kid. The toughest one to spot is the sincere one. 'Trust me,' she'll be saying right up to the minute she puts the blade in your back."

I look into her eyes, intelligent eyes, bold and filled with desire. And there is not a flicker of anything else. We come together for a long kiss and fall back on the bed.

I feel Julie's hand on my body. "What are you going to do about Johnny?"

"I don't know."

"You're worried about the gun, aren't you?"

"Sure. If Foley finds out I used it on Joe junior, he'll have all the leverage he needs."

Julie lights a cigarette. "Okay, let's do the worst-case scenario. That's how we prepare when we go to court. The Justice Department comes to you and says they have the gun and it matches up. What do they want from you?"

"I already dangled it in front of them. They want somebody on the inside. Somebody to rat for them."

"And if you say no, they'll put out the word that you killed Joe Dante's son. What would you do, Davey?"

"I don't know. One way, I'm a rat; the other way, I'm dead."

"You don't have much of a choice, then."

"Who would I rat on? My father, my brother? If the mob catches me, I'm a dead rat."

Julie looks at me. "The Justice Department wouldn't ask you to rat on your father; they'd ask you to set up Dante or Dino Manfredi."

Now I look sharply at her. "How do you know that?"

"Because I'm an attorney and I'm paid to anticipate what others would do. You'd be a terrific plum for a guy like Foley. The last thing they'd ask you to do is turn against your family. The natural thing for them to do is to ask you to destroy your family's enemies. That's how it works."

"Once you start informing, where does it end?"

"You cut a deal. It's like a contract."

I lean toward her and smell the perfume she uses. What we're talking about is very close to home and upsetting, but I am still aroused. Johnny's laughing words come back to me: "Hey, the man downstairs has no conscience. He's just a hungry, relentless bastard."

"You sound like you know this racket."

"I have to because of my clients. Davey, listen, if something went wrong, I'd help you. I'm not saying it will. I feel bad. I should have let you get rid of the gun right away. But the chance of their matching it up to the killing is remote. If it does happen, then there's always a way to maneuver."

She is watching for my response.

"Everybody is squeezing me, Julie."

"Then squeeze back. What do you owe Joe Dante or Dino Manfredi or Carlo Scola or any of them? They're evil men. They use and discard you. They're out to get your father. You'd be helping him."

"Vince would never forgive me for that. He never wanted me in the Life, but the rules for his son are the same as for him."

"If you saved his life, would he disown you?"

"I don't know what he'd do."

Her eyes search me out. "Davey, who else killed Nails Gordon?"

I blink my eyes. "They all did. They were all there."

"Davey, you have to save yourself. If it comes down to it, that's what you have to do."

"Save myself or put myself up on the cross for an ambitious prick like Foley? He's no different from the rest of them, Julie. They all want to use me."

She is quiet now, her eyes locking in on something. Her hand finds mine. "I'm here for you, whatever happens."

I don't respond.

"What is it, Davey. Is it Johnny?"

"He's got his own game and I can't figure it out. Vince doesn't trust him."

"Vince?"

Watch it, slick Davey. Vince is between you and Johnny. Vince is your way out of this vise. Julie can't know about that.

"Vince and Johnny have had something between them for a long time. It goes back in time, but I don't know what it is."

"Does that mean they're not together on what is happening now?"

I toy with that one for a moment. "I don't know. I'm not in the family business. None of this was supposed to happen."

The feeling in her eyes shows now. Feeling for me. Do you really care, Julie? Do you?

"I'm here," she whispers. "I'm here."

"And here," I whisper back. "And here . . . and here . . . here."

I roll over on top of her and Julie is mouthing *yes* to me over and over. I come alive, pulsing and hard, surging into the wet cocoon that envelops me in velvet, all the while hearing Johnny's voice: "It's the oldest hustle in the world, kid. The broad will be saying 'Trust me' right up to the minute she puts the blade in your back."

You're not hustling me, are you, Julie?

# 25

A SMALL RECEDING ROUND CIRCLE of sunlight falls on the man-made lake that intersects Central Park. It is late afternoon and the lake is empty, the rowboats stacked along the edges of the boathouse. I can see Red standing near a cluster of rocks that overlooks the water, flanked by Freddie Gold and Jake Kramer. Freddie and Jake were waiting for me when I left my building a few hours ago. Sent special delivery over the Williamsburg Bridge by Abe Mortkoff. Freddie is a little guy with a caved-in mouth and squirming eyes. He has a ready smile that says, I know the world and its treachery; I wouldn't have it any other way. Jake is stocky and doesn't say much. He has a ham hock of a face. But there is a fury in his eyes, and when aroused, he will defy anyone. The lips are protruding pieces of thick flesh that droop forward almost to his chin. But only close friends dare call him "Lips."

They came up quietly beside me and Freddie said, "Red says you're being picked up more than a beautiful broad."

"Could be."

"Show me a dago who hasn't got muscles in his head. They're all spaghetti, spumoni heads. No saichel. No offense, Davey, but I hear you're one of the tribe. Welcome home. Say hello to Jake and don't worry about your back no more."

Now they are at my side as I approach Red. It occurs to me that the picture we present is not unlike the face Nails Gordon showed the world. Red shakes his head. "For a minute, I thought I was back thirty years. Let's walk, Davey."

He is wearing an expensive brown overcoat and matching fedora. He catches me watching him and grins. "Max always wanted his boys to look good. 'None of this black shirt with white tie stuff,' he would say. 'We don't cut our whiskey and we dress respectable.' "

Freddie and Jake are behind us as we circle the lake. I fill Red in on the events of the day before, omitting my visit to Vince. Red listens, chewing on the stub of a cigar. I describe the town house on East Sixty-seventh Street and the visit by Brendan Foley after he picked me up. Then I tell him about the guy I followed to the Pierre. He waits until I finish. "What did you do after that?"

"I went home."

"Have any company?"

"A lady."

"The lady I met? What was her name?"

"Julie Alpert."

The trail in front of us leads into a dense area enclosed by trees and shrubs. The lake is no longer visible, nor are the towers of Central Park West. Red stops to relight his cigar. "Ladies don't usually carry pieces."

"She had a bad experience once."

"Oh yeah, what was that?"

I start to circle around it and Red cuts me off. "Listen, Davey, you're both in trouble if this Foley figures out where you used the gun. Give it to me without the relish and pickles."

I tell him about Frankie Tenuto and Julie's mother. Red nods. "She did a gutsy thing that day jumping in the car. If you got rid of the gun that night, neither of you would have to lose any sleep." Red chews on his cigar. "This other guy you tailed to the Pierre, we need to find out who he is."

"So where does that leave us?"

"It leaves us, Davey, with the chance that maybe the government is doing business they don't want to talk about."

The sun is going down and it has suddenly become dark where we are standing.

"What kind of business?"

"Maybe we have to watch Johnny to find out. I could put somebody on him."

The sky is turning a purplish red and the sun is rapidly slipping away. I shake my head. "He'll pick up a tail. Let's leave him to play out his hand."

I hear my words and the command in my tone startles me. I have made the decision not to trust Johnny. In three days, I have gone from being a noncombatant to a killer. It is no longer just Vince's life at stake; it is mine. The first threads of night show in the sky above us. And none of us knows what will happen.

Red has been watching as if somehow attuned to this transformation within me. He signals Freddie and Jake to back off and we are alone in a small clearing. "I spoke to Vince. He wants you to see Scola and give him a message."

"When?"

"Tonight."

"What's the message?"

"Vince is willing to come in and talk, but only at a Council meeting."

It all swirls around me as fast as the oncoming night. A trap laid for Scola. Part of an intricate plan Vince has for revenge, as ominous and dense as the small patch of ground we occupy now. There is a sudden crackling of twigs nearby and a figure appears. Red reaches for his piece. It is the shambling figure of a wino who has stumbled upon us while seeking refuge. Unshaven, wearing a rumpled plaid jacket and old boots. He sees the two of us and Red's menacing hand inside his coat. Behind us, Freddie and Jake close in. The wino's eyes look like they have been pumped open. No words have been exchanged, yet he knows he has come upon men involved in the violent art of survival, men whose stance implies their lethal character. He holds up a hand as if to signify his peaceful intentions and backs off.

The pause has given me a moment's respite, like a clinch after a staggering blow. When Vince saw me yesterday, he knew he would ask me to do this. But he kept it apart from our business with the abbot. That means he is separating those involved in approaching Scola from the way he will strike at his enemies. Red doesn't know about the abbot. Only Vince and I share that solution. And Vince is instructing me how not to let your left hand know what your right is doing.

"Why not you?" I ask.

Red pulls out a fresh cigar. "They can't face you, they can't trace you."

"What am I supposed to get from Scola?"

"Nothing. He'll tell you he has to talk it over with his *compares*."

"It'll make Vince look weak, like he's caving to the pressure."

Red lights the fresh cigar. "That's what he wants them to think."

My head is pounding. It is all closing so fast. Vince is making his move and I'm his point man. Once, this would have been Johnny's role, but Johnny is out. When I see Scola, it will be official. But will they buy it? If I were in their place would I buy it? Vince has lived as a wolf. Are they suddenly to believe he will make the peace? Why send me? Because it will be clear that I am a symbol. Scola has held me hostage all these years. I was the price of the ransom Vince had to pay. By sending me now, he is giving Scola a message: I will make the peace on behalf of my son. It is clever. A plea from an aging don: Joe Dante has just lost his son; I do not want to lose mine.

Red is watching me. "You ready?"

"I'm ready. When do we go?"

"Now. Scola is dispensing benedictions at St. Ignatius. They catch sight of you and they'll put you right up front."

We follow Freddie and Jake through the shrubbery till we find a path. I can see the lights of Fifth Avenue. The city is aglow with night. It is a mild October night. The missile crisis is over; Kennedy has won. The prince has come to our rescue. The world is young forever, except for those of us who grow old quickly playing this game. With a smile on my lips, the sprig leaf of peace in my hand, and malice in my heart, I go to trap Carlo Scola. He will be informed of my Jewish entourage and think that the son of Nails Gordon has returned to his roots. In the end, as in the beginning, it is Vince and a Jew who oppose him. He will smile, pat my arm, and tell me to await good fortune. Then he, like Vince, will make his plans. You have to get him Vince. You'll get one shot at him and that's it. If you miss, he'll kill us both.

# 26

WE STOP ON FIFTH AVENUE while Red makes a call. Traffic buzzes quickly by me, lights flashing incessantly. It is like a message. Do it. Do it fast and get out. No, wait. Then you will look like a scared errand boy. Scola will be gauging you. You represent Vince. If it looks like you're anxious, he may string it out and give Dino's guns more time to look for Vince. Vince took their advantage away by disappearing. He has made them uneasy. You have to maintain the edge.

Red walks toward us, the cigar jutting firmly from his mouth. "Let's go."

Freddie flags down a cab and we pile inside it. Jake sits in the front, next to the driver. I can see Red eyeing me. He is wondering if I can handle it. Can I hold on to my temper? Among big-time racketeers, two characteristics separate them from the pack: their lack of fear and not being intimidated by the moment.

Red shifts the cigar out of his mouth. "What are you going to say?"

It is a little test, and I don't respond immediately. "I'm going to give him the word, Red."

"Isn't that what he does?"

Carlo Scola has been holding audiences in St. Ignatius Church for as long as I can remember. You want your son to go to West Point or open a new bakery, you see Uncle Carlo on Monday night.

We pull in on Canal Street. It is crowded with traffic heading for the Manhattan Bridge. Canal Street divides Little Italy from China-town. It is just a few blocks away from the house I grew up in on Prince Street. There is a war going on, but Scola has a special status in the underworld. He is always the unseen power. He has carefully cultivated this aura over the years. He has made himself seem indis-pensable. "They come from all over the country to see Uncle Carlo," Vince once said to me, his words dipped in acid. Taking him out will have its repercussions.

Red takes my arm. "This is where I get off."

He sees my startled look and explains. "Freddie and Jake will back you up. Then we'll get some dinner. Go get them, boychik."

We walk past Mulberry Street and turn left on Elizabeth Street. The old church with its gray stone facade and single sphere looms in front of us. There is a single line of people formed on its steps. People go in and out. I walk toward them, then stop and wait.

There are several sedans parked in front of the church. Four men get out of the cars and walk toward us. I have never known by name the men who make up Carlo Scola's armor. There have been many of them over the years. The one who is their leader is thin and has tightly chiseled features. His suit is dark and expensive, his hair heavily pom-aded. He surveys me, then Freddie and Jake. "You're on the wrong side of town, Davey."

"I thought I'd teach my friends about Communion."

"We already taught them."

"What's your name, greaseball?"

It is just a parry to see what he's made of. He doesn't respond, but his body seems to shiver and his eyes recoil.

"Anthony."

"Well, Anthony, tell Uncle Carlo I would like to see him." He stares at my backup. "Just me."

He watches us and I know he needs to get in the last word. "No kikes allowed in church, Davey."

He smiles. He has pointed the finger at me.

From behind me, I hear Jake. "Why don't you bless my meat."

Anthony turns back to us. "What'd you say?"

I get in their way. "He said, errand boy, that you should tell Uncle Carlo I want to see him."

Anthony bristles and comes toward me. He starts to say something more, then cuts it off. As he backs off, his finger stabs the air in my direction. I hear Freddie chuckle. "I could cook spaghetti in his pretty hair."

We stand facing the rest of Uncle Carlo's breastplate in the middle of Elizabeth Street and it strikes me that I am re-creating the past.

It takes a few minutes, but then Anthony is coming down the steps toward us. I see the people being herded out of St. Ignatius.

Anthony stands in front of me. "Okay, he'll see you. Just you. And I gotta pat you down."

"I didn't know you cared."

"Fuck you, Davey."

He does the pat-down and then, flanked by three of them, I am led inside. The lights are on full and I can see the sanctuary, which holds the bleeding, crucified Messiah, as I walk up the narrow aisle. Just to the left of Jesus, below a raised altar, seated in a great chair and wearing a camel's hair coat, is Uncle Carlo. In that moment, I recognize the seat he has made for himself. It is a replica of the archbishop's throne in St. Patrick's Cathedral. Carlo Scola sits here in the chair of the cardinal as he dispenses his favors.

He slumps in the wooden chair, his head twisted to one side. As I draw closer, I can see the coat is draped over his shoulder like a king's robe. He seems almost to be sleeping, but that is fake. I can see movement behind the curtains of the sanctuary. He is never unprotected. I reach the foot of the sanctuary and he focuses on me with those child-like milky eyes. He dismisses the three triggermen behind me with a wave of his hand. I stand before and below him. This is the way our audience will be conducted.

I search for the sense of surprise in his eyes. Does he think me arrogant for coming this way? How much does he fear Vince? How hungry is he for a truce?

He straightens himself now, sitting up in the chair. "They tell me you come with a coterie of Jews and your manner is arrogant."

"I did not come to be arrogant, but I was challenged."

He regards me with a cold look on his ancient face. "I would have seen you had you come alone. You have nothing to fear from your uncle Carlo."

I would like to let that one go, but I cannot. "But there are others I have to protect myself from."

"From who?"

"From Dino, from Joe Dante."

"But they are your father's friends. He has forced them to the mattress."

He is doing this to provoke me, to see how much of a hotblood I am. To learn how much of a threat I am. He has his own version of what happened during the shoot-out on the Palisades Parkway. I can play the same game.

"Tommy is dead. My father has disappeared. We're the ones driven to the mattress."

"But you come here with Jews. They are not our friends. We dealt with them in the past."

He has driven the knife in up to the hilt. He is trying to bait me. How much do I know? How vengeful am I?

"I wasn't a part of that. That happened before I was born. But I can't be unprotected."

"But them," he says, dipping his head in the direction of outside, where Freddie and Jake remain, "they have been our enemies always. If you travel with them, you will suffer what they suffer."

The threat is clear, as is the sharp knife point he keeps jabbing me with. The hot answer is there on the tip of my tongue, but I suppress it.

He leans forward, fixing me with those saucer eyes. "Is it that you have gone back to them? Those who know and respect me do not come this way. Your brother cannot know of this. He would approach me with respect. Your father knows our rules. How have you come to this?"

He wants me to genuflect and kiss the ring. This is a great show to take my measure. If I tell him to fuck off, then he has me. If I kiss the ring, he will hold me in contempt. I have to get his attention. "This is a time of war, Uncle Carlo, and I do what I must for my family. I have been picked up twice, and Tommy is dead. In times of war, you need men you can trust to protect your back. These mercenaries are loyal to me. When the peace is made, they will be sent away."

Scola closes his eyes to underscore his indifference to me. I stare at this man who arranged for the killing of my father and of Vince's brother and in doing so turned them against each other. He is small, and bent. His hair is white and his skin wrinkled. The charcoal suit he wears is inexpensive, as is the red turtleneck sweater. Put together, he seems like just another old man whose clothes do not fit him well. Only the soft leather shoes on his feet clash with the aura of simplicity he attempts to present.

The eyes snap open. "Why have you come?"

More pitter-patter. "Johnny told me about the date of the rematch. It's too soon. My cuts will barely heal. Simpson is a great fighter. I need a few more months."

"How many?"

"Five months. Two for healing and three months to train."

He sits back again and rubs his chin. "Can you beat him?"

What is he after? "I can beat him."

A funny little smile engages his mouth. "He is younger than you are and he hits harder. He beat you badly the last time."

"This time, I will be motivated."

"But so will he. I am told he will fight for the welterweight championship. He will hold two titles. And he is stronger than you."

"Stronger isn't always smarter or better."

"Smart isn't fighting a younger opponent when you are not well trained."

So you have done your homework, Uncle Carlo.

"I made a mistake. I have learned from it."

He shrugs. "What can I do? He is the champion now and he makes the terms."

He turns away, but I bore in after him. "You can do great things, Uncle Carlo. Greater than any man in these matters."

He turns back to me and rewards me with a superficial smile. "So you think, but I am a simple man."

"Simplicity is looked upon as a virtue by those who know."

The smile broadens, but now there is a cutting edge to it. "So some people believe. But this is a great thing to accomplish, and Simpson is as ambitious as you are. I cannot ask it of him."

"If I were given this, I would not be ungrateful, nor would my father."

He raises his eyes. "Your father . . . but you say he has disappeared."

"Only to protect himself."

"Some think him dead. How can you be sure? Do you speak for him?"

God, he has anticipated me. "My father was greatly shocked at the death of his good friend Tommy Costanza. He thought his life was in great danger. He had to go into hiding."

Scola nods. "So then, he is well?"

"He is well and wishes to make the peace."

Again the eyes close momentarily while the wheels spin. "But why does he do this? He could have come to me. I have always been his friend and adviser. Does he not trust me?"

"I think he was greatly shocked when Tommy died. Perhaps he needed time to think."

"Bene, he has his time to think. Does he think differently about the drugs now? Will he no longer oppose the will of the majority? After all, this is a business we are in. It is selfish and arrogant to stop your friends from making money. We are not men of virtue; we are in business."

I give him his victory by not answering him. He rubs his pointed chin and picks hurriedly at something in the large angular nose. "Why have you come here?"

"Vince wishes to make the peace. He wants a meeting of the Council. The Rossi family does not want any further bloodshed."

"So you speak for him. What of your brother?"

"This is the way it is. I have come to ask for this on behalf of my father."

He rubs his hands together and draws the coat around him. Your blood is thin, isn't it, old man? Time is running out for you. With all your power, you can't stop that, can you?

"Are you his consigliere, then?"

"Just his son, come to ask for this meeting. It is our show of good faith. The Rossi family asks for this meeting, and as a show of good faith on the Council's part, we ask for special consideration in changing the date of my fight."

The small smile is back on his lips. "Worthy of a skilled consigliere. Is this a trade you propose? One favor for another?"

I answer in Italian. "Una mano lava l'altra."

He nods his head in approval. "Bene . . . bene. Vince has taught you well. But of course it is not up to me. There are the others, and I must put it to them."

"I understand."

He studies me. "You have shown wisdom beyond your years. I am unhappy to see there is friction between you and Johnny. He has worked for all of us and we must find a way to end this disagreement. But perhaps now that your fighting career is over, you will come into our profession. You show a bent for it."

He is wondering if now there will be another Rossi to contend with in years to come. That will be on the table when he speaks with the others. "I am trying to help my father; that is all. My career is not ended yet."

He leans forward, the words hurled at me in the searing voice I remember from childhood. "Your father has cost us all a great deal of money over the years. He has forced our hand. Do you understand this? It is Vince who must make the peace. We will listen to him. We have all been together for years, so of course we will listen. But you cannot beat the nigger in two months or five. Do you understand what I am telling you? You will bleed and the fight will be stopped and you will suffer an honorable defeat. Sandy Simpson will win the fight and the welterweight title after that. You will be taken care of. It is all arranged. Do you understand what I am telling you?"

"Joe Fletcher is going to tank his title and you'll pay him off."

"Bene . . . bene. And then in less than a year, Simpson will fight for the middleweight title. It will be the biggest fight in years. A chance for Simpson to hold all three titles if he beats Ray Ramirez. In Yankee Stadium, before seventy-five thousand people." He sinks back into the archbishop's throne to contemplate his grand design.

"Have you decided who will win that fight yet?"

The little head is tilted toward me, the malevolent face thrust into mine. "You are Nails's son after all. You come with your friends and your tricks and try to take something that is not yours. And you must pay the price. You will not have your championship. Tell Vince that."

The church seems very small now. My head and heart are pounding with fury. Vince may be welcomed back by the Council, but I can't have my title back. I look up at Scola and the words to match my fury are there. As easy and natural as letting fly with a left hook, but I do not. It would be giving something away, something I will need later on.

Scola's eyes search me out. He is waiting for me to show him I am his undying enemy.

"As you wish," I answer.

He nods and waves me off. The gesture of fatal arrogance in a man who thinks he can never fall. I start to go, then hear his voice and turn back. "Tu sei un Ebreo, ma sei più, furbo di tuo padre." In the end, you are a Jew. But you are smarter than your father.

We stay that way for a long beat, exchanging a stare of mutual understanding. Then it is over and I am walking down the aisle. If Vince doesn't survive Scola, and I do, then he will come for me. He feared Nails and Vince and now he fears me. It is all coming. Let it. Because I know how to kill you, Scola. The edge is mine.

# 27

THE CAB LETS US OFF on Fifth Avenue. We walk to an Oldsmobile sitting next to the curb. The door opens and a man steps out. Red calls to him and the two of them go off to the side for a discussion. The man is of medium height, wearing a hat and a scarf, although the night is mild. He uses his hands a lot as he speaks. Red does most of the listening. He nods, whispers something, and the conversation ends. Red opens the car door and gestures for me to get in while Freddie and Jake join the man who met us. We are seated in the front of the car, facing the Pierre Hotel. He inclines his head in its direction. "We are waiting for a party to come out. Could be awhile, so let's talk."

I remember the tall man I tailed here last night. "Is this about Johnny?"

Red rolls down the window and throws his cigar out. "It's about you, Davey. The gun the Justice Department took off you. What do you remember about it?"

"It shoots. I killed Joe junior with it."

Red takes out a package of gum, peels off a stick, and offers me a piece. I decline. He unwraps it and wedges it into to his mouth. The pungent aroma of Juicy Fruit comes to me. "It's an eight-shot thirty-two semiautomatic with a magazine you slam into it. When it runs out, you just ram another mag inside it. Fancy artillery. How come the lady carries it?"

"I told you once. She and her mother got worked over by a professional named Frankie Tenuto, who the mother was involved with. It was very traumatic."

"I can see it was. So the lady gets herself a chrome semiautomatic pistol, silver-plated and pearl-handled. You know what I'm saying, Davey? It's a Browning, a pro's gun, you understand?"

I understand, but I don't want to understand.

"I mean a cop, Davey, he runs out of bullets, he has to push his bullets into the barrel one at a time. But not this lady; she just rams another magazine home into her Browning thirty-two and she's in business. And now this silver-plated, pearl-handled beauty with your prints all over it is in the hands of the Justice Department. How long before those guys figure out you used it?"

I roll down the window to get some air.

"Think about it, Davey. That gun should have been dumped the same night you used it. You said you would, but somehow it stuck around long enough for you to get picked up with it in your pocket."

"You're saying she set me up."

"I'm saying she's a Justice agent; that's why she packs that kind of artillery."

I stick my head out the window to fight the queasy feeling. Scenes from the last forty-eight hours unreel inside my head. Just two days ago, Joe junior picked me up. Bang-bang, the next day I get conveniently rousted by Brendan Foley while carrying the gun after leaving Julie. And last night she offers to handle it for me if anything comes up.

"The Justice Department got the hook in your mouth and they'll reel you in."

"What will they offer me?"

"The big squeeze. Fink for us and we'll let you go on living. Otherwise, we tell Joe Dante who killed his son."

I open the car door. The street feels like it's coming up to meet me.

Red's hand is on my shoulder. "Here, chew this gum; it'll make you feel better. Take it."

He watches while I unwrap it and jam it into my mouth. I look at Red and then at the hotel. "Why did you bring me here?"

His hand goes to my arm and he squeezes my biceps. "Because she's up there now with him."

I feel the pressure of his hand as it tightens. It hurts. It all hurts. "Up there with who?"

"With her boss."

The words echo through me. Boss, boss. Brendan Foley. Foley, last night, me following the tall man to the Pierre, where Bobby Kennedy was staying. "Kennedy. She's up there with Bobby Kennedy?"

Red's hand is still there gripping me. "She went in while we were having dinner. You want to wait to see for yourself?"

I look toward the classy hotel with the gray facade and white awning. I gaze up at the lights in the rooms. Which room are they in? Are they talking about me? The light from the room seems to be in my head now, bursting to get out.

Red talks softly in my ear, the ever-present hand still supporting me. "But we got this setup made, Davey. We couldn't see it the last time until it was too late, and then we had to take our lumps."

I whirl toward him. "What'd do you mean, 'too late'? Are you saying Nails knew?"

"Are you ready to hear it?"

I close the car door and sink back on the seat. "I'm ready."

"Nails came in late. It was past one. The rest of them were playing cards next door. I didn't feel like playing and I was lying on the bed. My gun was under the pillow. Nails had told us to come to the Rodman Arms and to wait while he tried to make a deal." Red looks past me toward Central Park, his eyes focused on a vision only he can see.

*There was a soft rap on the door; it slowly opened and then Nails Gordon let himself inside the room. Red Miller relaxed his grip on the gun he was holding and fell back on the bed. Nails raised his eyebrows and Red gestured in the direction of the next room. "They're playing poker."*

*Nails took off his jacket and draped it over a chair. "Maybe I'll sit in on a few hands."*

*"How about the one we're holding?"*

*Nails reached inside his jacket, fished out a cigarette and lighted it with a kitchen match he struck with his thumb. His dark hair was disheveled and his eyes looked kind of dreamy. It was not an expression*

Red had seen before. He was used to the dark energy that emanated from Nails. The sense of command always so apparent wasn't there. Red felt distinctly uneasy. He spoke now to calm himself as much as anything else.

"Any bargains out there?"

Nails grabbed a pillow and, propping it against the couch, fell back. "Everybody's selling shmattes."

"Then maybe we should go to the country."

Nails watched the smoke from his cigarette drift out the open window. His eyes flickered around the room, taking in the simple decor. Red lay on the double bed in the center of the room. There was a smaller single to its left. In the corner of the room was a desk with a small lamp on it. The chair next to it had been pulled away, as if somebody had gotten up in a hurry. A solitaire hand was laid out on the top of desk. There were three windows, all with drawn shades. Over them were brown curtains, which had been pulled back. A light brown rug covered the floor. There were cigarette burns along the edge facing the door.

"If nothing comes in by the morning, we'll leave after breakfast."

Red slid the gun back under the pillow. "We should have gone this afternoon, Max. This is like being in a closet. We could still do it. Get hold of Lazar and tell him we're coming. Who would look for us in Rhinebeck?"

A playful smile tugged at the corners of Nails's mouth. "They wouldn't have to. Somebody will go for a paper and the whole town would inform on us."

"We'll stay on the farm and drink milk."

"Then the milkman will sell us."

"Max, how long can we stay on Madison Avenue?"

"I got something working. I made somebody a proposition."

"Who's the messenger?"

"The Wax Man."

"Max, every dago in town is looking for us. Let me call Lazar and then I'll get Petey over at the garage and we'll be out of the city in half an hour."

"And then what? I can't make a deal from Rhinebeck."

"What deals, Max? The dagos are holding a royal flush. We're left holding the marker for the hit on Nick Rossi. We brought the heat down on the Syndicate. The fucking Pope couldn't get us off now. We should go right at them."

Nails reached for a ring of smoke and watched it dissolve between his fingers. "Leave the dagos alone and they'll kill each other off. Isn't that the way it's always been? There's always one dago you can turn against the others. And he'll fuck them because he thinks they've always been out to fuck him. That's our chance. We can't shoot our way out of this. I made someone an offer. If I don't have an answer by the morning, we'll go to Rhinebeck."

Red tipped the window further open. He was sitting in his undershirt, a ring of sweat around his throat, his face flushed, beads of water resting on his forehead.

Nails unbuttoned his shirt. A thick mat of wet hair showed itself. "The country would be nice."

"Remember that girl Lazar had working the cows? Rachel. Could I milk her."

"We'll bring Lazar bad luck. Our time is over, Red. I got nothing to pass on. You know what we're good for? We're good for tomorrow's papers—for them to read on the train to Westchester and then toss away at some railroad station and go home to the wife and kids."

Red looked up at Nails Gordon, who had risen from the couch. "Do you want a wife and kids?"

"I want something to leave someone. I'm Nails Gordon, with my pictures in all the papers, but I'll be forgotten in a year. Look at the East Side, Red. The people are moving out. To the Bronx and to the Heights. How many will remember me? Nails, he was a tough guy, a regular hero."

"That's for them, Max. We never had a shot at that."

Red poured some whiskey into a paper cup and handed it to Nails. He downed it and gave it back for a refill. "They used me, Red."

"The dagos?"

"No, I mean the Hebes... the ones who will get away from this." He downed the refill and threw away the cup. "Lead your people out of the ghetto and then take the rap for them. The hell with it. Listen, someone's coming to pick me up for a meeting. If you don't hear from me in a few hours, then something's wrong. Go up to Rhinebeck, lay low. Any trouble, there's a package with Lossy Beiderman. He's got it in his office. Tell *him I sent you. He'll be expecting you. There's instructions inside. You do that for me, Red. You do it."*

*They stood facing each other, knowing what all the words meant and knowing about all the words they couldn't say. A tantalizing wisp of wind blew through the open window, carrying with it a hint of a fresh breeze. A little night wind on a June night on Madison Avenue in the year 1933.*

Red's voice has dropped now, soft as that of a seer. "I remember thinking, Jesus, he wants out. He wants out. The great Nails Gordon has had his kishkehs full of it. For a few minutes, he let me see his heart, until Bo came in and said the guys wanted some girls. Max said it was okay. He went downstairs and called Polly Adler to send some girls over, and then he went out for a while. He came in around four, when we were throwing the girls out. I don't know where he went, but he was very quiet. I remember he was lying on the bed, smoking a cigarette, remembering World War One. He joined the army to beat a murder rap, won some medals, and came back a hero. He was talking about Paris and the girls of Montparnasse. He said the hookers there really knew about making love. There was a girl named Michelle, beautiful. You couldn't believe she was a whore. Michelle of Montparnasse. He was smiling as I walked out of the room. Twenty minutes later, the dagos came through the doors blasting. My gun was on the table. I hit somebody before they gutted me full of slugs."

I turn my face toward Central Park, watching the swaying trees. "What happened to the package?"

"I never found out. I was in the hospital a long time and I snuck out of there in the middle of the night."

"Who's Lossy Beiderman?"

"An old theater producer. He's long buried."

You wanted out, Nails. In the end, you felt bitter, alone, and used. Trapped by the image of yourself as the tough guy, the fearless savior of your gang and your people. So how could you leave me to Vince? All roads led me to where I am tonight, right back in it. What was it you told Red? "We can't shoot our way out of this." You made someone an offer, Nails. Who?

"Davey."

I turn, and there is Julie coming out of the Pierre. I feel myself tighten and Red's hand is on my shoulder. "Let her go, Davey. Don't see her tonight. You have to keep the edge. If you see her, you'll give it away. You'll go to her place or she'll come to yours and there will be all those hot words and then the other hot stuff, and tomorrow you'll be cooking in the stew. You have to figure out a way for yourself. All things end. Leave it alone tonight. You have to plan what you're going to do when the Justice Department comes for you."

"What would you do, Red?"

"Play them and play her. Are you good enough for that?"

I watch Julie walking uptown on Fifth Avenue. Watch the nice legs and the graceful sway of her body. The body that wraps around me in the night. I watch till she is out of sight. Only then does Red's hand release me.

"C'mon," he says. "We'll get ourselves a drink." He calls to Jake and Freddie. We cruise over to Lexington Avenue, looking for a bar. At the corner of Fifty-third Street, we pull in front of a place with blinking neon called Goldie's. Red leans over and says, "They have the best whiskey in town here. Goldie's husband used to meet us on the beach on Long Island with a lantern during Prohibition. Harry Tendler. Can you imagine they tried to outlaw whiskey in this country? The smart goyim made a fortune; the dumb ones drank up their money."

Many drinks later, I lie in bed thinking about how cute Red is. He wouldn't let me go home in case Julie was waiting for me. The trouble is, she is here right now. I reach for the phone each time it rings. Each time, I don't answer. It rings till very late in the night.

# 28

IN THE MIDDLE of a tossing dream pregnant with betrayal and death, the phone rings. I fall away from a stabbing image and hold the receiver as if it is a lifeline. Carrying me back to consciousness from a nether world of pictures and faces I suddenly cannot recall. I hear Johnny's voice.

"You alone?"

"Yeah."

"All right, listen. We're signing for the Simpson fight tonight. Six o'clock at Funicelli's."

I struggle to comprehend. "What's the rush?"

"That's the way they want it. You're getting a split on the gate. But they won't budge on the date."

"When is it?"

"December twenty-first . . . a Christmas special."

Johnny hears my groan. "You said to get you the fight."

I fall back on the pillow, still reeling from dreams I can no longer remember.

"Go back to sleep. Six o'clock. Funicelli's. Tell your Hebe bodyguards to get you there on time."

He clicks off. I lie there with the phone in my hand until it signals it is out of order and then hang up. I toss the sheets off me and walk to the bathroom. I urinate and feel the nudging approval of my still-sore kidneys. Then I move to the sink and study my face in the mirror. The swelling has gone down, but there is still discoloration around my cheekbones. I have a sullen look. My beard is heavy and dark. I look like I'm posing for a mug shot you see on the felon posters. The wanted and hunted, their eyes numb and detached from a repetitious life in which there are no surprises, only pain. Faces molded by the knowledge that you can never make it right. The designated heirs of some lifelong curse. Is that me? No. I have to know it all. That is my only chance. Don't trust anybody. Just find out. Find out and be free.

Minutes after I get out of the shower, Freddie and Jake arrive with coffee, bagels and bialys smothered in cream cheese. The banter is sharp and Freddie is expert at sticking the needle into Jake, who has long since given up trying to trade repartee shot for shot with little Freddie. After a couple of exchanges, he lapses into silences punctuated by grumbling snorts and mumbled replies, "Yeah, yeah, I know."

I give Freddie the high-sign and he dispatches Jake to watch the street. We are seated in my living room, separated by a thin glass coffee table on which the remains of our breakfast are strewn.

"Freddie, I want to play a hunch and tail somebody who is very good at spotting it."

"I get you, Mendel. You want us to be inconspicuous. That's the word they use in the movies, ain't it?"

"That's it."

"What's the setup?"

"It's a government safe house. Johnny is going to turn up there."

Freddie's eyes widen. "I'll get us a cab. Just give me the address."

The phone rings. I get it on the third ring. It is Julie. "Are you all right?"

I put a clamp on the angry feelings. "I'm okay. I slept late."

"I called you until late."

"I had to go down to Philadelphia on business."

"I missed you."

"Yeah, me, too."

"What's wrong, Davey?"

"There are some people here. It's okay."

"I'm free for lunch. I want to talk to you about something."

I run the script in slow motion. We meet for lunch and the boys in the blue suits with blue shirts and ties pick me up. "Lunch is no good—there are some things I have to take care of. I'll call you this afternoon. Maybe tonight for dinner."

To my surprise, there is no quick acceptance. "I have something on with a client tonight. Sort of business on the town."

"Maybe we can do a nightcap."

"It might be late."

There is a short, uncomfortable pause. "Davey, what's happening?"

Funny, I wanted to ask you that. "Just stuff. I'll call you later."

"I'll hold you in contempt if you don't. You know what that means, don't you?"

"What?"

"No nooky, cookie."

"We can't have that."

"No, we can't, Davey. I'll speak to you later."

I hang up. If this were a movie, I know the camera would move in for a close shot on Julie as she looks at the phone, knowing something is wrong. How am I going to play it with her?

Freddie moves past me and starts working the phone. It takes him exactly twenty-seven minutes, with three calls coming in from a man named Lutsky, who has a voice like a braying donkey.

When the cab is lined up, Freddie pounds the wall in mock delight. "Fuckin' Lutz, he can fix anything. All right, what we got is a cab on loan from Philly Tessler. Anything goes wrong, we gotta cover damages on his cab and give him three hundred bucks."

"And if nothing goes wrong?"

"We give him a hundred and fifty, plus whatever's on the meter. And fifty for Lutz. He's the broker on the deal. What are you looking at, Davey? I got you basement prices."

I retreat into the bedroom to finish dressing. The call from Johnny comes while I'm knotting my tie.

"Davey, something's come up. I have to go down to Miami Beach."

"Bad time to freshen up your suntan."

"It's not about a tan."

"When you going out?"

"Late afternoon. From LaGuardia."

"I'll come out and see you off."

"You won't make it back to Funicelli's in time."

"You want me to sign without you there?"

"Hey, my lawyers have been all through the contract. It's sanitary. You make some small talk with Matty Clark, drink some espresso, and beat it. Bring the little Jewish navy."

"What's that?"

"That's some ancient history out of Detroit. Ask Red."

Nothing gets past slick Johnny.

"How long, Johnny?"

"A day."

"What about the home front?"

"I left Dago Pete in charge. I'm just a dime away. It's gotta be done, Davey."

"What about Vince?"

"I haven't heard a peep. You?"

I say the word without the hesitation that would give me away. "No. We gotta talk, Johnny."

"I'll be back tomorrow night. Let's have dinner at Chandler's. Seven-thirty."

Some instinct I cannot identify pulls at me. "Where are you staying?"

"The San Souci. I gotta go, kid. Just stay cool, keep off the street, and get a good fountain pen."

"Have a good flight."

I hang up and feel my face twist into a frown. Something's off, but I'm not sure what. For Johnny to go out of town means something big. But the fort can't go unattended. People have taken to the mattress.

# 29

FREDDIE AND I are slouched down in the back of the yellow cab, eating tuna fish sandwiches and drinking hot coffee. Jake is at the wheel, working on a cigar.

The door to the brownstone opens and a tall man, dapper in a well-cut gray suit, steps out into the bright sunlight. "That's him."

Freddie whistles and nudges Jake, who already has the ignition on. "Get a load of the fashion plate."

It is the man I followed to the Pierre. There is something aristocratic in his stance and manner and a touch of arrogance in the way he poses on the step, the sunlight glistening on his light brown hair. He looks like he's being featured on the cover of *Gentlemen's Quarterly*. He slips on sunglasses, completing his ensemble, as he comes down the steps and looks east.

"He wants a cab," Freddie says. "Maybe we should offer him a ride."

His arm goes up as he sees one. The cab pulls up and the mystery man disappears inside. The cab starts up again and Jake pulls out. We follow him west until the cab turns and heads uptown.

"So where's our lord of the manor taking us?" Jake rumbles through teeth clenched around his cigar.

We blend into traffic behind the cab as it makes its way through the Eighties and then the Nineties. At 112th Street, the cab turns the corner and Jake slows down before doing the same. We make the turn in time to see the cab swing around on Second Avenue.

"Don't lose him," I say to Jake.

I can see Jake's heavy features in the rearview mirror. Some instinct guides him into slowing the car. We come around the corner as our quarry is getting out of the cab. "El Barrio, baby," Freddie croons in a soft voice. We drive past and Jake again slows down for me to take a look. The tall man is heading across the street.

Freddie snaps his fingers. "There's a restaurant there. Let me out here and I'll watch it. Jake, come back around the block and pull in across the street."

Freddie jumps out and Jake cruises around the block and pulls in when we reach Second Avenue again. He stops but leaves the engine idling. The restaurant across from us has the name Hector's emblazoned in yellow. Second Avenue is run-down here—small tenement houses, grocery stores, and cheap restaurants.

There is no sign of Freddie, and then he appears and slides into the back. "Bodega heaven."

"What's that?"

"That's where you go when you get your piece of the good life in the Barrio. El Arrogancia is inside at a table in the back. You think maybe he came here on a tour?"

"Let's see who else turns up."

We sit idling for ten minutes before the birdie shows up. The birdie comes with another birdie and they step out of a big brown Caddy. The birdies are brother Johnny and a small man in a dark coat.

Freddie whistles.

Johnny is wearing a light tan raincoat with the collar turned up. He looks both right and left. A cigarette is wedged into the corner of his mouth. Damn, what the hell is going down here?

The small man next to him has thick glasses, dark hair, and a mustache. He seems both myopic and sinister.

"Major greaseball," Freddie announces after close inspection.

Johnny looks edgy. Why is he here? What's the play? Could this have something to do with Johnny's Miami trip? Miami is just ninety miles from Cuba. What's Johnny doing meeting with a sinister-looking greaseball and the tall lord of the manor who works for the feds?

Sometimes you fight a guy and he fakes the right all night and saps you with his left. And sometimes a guy comes at you with a right and that's all he has. There's nothing tricky here. I just can't read it.

Freddie's eyes look bigger. "So what do you think, Mendel?"

My eyes are riveted on Johnny as he goes inside Hector's with the little man. Freddie whistles. "They come a long way to eat spic pot roast."

"It's called ropa vieja," Jake informs us.

Freddie's eyes are fixed are Johnny. "It's called give a man enough ropa and he'll hang himself."

All right, Johnny, we'll put this on hold till you come back, and then we'll settle it. But I'll tell you this, Johnny, you better have a good story to tell.

# 30

NIGHT HAS FALLEN as I walk across Sheridan Square and head toward Sixth Avenue. Freddie and Jake cruise behind me in a car. There is a light chill in the air. October is turning into November. It is the season I have always loved best, the time when we pass from Indian summer into the crisp, cold days of late autumn. The corduroy jacket and turtleneck I slipped into at home hug my body. It is the night before Halloween and the windows of West Fourth Street are bright with pumpkins, witches, and masks. Some boys in costume and painted faces skip quickly by me. Across the street, two young girls in elaborate costumes approach a couple, loudly proclaiming, "Trick or treat."

I reach Sixth Avenue and veer toward Bleecker Street, walking past the basketball courts, which are packed in the afternoon with leaping, agile bodies darting and driving to the hoop. As I come around the corner of Bleecker Street, I see the neon lights of Funicelli's in the middle of the block. A couple of big Caddys sit across the street from it. Waiting at the entrance to the restaurant is Anthony. A cigarette dangles from his mouth and he leans indolently against the building, filing his nails. He sees me and the file stops its work. He flicks the cigarette away and steps toward me for the frisk.

Anthony does a quick but thorough job. He must bathe in the cologne he uses. He steps back, a smirking smile painting his face, and jerks his thumb in the direction of inside. "The champ's waiting."

His emphasis on the word *champ* is meant to express his lack of respect for me. The smile abruptly fades as Freddie and Jake pull up in front of the restaurant. Freddie leans out and calls to him. "Hey, baby, how are you?"

Anthony stiffens.

"He's smelling very sweet," I call to Freddie as I walk past Anthony and into the restaurant.

Funicelli's is a big old-fashioned trattoria with booths lining both sides of the wall. A steaming espresso bar is to the right of the check-room as you enter. Large Renaissance-style paintings cover the walls. Two Cupid-faced angels depicted over curtains cover the entrance to the back room. A couple of large hoods stand next to it. I spot a tall coffee-colored man joking with the hatcheck girl. She is blushing and he is smiling. He leans toward her now, turning that angular body in her direction. He is putting the make on her and she is both eager and disconcerted by his approach. I walk toward them.

"Hello, champ."

Sandy Simpson whirls with amazing catlike grace, making it look like a choreographed dance step. His brown eyes leap with exultation when he recognizes me. He doesn't think I can beat him. This is a champion who is looking at being a triple titleholder. The last man to do it was Henry Armstrong.

"Say, Davey, I didn't think you was coming."

"Oh, I wouldn't have missed it."

Sandy has about four inches on me and he emphasizes them now. "You should have stayed home, because you ain't never getting that title back."

"Well, I'm still planning on being there."

Sandy looks at the hatcheck girl, who is somewhat goggle-eyed at all this. He points to me. "I'm going to beat him bad. What you think of that?"

She looks over at me to see how I am taking this. She has long brown hair and limpid brown eyes. She has come from far away Hicks-ville to see the stars of Broadway. This may be as good as it gets.

Sandy is full of himself. Why not? He muscled me all over the ring and left me bloody and helpless. He watched Kid Bassett put me down six times. I look like pork chops to Sandy Simpson.

"We're even, Sandy, so let's see what happens."

"Shit," he says, pronouncing it like he was saying *sheet.* "I still owe you for that time in the Golden Gloves. I wasn't nothing but a little boy then."

"You were full of shit then also."

His eyes tighten down and the gleam in them is replaced by something hard. "I'm going to beat you worse this time. No pity on you, Davey."

We have squared off and there is less than an inch between us. The eyes of the hatcheck girl are prominent and frozen.

"Hey guys, save it for December twenty-first." Matty Clark, Sandy's manager, edges between us. He is a short, barrel-chested man with a thick crop of white hair. "C'mon, you don't want to give it away free. How's it going, Davey?"

Clark turns toward me and regards my face. "The Kid hit you with some shots; I never saw you take punches like that."

"I was training my face."

He taps my legs. "What about them?"

That's his way of telling me I'm shot. They are both supremely confident. That's the way of the fight game. One day nobody can touch you and the next it's poor Davey.

"We could do it tonight, Matty, then none of my cuts will heal." The left hook has caught him flush and Clark looks down at the floor. "I'll see you December twenty-first, Sandy."

I make my way toward the back of the room, where two gorillas stand guard. They step back and make room for me. A long table has been drawn to the center of the room. Scola sits alone at its head. He is wearing a camel's hair coat and a green shirt open at the neck. A bottle of red wine and a half-filled glass rest on the table. An unfinished plate of antipasto is before him. He spears a piece of cheese with his fork and beckons me with his hand, pointing to the chair across from him at the far end of the table. A thick envelope lies on the table. I slide into the seat.

Scola finishes his cheese and picks up the glass. "Your brother and I went over the contract. Everything is arranged."

"What about a return match if I win?"

A thin smile paints his mouth. "You are getting forty percent of the gate. You already have won."

He takes an envelope from his pocket and pushes it across the table. "There is a hundred thousand dollars in it."

It sits there in front of me. "What's that for?"

"So you will lose in an early round."

It's smart business. He expects Vince to step down. Someday he may have to deal with me. What's my price?

I hold the envelope in my hand and feel the wad inside. "What about Vince?"

Scola eats a piece of provolone and washes it down with wine. Finished, he wipes his hand across his mouth. "The Council has agreed to meet with him. The heads of the Five Families will sit down together. He comes with one man of his choice, as we all will."

"Who guarantees his safety?"

"The Council does."

"The Council?"

He looks at me mildly. "Frank Bruno has long been a close friend to Vince. He personally guarantees Vince's safety, as he does for all of us. Tomorrow night at nine o'clock in the Villa Capri."

Scola unwraps a cigar. "The doctors say I mustn't smoke, but I do it anyway. I haven't much time, you see."

"My brother is away."

"We cannot wait for Johnny to return. Tell Vince that Dino will not wait. Joe Dante has lost a son. This must be handled now, before something else happens."

My fingers press against the wad of money. I can feel the wetness underneath my arms. I don't like the idea of Vince walking in there without Johnny. I don't like Johnny disappearing on the night before this is to take place. I remind myself that Vince has a plan. I have to see the abbot. Soon.

"Sign the contract."

He slides a pen across the table. I look at this wizened old man, throw the envelope back to him, and pick up the pen.

Scola looks first at the envelope and then at me. "You will take a beating."

I go through the pages of the contract until I find the line with my name on it. I sign just above it. He looks up at me, the cigar in his mouth.

"You are stubborn."

"Like my father."

"Vince is older than you. He is being reasonable. We will work something out and put this behind us. Tell him that. Tell him that the time for opposing the drugs is over. The younger men must have their chance."

He picks up the envelope and holds it out to me. "We all help each other. You may last for more than four rounds, but you cannot win."

"If it's such a sure thing, you have nothing to worry about."

"This money could be placed on the exact round you will lose the fight. In the right place, this could win you half a million dollars."

I look at this malignant creature I could crush with one blow. I warn myself that he is testing me. With each canny enticement, he learns something he can use in the future. I must do the same.

"I'll give Vince the message."

"By tomorrow at noon, bring me Vince's answer."

"And if he says no?"

"Then, like his son, he will take a beating."

"If Vince agrees to come in, I'll call you."

Our eyes meet. My message is clear. I don't run errands and I don't kiss the ring, Uncle Carlo. I break our clinch and leave the room, brushing past the two goons, and then I am out in the street. I signal for Freddie to follow me in the car as I walk east on Bleecker Street. The Council meets tomorrow night and Vince has to activate whatever he has in mind. I have to call the abbot, but not before Sister Mary contacts me. It better be soon.

I see a phone up ahead and fish in my pocket for change. I dial the number and ask for Red. He comes on quickly. "It's tomorrow night at nine o'clock at the Villa Capri in Hoboken. Frank Bruno owns it. He guarantees Vince's safety. They want an answer by noon tomorrow. He can bring one man with him. The same as the rest."

"What else?"

"Tell Vince that Johnny flew to Miami."

"Don't do anything romantic tonight, Davey. Go home and wait."

He clicks off and I am left standing on the corner, wondering which way to go. A car pulls up and Freddie leans out. "Get in, Mendel. Let's get a nosh."

I look back in the direction of Funicelli's. I am troubled by what happened, but I can't isolate why. Vince is coming in to meet with Scola, Dino, and Joe Dante. What's his plan? Where's the abbot? There isn't much time. It's almost Halloween, the night when all manner of creatures change their shapes.

# 31

**DRESSED IN A ROBE,** a beer in my hand, I stand at the window, watching the lights of the city glistening with hard brilliance, realizing how much I want her. Play it cool. Don't let on. Grudge-fuck her. Anything to get that lush body beneath you. Anything to part those legs and move inside the velvet. Anything to hear those silky cries as her legs tighten around you. Anything. The movie in my head drives me to the phone for the third time. Endless dial tones and no pickup. I have to see her. I dress quickly and go downstairs.

I move deftly away from the basement exit of my building. A cab approaches and I raise my hand to flag it. As he pulls in, I wave him off. Some instinct tells me to go on foot. I check my watch. Ten o'clock. It is two hours since dinner with Jake and Freddie. I told them I was going to sleep. They could divide up the watch in the front of the building however they wanted. Since I was a boy, it has been my habit to lie on cool, fresh sheets in a darkened room. At those times, the dark seemed like an ally, offering me a gilded sanctuary. As if a gift had been bestowed upon me. But tonight, some feeling of dread came upon me. The sweat formed around my neck and the sheets became hot and clingy. I escaped to the shower, the images of Julie flooding over me, the pictures of our lovemaking bringing me to erection as the water cascaded over me. You still want her even after she set you up for Brendan Foley. Why didn't Foley pick you up today? Why is he waiting to make his move? You have the murder weapon, Foley. What are you waiting for?

I walk down Third Avenue and fall behind a bearded man in a dark suit and hat. I see the pigtails curling down his neck and I recognize him as one of them. "The Sids" we used to call them. Young men who looked like caricatures of old moneylenders. When I was a kid, it was considered great sport to torment them, to knock their packages or bags flying. Running by them to tweak a long beard got you laughs and applause. Stealing their eyeglasses was another big favorite. I participated in those games in the beginning. There was something about the Sids that made them seem victims and yet more. They seemed to be asking for it. Thousand-year-old men. As I grew older, I stopped tormenting them. They repulsed me. It seemed like they had given themselves over to an unnatural life. Once in a subway station, a group of my friends mocked one of them and I moved away, strangely embarrassed. Did some ancient instinct warn me that I was one of them? Was it shame I felt about what my friends were doing, or did I have some intimation that this bearded man with the pigtails was bonded to me? But they aren't the only Jews. There are Jews like Nails Gordon. And what does that make me? I am dago-bred and in the middle of a dago war. When it is finished, who will I become? What happens the next time I see a group of young boys crying, "Get the Shy, get the Shy."

I reach Sixty-fourth Street and turn right, heading in the direction of Fifth Avenue. At Sixty-first, I cross the street and stand looking at the Pierre. This is crazy. Why do this to yourself? You know what you have to know. And what if you do see her? I don't know. I don't know.

I feel helpless and dumb lurking in the shadows like some spurned lover. You have bigger problems. What does Scola want? To see if I'm a threat if the war continues? To see what I think my chances are? All of the above. How did he do it to you, Johnny? What did he dangle in front of you that made you bite? What happened to that tough little kid, Johnny Baca?

A cab pulls up. I see a woman getting out and I start across the street. Somehow, I know it's going to be her. She's dressed in a black raincoat, her hair let down. I reach the sidewalk as she starts inside.

"Julie."

She turns and I see the startled expression on her face. She looks beautiful. Her eyes are intense and the lips are painted a deep, voluptuous red. This is not about a meeting on organized crime. This is about something else. This is a rendezvous with the attorney general.

Her lips move, but for a moment no words from there. "Davey . . . I—why did you come?"

"To see for myself."

"I'm sorry."

"It's all a setup, isn't it? Kennedy decided to go after the mob here in New York and I was your project."

"Davey."

"You got guts. To jump into the car with me that way. You went for a ride, you saved me, and then you gave me up to Foley."

"Davey . . . listen . . ."

"What's this tonight? Homework? Animal attraction?"

"You wouldn't understand."

"No, I wouldn't. I was raised with simple dago virtues. When it's good, it's good."

Something in her eyes makes me stop. There is a mixture of compassion and intelligence, as if she is seeing me more clearly than I see her. And I go cold. The words stop. No more of the outraged lover. That's chump change. This is the way they do it in the upper echelons. You see somebody you want, you bed them. Where I come from, it could get you killed. Enough. You came, you saw, you got your lumps, now go. She works for the Justice Department and she sleeps with Robert Kennedy. She sleeps with you also. It is good for her with both of you. She is not a girl of simple virtues. She learned from her mother's words. Degradation is wanting a man so much, you'll do it anyplace, anytime, anywhere, even though you know he has others. He'll have someone else in the morning and you won't care. I turn and walk away, hearing her call my name.

The streets and the lights are a blur as I travel like a nomad in the night. I walk downtown and then across and then back uptown in a whirling circle. Chump. You gave away the edge. And they'll still use you. Foley will pick you up tomorrow and he'll squeeze you like an orange. Help us or we'll give you to the police. There will be an investigation, you won't fight Simpson in December, and Joe Dante will be your lifelong enemy. And no more Julie. Funny the way she looked at me. Seeming infinitely older than I. She cared for my hurt in that moment. Cared less for herself than for me. But she's upstairs now with him. Johnny would understand. He would explain it to me. It's the way of the world, kid.

I turn in and somehow I am on my block. Up ahead, I can see the Dodge sedan. Inside it will be Jake or Freddie or both. As I approach my building, someone starts toward me. A nun. Sister Mary.

"Good evening," she says.

"Have you been here long?"

"Not long. But I'm glad you came home."

Behind her I see Freddie approaching us.

"It's time for you to call the abbot."

"I know. Thank you for coming. I'll have someone take you back to the convent."

"I've arranged to stay in the city tonight."

I wonder if she knows what this is all about. Yes, this is revenge. Vince has told her about Scola. She has been waiting for a long time.

"When this is over, we should talk."

I take her hand. "We will. Thank you for coming." She turns and walks away.

Freddie shakes his head. "Bad boy, Mendel. It would have been my ass if someone grabbed you."

"Call Red. Tell him to get over here and leave us the car."

"You could stash me in the trunk, Mendel."

"Thanks, Freddie. Call Red."

The elevator takes me upstairs, humming to the beat of my heart. I unlock the door and step inside. It is cool and dark, the way I like it. I switch on a small light and pick up the phone. The number is right there in my head, as it has been since the day Vince gave it to me. I dial it. I am very calm now. All the emotion has gone out of me.

A thick voice answers. "Yeah."

"I'm calling for the abbot."

There is a pause and then he says, "Just a minute."

The man has a rough, dago voice. He's mob. Now another voice, also thick, but muffled. He has something over his mouth. "This is the abbot."

"I have a message for you. The priest is finished with his devotions. He seeks an audience with a higher authority."

"Then we should talk."

"When?"

"Tonight. In an hour."

"Where?"

"I'll give you instructions."

# 32

THE ROUTE TO THE ABBOT takes us across the Fifty-ninth Street Bridge and into Long Island City. A cigar is clenched firmly in Red's mouth as he drives. No words pass between the two of us. The clock in the car reads 11:55. Red slows as we reach a landmark, an old diner, the Pit Stop. He swings into a right and I get a view of the faces in the diner. Tired men hunkering down over coffee, heads bent to receive a forkful of scrambled eggs and home fries. We cruise for two blocks, until we reach a large sign that reads ACME MOVING COMPANY. We drive past the large warehouse and dip left, which puts us on a street with several more warehouses. The smell of freshly baking bread assaults us. Red grins at me. "Sometimes, back in the old days, we'd finish a run and stop off here. We'd bring the bread back, load up on coffee, and feast. In them days, I could drink a cup of coffee at two o'clock in the morning and sleep like a baby."

Up ahead is a building. In black lettering is the name Smythe's. The product word is faded out. Lights burn on the top floor of the building. Another right and Red slows the car appreciably. We are on a dead-end street and two cars with their lights on face us at the far end of the block. They are parked in front of a darkened warehouse. Red brakes the car and pulls in. He turns off the ignition and I get a final look at the clock as he douses the lights. Midnight. Halloween has begun.

As we walk toward the cars, four men step out. The lead one is tall and muscular. He is coatless and has a bulging forehead under a thick splash of dark hair. As he gets closer, he switches on a flashlight. I can see a vivid tomahawk of a scar running down his right cheek. Someone's blade opened him once. I'll bet the other guy paid a high price for using that blade.

He scans us both before he speaks. "I'll take you inside. Your friend can wait in the car."

Red removes the cigar from his mouth. "I'll wait with you, friend."

The big guy lets it pass. "Sure. But it's chilly out here for an old guy."

"My hands don't shake."

They survey each other, measuring what they read in each other's eyes. The stares hold for another second and then the big guy breaks it. "Here or there, you're still waiting outside."

He shines the flashlight in front of me. It shows me the path up the steps into the warehouse. We walk past the other three men. I don't recognize their faces, but I know the breed. They are hard-eyed vultures. Guns for hire.

The big guy reaches over and opens the door. It creaks sharply and then I step inside. The room that composes the warehouse is huge but empty. The floor is gray and cold. A bank of dim lights illuminate a table at the far end of the room. Sitting there is a lone man. A wisp of smoke spirals from the cigar stuck in his mouth. A bottle of whiskey and two glasses sit on the table. He looks at me and beckons for me to come ahead. I walk toward the table until I am standing in front of it and the abbot.

Frank Bruno gestures with his hand. "Sit down, Davey." He inclines his head. "Take a load off."

I drop into the chair and look at this big bear of a man I have known all my life. He points at my face. "Until the other night, I thought the Graziano-Zale fight in Chicago was the best I'd ever seen. But your fight with the Kid ranks right up there with them. I love your face, Davey. You look like shit." He throws a mock right at me. "Farlo fuori. The spic is dead."

He pours two whiskeys and signals me to pick up my glass. "You got moxie, Davey, the real kind. I'm going to put a bundle on you to take Simpson. It's not the smart bet, but it's from the heart. That's the way you fight. Salud."

The bourbon goes down fast and warm. The Executioner refills his glass and points at mine. "It's the best. Old Grand Dad. You have to develop an appreciation for bourbon. I learned about whiskey when we had to water it down back in Prohibition. Sometimes you didn't have enough booze and you had to cut it a little. For the chumps. As long as it smelled like booze, they thought they was getting the real goods. And if you cut it, your profit went up. For the scotch, we added some medicine. Did you ever notice that scotch tastes a little medicinal? Here's to Vince."

Sweat has created a damp glow on his face. His hair is an olive oil black. I don't see a gray hair in it. It is a strange face. The nose is that of a haughty Roman. The cheeks hang down shapelessly. He has a little boy's quiver of a mouth. A weak sliver of a thing. But his eyes atone for the mouth. They are dark, twisted things, which tell you this man is capable of the most horrific vengeance. This is a man who revels in violence. It is his life's orgasm.

"What about Vince?"

The Executioner flicks an ash off his expensive black coat. He is wearing a black tie and white shirt. A brown coffee stain is prominently displayed on the shirt.

"It's all set, Davey. They're coming to us tomorrow night. And you know what's going to happen?"

"No."

He refills his glass with the third hit. "They're going down. All those bastards who hit Tommy."

"Dino?"

Frank downs the glass. "Especially Dino. He gets it first."

"And the others? Scola? Joe Dante?"

"Them, too. Drink up, Davey."

I hold up the glass, but I don't drink. "But this is a Council meeting. You're breaking all the rules."

His eyes light up. They are the eyes of the true believer who has seen paradise. "That's the beauty of it. It's never been done before. They'll never see it coming. Fuck the rules. We'll write new ones. Johnny will think something up."

Handsome Johnny, slick Johnny. Somehow he manages to be in Miami when this is all going down. His hands are clean. It couldn't be better if he'd planned it.

"What am I doing here, Frank?"

"You're an important man, Davey. If you didn't come here tonight, it wouldn't happen. If I didn't see you, then I wouldn't have my people in place tomorrow. And if you didn't see me, then Vince wouldn't know it's okay to come in. We worked it so it would be in my restaurant. They want to push Vince out. Make him step down. So they think, where would Vince feel safe coming in for a talk? In my joint. So once we got inside their thinking, we waited for them to suggest it. When they did, we had them by the balls. When you leave here tonight, you send word to Vince that it's all set. They're all going down tomorrow night. The abbot has turned a penitent face. That's what you tell him."

The violent dark eyes are alive with a lethal shrewdness. "Tomorrow night, go to some big restaurant or a club. You're spelling it out for the law and everybody else: I wasn't in on it; I was out living it up."

"That's a lot of bodies, Frank. What about the Five Families?"

"They'll recover—they always do. We'll put Johnny in Tommy's place. With me and Vince, that's three. The other spots will fill up. In the Life, we deal with the treacherous ones."

"Vince is coming in too soon. He should have made them sweat more."

He frowns. "The hit depends on timing. If we wait, they'll keep looking for Vince. A lot of stash is being waved around for someone to give him away. Somebody will sing. This works for us. It makes Vince look like he wants a deal real bad."

"What's Dino thinking?"

The Executioner puffs on his cigar. "He's thinking that once Vince steps down, I'll wait awhile, then kill him."

It makes sense. Once Vince retires, he has no power. No one would take a contract from him to do Dino. Then Dino will have him whacked.

Frank Bruno grasps the whiskey bottle and waves it in the air.

"Tommy always took care of me. He backed me as head of the Gardena Family after Augie Gardena died."

Someone shot Augie down. That was convenient for you, Frank.

"Tommy was the Eminence. He deserved to live out his golden years in class and style. He earned his retirement. He made us all rich. And what do they do? They crucify him in a barber chair. Tommy was a gentlemen and a gentle man. He hated the hit. I begged him years ago to let me finish Dino. He said, 'No. There will be a war. We'll find a way to live with Dino.' He told me, 'Frank, it's dumb. I'm too smart for Dino. Don't worry about nothing.' "

"Johnny says the drugs can't be stopped."

"We let those who wish to wet their beaks do so. Give your father some credit. Vince understands that progress cannot be stunted."

"You want the drugs, don't you, Frank?"

The Executioner's eyes bore into me. "They took you for a ride, Davey, and only you came back. Two different guns were used. Two sets of bullets. Joe junior was killed by one gun and Nuñez died from another. What happened, Davey?"

"I have good friends," I reply, but the lesson is clear. There are certain things you don't ask. We all have an agenda.

He rewards me with a big smile. "So I hear. Let's drink to the future." He tips the bottle again into our glasses. "A salud."

The fiery stuff burns its way into my chest and lights me up. Frank stands up and, leaning over, grabs my arm. "The abbot has turned a penitent face." He claps my cheek. "I remember you were a skinny kid, but I also remember your eyes. The same then as now. No fear. Like your father."

I stand up. "Like both of them."

Something passes between the Executioner and me. Like a jolt from a hot wire. I can see him measuring what he sees in my eyes. I am part dago and part Jew. Maybe more dangerous than both my fathers. He nods now. "Get going, Davey. Tell Vince it's set. Then get word to Scola tomorrow that Vince is coming in. And one other thing. He can bring one man with him, but it can't be Red Miller."

"Why?"

"It's an old rule. No Jews at the Council."

"Who made that up?"

Frank hawks up some mucus and spits it on the floor. "Scola. Get going, Davey. It's time for us to take our revenge." The word reverberates in my ear as I walk from the long room. Just at the door, I look back. Frank is drinking again. Stoking the demons he will release tomorrow night. The assassin plans murder. Our eyes meet. His face is marked by the dark deed he carries within him. Then I step back into the night. It is cold now and the chill bites into me. I make my way toward Red, who leans against one of the cars, his cigar shrunk to a little measure.

The triggerman with the tomahawk scar stares at me. He switches on the flashlight and for a moment it flickers across my face as if he is searching for something.

"Get that fucking thing out of my face."

But the light insolently remains there, as if probing for what is concealed inside me.

I come at him, my left hand reaching for the light. He grabs my hand. "Easy champ." He is incredibly strong. His hand encircles my wrist.

"Turn it off, sonny."

Red is there. The big guy eases off now. "Relax, I was trying to make it easier for you." The beam disappears.

We walk slowly away, the eyes of the four triggermen on us. We slide in on opposite sides, Red switches on the ignition, and we pull away. When we get around the corner, Red darts a glance at me. "What's the word?"

"The abbot has turned a penitent face. That's what you tell Vince. That means it's set. Frank says Vince can't take you there with him. No Jews at a Council meet full of dagos. That's Uncle Carlo's rule."

Red flashes an awry smile. "You mean you don't trust him?"

"I mean I want you there with Vince."

"Those're the rules, Davey. Always have been. La Cosa Nostra is not from kosher."

We are at the foot of the Fifty-ninth Street Bridge and I see the lights of the city sparkling in front of me. "I don't like that big guy with the tomahawk scar and I didn't like his flashlight in my face, like he was looking for something."

"What?"

"I don't know."

It all eats at me and I can't figure it.

Red rolls a fresh cigar into his mouth. "I'll tell Vince it's set and whatever else you want me to tell him."

I take a deep breath. "Vince and Frank are going to hit them all tomorrow."

Red doesn't answer.

"It'll break all the rules."

We are on the bridge, driving across the East River.

"What do you want me to tell Vince?"

Red is watching me. We come off the bridge, back in Manhattan now. "Tell him it's on for tomorrow night and he goes in there with you and Dago Pete. Tell him I said so. Tell him to fuck Uncle Carlo's rules."

Red's face splits into a big smile. "That's what Max would have said."

# 33

HALLOWEEN NIGHT is cool and crisp. I leave the car with Jake at the wheel and walk across the street toward the Children's Gallery. It occupies the first two floors of a gray stone building with a multicolored banner hanging above the entrance. Bright lights that decorate the lobby cast a golden glow on the museum's red awning. In front of the building, young children dressed as witches, monsters, and goblins are lined up, prepared to enter the museum for its Halloween show. Farther up the block, older children in masks and capes, traveling in groups, work the buildings in search of trick or treat. The museum is on West Eighty-third Street, facing an espresso shop, The French Café. On the corner is a bar with a red neon sign that reads RACCOON LODGE. The children flit by me, punctuating the air with yells and cries of delight, intoxicated by the adventure of the night and their youth.

I look up at the sky and the lights of the apartment buildings. In hotel and motel rooms across the city are men who will also be playing a game tonight. One with deadly intent, whose effect is permanent. Men who will write the headlines for the morning papers. The mechanics who wait to bring down the hit tonight have not spent the day with the wife and kids. They have been holed up in and around the city, waiting for the word to go. In some ways, it is like waking up the day of a championship fight, counting the hours till you step into the ring. There is a feeling of tightness in your gut, a feeling of apprehension. You're a professional and you know no matter how many times you've done it, the potential is there for it to blow up in your face. But the hit is final. There are no return matches. The shooters Frank Bruno has hired know they will be putting the blast on three dons and their bodyguards. If they don't get it right, their own lives will be forfeited. For these men awaiting a telephone call in their rooms telling them it is time to go, the only magic they believe in is death.

The shock waves will rock every one in the mob. A Mafia Council meeting is inviolate. The hit in such a circumstance breaks the rules set up when the Syndicate was first formed. It invites anarchy. But it is Vince's only play. Get them before they get him. And in the privacy of their homes and in hushed conversations with one another, the dons of the National Commission will have to acknowledge that Vince Rossi and Frank Bruno have got the kind of balls you carry around in a wheel barrow. I look inside the lobby on the off chance that I have missed Julie. Why the call and why the meeting here? Her words were, "I have to discuss something with you." Is this about the other night, or is it some kind of deal that she is proposing on behalf of Brendan Foley? She's quite a package, this lady who jumped in the car with Joe junior and me. The lawyer who does work for the mob is a Justice Department agent and sleeps with Robert Kennedy. It's somehow in keeping with everything that is going down on this Halloween night. A grotesque masquerade full of lethal deception.

Two women are crossing the street with a young girl between them. She is dressed in a cape and long dress and wears a Cat Woman mask. The woman on her left is Julie. She is looking straight at me, but there is no sign of recognition. Has something happened? I take my cue from her and fall in behind the two women as they line up at the Gallery for tickets. I am engulfed in a line of squealing, excited kids, and then somehow Julie is in front of me, her back touching my chest, slipping a note into my hand. I accept the piece of paper and tuck it into the pocket of my trench coat, my hand firmly around the message. When I get inside the lobby, I read it. The letters are printed in dark crayon. "Go upstairs to the balcony. I'll meet you there after the show starts."

I am the only one in the balcony as the lights dim. Below me, the excited babble of the kids has suddenly stopped and there is the hush of anticipation. The auditorium goes black. Chimes. Slowly, a light reveals hanging metallic disks blown mystically toward one another. The audience of kids is spellbound. As the chimes continue, the light changes, filtered through colored gels hung from the ceiling. The sound of a flute, mysterious, insinuating, is heard as a small puppet creature in a purple cape is lowered down. He approaches his audience, beckoning for their attention. As he speaks, a masked puppet figure holding a large knife stealthily creeps up behind him. The children cry out a warning. I am distracted by the intoxicating smell of Julie's perfume as she slides in next to me, but I remain fixed on the theatrics. The knife flashes through the air and the cloaked figure falls, his head hanging grotesquely. Crashing cymbals and darkness, then Julie's hand is in mine and she leads me to the back row.

I watch her, trying to ignore her obvious beauty. Meeting her in such close proximity and in the dark is unsettling. She is wearing a charcoal jacket over a white blouse that opens just below the neck. It is tasteful enough to emphasize her ample breasts without showing any cleavage. Her hair is a lustrous mass. I use my anger to fight my feelings.

"What's this about, Julie?"

I hear the rawness in my voice, fueled by the hurt inside me. I wait for the pitch about playing ball with Foley.

"It's about Johnny."

I feel my mouth full open. "Johnny?"

"Where is Johnny now?"

For a moment, I hesitate. "He's out of town."

"Where?"

"Down south."

"Like in Miami Beach?"

"Could be."

"Do you know what he's doing there?"

"You tell me, Julie."

"He's working with the Cubans to bring down Fidel."

"That's his business, isn't it?"

"Davey, there isn't just an effort to get Fidel out; the focus is on getting him period."

The words come out of me slowly, as if I am chewing on stale pieces of bread. "You mean a hit?"

"Cuba is very big business, Davey. It's big politically and it's big bucks. Castro stands in the way of all that. Just because the Bay of Pigs failed doesn't mean the undercover stuff has stopped."

"Where does Johnny fit in?"

"Who's losing the bucks?"

The answer is suddenly there for me in big blinking neon letters. "The mob."

"Castro shut down all the casinos when he took over. If he gets removed, then everything opens up again."

"How did Johnny get into it?"

"He's the point man for the mob, for dons all over the country who want back into Havana."

"You seem to know an awful lot about it."

She lowers her head for a moment as if gathering up courage for what she needs to say. "Everything is all tied together. It's about getting Cuba back, reopening the casinos, and getting rid of Castro. It's about Johnny and it's about Tommy."

My mouth opens but doesn't work. I take a deep breath. "Tell me about Tommy."

"Tommy made a deal."

"What kind of deal?"

"The government had him on that deportation rap. He was going away, Davey. To Palermo or wherever it was he came from, and he wasn't coming back. He couldn't face that. So he offered the government a deal. A deal they couldn't turn down."

She puts something to her mouth and I can discern a Coke bottle. She takes a careful swallow and offers me some, which I decline. All I can think is about whether I can share her with Bobby Kennedy.

"The deal was Castro, Davey. Tommy said he would get Castro for the government in exchange for the deportation rap being dropped. It's code named Operation Mongoose."

Tommy hated the hit; he thought there were better ways. If you asked him today what he thought of his own murder, he'd shake his head and say, Stupid. But they were sending him back to the old country. They had him. Oh Jesus, poor fucking Tommy. And once Tommy was in on it, then so was Johnny.

I look at Julie. "So that's what Johnny was doing at the safe house."

"The man you followed from there was Cord Waters. He's CIA. He's heavily involved in exile politics down in Miami. He was there at the Bay of Pigs. He runs teams of men into Cuba. Their job is to do damage, heavy damage. And Johnny is working with him. The target is Fidel."

My mind runs back to yesterday afternoon and Johnny there in the Cuban restaurant with Cord Waters and a little Cuban. The meeting was about the hit on Castro.

"What are you thinking, Davey?"

"The missiles in Cuba. How does that affect all this?"

"Everything goes on hold. The missiles are being dismantled and everybody is on their best behavior. An incident now with Castro and all the bottles could fall off the table. Mongoose has to be shut down. That's official. It comes from the highest echelon of the government."

Our eyes meet. "So Johnny is down there turning off a hit job on Castro. Why are you telling me all this, Julie? You're hip-deep in it and you spill to me. Where I was raised, that spells a deal."

I can see the shock in her eyes.

"Why else all this spy stuff up in the balcony? We could have met at the bar down the street."

Her eyes are blazing. "I'm not here to make a deal. Your brother is in trouble. Operation Mongoose is a terrible embarrassment to the CIA. The attorney general wants it turned off. Cord Waters's job is to smother it. Johnny is the link to the Cubans who are supposed to be doing the job. Eliminate him and the CIA has deniability. Johnny is expendable because the Rossi crime family is weak and on the run. We're here in the balcony because I'm at risk telling you this."

Her words rock me. The CIA is in the hit business, all in the name of national security. The eleventh commandment is Cover thy ass.

"I'll call him."

Julie bites her lip. "I already have. He checked out of his hotel and he's on his way here. There's something else." She hesitates for a moment. "What I am going to tell you is Justice Department business. I'm taking a big chance doing this."

"Go ahead."

"We have a wire tap on Dino Manfredi. He uses a Greenwich Village social club as his office. We have a recording of a call from

Cord Waters made to Dino. He said Miami Beach was shut down and now New York needed to be taken care of. Waters is sending the Cubans. Do you understand what I'm telling you? They're going to kill Johnny tonight."

It's like there is a trip wire hooked to my heartbeat. Someone has pulled it and everything is hammering inside me. Johnny is flying home. I have to reach him.

Julie reads my mind. "The hotel said he flew on Pan Am. He'll be arriving in about forty minutes at LaGuardia. You can still make it if you hurry."

She's gone out on the limb. Way out. Like she did that day when she jumped into the car. You're still there for me, aren't you, Julie? But you're still there for Bobby also. You get off on being with two men.

"I have to go. Thanks."

She nods. I start out and she calls to me. "Davey, your secret is safe with me."

She's talking about the gun and Joe junior. She hasn't given me over to Foley.

I want to say something, but I can't. The price is still too high, Julie. A scream from the stage and I look down and see the masked figure with the knife falling to his knees as he confronts a witch. She chants a magic incantation and waves her wand. He begins to grovel at her feet and then he is mesmerized into a frozen statue. Bewitched and helpless. The way I'll be if I join Julie's ménage. I turn from her and take the stairs two at a time, then burst through the door and onto the street. Standing in front of me is an evil wizard. He is very tall and his black silk costume glows in the dark. He is wearing a Richard Nixon mask.

I brush past him, knocking him off his feet as I run toward my car, where Freddie awaits me.

"What's the rush, Mendel?"

"They're going to hit Johnny."

"Who?"

"Cubans run by the CIA."

"Jesus . . . where?"

"Chandler's restaurant."

"You sure."

"I should be. . . . I'm having dinner with him tonight. Send Jake to LaGuardia. Johnny's coming in on a Pan Am flight. He's to tell Johnny to go home."

Freddie dashes for the car while I head up the street to the Raccoon Lodge. I find the wall phone, drop a coin in the slot, and dial the number I long ago memorized, listening impatiently. On the fourth ring, someone answers.

"Yeah."

"I'm calling for the abbot."

A short pause. "Hold on."

There is something about the voice I recognize. It's the big hitter I met last night at the warehouse in Long Island City. Scarface. He's gone to get his boss. Now the ominous baritone of Frank Bruno floats back to me.

"Davey, you got trouble?"

"There's a hit coming down on Johnny. I need backup."

"Where?"

"At Chandler's. Cubans."

"When?"

"He's got a seven-thirty dinner reservation with me."

"We got half an hour. Listen to me, Davey. Don't do anything crazy. Get over there, but stay down. I'll send Marty with some artillery. You met him last night at the warehouse. Don't do nothing till you see him. You got anybody with you?"

"One guy."

"You sure Johnny's going to show up?"

"He's got a reservation. He always keeps those."

"Get over there." He clicks off. I head back through the smoky pub and note the big clock on the wall. It's 6:55. Thirty-five minutes to save Johnny. Beneath the clock, a drinker at the bar shoots a fluff ball into a tiny basket. Swish. I look up and the minute hand on the clock has moved. Another minute gone by. Get going. You can't freeze the ball.

# 34

CHANDLER'S IS LOCATED on East Forty-sixth Street, between Second and Third avenues. A touch of old world class for successful people. Tommy dined there a lot. It's a natural for Johnny. The street is brightly lit and heavy with couples headed for cocktails and drinks. Halloween parties are the order of the night. A festive flavor permeates the city. And there's a real trick or treat surprise to spice up the evening. The big blast is coming down.

I check my watch: 7:10. Time for the cast of characters to start showing up. My vantage point is from the window of a pharmacy just across the street from Chandler's. Freddie is standing in front of the pharmacy, by our car.

A dark sedan pulls up in front of Chandler's and I stiffen. Moments later, Buster Minetta, wearing a dark trench coat and hat, steps out. He walks down the block till he reaches the corner of Second Avenue and stops in front of a phone booth. The sedan pulls around the corner. I leave the pharmacy, eyes roaming up and down the street, looking for a sign of the Cuban hitters, the varsity squad. No vehicle has lingered on the street other than a florist van, whose driver is just now pulling off. Everything else has been dinner traffic. People being dropped off and their cars moving away. So where are the Cubans?

Buster is still on the phone. It's all been carefully laid out. Johnny is Tommy's disciple. Tommy's philosophy was, Be punctual. Don't keep people waiting, whether it's business or social. It makes them feel important. You could lay money on Tommy to be where he was expected. That's how they killed him. You can depend on Johnny to be here in the next twenty minutes. So will the Cubans. No problem.

For some reason, my eyes flicker in the direction of a green neon sign just up the street. Hurley's. A big window fronts the bar and in the back are tables for dining. The window shows a huge pumpkin and hanging down from above it is a crepe edition of a witch on a broomstick. She is holding a gleaming green sign that reads HALLOW-EEN COCKTAIL SPECIAL. There is a vacant parking spot in front of Hurley's, which is only about twenty feet from Chandler's. I walk over to Freddie, who is leaning against our car.

"It's almost game time, Davey."

"And no reinforcements for us. What's Buster doing?"

Freddie points in the air. "He's the finger man. If anything goes wrong, he'll come up shooting and he'll have backup."

I scan my watch again: 7:15. No Johnny and no hitters. Everybody's cutting it very close.

I run into the pharmacy and dial Chandler's. Seconds later, I get Caesar, the maître d', on the line. "It's Davey Rossi. Anything for me?"

"Yes. A Mr. Jake called for you. He said your party landed and it's too late to reach him."

I can feel the sweat running freely under my arms.

"Mr. Rossi? Are you still there?"

"Yes."

"Can I give your brother a message?"

"If he calls, tell him I said to cancel dinner. It's not good for his health."

I hang up and go outside. Freddie is waiting by the curb. "You look like you lost your wallet."

"Jake called. Johnny landed; that means he's on his way."

It is Freddie's turn to look dazed. A thin smile appears on his face as his head dips in the direction of Hurley's. "Trick or treat."

A Buick has pulled up in front of Hurley's. There are two men in the back. The car has a perfect sight line on Chandler's.

"That's what Buster was doing," Freddie says. "He was telephoning the Cubans to pull in. When Johnny gets here, they'll be ready to give him a jolt."

My gaze moves in the direction of Chandler's and I see Buster standing just a few yards from the entrance, ready to point the finger at Johnny when he gets out of the cab. Two big men have come up behind him. They wouldn't last thirty seconds on *What's My Line?*

My throat gets very tight. "We have to do something, Freddie."

"We could ask them to move on, but they're pretty itchy right now. One Rossi is as good as another to them."

My watch reads 7:25. Johnny's cab will pull in and the big hitters will come out of the car spitting bullets. Frank Bruno's men still haven't shown up. They must have gotten stuck on the Fifty-ninth Street Bridge.

A cab pulls up and I go all tight. The door opens and a woman steps out, followed by her escort. Someone throws a shoulder into me, jostling me backward. I yell at the kid in a garish orange costume as he sprints recklessly down the block. Freddie pulls two Halloween masks out of his pocket. "Here, put this on and get in the car."

I start to snap at him, but I can see he is deadly serious. "We got one chance, Davey, and that's to ram the Buick. We're a couple of party guys out of control. The accident will bring the police. All the hit men go bye-bye."

We get into the car and adjust our masks. I gauge the angle between the Buick and us. I need to make a U-turn, back up, and then ram them hard. Freddie is sitting in the backseat, holding his gun. "Now listen, Mendel, here's the action. Soon as we crash them, you get out and weave around like you've had too much booze. Don't get too close. Point to our car and yell for them to get out. If they show guns, you hit the ground. It's my play."

"What about Buster and his boys?"

"Once the crowd gathers and the cops are on the way, they'll split also. And with the mask on, Buster won't recognize you."

I turn on the ignition. "Here we go."

I ease out and then swing into the U-turn. I can hear someone yelling, "Hey." I swing into reverse, back up, and get the angle on the Buick.

"Do it now," Freddie says.

I let the car fly forward at the same moment I see a cab coming down the block jam on its brakes. Our momentum drives us into the side door of the Buick. It is a good hard ram. I can see the heads bobbing up and down in the Buick. The Cubans are going off like Mexican jumping beans, jabbering frantically at each other and pointing at me. "Get out there and start yelling and pointing," Freddie yells.

I step out, looking toward the cabdriver, who is shaking his fist at me. Alighting from the back of the cab is a graceful, dapper-looking man with silver hair—Johnny. I call to him, but the cry is muffled by my mask. He is slipping a bill to the driver and pointing at me, a smile on his face. My masquerade has worked perfectly. Johnny doesn't know who I am. For a moment, I stand frozen; then I hear a man's voice. I pivot and whirl in the direction of the sound. Buster Minetta is pointing at Johnny, a signal to the two killers behind him. I hear myself yelling to Johnny, "It's a hit," but he just stands there laughing at this crazy drunk. Buster has his piece out and is walking straight toward Johnny, who is ten yards behind me. Buster also thinks I'm a Halloween crazy to be brushed aside. He pushes past me and I throw the left hook. He staggers and I am all over him, driving the right into his gut, hearing his grunt as he crumples. He is on his knees in front of me and I finish him with a left-right combination that leaves him lying on the ground before me. I spin around and hear the first shot. I can see the startled expression on Johnny's face and my hand goes out as if I can somehow intercept the bullet. The sound of the second and third shots pierce the night, accompanied by the screams of a woman. The bullets shatter the cab's window and the driver slumps over the wheel. His horn starts blasting. Johnny stands alone, silhouetted in neon. The two hitters close on him as another man with a gun appears from nowhere. It is Freddie, his arm thrown forward, looking like a deadly apparition. The gun spits fire and one hitter takes rounds in the neck and head. His gun discharges as he topples over. But the other shooter opens fire. Johnny throws up his hands. My cry of "No" is swallowed by the cab's stuck horn. The hitter is standing over him, poised to finish the job. A new burst of gunfire. The killer's hands go up in the air and his body contorts in agony, as if he were a tribal witch doctor seized by evil spirits. Freddie puts another slug in him and the hitter crumples.

More slugs rip the air. The Cubans have exited their car, firing wildly as they run toward the corner of Third Avenue, scattering people in their wake, using their bullets to clear a path. It seems like everyone is screaming and running. A vast kaleidoscope of colors, faces, and masks spinning before me. Another volley of shots echoes in the night as the Cubans make their escape. All the while, the cab's horn blares its accompaniment to the dance macabre engulfing Forty-sixth Street. From behind me a voice: "Go, Mendel." Amid the sound and the fury, Freddie and I are sprinting toward Second Avenue.

I know I am running in the wrong direction, away from Johnny. The picture is frozen perfectly in my mind: Johnny with his hands up as the shooter fires from just yards away. It was a head shot, and you don't survive those. A car on the corner and someone standing there. Frank Bruno. I yell to Freddie to follow me, then dart across Second Avenue as the light changes, leaving Freddie behind. Scarface is standing next to Frank as I reach the car. "Get the fuck out of here," Frank roars at me, and shows me his gun.

It's the mask. He doesn't recognize me. I whip it off.

For a split second, Frank looks at me as if he is in deep shock, and then he is pointing at the car. "Get in."

"They got Johnny."

"Get in the car, Davey." His hand is on my shoulder. I see Freddie running toward us, and I point in his direction.

"He's with me."

Freddie reaches us. The gun is still in his hand. He has on a Frankenstein mask. It's the first time it has registered on me. "This is Freddie."

Frank Bruno's arm is extended as if to welcome Freddie. He draws Freddie to him and then there are the two quick pops as the steel-jacketed slugs silently detonate inside Freddie. His eyes register surprise, as if he never knew how exquisite was the pain of death. Frank Bruno steps back and lets go of Freddie, who falls in a heap at my feet. At that moment, I realize the whole thing and realize nothing as Scarface is there to drive the butt of his gun into my head.

# 35

**ANOTHER SET OF MEN** guard me in the car. But it makes no difference, for they are mob men. One on each side of me as we drive through the countryside. The side of my head where Scarface got me throbs and my temple feels heavy. My eyes are open, but I remain dazed.

We pull into a place with winking yellow neon that spells out THE ROADHOUSE. It is a mob joint. We are in New Jersey. The mob owns the Garden State. The only things that grow here in New Jersey are deals. Two men pull me toward the restaurant, where there are just a few cars. On the window is a large sign that reads CLOSED. I am surrounded front and back as we enter the Roadhouse. It is a trendy spot with checkered tablecloths and a large bar. The kind of place that specializes in burgers and beer, the dance floor laid out in the back room. It is a place for pickups and watered-down drinks at expensive prices. Looking through the window, I can see the lights of a beckoning motel, the Trixie Inn. That is also a mob spot. You meet the girl here and she takes you over to the Trixie. The Roadhouse does $300,000 or more in business per year and there are a string of them in Jersey.

The walls are covered with large framed photos of football players and boxers. There is one of me on the far wall. Sitting underneath it at a table by himself is Dino Manfredi, dapper in a black jacket and deep red sport shirt. My escorts lead me over to him. Dino is eating a large hamburger. Its blood drips down Dino's hand. He likes his burgers very rare. A glass of whiskey rests on the table.

"Sit down, Davey. You hungry? No, I don't think so. I said sit down."

A huge paw descends on my back and pushes me into the chair. Dino looks at my face and then the bruise on my temple. "Frank did some damage, huh? Still not as bad as that Hebe you were running away with got. He plugged two hitters and you messed up Buster. Somebody had to pay for it."

He dives into the burger and rips off a large chunk. He chews the meat ferociously, greedily eyeing me like some beady rat come upon its prey.

"You figured it out yet?"

"I'm not that smart."

Dino puts down his drink and wipes his mouth with the back of his hand. "But you're good at surviving. You went from a ride Joe Dante arranged for you, and tonight you were in the middle of a hit and made it back without a scratch. That just ain't luck; it's talent. Have a drink, Davey. Hey, bring us some whiskey."

The whiskey comes courtesy of a swarthy hood. He sets it down and walks away.

"Hey," Dino calls out. "Where's your manners? Get the man a clean glass."

The glass comes and is filled to the top with gleaming bronze liquid.

Dino bites into his burger and more juice drips from it. "What's the matter? You're not drinking."

"I'm not thirsty."

"Sure you are. This is a celebration."

"Whose?"

"Mine. And maybe yours." He reaches for a cigarette and lights it with a match from a big red book that has the name of the joint on it.

Dino holds out his glass. "Salud." He drinks from the glass and sets it down. His eyes glitter with some inner reservoir of excited feeling he cannot suppress. He leans forward. "Sometimes, Davey, you take your chances when you got no chance at all and things work out for you. Like with the Syndicate. When Prohibition came, no one knew what we were getting into. We were just hustling a buck, and look how it worked out for us. We're bigger than General Motors. You follow me?"

"I never liked history."

Dino grins. "Me, either. I hated school. Especially those nuns. They used to whack the shit out of us. They'd really do a job on you with those rulers. Tell you to put out your hands and then whack right across the knuckles. When I was fourteen I just quit, but not until I laid one of those bitches out right across the desk. Sister Theresa. She was a hell of a hitter."

"I'm still not drinking."

A crafty look comes into his eyes. "You're like one of them old peasants back in Sicily. They didn't want to hear about progress and well water and flush toilets. They wanted the money in their hands. That's what they understood. You give it to them straight and they could deal with that. So here it is. Johnny's alive. You saved your brother's ass."

The breath goes out of me. The questions coalesce into one. How?

Dino takes up his whiskey and dangles it in front of me. "A toast to luck. To Johnny's incredible fucking luck. I mean, I seen hits go down and I seen hits get all fucked up. For every kind of reason you could imagine. I once had a hitter who tracked a guy all over town and then didn't do the hit because he thought he was hexed and it would bring him bad luck. But I never heard of a hit where the guy missed at less than ten feet."

He sees my incredulous stare. "It's no bullshit. Johnny should have got popped right between the eyes, but all he got was his temple grazed. He's going to be the second hottest story in New York. The hit that missed. The hit that lived. Now tell me you don't have something to drink to."

"Where is he now?"

"They're bandaging him up, but he walks out of the hospital in a little while and the flashbulbs will be popping. So drink up."

Dino drains his glass. My fingers close on the glass, but I don't lift it. "Why ain't you drinking?"

"Why am I here?"

Another big grin. "I know what you're thinking. I bluffed you once about Vince and then tried to pick you up. So you're figuring, What's the action now? What does Dino want from me? Ain't that right?"

"Maybe."

"Sure, that's what I'd be figuring if I was you. It's the smart move." Dino signals for a refill. His fingers move around the rim of the glass. He looks at me and his eyes are tight with anger. "You tell Johnny to keep his mouth shut or I'll do the job myself next time. Tell him if he plays his cards right, we'll let him back in."

Let him think I don't know about Cuba. "Why the hits?"

"We did the CIA a favor to get the Kennedy brothers get off our back. You just tell Johnny he's been given a second chance."

I look up at the clock above the bar. The gleaming dial indicates it's nine o'clock. Dino notices me staring. "Something eating you?"

"What's the first-hottest story in New York?"

Dino's mouth opens as if he would devour me. He has been waiting for this. "It's your old man. Vince thought he pulled a fast one. He was going to come in under a flag of truce and hit all of us. What do you think of that?"

"It was a hell of an idea."

"Yeah, it was. Only we smelled it out. Can you figure it, bright boy?"

"Frank Bruno finked."

"Can you figure the rest?"

The image of Freddie smothered by Frank Bruno, the gun exploding into his chest, floods back over me. This Halloween night is the cross to end all crosses. Frank Bruno put his signature on it when he killed Freddie. Vince made the deal with Frank to hit the Council. Scola, Dino, and Joe Dante were to get the bullets with their names on them at the Villa Capri tonight. But the Executioner sold the deal and sold Vince in the bargain. The lure of the drug money was too much for him, and Tommy was no longer here to convince Frank to line up with him and Vince.

"I don't want to figure. You tell me. What about Vince?"

Dino leans across the table. "I would have listened to what he had to say. He could have cut a deal, walked away, and enjoyed his golden years clipping coupons in Miami Beach. But no, he tried to put the knock on me. No one does that to Dino."

I am out of the chair, the words a primitive growl in my throat. "Where is he?"

I feel the gun in my neck. "Sit down," Dino barks. "I said sit down." He picks up his glass and studies the whiskey, then casually sets it down. "Vince is sitting in his car by the side of the road with Dago Pete. They got maybe a hundred slugs in them."

It is like getting a sharp slap in the face from a taunting bully when you can't move. The gun jabs me in my back and then the numb despair sets in.

Dino snaps his fingers and someone hands him an envelope. "This time, there's no bullshit." He tosses a polaroid on the table. The quality is not good, but it is Vince, his lifeless eyes staring at nothing, trails of blood covering his face. His neck is twisted grotesquely to one side, like the dead puppet in the show at the Children's Gallery.

"We moved him to his car. The Villa Capri is Frank's place, and it wouldn't be good for business if Vince was found there. He got it with respect. The way a don should. They called his name and gave it to him while looking in his face."

I sag back in my chair, fighting to keep my composure. At such moments, if you are in the Life, it means a great deal to be a man. Vince always believed that. "Save your grief for a quiet place," he told me. "If these men see your tears, they will think you are like a woman. Something to be fucked and discarded." I force the whiskey down in slow gulps. They saw Vince coming and cut him up in pieces. And there is nothing in me. No rage, no pounding in my chest, no oaths about vendetta. I grow cold all over and I see it clearly. This is the way it's done in our life. Do unto others what they would do unto you. Only do it first.

Dino's rasping voice brings me back. "So you go back and tell Johnny that it's over. Everything is too hot. If he keeps his mouth shut, I can use him." Dino points a finger at me. "But you tell him if he peeps to anyone, then we'll finish the job. As long as he's a good boy, Johnny will get a percentage from all of us on the casinos. That's the deal.

"Now I got a word for you, Davey. Frank done a stupid thing tonight. He popped this Hebe with you there. That's always his answer for everything. He was never too swift upstairs. You didn't see it. If anybody comes back to us with it, we know it's you who told them. Don't think because you're a celebrity you're immortal. We can get to anybody . . . anybody. You understand, don't you, bright boy?"

Dino is watching me. It is not what I say but what he picks up in my attitude. I show him nothing. It's all there in a private place. You crave being boss of all bosses, when the last man who wore the crown was killed for it. Uneasy lies the crown, Dino, for in your ambition lie the seeds of your destruction.

I nod my head. "I'll tell Johnny."

"You do that, and remember what else I told you. Now here's your story. You were at a private party. We have witnesses who can place you there. Then you were shacked up with a broad. We'll supply her also. And you just now found out. Gene and Gombo will drive you back to the city. The cops will have Johnny down at the precinct and you bust in all upset. You let them tell you about Vince and then you get all sad. You got that?"

He watches me closely, searching for the anger or the revenge in me. But I have put it all away in the same place as my tears.

"And wear a hat when you go down to see Johnny so no one will see where you got sapped."

I finish the whiskey to get away from his eyes. They got Dago Pete along with Vince, but what about Red? If they got him, Dino would have mentioned it.

"I have to go to the bathroom."

"Hurry up."

I stand in front of the washbasin, turn on the water, and run it over my face. Why am I so cold? Because you knew it was coming, a voice inside me answers. Somewhere, somehow, you knew. Like Nails knew it was coming and Vince didn't. In this killing time, you are more fatalistic than hot. More Jew than dago.

Something falls from my pocket. The mask Freddie gave me. The one I wore when I tried to save Johnny. It is the face of the Wolfman. I put it on and stare at my savage reflection in the mirror. The beast within me. The same creature that lurks inside Dino, Scola, Joe Dante, and Frank Bruno. Remember what Nails said. There's always one dago you can turn against the others. Because he thinks the others have always been out to fuck him. They distrust one another even as they embrace, and by cunning and stealth I will turn you one against the malignant other. Play you and ply you until the betrayal in your hearts devours your insides like a nest of hungry maggots come upon a festering corpse. Then I will strike.

I leave the bathroom and the two hoods march me over to Dino. "Get going. You know what to do. Get Johnny alone at the precinct and tell him the score. And don't forget this." He throws the photo at me. There is a malevolent smile on Dino's face. He cannot believe that his triumph is reversible. He cannot comprehend that his throne is not secure. Cannot visualize that he's going to die. Cannot imagine that I'm going to kill them all. Anybody can be gotten to, Dino. You're not immortal. After all, the hit is good for business.

# 36

**IF I AM GOING** to beat Sandy Simpson, it will take great legs to do it. Legs that will let me push off and beat him to the punch. Legs that will carry me around the ring and away from his lethal punches, that will hold up when my chest is heaving and my lungs are gasping for breath. Legs that will keep me up bouncing on my toes instead of back on my heels, where I become an easy target. So I run twice a day, five miles around the lake and through the shelter of the trees, plotting my fight. As I run, I see Sandy Simpson's coffee-colored face in front of me, the expression of cool contempt he wears as if it were painted there.

As I circle the lake, there is a patch of ground that breaks left and leads you into the woods. It is always cooler here. In the morning, I can see the sky change from dark to light as a line of silver marks the coming of dawn. Then come streaks of gold as the sun begins to crest above the lake, hues of shimmering bronze that momentarily blind me before I plunge deeper into the woods. But in the late afternoon, when I begin my run around the lake, the sun plummets fast into the all-enveloping night, a rapidly dying red sphere bent on displaying its fiery brilliance in one last extravagant gesture—like the final burst of flame from a fire that has been extinguished. Then the woods swallow me up and I am running in darkness into what seems like oblivion. Running alone, the smoke pouring from my mouth, the picture in my

mind changing. The image becoming a dago face. First one, then another. Freshly painted portraits of the men I must kill. When I fix
them firmly there somehow, my pace always picks up and my knees
come up higher as I run, my arms become driving pistons, and I emit
furious grunts. I look up ahead, toward the clearing where the woods
fan out, see the car, and break my stride as I reach it. The door opens
and Johnny steps out.

He is dapper as always in a camel's hair overcoat, white silk scarf,
and dark hat with a pointy brim. He points to the car, but I shake my
head. I lead him toward a tree, where I bob and weave to the punches
of an imaginary opponent. Shadowboxing with an opponent who
would kill me. More dangerous than even Sandy Simpson.

He lights a cigarette and the flare illuminates his face and eyes.
They are snapping with tension and energy. He inhales a lungful of
smoke and punches my arm. "You look ready to go, kid. You going
to win this fight?"

I dodge an imaginary left hook and slip away from a right uppercut.
"Bet your wad on it."

Johnny steps back and appraises me. "Maybe I will."

I throw a left hook at him and then pull it back. "What can I bet
on?"

A circle of smoke from my mouth drifts toward Johnny and evaporates. The night and the woods absorb everything. The sun is gone
and the sky above us has turned inky blue. We are creatures of stealth
covered by pitch.

"You can bet on Frank Bruno," Johnny begins. "He bought it. All
we need is for the feds to show up tonight. I'll have Frank sitting in
my car, watching the bust go down."

"How did he take it when you told him he was being sold out?"

Johnny flicks an ash from his butt. "His eyes got big and the saliva
was running from his mouth. 'Why you doing this for me, Johnny?'
he says. 'Because I hate that rat bastard Dino,' I say, 'and I don't have
the muscle to do nothing about it. Dino's going to take us all down
with him. Him and his dreams of glory. And he's scared of you, Frank.
He figures even when he's boss of all bosses, you're going to come
after him.' All the while I'm talking, Davey, I can see Frank's wheels
spinning. Frank's always hated Dino. So he sits there trying to figure

it, and all I have to do is whisper in his ear, 'Dino wants you out of the way, Frank, but he doesn't want another big hit now. He knows the Five Families can't take any more heat, what with Vince being clipped, so he's selling you to the feds. Papa Joe set it up. They both hate your guts.' Frank gets that crazy look. I can read his mind. Farlo fuori. He's going nuts. Then he wants to know why I am telling him this after he put the hit on Vince." Johnny smiles and shakes his head. "I look him in the eye and say, 'I wasn't that close with Vince anymore, Frank. The drugs are good for business, and Vince would never have let that happen.' I don't say anything more. Frank chews on his cigar for a long time and then finally he says, 'I gotta have proof, Johnny.' 'You'll get your proof,' I tell him, 'but you're going to have to lose a couple of good boys to the feds.' He chews on his cigar some more and then says, 'Okay, I'll watch from your car.' It's all set, Davey, but the bust has to go down."

"I'm seeing Foley in a little while."

Johnny throws the butt away with a swift, angry motion. "You're cutting it tight, Davey. There's a couple of hours to go, and if the bust doesn't happen, I have to do some very fast talking."

"Foley will buy it, Johnny. He'll drool for it just like Frank Bruno did. Look what I'm offering him."

Johnny scoops another cigarette out of his gold case. He looks old now, a womanizer too long debauched, who has been corrupted by his greed and his fear. He has the brain for this, but has he the stomach? We are taking them all on. Frank Bruno, Joe Dante, Dino. We must turn them against one another and strike before they can figure it. Before they realize who is behind it. It is a bold plan, but there is no hedging our bets. If we don't win, we die.

Johnny stamps his feet. "Christ it's cold. Let's get in the car."

We slide into the car, where it is warm and smells of cigarette smoke. He pulls a hip flask from the glove compartment and takes a swig. Getting nervous on me, Johnny?

The smoke from his cigarette swirls up and around us. Johnny traces a line through the smoke with his finger. "It's tricky what we're doing, Davey, promising the Justice Department Frank Bruno and then double-crossing them."

"That's their problem. Besides, we have another plum for them, in case something goes wrong."

Johnny looks at me hard. "Do we?"

"Sure. The time and the place where Dino is going to anoint himself boss of all bosses."

"But that's a tease, too. And you can get by with teases just so many times."

"What are you saying, Johnny?"

"I'm saying you can promise them anything you want, but I'm not telling you when the big meet is going to take place."

"What's the matter, Johnny, getting cold feet? Did you forget what Vince looked like in the car with thirty slugs inside him, his face plastered to the windshield and his eye shot out? Well, don't forget it, because that's what's waiting for us just a few steps down the road. One day, Dino is going to look around and say, Okay, the heat's off. Let's cancel their checks. Did you forget already?"

His eyes cloud over and he looks away. "I'm still not telling you when the meet is, because you're crazy to get even. All you need to know so you can hook Dino is that it's at Joe Jelly's place upstate— Chatham. But I'm holding on to the exact time. That's my ace in the hole."

"What's wrong, Johnny?"

"Nothing's wrong. If we can get Dino and Frank to go after each other, then our problems are over." He bangs his hand against the car door. "We should have waited until the fight was over."

"We both agreed this was the right time, while I was training for the fight and they weren't expecting anything. This thing with Dino making himself the big boss has everybody nervous. This is the time to play it for all it's worth."

Johnny rolls down the window and throws the cigarette away. His eyes remain focused on the woods. His finger is pointed toward a cluster of trees. "Can't see nothing out there, can you?"

"There are no sure things here, Johnny."

"So where's the edge, Davey?"

"Maybe there is none and we just have to take our chances. But we already got Frank Bruno talking to himself."

Johnny reaches for the flask again. "Dino won't be so easy. He's going to want something more than information from you, Davey."

"That's my ace in the hole, Johnny."

We stare at each other as the cold air pours in through the open window of the car. It is a chilling reminder of the finality of the game that we play against men I have known all my life.

"How you sleeping nights, kid?"

"Pretty good on some nights, not so good on others."

Johnny eyes me, but we both know it is too late for second thoughts. "You should be concentrating on the fight. That's all Simpson is thinking about."

"I've had a good camp. I'm in the best shape of my life."

Johnny runs a finger over my eye. "It'll open easy, kid. The tissue is soft."

"Don't call me 'kid' anymore."

Johnny eyes me again. He taps my legs. "Are they going to hold up?"

"You'll be down at ringside, so you'll find out."

"Stick and run?"

"Maybe. Maybe a few surprises."

He doesn't think I can win. I can read that in his eyes. If it was Tommy sitting next to me, he'd say, Go out with class.

Johnny checks his watch. "Quarter to six. When are they coming?"

"Soon."

"Julie with him?"

"Yeah."

Johnny pulls a cigarette from the case. "Is she your edge with Foley?"

"Maybe."

"She likes you, kid, and she's got guts."

"I know." But the edge in my voice gives me away.

"She got under your skin, didn't she?"

"That's my worry."

"Is she two-timing you, kid? She knows a lot of guys."

"I told you not to call me that."

"Look, she's a great broad. Why can't you just enjoy that?"

Johnny leans over. "Tell Foley the buy is going down in a warehouse in Long Island City. It's on Sixty-seventh Avenue. There's a big sign on it that reads ROLL AWAY TRUCKING. Eleven o'clock. Frank will be sitting right next to me, watching Foley bust his drug sale. Then I'll whisper to Frank that Dino keeps a mistress out in Red Hook. Her name is Annabelle. I have the address. When you see Dino, tell him that Frank has a couple of men on the rooftop across the street, watching for him."

"How can I be sure of that?"

"Because I'm putting them there, Davey. They don't call me Johnny Silk for nothing. You get Foley there tonight and I got Frank Bruno in my pocket. Dino is up to you."

We turn away and my eyes lock on the woods in front of me. If Johnny knew why I was on edge with Julie, he'd call the whole deal off. He'd recite in that metallic rasp of his the entire litany of how you handle a woman: Is that why you're sore, kid, because she's fucking Bobby Kennedy? Never take a broad seriously. Kennedy doesn't. Never come on sincere. You gotta be the one to two-time the broad. That's how you keep the edge.

Johnny taps me on the shoulder. "I gotta go. Call me in the morning."

"Dino's going to wonder how I know that Frank Bruno has got a couple of men watching his mistress."

"You tell him that you made it your business to know."

He lights the cigarette. "Good luck, Davey."

We exchange stares. It has nothing to do with luck. It has everything to do with being good. Then I get out and Johnny drives off, leaving me alone in the woods, which are impenetrable in the darkness.

# 37

SANDY SIMPSON is right there in front of me. I go under his left lead and dig him with a hard right to the heart. Take his heart. Take his heart. A car pulls into the clearing and then a second one behind it. I told Foley not to come with an entourage, but that wouldn't be Justice Department protocol, would it? The two cars park and form a semi-circle, like a wagon train drawing together to fight off an attack by hostile Indians. Even though I am alone, Foley is clearly uneasy about meeting me here in the woods. It is some moments before the back door to the first sedan opens and he steps out. He is joined by another man and they walk toward me. I search for a sign of Julie in the car, but it is too dark to tell if she is there.

Foley reaches me and I hold up my hand and point to the backup man. "It's just you and me, Foley."

He stops and nods to the husky guy, a fullback type. His disappointment at not being able to document the deal I will offer is evident as he lingers for a beat before Foley walks over to him and says something. Then we are alone.

"Let's go for a walk," I tell him.

Here in the dark, with his trench coat wrapped tightly around him, the sharp contours of his face shaped by his eagerness, Foley resembles Dick Tracy in the cartoons I remember reading as a kid. But this isn't a cartoon; it's the big time. People are going to die the way Vince did. One mistake and it'll be me or Johnny.

We walk in silence till we reach a point where two large trees form an ominous sanctuary. Foley turns to me. "Let's talk, Davey."

"I have a deal for you."

Foley doesn't say anything. He looks down at the ground, then back at me. "I can't make any deals with you. I can listen and take it back to our people and we'll let you know."

"The deal is on a onetime basis, Foley. Right now. I'm risking my ass and I'm not going to play any chickenshit games with you. So let's not dick each other around."

Foley kicks at a twig. He's looking for some kind of leverage going in. That trained lawyer's mind is whirling around, looking for the edge. But I have grown up among men who've defined their lives by having the edge. It belongs to me now because I have something Foley wants—an arrest. Getting one of the major players in the mob is what the Justice Department dreams about.

"I'm listening, Rossi."

We're back on an official basis. Let's see how long you stay official after I make my offer.

"There's a drug buy going down tonight. You interested?"

"Who's buying?"

"Frank Bruno."

Even here in the dark, I can see Foley's eyes recoil. His mouth, which is always clamped tight, falls open as his lips part. I have just offered him the head of one of the Five Families. Frank Bruno, the Executioner.

"You're offering Frank Bruno in exchange for what?"

He thinks this is about Vince. He's right. Foley is linking Bruno to Vince's murder. He's not going to be prepared for what I ask.

"I want you to set someone up for me."

His eyes leap out at me. He figures he's come upon the hidden treasure in the lost city of legend.

"Who?"

"That's my secret."

"What do you want us to do?"

"I want to borrow one of your people."

"Who's that?"

"Julie Alpert."

The briefest flare of anger shows in his eyes; then he covers it. I'm not supposed to know that the lady they planted in the mob works for them.

He doesn't confirm or deny. "What do you want her to do?"

"I want her to meet with somebody."

"Who?"

"That's a secret also."

"Somebody from the mob?"

"Could be."

"I can't do that."

"Sure you can. It's very safe, but it will look very unsafe to somebody else."

"You're asking me to let you run your own private little sting operation."

"That's right. And in exchange, you get Frank Bruno."

Foley's eyes glitter with ambition. He's turning the whole thing around in his mind now, looking for the flaw in it. He knows he's not going to be able to call and get his boss to approve it. The eleventh commandment: Cover thy ass.

He does a little circle away from me while he runs it through the hoops. And then he comes back at me with probing words. "You're saying this sting operation is very safe. But if it looks unsafe to somebody, then there's got to be a reason."

"There is."

The picture is there for him, and Foley, to his credit, sees it very clearly. "You're saying Julie's going to make somebody look like they're selling out. That only works if whoever is being set up knows she works for Justice. You want to blow her cover. That's it, isn't it, Davey?"

We're back on a first-name basis again. That means his pants are down and going to bed is a distinct possibility. But it is also about who does what to whom. And that comes down to having the edge.

Foley gives it the big theatrical take. "If we do that, then it blows a lot of things we set up. And it puts Julie in danger."

"Julie hasn't gotten that far, Foley. She fooled Tommy, but he's dead, and you're operating on a maybe for the future with her. Maybe somebody else will hire her. If the mob finds out about her, they'll write her off. That's all. The logic will be that Tommy got what he deserved for being soft. Nobody will go near her. And you still get Frank Bruno."

"You don't know what Julie has developed for us."

Sure I do, but I'm not letting on. "That's not my problem. The buy goes down tonight."

Foley doesn't miss a beat. "Once we get Bruno, we'd like the lines kept open."

You mean once I become an informer, you've got the hook in me and you'll want some other choice cuts.

I don't want to disabuse him of that notion. "Let's see how it goes. I remember once my father telling me how some guy was set up twice for the G-men and both times you guys fucked up."

Foley thrusts his jaw at me. "We don't fuck up."

I push into his face now. "Sure, it was some other guys. You want Frank Bruno or not? I have to get back to my training camp."

Foley rubs his chin. "I'll have to ask Julie."

"Ask her. She's in the car, isn't she?"

Foley's sharp eyes bore into me. He'd love to know how I found out about Julie working for him. I'd love to tell Foley I found out because I caught her sleeping with his boss.

"What if she doesn't want to do it?"

I look at Foley. She'll do it all right. I asked her when we were in bed at her apartment last week. But I can't tell you that, Foley. "Then you don't get Bruno."

We stand there measuring each other and finally Foley turns and heads back for the car. I follow him at a distance. He is walking briskly, the blood pumping in his veins. This is the kind of a break that comes once in a lifetime. Wait till he tells Bobby. We have a line to the mob. The son of the don who was hit. We can break the Five Families wide open. Talk about drooling. He reaches the car and slides in.

Julie is inside and she'll play it cool. Not like last week. Neither of us was cool then. I had started thinking about her as I was running that morning. I thought I could put her away, but I couldn't. And when it came time to do my evening roadwork, I told Sy something important had come up and I had to go into the city. I remember Sy spluttering, "You're fighting for the championship in less than two weeks." Then I was in the car and the feeling of excitement took over. Somehow I knew she would be there waiting for me in her apartment, and she was. And in those cool eyes was that expression that said, I knew you'd come. Those eyes kept appraising me as she mixed us drinks—a drink I never tasted because that line that had been building in me all day and all through training camp exploded and either I reached for her or she tumbled into my arms.

We stayed in each other's arms for two hours, me surging and Julie yielding till the fever in me went away. Then I told her what I needed her to do. She lit a cigarette calmly and, looking at me, said, "Now that you've grudge-fucked me to jelly, you want to use me."

I got up and began reaching for my clothes, but Julie put her hand out. "Tell me what you want me to do."

I told her and she listened. She's a good listener, and I always want to tell her more than she should know. This time, I didn't. I told her just enough and she said she would do it. She even told me how to handle it with Foley. "It'll work if you do it this way," she said. Somehow, I knew she was right. She's smoother than I am and she's wiser in the ways of the world. It seems to me that my anger makes me less than her. Is that why I don't trust her? Or is it because of the Sicilian in me?

She comes out of the car now, walking next to Foley, wearing a fur coat, her hair up. The feeling that makes me want to surge inside her comes back for a moment and then I force it away.

Foley takes the lead. He wants Frank Bruno. "I've spoken to Julie and she's willing to do it. We'll help you on this thing, but we have to know who it involves."

I play it big for him. Enough so he thinks he has me off balance. "Let me think about it while I talk to Julie."

Foley checks his watch. "If we're going to go tonight, I need to set it up."

"Five minutes," I say.

We walk away from him. I try not to smile. Foley has the hook in his mouth.

Julie brushes my shoulder and I come alive. I do a little jig in place
to stay warm.

"You must be cold."

"I'm trying not to cool down. Sy will have a fit." I look back at
Foley to avoid her eyes. "It went just the way you said it would."

"Will it go the way you said it would?"

We have stopped walking. "What do you mean?"

"Will we get Frank Bruno?"

It is the "we" that digs hard. Reminding me she is still one of
them, still Bobby Kennedy's, no matter how good she is in bed with
me.

"If you're sharp, you'll get him."

"Meaning there's many a slip twixt the cup and the lip?"

"Something like that. But the buy is definitely tonight. That's fresh,
hot off the press."

Julie nods and I can feel the syringe go in deep where the ambition
lies. They're all that way. She and Foley and their boss. Easy, don't
get emotional. There is a bigger game than this to be played.

Julie's hand comes out and for a moment I think she is going to
take my arm.

"I almost took your arm."

"I know."

"You're still angry aren't you, Davey?"

I brush away a branch that touches my face.

"Aren't you?"

"I'm old-fashioned. That's the way I was raised."

"I understand."

"But I don't."

"You can't come back and do it that way to me anymore. If you
come back, you have to be different."

"I don't think I can."

I look back again at Foley. "He looks very impatient."

"He is. Let me tell him you want to sting Joe Dante next."

"You mean you haven't told him?"

"No, I haven't. Davey, if you want me to look real to Dante, I need
to work up some kind of deportation case against him. Enough so it

will seem legitimate to Dante and I can pose as his friend. Foley can help me with the frame. Trust me . . . in this."

"Okay."

She stands facing me and I stare hungrily at those moist lips. But nothing has changed. I'm old-fashioned and she doesn't want me to come again unless it's different.

I can see in her eyes that she knows what's going through my mind. "Let's go back," she says softly.

Foley is waiting for us, trying not too look too anxious. I walk up to him. "It's a deal. Julie can tell you about who we're going after. About tonight . . ."

"Hold it." Foley pulls out a pad, his fingers moving quickly to a fresh page. "Go ahead."

As I start to say the words, I remember a long-ago winter night when Joe junior called a kid at St. Joseph's Prep who snitched on us to one of the sisters a "rat fink." "Long Island City. Eleven o'clock tonight. There's a warehouse on Sixty-seventh Avenue. The sign says ROLL AWAY TRUCKING. Don't screw it up and you might have yourself something. That's it, Foley. You have to do the rest."

Foley wheels and calls to the big guy, who hurries over. The Justice Department is going into action.

Julie has been watching me. "He'll get back to you."

"I know he will."

"And you?"

"I have to go, Julie."

For a moment, it seems like I will say something else or she will. But the moment slides by. "Take care of yourself, Davey."

I nod and start moving away. Then I am running back to the woods. I look back once, but Julie is no longer there. I keep up a steady pace till I reach the lake. It is exhilarating running now. My legs are strong. I want Sandy Simpson. I want him. When I reach the lake, I slow down and stare into the water. It is clear and fresh and I can see my reflection. It is like looking into glass. The water ripples and the image changes. It becomes Vince with his eye shot out and his face stuck to the windshield. I shiver and realize how real this all is. I pick up a pebble and throw it into the water, dispersing the image. Then I run again, alone and cold, trying not to shiver.

# 38

**I BREAK OUT** past the lake headed for the woods, trying not to let a case of nerves overwhelm me. Good nerves is the feeling in the pit of your stomach before the bell for the first round, the anticipation of the fight you have long trained for. Bad nerves is when you know what awaits you may be fatal. Dino Manfredi is sitting in a car a hundred yards or so away, waiting for me. What I have set in motion must now play out. There is no turning back, no sign I can give to ask for a time-out. This is the real deal.

The sun is dipping low in the sky as I enter the woods. A bright, shimmering ball of red daring the night to eclipse it. The woods swallow me up as I run on the path leading inextricably toward this meet. I slice between some trees and my eyes blur. I feel dizzy and my legs wobble. I slow and there up ahead I see the headlights of a car. For a moment, I fight the urge to turn back. I take a deep breath and slow my stride, then walk deliberately toward the car.

A couple of Dino's men are leaning against a tree, smoking. The back door to the car is open and standing next to it is Buster Minetta. He gives me a sharp look as I approach. Halloween night resurrects itself. I see Buster holding a gun, going toward Johnny as he gets out of the cab, and me throwing the punches that make Buster crumple. Buster walks toward me as Dino calls from the car, "Hey, leave him alone."

I brush past Buster, and there is Dino, spread out in the backseat. A hero sandwich bolstered by a wrapper rests on his lap. The pungent smell of onions and cheese reaches me. A large container of coffee is in his left hand. Smoke billows from it. A dark overcoat is draped over his shoulders and his hat is pushed back from his forehead. He beckons with his free hand for me to come forward. I lower my head and slip inside next to him.

He wolfs down a large bite of the sandwich and washes it down with some coffee. His teeth flash as he chews on the remains of the food. "You should try some of this stuff. But you're in training." He looks me over. "You going to win?" He taps my leg. "How far can you go? Remember what Joe Louis said. You can run, but you can't hide."

"I'll be there."

"For how long?"

Dino doesn't think I can win. His money, the smart money, will be on Simpson.

"The odds are three to one against you, Davey. I might go for some of that."

"You should, but won't."

His eyes flicker momentarily; he takes another bite of the sandwich and drains the coffee. The remainder of the food goes into the container, which he throws out. "Close the door."

I reach over and slam it as Dino lights a cigarette. He eyes me as if I'm a piece of merchandise. "You got word to me that what you have to sell is vital. I like that word. My guys can't even spell it. Vital. I like that."

He is saying this better be good.

"What's being sold, Dino, is you."

I let it sit while he chews on it like he did on his food.

"Yeah, and who's doing that?"

"Your friends."

"And how did you come by this?"

"That's show business."

"Yeah? Since when were you looking out for my welfare?"

"I'm not, but it's useful when you come across this kind of information."

"I ain't heard any yet."

He draws hard on the cigarettes and I can see his eyes flash. He is ready to hear tales of betrayal, ready to strike.

"There are people who don't want you sitting on the throne, and they're speaking to other people."

"What kind of people?"

"The kind of people who will be coming to the party you're throwing upstate at Joe Jelly's estate in Chatham."

That rocks Dino. He recoils as if I just nailed him with a straight left jab. This is information I'm not supposed to have.

"There's a list being put together of people who don't want you to be capo di tutti capi."

"Like a Christmas list, huh?"

He has given me my opening and I skip to the main course. "And Santa Claus is Joe Dante."

Dino's eyes narrow and he draws hard enough on the cigarette that it seems like he will swallow it.

"How do you know so much?"

"I have sources. I put one and one together and I'm here with you."

"Who's one?"

"Johnny. I told him what I heard and he said I should give it to you direct."

"So he chirped about Joe Jelly's place."

"No, that was a different bird. One who sings sweet and smells good."

"A broad? What kind of deal is this?"

"The kind of deal that your uncle Sam is cutting."

"I ain't got no Uncle Sam."

"I mean Bobby Kennedy."

Dino jams the cigarette into the back of the driver's seat. "Fuckin' Bobby Kennedy. What kind of story are you peddling?"

"I'm giving you an inside seat, Dino. The skids are greased and you're going right down the tubes. Your friend Joe Dante sold the meeting at Joe Jelly's place to a federal agent."

"What agent?"

"Julie Alpert."

Dino shows his teeth now like a fierce rat trapped in a corner. A bitter smile paints itself across his mouth. "Tommy's lawyer? The bitch is a fed?"

"She works for the Justice Department."

The lie is halfway down his gullet. But he won't swallow it whole unless he can establish how I'd know it.

"Why would she tell you?"

"Because I'm good . . . where it counts."

His eyes are on fire. My lie is roasting his insides.

"What else did she tell you?"

"She's meeting Joe tomorrow at four o'clock in Diaglio's."

That shakes him. His voice drops to a whisper. His eyes get small and hard. "Oyster Bay." He says the words as though pronouncing an infamy. In Dino's league, when you go out of town for a meet, that's grounds for treason. He reaches for another cigarette and lights it. It takes a second effort for him to do it right.

"If you're jerking me around, you won't live to fight Sandy Simpson."

"I didn't come here to risk my ass on chump talk."

"Yeah, well, we'll find out about that in about twenty-four hours. But that don't tell me why you're all of a sudden my friend. I was one of the guys who put the hit on Vince."

"One of them, but there are three others, and they're all selling you out. Joe Dante, Frank Bruno, and old man Scola. He's back of the whole thing."

"Did the bitch also tell you that while you were screwing her?"

"She didn't have to. Scola's always behind everything."

Dino shows his teeth again. Old man Scola sticks in his craw.

"They're sewing you up in a bag, Dino. Next time you go to see Annabelle in Red Hook, check the rooftop across the street. There are some heavy hitters up there. One of them has a big scar on his cheek. He's Frank Bruno's number-one hitter. You know who I mean."

"Marty Dolan."

Dino turns away and his eyes wander off into the night. 'Twas the week before Christmas and visions of hell dance brightly before him.

Just to make sure, I hold the picture of betrayal in place for him.

"So if you don't get busted at Joe Jelly's place, then Frank Bruno is going to whack you on behalf of the boys."

"Yeah, well, we'll see about that." Dino licks his lips. A wolf debating whether to devour a rabbit. "So I knock them off and then you figure out some way to get me hit."

"I can't do anything to you, Dino."

"Yeah you can. 'Cause you're either with me, kid, or you're against me. Like they say, if you can't beat them, join them."

I watch Dino as his eyes work on his singular vision of revenge. "What do you have in mind?"

"I'll take care of Bruno and we'll see about Joe, but Scola, you're going to kill him for me."

He has come right at me. "I'm no killer."

"If you're not with me, Davey, you're dead."

Oh, I'm with you, Dino. I'm with you right to the end.

I play it coy so he can lead me right to where I want to go. "He's never alone. How would I get near him?"

A crafty smile crosses his face. "During the week before Christmas, Scola likes to sit in that big fucking chair of his down at St. Ignatius Church and play the Pope. His great fucking Eminence himself. You ask for a meeting right before the fight. He'll see you. He owns Simpson. You tell him you want to make a deal. He'll see you alone. When he does, you whack him."

"You're crazy."

"No I ain't. You'll figure out something."

"I got a fight coming up. I save your ass and you ask me to commit suicide."

"What the hell do you think you're playing at, potsy? You come in asking me to hit Frank Bruno and Joe Dante and then you think you're going to say, Dino, I can't get my hands dirty; I'm a fighter. Nails was your old man and Vince brought you up. You're just stepping up in class. Capisce, assassino?"

There is a trace of whiskey on his breath. Dino had a few belts before he got here. He isn't sleeping so good. Betrayal shares his pillow. He knows how they cut up the last man who tried to make himself the big boss. Dino was ready for the big lie before I ever thought it up. He hates Frank Bruno, fears old Scola, and expects the knife in the back from Joe Dante. And now he figures he has me. Well, you're right, Dino. I'm in.

I nod. "Okay. But not till after the fight. That's the deal."

He edges forward and whispers, "You'll get a call tomorrow night. Somebody will say, 'It's on.' That means my boys went to Oyster Bay and seen Joe Dante flagrante delicto. That means we're in business. Don't try to contact me. I'll be in touch when I need you. And no Johnny. This is our deal. And one more thing . . . the Rossi family is now headed by Albert Molina."

"What do I get out of this?"

"You get to live under my protection."

"Fuck your protection."

"What do you want?"

"Points on the boxing action in the Garden."

"We'll work out some numbers, nothing big."

Dino sizes me up. He's not sure I can get to Scola, but it's worth a try. Maybe I'll get lucky. Either way, he'll whack me when things quiet down. I know too much.

Dino throws the door open. "That's it. We both got things to do. Just listen up for a call tomorrow night."

When I get out of the car, Buster is there. "Trick or treat, Davey?"

He stands there smiling. I wait a beat, feint with the left, then, when he covers up, cross the right and pull it back. He is all bent over like an old man with his hands flailing in the air. "Have a good Christmas, Buster."

I jog back through the woods without looking back. I hear the car pull away as I reach the lake. A cool wind whips across my face. I pick up the pace, thinking about what lies before me. Sandy Simpson and then Scola. I'll do it, Dino. I'll do it. But it's for me, not you. It's for me.

# 39

RED SWINGS THE CAR off the Long Island Expressway and onto the service road that leads to the Montauk Highway. It is a crisp, clear night, the stars firmly entrenched above us. We pass a small cluster of houses. A large Christmas tree occupies the front lawn of one of them, its lights blinking in green, red and gold invitation to us. We've been on the road for two hours. When Red picked me up earlier at my training camp, Sy followed us to the car. "What kind of behavior is this, Davey? Sandy Simpson will be in bed early, getting his rest. Davey, this is not the first time you disappear on me."

As Red started up the car, he looked over at me. "You sure you want this?"

I didn't answer until we had been driving for twenty minutes. "I want it."

Now as we approach the Hamptons, I feel a tightness in my chest. You can't always see to the end of things, but the past has a point at which it all began, a place from which everything flows.

Red rolls the cigar around in his mouth. "You know, Davey, sometimes when you go looking for things, what you find is not what you expect to find. Life is funny that way."

"Yeah, I know. Vince wouldn't let you go in with him that night and it saved your life."

Red is silent as the sign for the Montauk Highway looms in front of us. He makes the turn behind a station wagon. "I didn't like not going with him. But in those moments, you can't say, Well, I got a feeling things might not work out. Vince thought he had the deal figured. Where he made his mistake was that he thought Frank loved Tommy the way he did."

And Scola figured out that Frank Bruno loved money even more.

Red reads my mind. "In this racket, someone always figures your weakness. That's how they get you."

We pass through Hampton Bays in a couple of blinks and then a sign next to a plant nursery announces Southampton.

We slide past some small stores festively decorated with holiday lights and a diner with a Christmas tree. Christmas bunting is draped over a Ford dealership. The Hamptons is a world unto itself into which I have come looking for an answer.

Red hooks a turn and we head in the direction of the center of town. We swing past several gas stations and a brightly lighted pizzeria. My hand goes inside my pocket and I feel the magazine article— the one Julie sent me. The date is July 16, 1934. The writer's name is Franklin Radford. I have read it over many times. Parts, I can recite from memory.

*I remember the first time I saw Dolly Irving. It was at the Palais Royale with the Paul Whiteman Band in 1927. She was twenty-two then, the golden-brown curls swirling about her head as she sang. The sequined white dress seeming both to hug her body when she torched and fly off her as she dug into a tune with upbeat lyrics. The Whiteman band had taken New York and then London by storm in the years after the Great War. There was a trip to Hollywood and a movie for the King of Jazz. This soft May night marked the return of the Whiteman band to the scene of its greatest triumph. Ghostly strains of "Whispering," "Song of India," "San," "Japanese Sandman," and "Avalon" seemed to echo in the mind as the audience, steeped in the legend of this flamboyant decade, mindless of its impending crash, laughed and drank with great abandon. Flappers flashing lithe legs and debutantes mingled with Gene Tunney, Babe Ruth, Marilyn Miller, and Flo Ziegfeld to welcome Paul Whiteman back. The Palais Royale was ablaze with light as the band took its place onstage. The lights dimmed and a mournful clarinet sounded the first note to "Sun" as the audience broke into wild applause. The lights slowly came up on the band and its leader, dapper in a white dinner jacket. Mr. Whiteman raised his baton and the band raced off. When the song was finished, the audience greeted the band with frenzied clapping. It became even more vocal when Dolly Irving appeared in her clinging white dress. She had astounded Broadway last year in* Rosie's Rose, *becoming everyone's Dolly in the process. Now as the band swung into "You're Driving Me Crazy," a stream of bubbles was released over the entire floor. Bright, brassy notes of gold serenaded us with their bouncy flavor, which seemed to stir the crowd to even greater heights of adulation. One wondered if the starving Parisians of the French Revolution clamored louder for their bread. If that allusion is apt, then Dolly Irving quickly gave them their cake and let them eat it. She soared through a series of upbeat tunes, then segued effortlessly into songs of heartbreak. The word* love *was on everyone's lips and minds. And just as she had won the hearts of the audience at the Winter Garden last year, she grasped control of this crowd only too eager to capitulate to her. One would have thought they were present at some great event that would be recorded for posterity in books and on film. Participants in a night of glittering enchantment that affirmed the belief that this euphoria would never end. There would be no end to this decade, only a headlong plunge into another ten years of epic hedonism.*

*But it was just as the band was finishing up that the truly memorable moment of this evening occurred. The last notes of "Who's Sorry Now" gave way to a slow downbeat glide into softer sounds and dreamier preoccupations. The caressing rhythm of "The Man I Love" sounded in the night, Gershwin's ode to the lovelorn and the lonely, to the eternal wish for that magical someone. It was precisely then that he entered, backed up by members of his gang. Wearing a dark suit, roughly handsome, with mesmerizing dark eyes and just the right touch of five o'clock shadow. Epitomizing in his stance and bearing the romantic image of the bootlegger. It seemed as if he must have just come in from a rum run along the coast of Long Island, where he had fought off rival bootleggers with his gun and his courage. The men around him were just shadows, yet there was no doubting their lethal character. One in particular caught my fancy. His name was Bo Sussman. A hulking creature. A powerful brute who conjured up tales of my youth. Little John to Nails Gordon's Robin Hood.*

*Now as Nails Gordon stood there flanked by his mob, he seemed to take on a dimension much larger than life. For who among us was not both awed and envious of him? Especially in that electric moment when Dolly Irving turned to him and it became evident to all of us in the Palais Royale that she was singing to him. To him and for him. What man in the room wouldn't have died to be loved that way and what woman wouldn't have given ten years off her life to love a man the way Dolly loved Nails? They stood there separated by less than twenty yards, some tables, and a glistening dance space. And now that crowd of people seemed to part so that Nails Gordon could approach the bandstand. He stood there as she finished the song; the lights dipped and died. We all waited in the dark, hushed room for what seemed like an endless time. Abruptly, the lights came up and they were both gone. For a moment, we were all too stunned to respond. Then someone clapped and the audience broke into spontaneous applause at the magician's feat. Applause, it seemed to me, that was mixed with delight, regret, and envy for Nails and Dolly, who had left us for the misty shores of Avalon.*

*That moment in time was stamped indelibly on my mind on a recent hot July night at Club 52 when the lights came up on Dolly Irving sitting on Sammy Feiner's piano. Her hair was darker now and the curls had been smoothed out into a long pageboy cut. One lock reached down and touched her forehead. She was dressed in a black gown cut just below the knee and allowed us a look at the beautiful long stems. Around her neck was a string of elegant white pearls. But if her appearance on the upright was dramatic and arresting, the expression on her face was even more haunting. She seemed as if she was re-creating the role of a Parisian chanteuse lamenting a loss of the heart. But a close look into her eyes in the small room that is Club 52 told you this was no act, no stylized mock or even heartfelt impersonation of a woman's heartbreak. No, this was the real thing. A woman singing to the man she had loved and lost. Instead of the theatrical sob of the chanteuse, the notes were clear, the words perfectly enunciated. When I heard Dolly Irving sing "The Man I Love" seven years ago, it was the sweetness of her voice that enthralled me. It was pure and direct, an artful interpretation of a young woman's yearning. But while it stayed in my memory above all the versions I had heard from other singers, it was a pale thing in comparison to what I heard now. The voice was deeper, huskier, the emotion deeply felt and palpable. The feelings on display were naked and searing. For above all, this was no interpretation. They were the sounds of loss, pain, regret, and recognition that her man would not come this way again. Once again, as they were seven years ago, the words were directed to Nails Gordon. I remember him so vividly that night at the Palais Royale in 1927, standing on the dance floor surrounded by his gang. The ghetto prince become a figure of legend by virtue of the decade that spawned him. A creature of those gossamer nights when lawn parties tinkled with the sound of laughter and the popping of champagne corks, while in the distance gunfire echoed off the coast of Long Island. But while he stood at our center, I don't think he was unaware of how he had been elevated above his station. Gangsters are not dreamers. They are ruthless, shrewd, and practical. Above all, they know how to make use of the moment. Nails Gordon and others like him took advantage of our time. Most of them were thugs: a few had a crude style, which we romantically embellished. That time will not return, nor will the ideals and foolish sentiment that marked the era. I think that somehow Dolly Irving was singing her heart out not just for Nails but for those years when we were all inescapably young, romantic, drunk, and naïve. Thinking it could never end and that we would never die. And somehow I suspect that of all of us present in the Palais Royal that night, Nails Gordon knew best that the end of the line was close at hand.*

We are driving along the beachfront now. I can smell the ocean as we pass the rows of estates and houses hidden behind tall trees and large hedges. The sound of the waves hitting the beach comes to me. A little over thirty years ago, Southhampton was at the heart of the roaring decade that gave my father his chance. Lavish lawn parties, corks popping, girls surrendering on the beach while back at the house ukuleles strummed out paeans to Avalon. I can hear them now. Whispering voices call out to me while ghostly shadows silently clamor for recognition.

We turn down the road toward the beach and a large house partially hidden from view. This is where I had to come to know about the past. The past is a place from which everything flows. It is time for the mystery to be over. When I solve it, I can sleep again. Inside that house is the answer.

# 40

**As I REACH FOR THE DOOR,** Red puts his hand on my arm. "There's something you should know about her. After Nails died, she took up with a lot of young guys. Maybe because she was from show business or maybe because they made her feel young. She got involved with a dancer in one of her shows. Blond-haired kid. Real pretty. She married him, and then it turned out he was fooling around with a chorus girl. She caught him with the tootsie and used a gun on the guy. His name was Jack Doyle. He was lucky that her aim wasn't so good. There were lots of headlines, a big trial; she got off, but that finished her career. From time to time, I would hear stuff about her."

"What kind of stuff?"

"Guys were still interested in her. There was one who made a lot of money in sugar . . . like in sugar daddy. But mostly there was always a young guy around her." He jerks his thumb toward the house. "There's one in there now. His name's Jack also. Just so you'll be prepared."

"Thanks, Red."

His hand rests on my shoulder. "I don't know what you'll find out, but don't expect too much. A lot of things happen—we all make mistakes. In those days, it was fast and exciting. We were young. It was crazy."

"Did you tell her who I was?"

"She knows. He told her. I'll wait here."

I get out of the car and walk up the driveway to the house. It is not quite estate-size, but it is big. A large manicured lawn stretches out in front of the two-story house. The shutters on the windows are open. I can see the downstairs lights burning. I ring the bell and musical chimes sound. I wait and suffer through an onset of nerves. Is this where it all began for me?

The door opens and a blond-haired man with a trim mustache faces me. He is wearing a powder blue sweater over a blue shirt. His slacks are gray and the line of the press is sharp as the edge of knife. Black tasseled loafers complete his outfit. There is an awkward moment, that which he tries to smooth over with a nervous smile. He gestures for me to come in but doesn't offer to shake my hand, for which I am grateful. I follow him through the foyer into a living room that is furnished in wicker and wood-painted pieces. An Oriental rug covers much of the floor. A large grandfather clock is in the rear of the room. There are numerous photographs on the wall and cut flowers decorate the tables. The light is managed: Small table lamps with green shades are placed at strategic points throughout the room. The total effect is like something out of those old black-and-white films you see on television, where everybody always has a cigarette or a drink in one hand.

"Can I get you a drink?"

"No thanks."

There is a touch of curiosity in Jack's blue eyes. He has the kind of a face you see in the magazine on models wearing outdoor clothing. Everything clean-cut and perfect, but without any character.

Jack walks in the direction of a large velvet couch and waits for me to sit down. He licks his lips nervously before speaking. "I should tell you that Miss Irving—Dolly—has her days, and then there are the other times. Today seems to be one of the other times. I'm sure you know what I mean."

I keep staring at his clean-cut face and the perfect square jaw. I get a whiff of his cologne now. It is sweet, almost like perfume. A great feeling of disappointment comes over me.

"I won't stay long."

"That's good. I'll tell her you're here." He stands up. "I've seen you fight, you know. Against Jake Torrio."

"He's a very game fighter."

"You were really good." He looks away for a moment. "I know why you've come. Don't press her too much. She has a way of going inside of herself. But if you give her some space, she can also be incredibly direct. Do you follow me?"

"I think so."

He nods his head. "Make yourself comfortable. There's a bar in the dining room. That's just beyond this room."

He walks out and I can hear him on the staircase. I look around the room, wishing to hell I hadn't come. You just can't go back into the past. What are you going to say to her? Are you my mother? Why did you give me up?

I sit there for some minutes. The big clock chimes eight o'clock. I get up and wander over to some of the photos on the wall. There are shots from various shows and lawn parties, with Dolly at center stage, flanked by an entourage of celebrities I can't always identify. In one of them, a smiling composer with a cigar in his mouth is playing the piano while Dolly leans over his shoulder. There is another one of Dolly with Fred Astaire and a woman I don't recognize, all of them decked out in white. In another photo, she is standing on the lawn of an estate, holding a croquet mallet. A man is sitting on a horse next to her, a scarf tied around his neck. They are both smiling broadly. Her hair is bobbed in that picture. A shot of Dolly in a flapper's costume, cavorting to music, catches my eye. Her hair is longer and a flirtatious smile is on her lips and in her eyes. It seems she is doing a parody of a young girl. Kidding the audience about sex. And yet somehow in her expression is a look that tells you this is just an act and the real thing is so much more. Any man seeing the picture would think, this is a woman I would like to know. What is it about her? She is not so much beautiful as alluring. Beyond the sunny smile, there is an air of mystery. The mouth seems perfectly formed, the nose is a bit crooked, and the eyes, though not large, are somehow deeply provocative. Broadway adored her; the playboys and celebrities flocked after her, but she was Nails's girl. They were ghetto kids who'd learned about passion on tenement rooftops while growing up. There are no pictures of her and Nails together. What they had was too real for posing. Somewhere in back of the light in your eyes, Dolly, was a blazing inferno. Men couldn't stay away from its lure. Uncle Nick was one of them. Who else?

I look at my watch. Ten minutes, and she still hasn't come downstairs. Maybe she can't face me. What am I going to do then? Burst into her bedroom and demand an answer? What happened? Why didn't you stick around?

I wander into the dining room, which is almost completely in darkness. A small table light burns in the corner. Above it is a theatrical poster. Dolly Irving in *Girls on the Loose*. The poster is done in vivid red and her lips seem to jump out at you, begging to be kissed. Oh, she was some dolly, this lady. Footsteps on the stairs. I whirl as if expecting an attacker. A lasso tightens around my rib cage. Get hold of yourself. I take a deep breath and walk back into the living room.

I step inside just a beat before she gets there. She is smaller than I expected—maybe because in the photos she dominated my attention. Her hair is dyed a brownish gold. She is wearing a flowing black dress with white pearls. Soft black low-top shoes complete her ensemble. It is contrived artifice, as though she is indelibly etched in this role. The eternal ingenue in a silent film that runs forever. I force myself to look at the face. She is wearing lots of makeup to give her color. The bold lips in the poster are now covered with a pink lipstick. It makes her look cheap. And the eyes that promised so much in the photos are dull, almost sullen. Where is the expression that is so palpable in the still shots of her? The crook in her nose is gone. Replaced with a slightly flared look. Plastic surgery. A face-lift that has eradicated the features that made her so fascinating. I feel slightly nauseated. Everything is off. Get out of here. Let the past die.

"Would you like a drink?"

The voice is thick, the words slurred. She is sloshed. I have come here to the past and its guilty mystery and undone her. I won't get anything out of this worth keeping.

"Nothing for me."

She walks toward me a little shyly and then pushes past me. I smell her perfume. It is flowery and she is wearing too much of it. I walk to the couch and sit down. She exits into the dining room and I hear ice being dropped into a glass and then the jarring noise of the glass falling to the floor. She swears, and though the words are unintelligible, the tone is not pleasant. She calls out, "Jack...Jack...come down here and fix me a drink."

But he doesn't come, and she swears again. Again I hear the ice cubes, and this time there is no spill. Moments later, she comes back into the living room. She finds her way over to a chair in the corner, just behind one of the table lamps, and sits down. She has positioned herself within just the right confines of the managed light. I can see the outlines of her, but not distinct features. Her body, sheathed in black, is completely hidden. It is like looking at a figure presented in the dim light of an old projector. The image is real and unreal, the person two-dimensional, the darkness both her crypt and her sanctuary. Her words float thickly across the room at me.

"I've been expecting you for a long time."

I wait.

"You look like him, you know."

"I don't think so. I think I look more like my mother."

She takes a long swig of her drink. "It's in your eyes. There was the look he had sometimes when he didn't give a fuck. You have that. That's what drew people to him." She looks down at her drink. "He would be proud of you. Max loved the fights. He backed a couple of fighters."

Her words come at me surly and defiant. "Get yourself a drink. I'm not sitting here with no teetotaler. You think you can come here and screw me around with the past and not drink with me?"

For a second, it seems that she is going to throw the drink at me, but she finds better use for it and drains the glass. I stand up.

"Where you going?"

"To get a drink."

"Fix me one, too. A gin and tonic. Easy on the tonic. And put two pieces of lime in it. Don't squeeze them. I'll know. Two pieces or I won't drink it. And pour a stiff one for yourself. You'll need it if you want to sit here with me."

I find the bar in the dining room and fix the drinks. Gin and tonic with two limes, unsqueezed, for the lady and a stiff scotch on the rocks for me. It takes some minutes and finally she calls to me. "Hurry up,

I'm thirsty. And I'm lonely. I'm always lonely. That's why I have Jack. I always have Jack. I knew the whole world, and now it's just me and Jack."

I reenter the room and walk toward her. She seems to recede into the darkness as I hand her the drink. I make my way back to the couch. She is already working on this gin with gusto.

"What do they call you?"

"Davey."

"I've seen your picture in the papers and I heard things. I knew about you all right. Why did you come?"

The words stick in my throat and I drink the scotch to hide my loss of control. It is strong, which helps. "It seems like there's a lot to talk about. You knew Nails and . . ." I stop. The words just aren't there.

"Yeah, I knew him. I know a lot of things. A lot. But you came out here on a goose chase. I'm not your mother, kid. I'm not her. I could have been, but I'm not. And I don't know who in the hell is. So you wasted your time."

It is like being hit with a bomb and having your skin peeled off. I feel all raw and exposed.

I drink some more scotch to numb myself, so I can go on. "But you were Nails's girl."

"I had a lot of guys, not just him. And he had girls. Plenty of them. Both of us traveled in fast company. He was a good-looking guy; the dolls loved him. And I was a knockout. Did you see those pictures? I'm not so bad now, either, am I?"

Watch it—this one is a minefield. "You're a beautiful woman."

From the corner where she is sitting, her eyes penetrate like sharp daggers. "You think so?"

I take a long swallow of air. "Yes, I do."

She gives me a wave of her hand. "It's all front."

Keep her talking. That's the way. If I can keep her going, she'll tell me something.

"I've heard things."

"Like what?"

Do I tiptoe around her or come right at her? My guess is that she likes boldness. Men who don't give a fuck.

"Things about my uncle Nick."

She swallows some of her drink. "Your uncle Nick, huh? What did they tell you?"

I don't answer.

"He was pretty . . . curly dark hair." She laughs as she lights a cigarette. "But he didn't lay a hand on me. Never touched me."

"That's not what I heard."

"Who told you different?"

"My father . . . Vince."

"The dago. He came to see me after it was all over and wanted to know what happened. You should have seen the way he looked at me. You should have seen—" She goes into a long coughing jag. Her head dips as the coughing subsides. She speaks softly now, without looking at me. "Your uncle Nick was a beard."

She smiles at my incomprehension.

"You know what a beard is? A front. And they killed him because of it."

"You're saying he took the bullets that were meant for somebody else."

"All those smart dagos had it wrong. I should have told that to your dago father when he came around with his questions."

"Why didn't you?"

"Because he couldn't have took it . . . because it didn't matter anymore."

She was going to say something else. What couldn't Vince take? I can see her watching me. She has said too much and moves away from it.

"You got to understand what it was like for me and Nails. We were like tar babies, always stuck together when we were around each other. But there were others. That's the way we both wanted it. I had the whole world chasing me. I was too beautiful to hang around waiting for him. He always said the same thing. 'My number is going to come up one day.' I didn't see how anyone could lay a hand on him. I was a young kid and I was crazy for him. But he would shake his head like he knew something." She takes another swallow. "And he was right. Get me another drink."

In the cool darkness of the dining room, I make it heavy on the gin, with just a sprinkle of tonic. This one she won't get through so fast.

I am back in the room, waiting ... waiting. She keeps her eyes averted, staring instead into the depths of her drink like a seer. She begins talking again, her eyes still fixed on the booze swimming in her glass.

"I was nuts about Nails, but I finally got to believe him. He said to me, 'We'll always come back to each other.' And we did, but there were others ... after awhile, there was lots of others."

"Tell me about Uncle Nick."

She finds a better use for her drink than staring at it.

"He was a cute kid. He would take me out to the speaks and then he would drop me off."

"If Nick was fronting for somebody, there had to be a good reason."

I can see the flare of her cigarette as she takes a deep pull on it. "You figure it."

"Nick was fronting for Johnny. That's it, right, Dolly?"

Her voice seems to come from far away. "Johnny was just a young kid when I met him. He was always staring at me. He would bring me coffee and cigarettes and a lucky flower after the matinees. It seemed like he was always around when Nails was there. He was cute and he knew his way around. There would be times when Nails wouldn't show and we would go out for laughs. That's how it started. He was different than Nails. Quick and funny. He worshiped Nails. That's why it hurt so much when it happened. It was on a weekend when Nails was away. We drove down to Atlantic City after my last performance. Just some laughs at the Jersey shore." She pauses for a fresh hit of booze. "Well, it turned out to be more than laughs. It was good, very good. We woke up and we were in very deep, because we knew it wasn't going to stop. And we were stabbing Nails in the back. But we couldn't stop. We both figured it would burn out ... that there wouldn't be any harm. . . . No one was supposed to get hurt."

"But someone did. Nick escorted you around to cover for Johnny and he got clipped when war broke out. Scola sent the killers because he needed a way to turn Vince and Nails against each other. Nick was perfect for the role. Everybody in the mob thought Nails had ordered the hit."

The silence rolls over us like a big wave soaking the shoreline.

She leans forward out of her dark corner, this siren out of the past, who trapped all manner of men. "So now you got what you came for. Get the hell out. Jack . . . Jack. Come and get me. Where the hell are you?" I stand up, which seems to frighten her. The voice drops now. "I told you I'm not your mother."

"Tell me about Johnny. When Nick got killed, he must have been crazed."

She puts her hand over her eyes and rubs them. "He busted into my hotel room. He was crazy scared what Vince would do."

I look down at the Oriental rug as the design of it evolves into a definable shape I can understand. "Johnny was afraid to go to Vince and tell him what'd happened and he couldn't go to Nails and tell him he had been sleeping with his girl. So Johnny went to Scola, not realizing that Scola paid for the hit on Nick. What did Scola tell him, Dolly?"

Her voice comes to me very gently now, like a little girl's. "He told Johnny to bring Nails to him and they would cut a deal."

"Without Johnny telling Nails what had really happened between you and him."

"What was there to tell him? It wouldn't change anything. The Gordon mob was going to be fried."

Something is jogged loose in my brain. Red told me that Nails came into the Rodman Arms and said he had made somebody a proposition. Scola. It had to have been Scola.

"What was the deal with Scola, Dolly? Tell me what it was."

She takes a deep slug of a very strong drink. "The deal was that Max would go to the Rodman Arms and wait."

Everything is spinning around. "Wait? Wait to be hit? Is that it?"

Her voice is like a distant trickle of water. "Max came into my hotel room and told me he would be going out of town for a few days. He said he had made a deal. He had met someone else and she was pregnant. It knocked me off my pins."

"Why would Nails tell you about having a baby with another

woman? That doesn't make any sense." And then I see it. "Nails didn't tell you, it was Johnny. You got all of this from Johnny." Dolly turns from me as the past rushes over both of us. "Johnny knew about Nails's deal because he was working with Scola to make sure nobody knew how it all happened." I grab her and she pulls away. "That's what happened, isn't it Dolly? After Nails was killed, Johnny saw to it that I was put up for adoption. Johnny just fudged the date of my birth from June to July. He fixed it with the orphanage. He's good at fixing things. But Vince found out and he adopted me. And what haunted Vince all the years, the question he kept asking himself was about where Johnny was that last night when Nails got killed. It didn't make sense to him that Johnny couldn't find Nails to warn him to stay away from the Rodman Arms. Vince was right. Johnny has been beholden to Scola ever since that time. One call from Scola and Vince would have known that Nick took the hit that should have been Johnny's. All these years and Vince was right. He couldn't put his finger on it, but he knew inside someplace that Johnny was rotten."

Dolly's head is bowed as if in homage to the drink she holds which promises sweet oblivion.

"Johnny tipped you I might show up, didn't he? Well, didn't he?"

Her eyes remain averted. "It didn't matter about being tipped. I always knew you would show up on my doorstep someday. You're the kid I should have had with Nails." She looks up at me now and thrusts her face from out of the shadows of exile. The eyes are fierce with possession. A fleeting image of the woman who sat on the piano in Club 52 and sang homage to the man she loved.

"Max was the real one. The others, I filled time with. But his life wore him down, and me with it. He would go away and come back, and each time a little bit of me died. We burned for each other, but the fire got us. I told him to quit the rackets, but he said he couldn't. There was nothing else for him, he said. One night when he'd had a few, he got this sad smile and said, 'The rackets are quitting me.' It was all closing in on him. The last year, I didn't see him much. He wasn't the same—he looked heavy and his eyes looked empty, instead of being filled with moxie. They were sad eyes. I didn't understand then. He knew he wasn't going to make it."

She takes refuge in her drink. I feel the magazine article in my pocket. This is what the Life did to Broadway Dolly and her gangster prince. One is a relic of history and the other dead before his time. The twenties were an illusion and their players were puppets dancing on a string.

Abruptly, Dolly looks up at me. "You got what you came for. Get out of here. Jack . . . Jack, goddamn it, get down here." She throws the glass across the room, where it crashes against the wall. I hear footsteps on the staircase. She gets out of the chair and lurches past me. Jack skips down the stairs and catches her as she crashes against the banister. She hangs like a limp rag doll in his arms.

He pats her head and then looks up at me. "I think she's reached her limit."

"Tell me the rest of it, Dolly."

"You better go. When she gets this way, nothing matters."

"This is my last chance, Dolly. Don't let it go this way. Finish it. Don't leave me without both of them."

For an indefinable moment, she doesn't move, and then I see her shoulders twitch. She pulls herself from Jack and throws herself on me. She reeks from gin, this tiny creature, but for a moment her eyes are alive. "You want it all, don't you? I was that way once. Max was that way, too. He told me he wanted to squeeze the juice from the world. We burned for each other. Did you think Johnny would have had a chance if Max had stuck around? We——" She collapses against me and I hold her. To whoever decides the nature of these things, I offer thanks that she is not who I thought she would be when I came here.

She looks up at me and touches my face. Her hand is unbelievably smooth. "I'm glad for Max that you're here. You should have known him. He was something."

In her eyes is pain from a life that no amount of applause could compensate her for. Jack moves in behind her to give support. She thrusts herself against me. There is something both bold and desperate in her gesture. So many times you did this, Dolly, with so many men. Where are they now, these men who responded and promised you the world in seductive whispers?

The words are half croak, half whisper. "Picture in the other room . . . left-hand side. Water lilies." She sags back now into Jack's arms.

Her eyes are closed. He picks her up in his arms. What does he get for being her caretaker? Sodden memories and nights of hell. I can see by the expression in his eyes that he has read my thoughts. "You can let yourself out."

He walks up the stairs, carrying Dolly's inert body. As he reaches the top, she lets out a scream.

I walk back into the dining room, find the light switch and flick it on. I move past familiar photos, until I reach a row of shots on the left side of the room. Water lilies. What about water lilies? Here it is. Dolly all in white, standing in front of chorus girls perched on artificial white lilies. A girl on each one. Long-stemmed beauties who have faded like the artificial flowers they pose on. Gone heavy, gone to children, gone to being grandmothers, gone to the grave. For a brief moment, they lit up the theater like so many fireflies, only to be eclipsed by the incandescent Dolly Irving. I stare at their faces. Four of them in clinging bathing suits. The second one, the brunette, has a nice smile. It is not forced like the blonde's next door to her. What is it about the smile that draws me back to look at the picture another time? It is a sweet, caring smile. The smile of someone who seems decent. Not glamorous like the two next to her. Which one would draw Nails Gordon? The last girl is chunky. More like a lily pad then a lily. My eye goes back over the four girls and stops again at the second one. Why her? Who is she? It is the way her lips smile. That's it. The smile that lends itself to an expression of caring. A chill line runs down my back. All these years, and she was right there for me. Right there and I didn't know it. I know how you met Nails. Backstage when he went to see Dolly and struck up a conversation with you. That's how it began. And I even have an idea why you couldn't keep me and Nails had to make a deal with Scola. I don't know all of it, but I know a hell of a lot more now.

I remove the picture from the wall. Thank you, Dolly. It must have been a knife in your side all these years, knowing who she was and keeping the picture here. But Nails belonged to you more than anyone else, Dolly. Hold that close on the nights when the pain is too much and the booze can't help you. I'll take the picture and we'll both be free. I trace my finger along the photo and stop when it reaches the second chorus girl. It rests there right on the face of my mother.

# 41

**IN THE AFTERNOON,** before I do my final run, I lie here in the cool quiet of my bedroom, but sleep doesn't come. There is too much on my mind. We'll break camp in the morning and drive to New York. The weigh-in is at noon at the Garden. I will spend Thursday night at Sy's apartment and Becky will make us a thick steak. The bookmakers have made Simpson a three-to-one favorite. At four to one, he would be an overwhelming favorite; this way, the odds reflect that he is the solid choice to win. Next to my bed is a table and on it is the column that Pat Gavin did in the *Daily Mirror* this morning. I have read it three times. He analyzes the fight, our styles, and picks Simpson. It is the last paragraph that stays with me.

*In a career that covers fifty fights, with just two losses and two draws, Davey Rossi has been an artistic, sometimes terrific fighter. But he has never been a great fighter. I thought he was on the verge a couple of times. His deft boxing skills, his superior footwork, and his fast hands have produced some of the most extraordinary boxing I have ever seen. So why not great? Because greatness in the ring is almost impossible to define but impossible to ignore when you view it. Sometimes it is fifteen rounds of greatness and sometimes it is in one round, as displayed by Ray Robinson when, bleeding from an eye cut and knowing he needed to knock out Randy Turpin, he went out and did it. Davey*

*Rossi had a round like that with Kid Bassett, and perhaps that was his bid for greatness. But to be remembered and persevere in the mind, greatness must come in a big fight, such as the Robinson-Turpin middleweight title fight. It is the feeling in this corner that Rossi has had his great moment. This is not to dismiss him. He has been a classy fighter and has given boxing fans and this reporter some big thrills. But he is twenty-nine to Sandy Simpson's twenty-six and Rossi has seen his best days. Sandy Simpson can start a knockout sequence with either hand and finish you off with either hand. He is that lethal combination of boxer and puncher. Against this, what can Rossi hope for? It says here that only a great fight from Rossi, a night of inspiration, will carry him to victory. I think Rossi is determined, but so is Sandy Simpson. A victory here would put Simpson in line for a welterweight title bout in May and a summer shot in one of the ballparks for Ray Ramirez's middleweight title. So Simpson has even greater motivation going for him than Rossi does. Simpson has too many guns for Rossi, who hasn't the legs anymore. Rossi was brutally punished in their last bout and was out on his feet, slumped over his stool in pain, when the referee stopped the fight after the eleventh round. Then there is the hidden factor of Rossi's grief over the recent murder of his father, Vince. It is less than two months since the Mafia boss was found in his car, riddled by bullets. It is too soon for Davey Rossi to be fighting again. The cuts over his eyes are barely healed; the broken heart is not yet mended. This bout won't go nearly as far as the last one. Sandy Simpson to retain his title by a knockout in the fourth round. Sorry, Davey, and thanks for the memories. And remember you read it here, fight fans.*

It doesn't help my mood. I got a call last night from Buster Minetta, who said only, "It's on." That means I have to kill Carlo Scola to keep my end of the deal with Dino. That's even tougher than beating Sandy Simpson. Not that beating Simpson will be easy. He is a hell of a fighter, one who is on the verge of greatness. But I'll tell you this about great fights and great fighters: Styles make fights, and maybe I've never really had the one that brought out something in me called greatness. Sandy Simpson is by all measuring rods a great fighter. So if I beat him while he is in his prime and I am past it, what does that make me? And if I beat Sandy Simpson and kill Scola all in one night, what book will record my deeds?

There is a soft knock on my door. I look up and see Johnny framed in the light of the second-floor landing.

"You up?"

"Come in."

I reach over and switch on the light above the bed. The room we are in has walls of cedar. It is furnished simply with a bed, a table with a radio, and some fight posters.

Johnny picks up the Pat Gavin article and shakes it in the air. "I thought you never read these things."

"Maybe I'm getting old."

Johnny's shrewd blue eyes flicker over the article, then back at me. "So what do you think?"

"Words don't win fights. But one thing Pat is right about is that Sandy will be motivated. If he wins this fight, he's got the welterweight title also. Scola has Joe Fletcher in his pocket."

Johnny pats my shoulder as he sits down on the bed. "Beat his nigger ass, Davey." He lowers his voice now and I know our discussion about boxing is through. "It's all in place for Friday night."

I sit up.

"Frank set up a steak dinner with Dino and Joe at Angelo's for before the fight. He'll bring his artillery with him. If you played Dino right, he'll have the same idea."

We exchange looks. There is a palpable hush in the air. Johnny is wondering if I really sold Dino on the double cross.

"Dino is primed," I answer. "He and Frank will have each other for dinner, and Joe Dante becomes the free dessert."

"What did Dino say he'd give you in exchange for our phony information?"

"I asked him for points on the Garden fights."

"How many?"

"What does it matter? Dino won't be around to negotiate."

Johnny is quiet. He's checking all the angles. "How did you handle the feds when they didn't get Frank the other night?"

"I said I'd give them the date of Dino's coronation in front of the

National Commission at Joe Jelly's place. I told Foley he could get everybody there."

Now it's my turn. "What about Scola?"

Johnny fishes out a cigarette and casually lights it. "What about him?"

"How's he going to take our little Christmas pageant Friday night?"

"He considers Frank Bruno a thug . . . no love lost there. He won't miss Dino's ambition. That kind of publicity brings the law. He'll miss Joe. Joe's a good businessman, but someone will take his spot."

"Everybody will be dead and Scola will shape the Five Families so he can rule forever."

"Could be."

"What happens then, brother?"

"We cut a deal with him, Davey. He'll need someone like me to handle the transition. Scola will do what's right for business."

"As long as he doesn't know how we set up Dino, Frank, and Joe."

Johnny stands up. "It's just going to look like they cut each other's throats. Everybody will buy it because it's such a natural. Frank and Dino have always hated each other, and Joe just got caught in the line of fire. If it works, it's the slickest deal ever pulled."

"Tell me about Dolly Irving. She must have been really special."

Johnny's eyes wander off in space. "Everybody who saw her fell in love with her."

"You, too?"

Johnny is quiet for a moment. "Sure. But I knew better. Uncle Nick didn't."

"It was tough to swallow, I guess."

"Tough on all of us. Everybody felt sorry about what happened."

I get up. "Time do my roadwork. We all set?"

Johnny claps me on the back. "Try to put it all out of your mind. Concentrate on the fight." We are standing just inches apart. I go slack so he can't see my tension.

"You okay, kid?"

"I'm okay. It's the fight."

He braces my shoulders with his hands. "I don't give a fuck what Pat Gavin says. You're a great fighter. Tommy said that to me just before he got it."

"Did he?"

"Yeah. No matter what happens Friday night, it's been great being with you. In the end, it's just you and me. The way Vince would have wanted it to be."

"Yeah, Johnny, that's what he always wanted. All of us together."

He holds out his arms and embraces me while whispering in my ear, "My kid brother came up with the greatest triple cross ever."

I step back. "Not yet, Johnny. Soon, but not yet."

He goes out and I reach for my sweatshirt and pants. After slipping them on, I bundle into my jacket and put on my gloves and wool cap. I head down the stairs and get to the door, when Sy calls out, "You want Joe should ride behind you in the car?"

"No. I think better when I'm alone. See you in an hour."

"See you . . . champ."

I stop and look back at the little man. "Thanks."

Then I am out the door and jogging down the road. A hundred yards later, I reach the lake and lengthen my stride. The wind in my face feels good. It washes me clean. My mind is clear. Everything is all in place. Friday night will tell the tale. I reach the lake and dip left into the woods. Once more, I am running alone in the dark, the setting sun just over my shoulder as it dives to its death in the lake. I pick up the pace and soon I am deep within the forest. I see the clearing up ahead and then the car in which she waits for me.

# 42

**I GET TO THE CAR** and slide in next to her. Her face is fuller than it was in the photo at Dolly's house. The contours are more rounded. But the kindness is there in the eyes, which are also touched by grief. She has lost a son. Anna Dante is wearing a brown cloth coat and her hair is down. I have seldom seen her hair not worn up. Perhaps her way of hiding the brief fling as a show girl. There are more lines in her face than ever before, as if the weight of the last few months has cut into her skin the way it has lacerated her heart.

It seems that neither of us is willing to speak. I wonder if she can read what is inside me.

"You must have a very great secret, Davey, to bring me all the way out here."

"I thought we could talk."

"I wanted to talk to you also, but I didn't want to disturb your training for the fight. I sent you a note asking you to get in touch with me."

She takes in my face and the scar tissue over my eyes. "You will bleed again, won't you?"

"It will be the last time."

The mouth twisted by hurt softens. "That's good. I never liked when you fought."

I want to tell her that I know, but the words are not there. "I saw a picture of you, Anna."

She looks at me expectantly. "You were standing on a water lily."

Her expression changes, but it is a subtle change. She has worn a disguise so long with me that it is almost impossible to discard. She nods in silent affirmation. "I hoped for this day, but I prayed it would never come. I knew if you learned about Max, the trail would lead to me."

We stand frozen in place, trapped in roles played for so long. Even casual affection is out of place. Anna stares out the window of the car.

"It is hard for me, Davey. I trained myself to let you go, not to touch you too often when I saw you and not to think too much about you. That was the hardest part. I lived a secret life with you. But I knew Rosalie took good care of you."

"Did she know about you?"

"No. Not her and not Vince."

"But Johnny knew."

"Yes. He has always been very good to me."

"And Joe?"

She hesitates for a moment. "He didn't know. He came later."

She looks away toward the woods and I can see her struggling with it. It is just as hard for me. How do you ask your mother why she gave you up?

The darkness closes in around us and abruptly Anna opens the car door and walks toward a tree. She bows her head as if in silent prayer, but I can see her shoulders shake. The past flows to us on tears of regret.

I leave the car and walk over to her. "I saw that picture of you at Dolly's house."

She looks up at the sky, which is a patch of purple. "She was a great star. I was just a young girl from Naples. I sang in the dance halls there. My voice was sweet and everyone told me I had beautiful legs. When I came to New York, my family remained behind in Naples and I lived with my aunt. I knew some English and I studied in night school after I came here. I had a funny way of saying words, and when I auditioned for *Water Lilies,* the chorus director thought my accent was cute, so he hired me. He liked my legs very much and he was always after me. I was just nineteen and I knew little about men. My father had been very strict with me. He pulled me out of a show in Naples because he was afraid people would think I had the morals of an actress. If he had been here, he never would have permitted me to be in *Water Lilies*. My aunt was just the opposite of my father. She wanted me to enjoy being young. She never let my father know what I was doing. The theater was like magic to me. Dolly was a great star, and all the men chased after her. Every night backstage, men came and left their cards for her. Some men, she went out with; some nights, she just tore up their cards. But when Max came, it was different. There was a look in her eye that only another woman would recognize."

The night is upon us and it is quite cold. I try to take her arm to lead her back to the car, but she resists. It is as though the cold is some kind of purgatory she is obliged to experience.

"He came one night with several of his men and you could see everybody move away from them, as if they were clearing a path. He was not a big man, but there was a feeling of strength that came from him. He stood there with his shining black hair. I couldn't keep my eyes from him and I didn't know enough not to stare. And maybe because I kept looking, I saw that he was unhappy. He was sad, like he knew something nobody else did. Dolly missed the performance because she was sick. As he was walking away, he turned to me and said, 'You want to go out?' "

She shivers and looks toward the lake. "He could have asked any girl in the chorus and she would have run to get her coat. I couldn't move or speak. It was a great business before I could say yes, but finally I left the theater with him. He told me while we were driving in his car that he had seen me staring at him all those times and had asked about me. It was a summer night and we drove to the beach and had drinks. He asked me a lot of questions, but he didn't speak much about himself. I could see that he was lonely. That must be what is making him sad, I thought. He took me home in his shiny car and all the young boys on the block were crazy with excitement. I never thought to hear from him again, but the next night we went to Atlantic City, and when he brought me home, it was morning. My aunt was very worried and when I told her who I'd been with, she thought the worst had happened. But nothing did. Not for a while. He went away, but when he came back, we were together again. He was happy with me. We would laugh. So it went on all through that summer. And then one night when he left me at my house, I went to bed and I longed for him. When I awoke in the morning, I knew we would be lovers. We were together only a short time when I became pregnant. I didn't tell him for a few weeks. We drove to New Jersey to eat and I suddenly began crying. He asked me what was wrong and I told him I was carrying a child."

The wind from the lake cuts across us and Anna turns toward me, her eyes moist from memory. "He smiled. I thought he was crazy. He said, 'So what do you want to do?' He said he would give me money. I was frightened. My mother and father had arranged to come here in the spring and I knew I couldn't meet them and tell them I was pregnant. I would put them in disgrace. I got morning sickness and I quit the show. I just lay in bed with my hand on my stomach, feeling for the little baby, feeling for you. I thought for a week that I wanted to be free, and then one night Max came to see me. He said he wanted me to have the baby. And I knew it was wrong to stop a life. We made a plan that I would go away for a few months, stay with some people, have the baby, and then come back to New York. I stayed on a farm with a nice Jewish couple and they did everything for me. I did nothing but eat and sleep. Johnny would come every two weeks with money and check if I was all right. He had my aunt write to my parents that I was traveling with a road show. For a while, I thought everything would be all right. One day, Max came. I remember he put his hand on my stomach. I was so big. He said, 'I want this baby.' It was in May and the sun was warm. The wind blew his hair, and for a minute he looked like a little boy. Max turned to me and said, 'I want a son. His name will be David. For the King of the Jews. And after he is born, he'll be circumcised. I want him raised as a Jew.'"

The wind gusts in my face. Johnny told me Vince gave me my name. One more lie.

"And then just days before I was due, Johnny came. He said Max was in a lot of trouble. Somebody had been killed. Somebody named Benny and the gang was in a terrible war. But he knew a man who would help me. He would take care of everything. I was very scared. My parents had arrived in New York and they found out I wasn't traveling with the show. Johnny said he would call them and tell them I had gone on a short trip and would be back in two weeks. But I had to go with him now and meet this man who would make all the arrangements so I would be all right."

"He took you to see Carlo Scola."

Anna's eyes flash and settle into a piercing stare. "He was called 'Uncle Carlo' even then and he looked much the same as he does now. I don't think he was ever young. He talked to me. He talked and he talked. He talked me into giving away my baby. He said no Italian would have me if he knew what I had done, and that my parents would live out their days in disgrace. He said it would be infamy to be an unwed mother and raise a Jewish baby. I would be all alone, and what would I do then? He promised me if I gave up the baby that a good family would raise it. He said Max was in such trouble that if it were known he had a baby, nobody could guarantee the baby's life, especially if it was a boy. That boy would grow up and one day Max's enemies would come after the boy and take their revenge. He said so many things. I was young and frightened. I wanted everything to be all right with my family, and I knew Max was in danger and couldn't help me. Johnny was his good friend and he told me he feared for Max. Uncle Carlo held my hand and said I would go to a hospital that night and stay there until the baby was born. He promised me he would take care of everything. He kissed my hand, made a telephone call; then Johnny came in and took me to a private hospital in the Bronx. You were born there three days later."

It is like I have been rubbing the surface of a slate covered with hieroglyphics for a long time and suddenly the signs and letters have arranged themselves in a coherent shape. I see it all now. You were in deep, Johnny. And you played right into Scola's hands. You told Scola about Anna's pregnancy and he suggested that Nails should come in and have a talk. So you arranged it Johnny, like you arrange everything else. Scola pointed out to Nails that he would never get out of this war alive, so why not save his unborn child, and they cut a deal. Nails would go to the Rodman Arms and go down with his gang in return for my being spared. What Nails never suspected was that Scola feared that this child might someday find out what happened and come after him. So he double crossed you, Johnny, and forged a note from Nails telling Vince about me. Vince was perfect for the patsy role because of his guilt over Nails's death. And I became the perfect hostage Scola dangled over Vince.

Oh, Johnny, how you did it to everybody, all to save your ass. You two-timed Nails and got Uncle Nick killed. And you chose Scola over Vince. You figured by being with Scola, you'd always be okay. It all worked out for you, but it wouldn't die. Nails's shadow was always there. And when Scola played his nasty trick, you had to watch me grow up and hope I'd never find out what happened. But I do know, Johnny, and I'm calling in all markers.

The wind whips us both and I put my arm around Anna and lead her back to the car. I slam the door and look at my mother. Her eyes are bright with tears. "After you were born, I had three days with you while they made arrangements for you to go to the foundling home. I knew I had to do something that would show that you came from me and Max. I was very scared, but I knew all that Scola told me was not true. I didn't think you should grow up without some part of you being as your father was. So I named you David, as Max wanted, and I had you circumcised. Johnny paid for it."

"Johnny?"

"I told him I wouldn't go through with it unless he arranged for it. The man did it while you slept. You gave a little cry and then it was over. You were too young to know pain."

No, that came later.

"On the morning of the fourth day, they came and took you and I cried. There was a big man there who pulled you from me. I thought I would die. I cried so bitterly, they gave me an injection. For a week, they put me to sleep that way. I went home to my parents. They were in tears when they saw how sad I was. I told them there had been a man who'd rejected me but that I'd kept my honor. Two weeks after Max was killed you were born. For months after that, I cried. I called Johnny all the time and asked him where my baby was. He said he didn't know. He didn't seem himself. Then one day, Uncle Carlo called me in and said he had a man who wished to call on me. He was a serious man who was interested in marriage. I said I couldn't marry, that I had been spoiled. He told me that this was a man who had lived as a brigand in Palermo. He understood such things. His future was assured here in this country. He would call my father for permission to see me. My life would begin anew and I would have many children. But there was just one thing that could not be discussed with him. He must never know about Max or about my baby. If I could promise Uncle Carlo this, then everything would be all right. I was grateful to him and so desperate for a life, I agreed. He patted my head, sent me home, and said everything would be taken care of. And the next night, Joe came to my house and took me for a walk, with my mother as chaperone."

The tears have found their way down into the lines in her face. You married a man of the world all right. And for each year he lived as a mafioso, you had a new wrinkle to show for it.

"How did you find out about me?"

"Johnny. One day he came to me and he told me. He was very upset. He had been drinking. I had never seen him like that. He was always so controlled. He told me Vince and Rosalia had taken you in. I had been praying to the Holy Virgin for you, for your safety, and also for myself. I promised the Virgin that if she let me see you, I would consider myself blessed. If could just see you once, I would never ask for anything for myself again. It was like a miracle when Johnny told me. I knew I could watch you grow up and be part of your life. Some mothers might have thought it a curse to see a baby they could not have or touch, but I thought it a blessing."

Anna reaches over and her hand runs across my face. "All these years, I have been close by and there for you. I kept track of everything you did. On those days when you played with Joe junior, I would pretend you were brothers."

The ripping hurt is back inside me. How can I tell her about me and Joe junior? She lost me and then I took away from her the son she had raised. Spare her this. Confession may be good for your soul, but it will shatter hers.

"Davey," she whispers softly. "Come here." We move together and her arms encircle me. Huddled together, I can feel her body shake. But her tears are silent ones. We cling to each other as the wind rips at the trees and leaves in a soundless display of fury, as if expressing its displeasure over the life my mother lived. Isn't she twice widowed? First from Nails and then from Joe Dante, who left her while he murdered and plundered his way up the ladder to become a don. And then in the final betrayal, he turned their son into a hollow imitation of himself and cheated him of his life. She knows all this. Even the Holy Virgin cannot soften those kinds of blows. And what kind of blows do I hold in store for her? The truth? I shot Joe junior. How about that one? Or an even better one. On Friday night, I've arranged for your husband to be murdered.

"Anna," I say into her ear. "Are you coming to my fight?"

She pulls back from me. "I've never seen you fight. But I'll pray for you. I always do."

"Is Joe going?"

"Yes. He's meeting his friends for dinner and they will all go."

She says the word *friends* in a heavy tone. She knows who they are and what they are. He's meeting his friends at Angelo's Steakhouse, where he'll get laced up and down in a volley of bullets. And Anna will lose a husband and son in a space of two months. So what is it, Davey boy, hot revenge, or do you spare Joe Dante? Joe Dante, one of the machine gunners who stitched Nails's body full of bullets in the Rodman Arms and a year later married my mother. Don't do it, a cold voice inside me says. If you spare Joe Dante, he will find out your treachery and kill you.

I take a deep breath. "Maybe Joe shouldn't go to the city that night. Maybe it's bad for his health."

Our eyes meet. She knows what I mean. I can barely hear her answer. What is she saying?

"I told him about you and Max. I couldn't be alone with it anymore. All these years, I have kept it to myself, but since Joe junior died, the nights are long, so long. Joe sits every night in the kitchen by himself, drinking wine. I am alone with my prayers and he with his wine, and it became too much. So one night a few weeks ago, I told him. The past must die, and I didn't want anything to happen to you. You're all that is left of Max and me. I thought that in his grief, Joe would understand, would forgive the past. But he became cold with fury. All his bitterness had been focused on Joe junior. Now it rests on you. He is obsessed with the idea that you killed Joe junior."

She looks at me and her eyes fill with tears. I cannot escape those eyes. "He swore to me that you would pay for it. Then he said, 'I killed his Jew bastard of a father and I will take the heart of his son.' Davey, was it you who killed my Joe?"

Our eyes burn into each other. I can't answer, and that becomes my answer. Her hand comes toward me, but she cannot complete the gesture. There is more than one murder between us. "I know you did it to save yourself. Joe junior wasn't mine; he belonged to his father. Always he had to prove himself to Joe. When you fought as children and you beat him, his father ridiculed him. It never seemed that you wanted to fight him when you were boys. Joe junior forced you. He forced everybody, and he always lost."

She looks at me now, this woman I have known and not known all my life. More than all of the dons and mobsters I have known put together she is a victim of the Life, ravaged by the brutes within it.

"Tell me now. Did Joe speak the truth?" she asks ever so softly. "He killed Max?"

"He was one of them."

She lowers her head and closes her eyes. She must choose between us. Her eyes fly open. "It must be finished. All this ugly vendetta and the rain of blood with it. *Basta...basta.*"

"Keep him home."

Anna shakes her head like an obstinate child. In her eyes is the rage so long suppressed. "No, Joe has to meet his friends for dinner. They're expecting him."

She turns away and closes her eyes again as if she is praying. Is she asking for forgiveness or divine intervention? Or maybe it is simply that she wants peace. I take her hand. We stay that way for a long time.

It starts to rain as I come back to the lake, and I pick up the pace, running hard, legs pumping, fists punishing an imaginary opponent. I reach my cabin and bolt inside, going directly up the stairs and into my room. I turn the water on in the shower full blast and then go to the telephone and dial the number. When I left Anna, she touched my face. "Our time will come," she whispered. "The men murder and die, but the women endure."

I listen to the phone ringing, which is like an insistent theme: The women are stronger, better. The women endure. The women survive.

A woman answers and I ask to speak to another survivor who has endured the murderous deeds of men I have known. "Sister Mary Elizabeth, please. Tell her it's Davey Rossi."

I wait some minutes and then she comes on, her voice calm and strong. The voice of a woman made a widow before she could marry. Like my mother. A woman who has lived in exile and gained strength from knowledge of herself.

"This is Sister Mary."

"Sister Mary, it's Davey. The fight is on Friday night. I hope you can come."

"I will be there. And I have something for you."

# 43

THERE IS THAT TIME in the dressing room before the fight when it
has all been cleared out and the space belongs to me. It starts with
Joe Dunn taping my hands and giving me a massage. We have been
doing it this way for as long as I have been a big-time fighter. Joe
fought over 150 times as a lightweight and welterweight. He never
won a championship, but Sy has told me he was as slick as they come.

Joe kneads the muscles in my back and shoulders with those strong
hands. His left middle finger is twisted and bent from too many breaks.
And the knuckles of both his forefingers jump out in disjointed fashion.
But there is nothing wrong with those hands, which find the soreness
and tension in me and ease them right out of my body. Joe talks to
me in that soft voice, which is more like a croon with a touch of the
New Orleans bayou in his inflection. His voice is so filled with simple
humanity that I am mesmerized by it. "Davey, how come you let
Simpson get away with calling you a Jew boy?"

It happened at the weigh-in. I had just come off the scale and was
slipping into my pants and shirt when Sandy Simpson sidled over to
me. The reporters were all gathered around the promoter of the bout,
Blinky Dobbs. None of them heard the exchange, but Joe was right
there. Sandy walked over to me, a sly smile painted on his lips. "Hey,
Davey, all this time you go on playing at being Italian, but you ain't
nothin' but a Jew boy."

He stood there grinning insolently at me. Flexing his arms, taunting me with his eyes.

"You know the story about David and Goliath?"

"The one about the slingshot? Sheet, you gonna need more than a friggin' slingshot. Maybe a tank, Jew boy. You goin' down, Davey. You taking the count."

"I'll be there, Sandy."

Joe's talented hands find a knotted muscle in my back and ease the little ball right out of me. "How come you be taking that from him, Davey? Letting him behave like some swamp nigger."

"The fight wasn't yesterday afternoon, Joe, it's tonight."

"But you letting him rank you. He busted you up the last time and now he thinks you're backing off him."

"After he gets popped the first time, maybe he won't feel that way."

"You got to take the fight to him, Davey. You can stick and run once in awhile to confuse him, but you got to beat him to the punch. Otherwise, he'll cut the ring in half and chop you down."

I don't say anything. You're right, Joe. Sandy Simpson is thinking this is going to be easy. He's thinking he'll come out and set the pace because I won't have the stomach for what he dished out last time. My eyes will open easy. That'll be his target all night. But he doesn't want the fight stopped; he wants a clean knockout, and that means he'll take some chances. I'll be there waiting, Sandy.

Joe's words float to me courtesy of his soft southern dialect. "You going to keep fighting, Davey?"

"Why you asking?"

Joe doesn't flinch; he never does. "I think you're going to hang them up."

Again I remain silent.

"Then give them something to remember, Davey. Something they'll always talk about. And don't believe that shit in the paper. You a great fighter, Davey. Just let them all see it."

I turn over and look up at Joe Dunn. He's got big brown eyes and a lumpy, broken nose that he has trouble breathing through. His mustache is flecked with brown and white, as is his hair. I take his hand. "It's been a great privilege to work with you, Joe."

He squeezes my hand. "It's been an honor, Davey. You an artist with those hands. Give them something to remember. Go out on top. Not many do."

"I'll try, Joe."

I'm alone now. Sometimes I can sleep, not this time. But I am able to go away to that soft compartment where it's very private. I don't think about the fight. I know what has to be done. But I think about after. Can I kill Scola? Self-defense is one thing, but looking a man in the face and squeezing the trigger, that's another league. A long time ago, I asked Vince about the hit. His words have stayed with me. "You're looking at a man and you know that in seconds or minutes, everything he feels will stop. He will not eat, make love, or smile again. But if you start feeling sorry for him, you are finished; you will never do it. Yet I know if it were the other way around, this primitive would not think that way. He would empty his bullets into my brain, go out, and eat veal for dinner, drink to his heart's content, and have a woman. In the morning, he will wake up and think about me. You know what he will think? He will be glad I am dead. You cannot be sorry, Davey, even the next morning. That is weakness."

The door to the dressing room opens and Sy is standing there holding my gloves. "It's time to take a walk."

The crowd cheers as I come down the aisle of the Garden. Some of them begin chanting my name. A lot of them have gone for the long-end price on me. A lot more have put their money on Simpson. There is sentiment and there is the business of winning your bet. I climb into the ring and duck under the ropes. I do a little dance to stay warm and make my way to the resin box. I grind my feet in the resin dust as an explosive roar erupts from the crowd. The champ is coming down to ringside. The champ always comes last; that's tradition.

Sandy Simpson is long and lithe in his black satin robe, his first name stenciled in white on the back of the robe. He comes through the ropes, waving to the crowd. For a moment, our eyes meet and I can see the confidence there. Then the smile is gone. This is for the money. I make my way to my corner as he stops at the resin box. I look down at ringside and there is Johnny. I wish Julie were here, but I asked her not to come. The hand hasn't been played out yet and she has a part in a dangerous scenario. Johnny is watching me with dispassionate eyes. What does he see? I'm betting he thinks he is looking at a shot fighter, long on heart but short on legs and reflexes. Our eyes meet and Johnny gives me the thumbs-up sign. I nod and turn away. Let's find out how much I have left.

Johnny Addie makes the introductions. I hear him as if from far away as I concentrate on what I must do. "In this corner, wearing the dark trunks . . ." The hum of my nerves has begun. The good hum. No more thinking the fight, just do it. "In this corner, wearing the white trunks, weighing one hundred thirty-five pounds, from New York City, the lightweight champion of the world, Sandy Simpson."

The referee is Herb Gretz and he beckons us both to the center of the ring. Sandy is measuring me with his extremely confident eyes. "I want a good clean fight," Gretz begins. "When I say break, come out of the clinch, and no rabbit punches. Keep your punches up. In the event of a knockdown, proceed to a neutral corner. Shake hands and come out fighting."

As Sandy reaches forward to shake, I ignore his hand. "Beat this Jew boy, Sandy."

His eyes recoil in anger and he slaps at my hand. The seconds get between us, then I am in my corner and Sy inserts the mouthpiece. The bell sounds.

I come straight at Sandy and meet him in the center of the ring. I deke with my left shoulder and the little feint freezes him. I drill him with two sharp lefts and the crowd roars. He blinks his eyes and rolls his shoulders. He has very long arms, and that gives him the reach on me, but it takes him longer to throw a punch, and that is my edge. I see the left coming and pick it off with my glove. I start another left, come back with the right, and nail him. The crowd bellows for more. I move counterclockwise and he has no target. He shuffles around, looking for an opening. He is too anxious. He throws a long, wild right and I come under it and spear him with two hard lefts. I am on my toes, bouncing, bouncing, and he cannot find me. We are at long range and I rake him again and again with a series of quick combinations. My hands are too fast for him. He is confused; he was looking to set the pace, and I keep rapping him. He scores with a left to the head and a right hook, but I feint again and pepper him with a whole repertory of punches, hooks, and jabs and draw blood from his mouth. He lunges forward and I come under him in a move Joe Dunn taught me a long time ago, and spin Simpson around. I am waiting there with a hard left, and another, and another, and then I cross the right. He reels backward and the crowd is up roaring for more. This is virtuoso stuff.

He ties me up and pounds my ribs while I work on the back of his head. Gretz breaks us and I dip my left shoulder and cross the right, then follow with a jolting left-right combination that buckles his knees. The bell sounds. I whirl and walk toward my corner while the crowd is up giving its approval of my performance in a furious voice. Joe Dunn slides the stool out for me and his eyes are twinkling "Magic," he says.

Sy is there, his eyes dancing in delight, but he's all business. "Don't let up; go right at him. We'll get him dizzy and give him the bicycle act later."

The ten-second warning and I am up on my toes. No bicycle. It's just me and him. I come forward to meet him and go right after him. When you are on a roll, you must trust to instinct, like a dice thrower who keeps coming up seven-eleven. My blood is boiling and my legs light. All the deft moves I have ever practiced and displayed are there for me. I can beat Simpson to the punch. I make him miss and rip him with rights and lefts. He lands three hard punches in sequences where I connect five or six times. I can see the anger and frustration in his eyes. My hands are lethal. They haven't been this fast in five years. When everything is going for you this way, you take chances. It's time for the trick. It's not on the up-and-up, but this is a fight, not a potsy game. A flurry of punches thrown by Simpson don't connect. He stumbles off the ropes. I move forward and plant my shoes on top of his, leaving him unable to move or punch with leverage. I rock him with four straight lefts, cross the right, and come back with two stiff lefts. Then I flit away like a dancing moth circling a lightbulb while the crowd surges from its seats. The bell, and once again they are up applauding madly.

Joe Dunn swabs my head and body down, crooning softly: "The master . . . oh, the master."

Sy plays the counterpoint. "Don't get cocky. We got thirteen rounds. This is one dangerous shvartzeh."

But the crowd noise is music to me. They know they are seeing a great performance and they urge me on. This is everything I have ever learned about boxing, only I know it better now. The reflexes aren't as sharp as they once were, but the head is better. And there is the feeling that everything I do will work. I can't miss and Sandy Simpson can't connect. Each cheer from the crowd sends a tingle up my spine. I make moves I know and some I don't and always they work. I am there to score with rapid-fire left jabs and ripping left hooks. And every time Simpson forgets about my right, I joyfully remind him of it. I am landing most of the punches and I am landing the harder ones. The third and fourth rounds are dizzy celebrations of my head and talent working at the same time. I close out the fourth round by spinning Simpson around again, and I am there waiting to stick his face with straight lefts while I pirouette around him.

The crowd noise follows me to my corner as I plunk down on the stool. Joe is no longer saying anything, but the look in his eyes says it all. Sy is there with a rapid stream of words. "We got all the rounds . . . all of them. Pace yourself, Davey. Let's not run out of gas. Tie him up, use the clock, and then spurt on him. Then when he thinks we're low on gas, we step on the accelerator about the ninth round."

I stand up to meet the buzzer. Sy is saying, "Don't leave your fight here in the beginning with nothing to fall back on. Use your head, boychik." It is the smart move, the shrewd strategy, the one that will give me the edge. But I am on a roll and that is hard to give up.

Every crapshooter will tell you there is a point where he goes from being on a roll to a cold dice bust and he's not sure where or why it happened. The trick to avoiding it is noting when you lose on a couple of throws and then you have to pull back a little. Not bet so much on the next throw. For me, it happens a minute into the fifth round as I come off the ropes and trade with Simpson. For the first time, he has me leaning back, with less room to maneuver. And he scores with hard punches as I fire back. We both land, but now his punching power is starting to tell. They are heavy blows, reminding me of how tough he is with either hand. I get away and then, circling around, catch him, intent on following up. I assault him with a flurry of blows, and as the crowd surges to its feet, we trade again. He catches me with a left and the blood flow is there from my eye. I fight back with three stinging lefts as the bell sounds.

Joe sutures the cut as Sy delivers a nonstop summation of where we are. "I think we got the round, but the eye doesn't look good. Stay away, box him, and maybe we can steal the next round. The legs . . . the legs, maestro, we got to preserve them. There are ten rounds to go. Jim Corbett couldn't have danced for fifteen rounds. Don't trade; just make him miss."

But that is hard to do. Sandy Simpson is a good boxer and his corner has told him to be patient. They are confident my legs will betray me. In the sixth round, I fight at long range, rapping him with the left, and then spin away. But he is relentless and he cuts the ring with precision. There are two exchanges near the ropes and one at center ring, where he scores. The blows hurt and I am not moving so fast. I land, but he lands more. It's his round.

The seventh round is his also. He digs my body and then jolts me with those long lefts. When I don't begin the exchange, he can land to my body, bring down my hands, and control the tempo. The crowd senses the fight is going the other way and, like the fickle lovers they are, switch their affections to Simpson.

As I stand up for the eighth round, Sy calls to me. "Give him this round—stay away and don't let him get near you. Let him think you're plotzing and then we'll surprise him."

I jump on the bicycle and put on a classic exhibition of moving around the ring. Simpson doesn't land much, although the crowd greets every move of his with an approving cry. It is a great boxing lesson I am giving, but the judges will give Simpson the round on aggressiveness. He looks very confident. I need to take the momentum back. It is not something I can turn on and off as I desire. We wrestle in the middle of the ring and Simpson hurls me down. It is not a knockdown, but Gretz wipes my gloves off. Simpson comes straight at me, anticipating I will backpedal. Instead, I scorch him with a hard right and the crowd loves it. We stand there ripping at each other, both scoring heavily. His punches are numbing blows, while mine, though more frequent, lack his impact. I hear Sy yelling, "Get away . . . the left," but it is too late. The blow catches me over the other eye and a fresh claret of blood streams down my face at the bell.

Joe works hard on the cut while Sy is in my face, his mouth all twisted up. "Now he's got both eyes open. All right, there's no place to run to. Go right to him. We need the next three rounds."

I can see Herb Gretz looking at my cuts as I come out for the ninth round. I whirl around Simpson, setting him up for the next trick, the bolo right. The flashy uppercut thrown with exaggerated motion catches him flat-footed as it explodes on his jaw. I rake his head and face with a quick combination and duck under his flailing blows. The moment is there for me to seize. I weave in and out and then score again with three lefts. Simpson fires back and his right bangs my temple. The red river runs from my eye down my face as I burn him with two combinations, landing the hook off the left jab. It is my art against his power, while the crowd screams its tribute to the fight it is seeing. I can't see him as well as I would like, but I don't have to. He is right there as I nail him with left-right combinations. The round ends with a barrage of punches from me.

Still, Herb Gretz is there looking at the cut while Sy rags at him. "It's our fight, Herbie. Did you see it? Did you see what Davey did to him? Nothing to worry about. We'll be out there waiting for him."

Gretz is not impressed. "Those eyes don't look good, Davey. The cuts are deep. I'm watching you, Davey."

The bell for the tenth round. We come straight to the middle of the ring, hungry for each other. We hate each other's guts. Once again, I feint with my shoulder and pop Simpson with a series of blows. He grabs my gloves and we go into a clinch. I feel his body tense and then jolt forward as he brings up his shoulder and head at the same time and butts me. My left eye flares open. The flow of blood spills down my face again and I struggle to see him. The crowd noise gyrates in my ear. You must be pretty desperate, Sandy, if you can't do it with your fists. I gesture with my hands. You want me? Come and get me. Beat this Jew boy if you can. I brush Gretz away, bob and weave toward Simpson, offering my head as a target. C'mon, let's do it. My heart is pounding as I fake the left lead and land a big right. I dig him to the belly and then come back to his face. He has the look of the bully who knows he can't intimidate his opponent. I whirl around him and his face looms and disappears before me as the curtain of blood rises and falls. But my hands are like one-armed bandits in a crooked casino, reaching out for him, coming at all angles. I want the money. As the round ends, I have him backing off from an assortment of punches thrown from all angles.

The crowd is calling my name as I drop onto the stool. And there is Herb Gretz, and this time he means business. He reaches for my face and I punch his hands away. "This is my fight and my night. It's my title and I'm taking it home."

"Your eye is wide open. The other one will bust the same way the next time it's—"

"Fuck my eye. Go look at his. Ask Simpson how he's doing."

"His eye isn't wide open."

Sy jumps into Gretz's face. "Eye . . . pie . . . we're winning the fight. They'll hang you by your balls you try and stop this fight. Stop being meshugeh."

Gretz is intimidated. "I got a job to do." But the words are mumbled and he goes away.

Sy grabs my shoulder. "One more round, boychik, and we can coast home. Then we have eight rounds and you can go on the bicycle. One more round."

The bell sounds and I jump off the stool. It is about this round, but it is also about taking Simpson's heart away. If he surges in the last four rounds, he could steal the decision. You have to do it this round, boychik.

I peddle back and Simpson looks forward, thinking I am looking to protect my eye and sit on my lead. He wants to open either eye. This will give him the fight. Come catch me. We meet as I come off the ropes and he goes to the body and catches me. I grunt and dive into the clinch. He is trying to use his head again to butt me. I get my foot behind him and send him sprawling. The crowd boos, but Simpson has gotten the message. Gretz warns us both and we touch gloves and come out winging. I bang Simpson twice to the face, come under his punch, and paint him with more lefts. He stops me dead in my tracks with a right lead, and now we are there in the middle of the ring, punching away with abandon. He has the power, but I have the hand speed. I make him miss while I score. Here, take it. From me to you. Can you take it? Beat this Jew boy if you can. He can't do it. I can see it in his eyes. Eyes cloudy with resignation. Resignation leads to defeat. But he keeps winging at me. A sizzling right hook connects and my knees buckle as my mouthpiece flies to the canvas. I grab him, whirl around him, and then as he steps forward, I nail him with three pistonlike lefts. Now the right . . . the left . . . the right as I talk to him. "Beat this Jew boy . . . beat him . . . go ahead." His punches are slower now and his eyes misty with defeat. He can't win. It's something the heart tells you. The heart, which always knows the truth. The heart that I have taken from him because mine beats louder than his. I drive him into the ropes with a right hand as the bell sounds and I greet the crowd with a wave.

They love it.

I don't remember the last four rounds. It is crude stuff, sometimes dirty, but my legs are there, and my heart. Sandy puts on a good show, trying to stalk me, but he knows the night is mine. Then the bell sounds and Joe wraps me in a towel and his arms at the same moment, the tears streaking his face. "The master . . . the goddamn master."

Sy lurks behind us like some old grandmother who refuses to count her money, but I can see the smile in his eyes. The decision comes and Herb Gretz holds my right hand up in the air. Joe jumps in the air, with Sy right behind him. Everybody is up. Pandemonium in my corner—officials, broadcast announcers, reporters, and people I never saw before. Sandy Simpson is there, a new look in his eyes. We don't embrace. There is respect, but we will always be adversaries. "Let's do it again."

I look at him. "Sure. Maybe tomorrow in the street."

He bites his lips. "I took you too light. You won it, man. I want you again."

He has lost more than a title fight. The dream of a triple crown is over. I can see Pat Gavin watching us, and there is an expression on his face I will always remember. I have won more than one battle this evening.

I look for Johnny in the milling crowd at ringside, but I can't find him. Joe wraps me in my robe and soaks my cheeks with his tears. "I guess you showed him . . . Jew boy."

# 44

NANDY PECORA is just finishing sewing up my eyes. It doesn't take as many stitches this time and my face is not nearly as lopsided as it was after the Kid Bassett fight. Nandy leans over and talks softly to me. "Davey, if you plan on fighting again, you need to take six months off if you want to heal properly. Even then they'll open easy and—"

I put my hand on his arm to get his attention. "You don't have to worry about it. . . . I'm taking a lot more than six months off."

A broad smile shows itself on Nandy's owlish face. "I hear you, Davey, and I'm very pleased. When will you make the announcement?"

"As soon as I settle a few things. I can hold the title for at least six months without a defense."

His face grows stern. "Don't wait. Somebody will offer you a deal and they'll suck you back in."

"No deals."

"I've heard a lot of fighters say that . . . an awful lot. They never quit."

I sit up on my dressing table and yell, "I quit. Davey quits."

Pat Gavin slides over. "Is that official?"

"Next week. I'll give you an exclusive. Call me Monday morning."

The little sportswriter, his tie unloosened and his hat perched on the back of his head, sticks out his hand. "Thanks for the ride, Davey.

I owe you for tonight. You want I should eat my column?"

"You can buy me a steak and we'll call it even."

"You got it. How about Angelo's?"

"Some other place, Pat."

"You name it."

A photographer sticks his head in the dressing room and calls to Pat. I watch them converse as Joe cuts the tape off my hands. Pat grabs his overcoat and comes over to me. I signal Joe to leave us alone. Pat talks very softly. "I just got a tip. Somebody fell down dead in the parking lot over on Eighth Avenue. I hear it's Frank Bruno and he took a lot of slugs. I'm going to go cover it."

"Thanks, Pat."

He grins. "I guess this is your night, Davey." He claps me on the shoulder and goes out.

I call Sy over. "Seen Johnny?"

"He's making some calls. He don't look so good. What gives?"

"Get them out of here, Sy."

Sy jumps forward as if taking an electric charge. "That's it. Everybody out. The champ wants to shower in private."

Joe finishes getting rid of the tape while the dressing room empties. Gentle as a baby, he leads me toward the shower. He mixes it for me and I step inside the small tile square and drop the robe. This will be the last time in the old mausoleum for me. Another time, I might enjoy it more. Now it just feels strange. The night has only just begun for me.

The hot water, which is never hot enough, cascades down on me as I stand there soaking under it. On any other Christmas, I would walk out on the streets adorned by festive lights and embrace the season. The city is all ablaze and I love to be a part of it. If I make it through this night, I promise to live a thousand Christmases and be a sprightly old man who will delight his grandchildren with wonderful stories. But I can't think about that now. Frank Bruno has gone down. The deadly game is reaching its climax. If you want to live to be an old man, to no longer be Davey Rossi, the pug, or Davey Rossi, the don's son, then you must finish what you started. Then you can be anonymous and happy.

I soap myself down as the steam billows around me. Something catches my eye, a figure behind the shower curtain. I pull it back and see Red.

"Benny Leonard couldn't have fought a better fight." But he looks grim.

"What's wrong?"

"The hit went down at Angelo's. Frank Bruno's boys got Joe Dante."

"Dino?"

"He wasn't there. I had somebody on the scene checking it out." Red throws me a towel. "Get dressed."

I rub myself briskly. Our scenario didn't work. Dino was a step ahead of us. He let Frank's boys whack Joe Dante and then caught Frank in the parking lot. We got two out of three, but that's not good enough in this league.

I slip into my clothes. There will be banner headlines tomorrow. The fight will be eclipsed by the news. Two dons have been clipped in the city on a night when couples walk the streets while their children point excitedly to the Christmas displays in the department stores.

I pull up my pants and reach for the white shirt on the hook. "How did Dante get it?"

"He stepped out of his car and three guys plugged him full of a lot of holes. His driver got it also. He was holding the door for him. They're lying on their backs, side by side, on Forty-sixth Street."

Eyes open but unseeing. And Anna, what is she doing? Waiting for the phone to ring with the news that her husband of close to thirty years was gunned down. Set up for the hit by her son. One more blow to the heart. One more hammer that will shorten her life.

I finish off the shirt and reach for my tie. "How did Waxy Green find out about me?"

Red pulls out a cigar. "It could only be Lossy Beiderman, the old Broadway producer. The way I figure it, Nails gave Lossy something like a diary, which laid it all out."

"Why Lossy Beiderman?"

Red mulls it over. "He had to pass the truth on to somebody, and I guess he trusted Lossy." Red points the cigar at me as if it were some kind of lightning rod of truth. "Everything Lossy had when he died was left to his greatest star."

"Dolly Irving."

"She had Nails's diary, or whatever it was he left. She came up short for cash, so she gave it to Waxy to use for blackmail. He did the work, she stayed in the background, and they split the profits. But then Waxy got hit."

I knot the tie as Red lights the cigar. "For a while, I was sure it was you who hit Waxy, Red."

"That should have been mine. But it wasn't me."

"No, Red, it was Johnny."

Red looks stunned.

"Johnny kept in touch with Dolly. One night when a lot of booze went down, she must have told him about Waxy. The Syndicate's story was that Waxy fingered the Gordon mob. Johnny needed that story to hide behind. Waxy would have blown his cover."

I slip on my socks and shoes, then bend down to knot the laces. I can hear the water drip from the shower. One droplet after the other. Like the second hand on a clock ticking relentlessly down. Time slipping inexorably away. The door to the dressing room opens. I don't look up. I know who it will be.

Dapper as always in a camel's hair overcoat, framed in the light, is Johnny.

"We gotta go, kid."

"Where do we have to go, Johnny?

"We got to square it."

I take a long look at Johnny. "Square what?"

"We have to talk." He inclines his head in Red's direction.

"Red, give us a few minutes."

Red eyes Johnny coolly. "Just a few." He goes out.

I slip on the tie and knot it. "I haven't heard any congratulations yet."

Johnny comes toward me. "You fought a great fight."

"You didn't think I wanted it that bad." I finish doing the tie and turn toward him. "So what do we have to square and with who?"

"I went for Simpson big."

It is like having a grenade explode in your face. "How big?"

"Three hundred g's."

"Then cover it."

"It's not that easy."

"Win, you collect; lose, you pay. You know the rules."

"I gave somebody my IOU."

"What somebody?"

"Somebody important to us."

We are inches apart. Breathing space barely exists between us.

"You need to make deals, Davey. You give up something and you get something back. You trade something you need for something the other guy needs. That way, you both get something and you're tied in together. That's how the rackets work." Johnny looks pale. Sweat glistens on his forehead.

"What did you trade?"

He bites his lip, the tension lines making him look old and weary.

I look at Johnny and put myself in his place. He figures I'm a shot fighter. "You traded the fight. You bet against your brother and you guaranteed it to somebody." I grab him by his lapel. "Tell me, smart boy, who you traded the fight to."

I pull him to me and he pushes at me with hands. "Get your fucking hands off me."

But I retain my hold on him. "You traded it to Scola, didn't you? It's always Scola with you, isn't it, Johnny? It was Scola when you two-timed Nails with Dolly and it was Scola you ran to when Anna was pregnant with me. Vince was right: Scola owned you. You sold him the fight, Johnny. Why?"

"You gotta hedge your bets, Davey, don't you see? We got Frank Bruno and Joe, but we missed Dino. We're going to need a friend. Dino will figure out what we set up. Someone always figures it, Davey."

"So now Scola is our friend. Scola, who set up Nails and Vince, is in bed with us. The whole time we were working to get Frank, Joe, and Dino, you've been playing it back for Uncle Carlo. Uncle Carlo, who got to Frank Bruno and turned him around so he would hit Vince."

Johnny gets red around the temples. "Suppose we had made it and got Dino, do you think we could have gotten Scola, too? Jesus, Davey, you gotta cut a deal if you want to live. Vince is dead. I wasn't part of that. I just made the deal I had to make."

A trickle of water falls on the old shower tile and a pipe groans. "What was the deal, Johnny?"

He wipes the sweat from his face. "He gave us points in all of Simpson's fights from now on. Five points, Davey. That's an annuity. Plus, we clean up on the Joe Fletcher fight because it's fixed. Scola had it all laid out for Simpson to win the welterweight and middleweight titles. We make a fortune betting those fights. Don't you see it?"

"Yeah, I see it, Johnny. In exchange for the points, you told Scola I would lose. But I crossed you up."

Johnny's face is flushed with anger. "We still have to cover."

"Cover what?"

"Scola's bet and ours. That's three quarters of a mil . . . seven hundred fifty big ones."

"Is that all?"

Johnny turns and paces. "It can be done. . . . We go to Scola and tell him how we'll do it. And it will work. I know it will. But this time, you have to play ball, Davey."

I don't say anything.

Johnny whirls toward me. "You'll fight Simpson again. It's a natural. They'll put it in Yankee Stadium and sell it out. Simpson will win it this time and we're off the hook. Then he fights for the welter and middleweight titles."

"I'm retiring, Johnny."

"After the next Simpson fight, then you retire. Get it, smart guy? This is the rackets and this is the way it happens in the Life. It's not about glory; it's about protecting your friends and yourself and we all make a bundle. That's all there is. No glory, no honor, no parades. You got it?"

"No fucking deal, Johnny."

"Don't tell me no fucking deal. I already made it."

I stare at him.

"That's right. I've been on the phone for an hour squaring it with Scola. And we're going down there now and make it official. Once we do that, I give him two hundred grand tomorrow and the rest after the next Simpson fight, plus vig. I sold Scola this fight. He could have made a mil and a half on Simpson, and we're on the hook for it. We make a deal or we're dead. So you bet your ass you're going to fight again and lay down for Simpson."

"How do we make it official, Johnny?"

He takes a deep breath. "We give him your purse on this fight."

Again the solitary drip of the shower behind us. "That's quite a deal, Johnny."

"And you know why we're getting a second chance, Davey? Because I kept Scola in the picture the whole time about the big hit coming down. I covered our asses. And so he listened to me tonight. I explained to him that you lost your head. You were fighting for your honor and you couldn't lie down like you were supposed to. But we get another chance to redeem ourselves. I covered our asses. That's why they call me Johnny Silk. So we go down there and you tell him about honor and he'll buy it. Scola believes in honor. It's for suckers, but he buys it, so—"

"You sold me out just like with Nails. It's always about covering your ass."

"We have to go down there now!" Johnny yells it at me and I respond by slapping him across the mouth. The force of it knocks him backward.

The door opens and I spin around. Dino stands there. Behind him is Buster Minetta.

Dino is dressed in a sharp black overcoat. He is wearing a white shirt with a black tie. He takes in the scene and smiles. "Did I interrupt something?"

Johnny smooths himself out and reaches for a cigarette. Dino loosens his coat. "Great fight, Davey. I bet the fight both ways, so I came out all right. After all, we were partners on another deal and I didn't want to bet against a partner. We're all winners tonight. You know, I did some hard thinking about what you told me, Davey. See, I figured it this way. If, like you told me, Frank is after me and Joe is in on it, then when Joe suggests dinner at Angelo's, I smell hit. So I don't go. And guess what happens? Joe gets hit. Now what do you think that means? Should I tell you? It means Frank and Joe aren't in no deal together. It means Frank was out to hit me and Joe at the same time. I think somebody set Joe up. What do you guys think?"

Johnny is there like he always is with the answer. "Frank is a mad dog. You know how he is, Dino."

"Yeah, I know. Farlo fuori. But after you called me to meet you,

Davey, I made some inquiries. And I put some people on you, Johnny, and they told me they saw you with Frank, whispering in his ear. You know what I think? The Rossi brothers have been scamming me. Pretending to be my friend and setting me up for the knock. And guess what, brothers, you're both in the shithouse." Dino lights a cigarette and walks around us. "But maybe you can square the deal. There's always a way to square the deal, right, Johnny?"

"Sure."

He stalks Johnny and me as if he were a rapacious tiger deciding which of us to feast on first. "Me and Davey cut a deal. Remember? Well, maybe if you keep the deal, we let bygones be bygones. You guys took your shot at me and you missed, but if you get the other guy, you make it up to me. I'm a forgiving guy."

Johnny's eyes widen. "What kind of deal did you make with Davey?"

A thin smile shows on Dino's mouth. "You mean you didn't tell him, Davey? There sure is a lot of shit falling from the sky. Was that going to be a Christmas surprise? Tell him, Davey. Tell big brother."

I look over at Johnny. "I'm doing the hit on Scola tonight."

It is as if I had shot Johnny. For once, the Silk Man has no smooth words or ready lies.

Dino approaches us. "You know what? I think both of you had a little extra something going on the side. That's okay. I don't mind seeing a guy advance himself, as long as he don't hurt the number one. And you know who that is, don't you, Davey?"

"I didn't forget. I'm ready."

He jabs his finger into my chest. "Good. Because I don't like no one crossing me up. And just to make sure, I'm going to hold on to Johnny for a while. When you do the hit on Scola, then Johnny boy will be set loose."

His finger is still in my chest as I speak. "And if I don't make it?"

I can feel the pressure of his finger as he answers. "But you will make it. Tonight's your night. You're a winner. Right? Get your coat. You come with me, Johnny."

I reach for my overcoat. Dino checks me over. "Where's your piece?"

"That's my business. You just make sure your boys are there to clear the way for me when I get out."

"That's my present to you. It's Christmas, ain't it? How you going to do it?"

"He wants to talk about a return fight with Simpson. How I do it is my business."

Dino flashes me a hard grin. "You always had guts, kid. I like guts. I don't give a fuck how you do it. You don't mind going for a little ride, do you, Johnny?"

Johnny doesn't bat an eyelash. "I like the city when it's all lit up. A ride is fine."

Dino spits on the floor. "Good. Let's go."

"Hold it," I say, "Johnny gets set free soon as this is over."

"Sure."

I slip into my coat. "Why don't we meet somewhere real public. Let's say on the steps of St. Patrick's at two o'clock."

Dino breaks into a wolfish grin. "Then we can all celebrate and watch the big Christmas tree down at Rockefeller Center. C'mon, Johnny, let's go sit and watch the big Christmas tree and wait for your kid brother to save your ass."

I look over at Johnny. What is he thinking now? This is one deal he didn't have taped. One time he couldn't cover the bet.

We go out into the hallway, where Buster, backed up by four torpedoes, is waiting. Dino leans over and whispers something. Buster nods. He turns. "Let's go, Johnny." Buster eyes me. "Be good, Davey. Be very good, or I'll be seeing you."

"I'm always good. Give me a minute with Johnny."

I step over to my brother and he gives me a big Broadway smile. "No hard feelings, kid."

"I'll be back for you."

"Sure you will." His eyes say something else. They say, I have no chance at all. But he fronts it. "It was a hell of a ride, kid."

"It's not over."

"Hell no . . . you can do it." He claps me on the shoulder. "Don't worry about it—everybody dies."

I look into his eyes, watching for the fear, but there is none. With his life on the line, he is little Johnny Baca again. The tough street kid Vince rescued from a coal bin, who followed him everywhere. My brother, whom I love as much as Vince did.

Dino walks over. "Let's get the show on the road."

I look over to Johnny. "Scola sending someone for us?"

"Walk over to Radio City. Anthony will pick you up in a car."

"I'll see you at two o'clock."

Dino claps his hands and Buster takes Johnny's arm. He moves down the long, dark corridor, flanked by Dino's hit squad. They are like so many pieces of Dino's royal cloak trailing in his wake. They exit and Red slips out of the darkness.

Red licks his mouth. "When do you get him back?"

"St. Patrick's, two o'clock."

"I know a priest over there."

"Really?"

"Yeah, he works on collections."

"This should be a good night for him. It's almost Christmas, and everyone is feeling charitable. Give him my regards. Tell him if everything works out for me, Dino will be feeling real generous."

"Want me to walk you over?"

"No. I'll see you later."

As I start to leave, I feel Red's hand on my arm. "When the time comes, don't wait. You never let the hit become a person to you."

"Vince told me that once."

I walk up the corridor, hearing the cold staccato notes my shoes make on them. Red calls to me. The words he says ring in my ear all the way on my walk to Radio City Music Hall. "Once and for all, kill that old dago fuck."

# 45

I MAKE MY WAY through the flow of people heading toward Sixth Avenue, hardly seeing them. Everything is bright and there are a lot of people on the streets. It will be a long holiday weekend, with many gifts exchanged. In the spirit of the season, my gift will be given tonight. I can see Radio City Music Hall. To its right, just half a block away, is Rockefeller Center, with the great Christmas tree, which is surrounded by people. Below the tree is the ice-skating rink and the throngs of people watching, pointing and laughing at the skaters. It is the happiest time of the year and everybody is on holiday. Everybody except for those of us in the Life.

There is a late show at the Music Hall tonight and a long line running almost to Fifth Avenue. I cross the street and stand a few yards from the box office. I look up at the night sky dotted with stars. It will be a clear, bright day tomorrow. A hand is on my shoulder. I turn and see Anthony. "Where's Johnny?"

"He got detained. It's just me."

I can see his eyes leap. He is a literal creature and any deviation from routine presents great problems. "That's all you're getting to-night. Me. Or do you want to tell your boss that you took it on yourself to call off the meet?"

He struggles with himself, then decides that half a loaf is better than none at all. "You explain it, smart guy. Let's go."

He leads me toward Fifty-first Street, where a car is waiting. I slip inside. As the driver pulls out, Anthony gives me a fast frisk. Satisfied, he leans back and pulls out a cigarette. There is no freewheeling banter tonight. He knows his boss is very unhappy and that sets the tone of the evening.

We sit in silence as the car speeds to the East Side Drive and then makes its way downtown. Traffic is light and the East River reflects the lights of the highway. Each yellow globe of light drifting on the water reaches out to me like one of many tortured souls in purgatory waiting to be saved. If I do what I have to, then perhaps some of them can sleep at last.

We exit at Grand Street and make our way through the crowded streets of the East Side until we reach St. Ignatius Church. A bright orange cross burns fiercely within a glass case over the entrance. We leave the car and Anthony takes the opportunity to pat me down again. "I don't think this is going to be such a great Christmas for you."

"Don't think too much. It's not good for you."

"Get going." He gives me a push. There is a small cluster of people outside the church, waiting to see Uncle Carlo. They have been herded away and lined up against a side wall. A stone angel carved into the wall of the church silently observes them. Their patron saint got crucified on a fight he thought was fixed. Now he seeks the Resurrection.

I enter the church, with Anthony just behind me. I can see Scola sitting on his throne. From a distance, he looks like a lonely old man whiling away his time. There is no one else in the large room. As I approach the sanctuary, I can see a glass of red wine resting on a table next to Scola's huge chair. The sanctuary is bathed in soft light. Scola is wearing a gray jacket over a pale shirt buttoned to the neck. His eyes seem closed, as if he is oblivious to my presence. But that is a show for my benefit, meant to intimidate me by making me seen insignificant. He has a million and half reasons to be aware of me.

He lazily opens his eyes and regards me coldly. He waves an idle hand and Anthony retreats. Scola turns to me. "Where is Johnny?"

"He won't be coming. I'll speak for us."

Scola raises his eyes. "So you speak for the family. Perhaps, then, you can tell me about why your family broke its word to me. I shook hands with your brother on this fight. There was a great deal at stake."

"It was a matter of honor."

Scola edges forward in his great chair. "So I have been told. You speak of honor, but you have much to learn about it."

I am suddenly sick of this deathlike old man and his pretensions. "Are you the man to teach me about honor?"

He nods his head. "So the venom in you shows itself. I always knew that inside of you was the heart of your father. The Jew. You didn't win this fight because of honor; you did it to show who you are. You did it to defy me. Your father was that way."

I peek back to see if Anthony is still here in the room, but he is gone.

"The great Nails Gordon. When he came to me that last night, he was most humble. Spare my child, he said. Spare my child."

Something inside me starts to quiver. Hold it back. Save it. But I cannot. "My father came to you and cut a deal. My life for his. As soon as he died, you took me hostage and held my life over Vince's head. Honor in your mouth is infamy. It is a word you use to wrap your evil in a cloth of virtue. I made no deal with you on this fight. We did not speak of it. You made your deal with Johnny, not with me."

Scola drinks slowly from the glass of wine. He is using the respite to plan his next move. Just seconds, but he has had a lifetime of these seconds maneuvering for position. He is a cunning and deadly serpent, and no matter what he tells me, he has decided that my impudence will earn me death.

He sets the glass down. "You do not understand that you must take responsibility for the deal your brother made with me. Do you understand how much weighed on this fight?"

"I understand that you tried to buy what you couldn't win in the ring. Now you want it back, but I won't give it to you."

A cunning little smile shows itself. "Sei il figlio di tuo padre. In fondo sei più Ebreo che Siciliano." You are your father's son. In the end, more Jew that Sicilian.

I move forward toward the little man in his great chair with the red satin draped over it. "Thank you for the opportunity to be used by you, Uncle Carlo, but I decline. Isn't that what it's always about? If one can be used by you, then you let them live in the sunny warmth of your contempt. Like Johnny. And if they oppose you, like Nails and Vince, then they get the stiletto in the back. Johnny spent his whole life courting you. He fawned before a man who held him in contempt. That's what you want from me, but you can't have it."

I watch his eyes. In this moment, he has written off any attempt to recoup his loss with Sandy Simpson. Word will get out that I crossed Uncle Carlo. He can only wipe the slate clean when my body is fished out of the river.

He points his finger at me. "I always knew after you were born that I would have to kill you. That is why I kept you close by me so I could watch you grow up. If I had left you alone, you would have learned about your father and come at me secretly. But there is nothing that can save you. Nothing and no one. I will reach out for you when I am ready. I will take it all from you. You will die with your balls stuffed in your mouth, screaming for your mother."

"You got Nails and Tommy and Vince. They were better than you, but they underestimated how far down the line you planned. You always knew you would kill them and you lived each day with that in mind."

Scola drinks more wine and some of it runs down his shirt. "You think because you killed Frank Bruno and Joe Dante that you are worthy of Scola. I allowed you to kill them because it pleased me. Tonight, I offered you my hand and you spit on it. Now leave and wait for the time that it comes. Morte al gran brigante e a suo figlio Ebreo." Death to the great brigand and his Jewish son.

I drop to my knees. It is the signal, and I pray that she is there. Scola looks down and, seeing the desperate look on my face, his eyes get big and childlike. In the end, everyone falls before him grasping his knees, crying for mercy. His lips part in pleased affirmation of his ultimate power. I see the curtains behind Scola move as he waits for me to plead to him. He beckons me closer and I say the words. "Eminence . . . fuck you, Eminence . . . fuck you."

His mouth closes and his eyes fill with rage. Sister Mary comes from behind the curtains, hands held out plaintively. Another supplicant begging for an audience. Words fly out of her mouth like so many birds released from a cage. "Pietà. The child is sick. He must have medicine. God's mercy is needed."

She pulls desperately at him till Scola frees himself and pushes her to the floor. He stands up and calls, "Antonio...Antonio...come quickly. Antonio."

I hear footsteps. I help her up, and as Sister Mary turns to me, she slips me the gun.

Anthony is there, gun in hand. Scola waves to him to put it away and signals for him to remove the distraught nun. Anthony leads her away as she continues to plead for Scola's intervention.

Scola turns and sees the weapon I am pointing at him. My arm is held straight out in front of me, the gun aimed as if in accusation. And I hear Vince: "You know that in seconds, everything he feels will stop. He will not eat, make love, or smile again. But if you start feeling sorry for him, you are finished."

Scola rises out of his chair, screaming, "Assassino...assassino." I squeeze off three rounds and the silent explosion echoes in the church. The bullets send him toppling over backward in his great archbishop's throne.

I spin around and point the gun as Anthony returns. Standing above the body of his dead master, I beckon for him to come forward. Scola lies on his back. The bullets have left a jagged hole in the front of his head. He looks peaceful, as if he is an old man sleeping away the remains of his life.

"Get on the floor."

Anthony's lips quiver. I aim my gun and he falls to his knees.

I cross to him. "Don't say anything, just listen. You fucked up, Anthony. It was the nun. She slipped me the piece. You're not very good at this, are you?"

He shakes his head vigorously.

"The word is going to get out. You're better off dead, aren't you?"

This time, he doesn't respond. "Good-bye, Anthony."

I jam the gun into his temple and there is a hissing sound and a groan as his bowels give way and the stench comes pungently to me. The water released from his bladder stains him and the floor around him. He lies there completely befouled. "That's not good, Anthony. You've made a complete mess of the church, haven't you?"

He shakes his head affirmatively.

"Now listen, Anthony. I'm going to leave now. I have lots of boys outside and you have no friends. So you just lie here for fifteen minutes and don't say a word and maybe they'll let you live. You smell like shit, but you're alive. Then you know what you're going to do?"

Again the head shake.

"You're going to get up and go to the train station and get out of town. Don't come back, because everything changed tonight and you have no friends. If you ever do, I'll let it be known that you let Scola get hit while you shit your pants. Understand? Good-bye, Anthony. And change your outfit before you leave town or everyone will know. You're not really meant for the Life, are you?"

I leave him on the floor, soiled and shaking his head. I walk past Scola, who still seems peaceful in his sleep of death.

I duck through the curtain and walk down the narrow corridor to the emergency exit. I push the door open and I am standing in a garden, facing a large tree. Through its naked branches, I can see the sky illuminated by vivid stars. It is a fine winter night. I walk from the garden into the street and there is no one there. Dino has kept his word, as I have mine. I walk slowly to the corner, feeling the weight of the two guns in my pocket. I keep walking until I reach a sewer. Removing the clip, I drop Anthony's gun down inside it. My own gun rests comfortably in my pocket. That will be thrown in the river. I pull up my coat collar and keep walking. I don't feel anything. Not yet. But I know it will be different. I have been changed irrevocably. I reach Canal Street and see a cab, which I flag down. It is magically there, just like the gun was there for me so I could kill the old serpent, Scola. It was meant to happen this way. Like Uncle Carlo said, I am my father's son.

# 46

IT IS LATE as I walk up toward the tree that looms over Rockefeller Plaza. It looks like a million balls of fire dancing irresistibly before me. People hurry by me, laughing, happy. Balls of smoke leap from their mouths. I see their faces, but no one registers as I brush past them. A girl turns toward me and smiles. It occurs to me that she is pretty. Her eyes follow me as I hurry on. She is wearing a white coat and has long brown hair. A gift I have not the time to unwrap.

I check my watch. Just minutes before two o'clock. I pause as I reach the Christmas tree. People are wedged together, entranced by its magnificence like they always have been. Someday I'll bring my children here. A thousand Christmases to grow into a fine old man if I can survive this night. Someone next to me is holding a portable radio as the excited voice of the news broadcaster crackles in the night air. "Dante had just stepped from his car in front of Angelo's restaurant when three men in hats and trench coats suddenly confronted him, then opened fire, killing him at point-blank range. Police report that Dante took five shots to the head and chest and died instantly. His driver was also killed. Two hours later, another big-time mob figure, Frank Bruno, was cut down as he was picking up his car in a parking lot located at Eighth Avenue and Fiftieth Street, just across from Madison Square Garden. Bruno had been attending the lightweight championship bout at the Garden between Davey Rossi and Sandy Simpson.

He was killed by a tall man dressed as a car attendant. The killer pumped six bullets into Bruno and then fled. Bruno died still clutching the parking ticket for his car. Ironically, he had just viewed the bout in which Davey Rossi, whose father, Vince, was cut down in a mob-style execution less than two months ago, won back the title he lost to Simpson last spring."

I drift away from the sounds of the news broadcast and head for Fifth Avenue. The news of Scola's death hasn't been released yet. The police are there, but they are afraid of anarchy. One by one, the dons of the Five Families are being picked off. And the night isn't over.

I reach Fifth Avenue and St. Patrick's looms just across the street. Its tall double spires seem to extend beyond infinity. I cross over to St. Pat's, checking for Dino. Though it is late, there are still small clusters of people grouped together. As I reach the steps, I see a circle of young girls and boys singing Christmas carols. I climb the steps and look around. A car door slams and I turn. Walking toward me is Dino. A cigarette dangles from his mouth and his white hair blows softly in the air. Just behind him is Buster Minetta. I look toward their car for a sign of Johnny.

Dino greets me with an icy smile. "You done the job, didn't you?"

"You already know that."

A tuft of smoke leaps from his mouth and goes skyward. "There are enough cop cars around that fucking church to guard the Pope. Fucking Scola would have loved it."

"I don't think he can appreciate it right now. Where's Johnny?"

Dino inhales a large lungful of smoke. "He took the night off."

"We made a deal and I kept my end, Dino."

"Well, that's rough, because I didn't keep mine. But you're lucky you did what you said you would. Now you can go home and sleep good. You're sitting on top of the world and you got my friendship."

"Where's Johnny?"

"Like I said, he took the night off. It's a permanent move. Get it?"

Buster has moved in next to me, his hand in his pocket. As I look over his shoulder, I can see three priests with a collection box accepting donations.

Dino forces his way into my field of vision. "What did you guys think you were going to do, try to clip me and walk away? You set

Frank Bruno up to hit me, only I beat you and him to the punch. You and Johnny boy had it worked out so that everybody got it tonight. It was slick and it almost worked, only I'm better. But somebody had to pay, and that means brother Johnny. He got it clean and quick. Three slugs in the head while he wasn't looking."

I struggle for breath. "Where is he?"

"Never mind that. Here's the deal. You guys took your best shot and you missed. Johnny takes the rap for it. You walk because you got Scola. That wasn't no easy thing to do, and I know that. So we're even. If you keep your nose clean and don't start no trouble, you can walk away. I got bigger things to attend to. You know who I am? Capo di tutti capi. Get it? And you're just another pug. I'll take over the fight rackets, and if you behave yourself, maybe I'll let you promote some bouts. But that's it. You're a pebble on the beach and I don't want to hear anything more about you. Hey, things could be a lot worse."

I push into him. "Where's my brother?"

Buster is there, but Dino holds him back. "Easy. Listen, you're a lucky man. You came that close. This is a tough racket. Understand?"

We stand inches apart, eyeballing each other. A hoarse, racking cough attacks Dino. "I gotta go. You want your brother, check the river. He'll come floating by. But if you're gonna look, wear a warm coat. He's carrying a lot of weight. It could be awhile till he shows up."

A bitter smile paints itself across his features. There is the tinkling sound of a bell and Dino turns. The three priests have reached him. I slide down the steps, hearing the first one address him.

"Can you help us?"

I hear Dino's rasp of a reply. "Sure, Father, it's the Christmas season and I'm going to reach deep down. I got a lot to be thankful for. Is this enough?"

The muted explosion of a pistol equipped with a silencer is the answer to Dino's question. I turn in time to see the priest put two more slugs into him. The other two priests have opened fire on Buster and he falls at their feet as they continue to pump bullets into him. A woman screams and I recognize Jake standing over Buster. "That's for Freddie, you dago prick."

More cries as I run on quick feet down the steps and hurry toward Madison Avenue. I keep my head down, walking briskly, trying to keep cool. It's over. It's all over. For everybody.

Red is waiting for me in the car. He throws open the door. "Where's Johnny?"

I shake my head.

Red doesn't look surprised. He saw it coming; he beckons to me. "Get in."

"I'll walk."

"C'mon, Davey."

"It's over, Red. They got Dino and Buster. Tell Abe Mortkoff there'll be a bonus for his boys. I gotta go."

Red looks at me helplessly. "This is no time to be alone. You're all in. You won, but you took a pounding tonight."

He guides me into the car. "Losing Johnny hurts, and I don't want you to be by yourself. He just played too many angles. No one is smart enough to last forever. The rackets will always catch up to you. The ice Johnny was standing on was very thin."

"It's time for us both to retire, Red."

He reaches for a cigar. "Yeah, it is. I'm too old for the rackets anymore. But you, Davey, you're the best. As good as Nails ever was. You got them both tonight. Dino and Scola. It was beautiful. They never saw it coming." Red comes out with a flask and I take a slug. The whiskey hits me hard, but it also gives me the kind of jolt I need.

"You know, Davey, tonight was the end of a lot of things. It goes back even further than that night in the Rodman Arms. But that night will always stay with me. It runs through my mind like a song you can't remember all the words to. Just the melody stays with you."

"We have a lot to talk about, Red."

We ride east and I look up at the night sky once again. On a clear Bethlehem night almost two thousand years ago, the Three Wise Men came bringing gifts of gold, incense, and myrrh to the infant Christ born in a manger. That was the story they acted out in the Christmas pageant I watched in school. That is the story that most kids grow up learning. The one I know ended tonight. It tells the story of Nails, Vince, and Johnny and the serpent who corrupted them. The story ended when I cut off the head of the serpent. That old Sicilian fable, which presented its own dark vision, is finished. Maybe now I can live to be that fine old man I want to be. One who sits around and tells his grandchildren stories on Christmas Eve. But it will be the one about the Wise Men who followed the star to Bethlehem and found the Messiah. Not about tonight. This fable will always reside privately inside me. Flickering candles burning for Nails, for Vince, and for Johnny.

# 47

Six weeks ago, Johnny was found floating on the Jersey side of the Hudson. I had to make the identification, and it wasn't easy. He had decomposed in the water. I did it as best I could, but I had to wait for the autopsy before I could claim the body. Dino was right; Johnny took three slugs in the back of the head. Clean and quick. I had Gelardi the undertaker fix him up before the burial. He was Vince's longtime friend and something of an artist. But as he explained to me, "The water is nobody's friend, Davey, when you are in it for so long." Gelardi did his best and Johnny went to meet his Maker in presentable form. I had him buried next to Vince. They had come a long way from that time when Vince found Johnny alone and abandoned and took him in. Time separated them, but time is timeless also. I mean that it goes on and we come back to what we know. I don't think either of them has forgotten those early days and I think they love each other. And I also believe that their souls, which float somewhere in space, have staked their claim on forgiveness. And if you are one of those who think that because they were gangsters they had no souls, then I will come out of retirement to dispute that.

They're still talking about the night in December when four dons got whacked and Johnny Silk, the mob's consigliere, disappeared. New York has never seen a night quite like it. The papers were full of vivid details of the killings and the saga of the bloody men who died. My fight with Sandy Simpson didn't get buried because of it. Instead, it was treated as part of the panoply of a historic evening. After all, Vince had been killed only seven weeks earlier. There were some references to my relationship to the night's events, but they were meant symbolically. There has been a lot of speculation in the last few months about who put the hit on the heads of the Five Families, but it's all the stuff of fantasy. Greg Landers, the top crime reporter in town, swore he had been given an exclusive by a member of the National Mafia Commission. This informant told Landers that the Commission was sick of the fighting in New York and that a faction led by Benno Chiari, the don of Miami Beach, had ordered the hits. Benno Chiari has been senile for some years, but it makes for good reading.

I announced my retirement two months ago. I visit Nails's grave a lot. He's buried in the Bronx. On the tomb, it reads MAX GORDON, 1900–1934 SON OF PINCUS AND RACHEL. I don't know where his parents are buried. I've made inquiries, but the past has a way of zealously guarding its secrets. I talk to Nails a lot. He doesn't answer, but that doesn't matter. Being with him comforts me. I spend a lot of time by myself. Sometimes I drive to the country and eat in a nice old inn. I can't seem to go very far from the city. I get the shakes.

The thing that changes you is killing. When you look a man in the eye and shoot him, something goes out of you. Something that is visceral, throbbing, and alive. So you eat, you sleep, you breathe, you eliminate, and you wear a stolid expression. Life, it seems, cannot surprise you.

Red called me this morning and asked me to go to Friday-night services at a synagogue on the East Side. When I get there, the small room is crowded. The sanctuary is on a platform, the Torah encased in a bronze ark just behind the rabbi. The service concludes with the Kaddish, the prayer for the dead. Red taught me the words. It is a timeless ritual and I feel a chill go through me. All of us gathered together to pay tribute to those who went before us. There are a lot of people I have to remember, and even if some of them are not Jews, I don't think anyone would hold that against me.

I say the words *Yit-ga-dal ve-yit-ka-das she-mei ra-ba-be-al-ma di-ve-ra chir-re-u-tei.* I think of Vince and of Nails. Somehow, they are united in my prayers. The father I knew and the one I didn't. I was lucky that Vince was there for me when Nails died. Maybe there is a symmetry to life that we are unaware of. Born the son of a gangster, I was raised by another gangster. It was meant to be that I would be defined by the Life. And somehow, it was also meant for me to avenge the deaths of Nails and Vince and Johnny. If you could depict my life as a play, then all of the men I knew as I grew up would be characters in it. Dino and Joe, Frank Bruno, old Scola, and all the others, who were their followers. So the twin themes in my life seem to be destiny and revenge. But perhaps what I am struggling with is that I don't feel at peace with myself. The destiny of revenge should bring you to catharsis. I don't feel cleansed, just drained. I don't feel pity, only relief. I don't seem to understand what has happened, or is it that I am just empty? As I sit here with other people who chant the words and I hear a sob or a muffled cry, no tears come to my eyes, but I am moved. I feel grateful to be with these people who have also experienced death.

I've seen Anna many times. It's funny I still think of her that way. I can't call her Mother when we are together and I can no longer call her Anna, as I once did. We meet for walks or lunches. Sometimes we drive out of the city and talk over coffee. It is not an easy thing to fill in the spaces of a life not lived together. We have spent our days in close proximity without ever truly knowing each other. And I have made her a widow as well as taken a son from her. Once on a drive to the country, she brought it up to me. "I see pain in your eyes, Davey. Please let it go. I became a widow a long time ago. Do you think it would be better if Joe junior had lived and you were dead? All of us have paid for this thing they call 'the Life.' It is not about life at all. Now you must put it aside and enjoy your youth. That is what will make me happy."

We got out of the car and walked down to the water's edge. I picked up some pebbles and threw them. They kicked up water and then receded into small ripples that gradually vanished. Anna watched the small undulations in the water and finally said, "You know, Davey, if Max was here, he would be proud of you, but not proud of what you did. But he would understand. It was not that he didn't want you to be strong, but he wanted something better for his son than the life that is ruled by the gun. That is what filled him with so much sadness at the end. He had lived a certain way and then there was no escaping it. He was tired of it and he wanted peace. A peace he could never find. He saw what was coming for him and for the others around him."

"It's called seeing to the end of all things."

Anna nodded. "That is a good way to put it. One time he said, 'They won't let me walk away. In any other profession, you can retire. But in this profession, you go out in a box. That's your retirement.' What he looked forward to was you. Then his eyes would sparkle. But you must believe, Davey, that all this had to happen. There was no way Max and I could have been together. His life had run out. Who you are and who I am is the product of all this. We all have had to pay the price for our lives in order to be free. Do you understand that?"

I nodded, not knowing if I understood anything.

"I am moving in with my sister, Davey. She lives in Connecticut. You will come and visit me often and we will get to know each other. You are sad now, as I am. But one day you will wake up and be glad that your mother is alive and you can see her. And we will get to know each other and become good friends. Good friends."

She leaned over and kissed me and then for the first time in all these months, she hugged me. It is not easy to drop the restrictions and defenses of a lifetime. We drove back to the city in silence, but I don't think there was any need for either of us to say anything. We have both been prisoners of a lie for a long time. And tearing away the veil that covered the truth has left us raw. We need a time when seeing each other does not bring with it a painful reminder. The past will always be there for Anna and me. But there must be a time when the hurt makes you stronger because you have absorbed it within yourself. When that time comes, it means you have accepted your life. Right now, it is a ways off. But I will watch and feel for it the way you look for a harbinger of spring and one day a bird flies overhead and the soft smell of spring is there.

I am alone a lot these days and I have learned to embrace it. I take pleasure in simple things. I keep up with my roadwork, I eat well, and drink more wine than I used to. I visit with Sister Mary. She has never mentioned the last night, but sometimes in her eyes I can discern a look of satisfaction. Like Anna, she has paid the price for the deed of evil men, and while she is devout, turning the other cheek is not for her.

The last time I saw Sister Mary, we walked down to the woods near the convent and watched the dappled sunshine that bathed the grounds in soft hues. I turned to her and said, "Do you think Vince is at peace now?"

She didn't answer at first. She is not one to be rushed, nor will she speak without having something to say. "I think Vince will speak to you many times over, Davey. His was a tortured soul and I don't think he will sleep easily. But you have taken away the shame of his life and his death, and for that he would be grateful."

I booked a flight to Paris this morning. I need to get away from New York . . . from everybody here. To get away from all that has happened. Then I called Julie and asked her to meet me for a drink and talk. I want to say good-bye and part as friends. She said she could meet me at the Pierre Hotel at 5:30.

I am standing here on Fifth Avenue, across the street from the Pierre, wondering if this is a terrible mistake. A cab pulls up and Julie gets out. She is dressed in a pink suit and she is more beautiful than I remember. Her eyes are clear and strong. We shake hands and she asks me to walk with her.

We get half a block away and I stop. "Why here, of all places?"

Her eyes are bold now. "Because I have a meeting inside."

I get a pasty feeling inside me. "With him?"

"Yes. Want to wait?"

"How long will you be?"

"Ten minutes."

I don't say anything as Julie studies me. "Davey, I'm leaving the Justice Department."

"Why?"

"Because it's time to move on. But that doesn't solve your problem, does it?"

"What do you mean?"

"Because you'll always wonder. What happened will always be there for you."

"You know, Julie, you don't have to work for him to keep seeing him."

"No, I don't. But it's over."

"Are you sure?"

"Are you?"

I don't say anything and she turns back toward the Pierre and we walk together.

We reach the hotel now. It is a warm day, but a tumble of a breeze makes me shiver. This is a mistake.

Julie catches it. "You're sorry you came, aren't you?"

It is not easy to respond to her. She is so direct and so perceptive. "There's nothing left of me, Julie. I'm going away for a while . . . to Paris."

I can see her examining me and coming to some decision. "There's a lot there, Davey. Just give it time. Give yourself a chance." A pause. "Give me one."

"I've tried."

"No, you can't forgive what you learned about me."

"I can't help it. I'm old-fashioned."

"If you can't forgive me, how can I forgive myself?"

I can't answer her.

Julie gives me a firm look. "Wait five minutes."

I go across the street and sit down on a bench. I am there for a long time without being conscious of any coherent thought. I have lost my sense of time and purpose. It's time for that trip and then this thing with Julie will be over. I can see lovers holding hands in Central Park. The world is full of young girls and it's time to rejoin the human race. The past will always be there, but someone new, untouched by it, will help a lot. I'm sorry, Julie. I'm still old-fashioned. And I'm still angry at you.

I stand up and watch the sun sink and run rust gold over the grass as I enter the park. I make my way toward the pond and find a place next to a cluster of slate rocks. I watch the sun burrowing into the water and the beauty of it touches me. I leave my nesting place and walk along the edge of the water, watching the diving patterns of the sun. I love this city and I will be back when I am free again. Someone calls my name and I turn. Julie is running toward me. She has dropped her leather briefcase. I look at her and feel amazed. Is that for me? All that feeling? I start trotting toward her and then something in me tumbles loose and I am running, too. We are heading straight for each other, and I see a young girl watching us with delight. We are closer and closer, and then as the circle closes, we embrace in a golden halo of light provided by the sun. There is a long kiss and her lips are moist and taste of something fruity. Then Julie is laughing, whispering into my ear, and I hear myself say something about Paris.

# Epilogue

I AWAKEN JUST BEFORE DAWN, trying to fight off the vivid images of my dream. I raise the blinds and see the sun breaking free into the morning sky. I am flying to Paris in a few hours. Julie will meet me there on the weekend. But I don't have a good feeling. The dream is trying to pull me back. What was it Red told me? "It runs through my mind like a song you can't remember all the words to. Just the melody stays with you."

I close my eyes and drift back to my netherworld.

*Before me is a long table in a darkened room that I enter alone. Then in the semilight, I see them seated around a table like so many grotesques in a wax museum. Frank Bruno smoking a cigar, Joe Dante, Dino with a mocking smile etched on his face, and Scola sitting on his throne. Seated at his knees is Johnny, who winks at me. Their faces are a pale, chalky white, as if they had been raised from the grave in the mist of putrefaction. Dino rises, points his finger at me, and cries out, "Io ti accuso." The words echo in the room. I am here to answer to them for their murders. I turn to run, but the floor dissolves beneath me. I am falling through space. I cry out as I land. I am on the shore of a lake. The sky is fiery red. A mountain looms above me. This is Sicily. A peasant is lying on his belly, his face submerged in a lake. I am suddenly parched. I drop down beside him and drink the water. It tastes of blood. Suddenly, the peasant has his arm around me. He tightens the viselike grip around my neck. It is Scola and he is laughing. The sky turns ominously dark and his arm becomes a luminous green and slithers about my chest. The snake coils around my neck, choking me, flashing its red tongue as it hisses its accusation:* "Assassino ... assassino."

From far away, a jangled sound pulls me back—a succession of rings as I lurch toward the phone. It is Red. There is someone he wants me to meet. In an hour. I mumble my assent, still gripped by my nightmare.

We drive up Amsterdam Avenue and then turn right, heading east. He pulls up in front of a yellow concrete building and the sign reads MANHATTAN NURSING HOME FOR THE AGED. Inside, the reception room is pleasant and well lighted. A white-haired woman is at the reception desk and the sounds of activity are all about the place. Patients in robes are wheeled by every few minutes. Red finishes talking to the receptionist and beckons for me to join him. I walk over and he removes the stub of a cigar from his mouth. "This guy is an old-timer and he loves the fights. Give him three minutes."

We walk down a long corridor and past several rooms. There is a funny smell mixed with a more medicinal odor. I don't mind. I have been in places reeking of death. This is only a disembarkation point. We stop in front of a room and he leads me inside. The light is not on, but lots of sunlight pours in. The room is too warm and it smells of cigar smoke and whiskey. The old man in the wheelchair is very thin and frail. Tufts of white hair are spread in odd places over his head. His skin is red and splotchy. He has a sharp, angular nose and his eyebrows are a mass of thick white hair. He seems to be dozing. Red bends over and whispers something to the old man, then turns the wheelchair toward me. Red continues talking to the old man, whose eyes remain shut. Suddenly, they bolt open and he stares at me.

"Davey," Red says. "He knew Max from the old days."

The old man is trying to stand up, but it is a struggle. He comes toward me and I grip him hard before he can fall. He looks into my face and eyes as if he doesn't believe I am really there. The words are spoken in a scratchy, failing voice. "This is true? You are Max's *kinder*? You are his son?"

For a moment, I cannot speak, but finally I mumble a yes as I nod.

The old man's eyes fill with water. "You have come to Pincus and made a mitzvah. Thank you, thank you."

His arms go around me and he is crying. Soft tears at first. Now he is sobbing into my jacket. I can feel his frail body shake as Red's words come to me. "He's your grandfather, Davey. Pincus Gordon. I wasn't sure how to handle it, but I thought you two should have a chance to meet before more time went by."

The old man steps back and looks at me, his hands running over my face. I want to say something, but there is all this noise in my head and blood in my throat. Everything is pounding.

He looks at me with disbelief written all over his face. "Max's boy. You have come to be with Pincus?"

"They used to sell shoelaces and stuff from a pushcart down at Orchard Street. Him and Max. That was a tough buck, Davey. Help him sit down."

I edge him toward the bed, but the old man refuses to sit. "Thank you," he whispers. "Thank you for coming."

Red nervously clears his throat. "He's a champion, Pincus. A boxer. Full of guts, the way Max was."

Pincus Gordon inclines his head toward me. "He was a meshuga, Max. Too much fight he had in him. Like you, huh?"

He grabs my hand and forms it into a fist and tries to hold it up, but then his body starts to shake and his face wrinkles into a mask of tears. He pulls me to him and cries into my shirt. Shaking and crying, the old man whispers into my ear, "Kinder . . . kinder."

I have always trained myself to think first. And so now I think about how everything flows from the past as this old man smelling of whiskey and urine holds me close to him. And then it is no longer possible to think. He is the line to my father and to everything that came before him. The feeling erupts from somewhere deep inside me; then my chest gives way and everything so long stored up washes over me. Julie was right; I need to cry. Cry for what my grandfather also weeps for. For himself, for his grandson, and for Max, my father. And for this chance to meet each other and know it hasn't ended for Nails. Not while both his father and his son live. I look for Red, but he isn't there. There is just Pincus and me. Two Jews met on the road to Jerusalem.